A BRIDGE
BETWEEN US

K. K. ALLEN

A Bridge Between Us

Copyright © 2020 by K.K. Allen

All rights reserved.

Cover Design: Najla Qamber Designs

Cover Photographer: Regina Wamba

Editor: Red Adept Editing

For more information, please write to
SayHello@KKAllen.com

A BRIDGE
BETWEEN US

USA TODAY BESTSELLING AUTHOR

K. K. ALLEN

NOVELS BY K.K. ALLEN

British Bachelor

A steamy enemies-to-friends-to-lovers romantic comedy.

Coming January 24th!

Up in the Treehouse

Haunted by the past, Chloe and Gavin are forced to come to terms with all that has transpired to find the peace they deserve. Except they can't seem to get near each other without combatting an intense emotional connection that brings them right back to where it all started . . . their childhood treehouse.

Under the Bleachers

Fun and flirty Monica Stevens lives for food, fashion, and boys ... in that order. The last thing she wants to take seriously is dating. When a night of flirty banter with Seattle's hottest NFL quarterback turns passionate, her care-free life could be at risk.

Through the Lens

When Maggie moves to Seattle for a fresh start, she's presented with an unavoidable obstacle—namely, the cocky chef with a talent for photography and getting under her skin. Can they learn to get along for the sake of the ones they love?

Waterfall Effect

Lost in the shadows of a tragedy that stripped Aurora of

everything she once loved, she's back in the small town of Balsam Grove, ready to face all she's kept locked away for seven years. Or so she thinks.

Center of Gravity (Gravity, #1)

She was athleticism and grace, precision and passion, and she had a stage presence he couldn't tear my eyes from. He wanted her...on his team, in his bed. There was only one problem... He couldn't have both.

Falling From Gravity (Gravity, #1.5)

If I hadn't considered Amelia dangerous before, I certainly did now. She wasn't anything like I had expected. Even after all these years—of living so close to her, of listening to her giggle with my sister in the bedroom next to mine—I hadn't given much thought to my sister's best friend.

Defying Gravity (Gravity, #2)

The ball is her Amelia's court, but Tobias isn't below stealing-- her power, her resolve, her heart... When he wants a second chance to reignite our connection, the answer is simple. They can't. Not unless they defy the rules their dreams were built on and risk everything.

The Trouble With Gravity (Gravity #3)

When Sebastian makes Kai an offer she can't afford to refuse, she learns signing on will mean facing the tragedy she's worked so hard to shut out. He says she can trust him to keep her safe, but is her heart safe too?

Dangerous Hearts (A Stolen Melody, #1)

Lyric Cassidy knows a thing or two about bad boy rock stars

with raspy vocals. In fact, her heart was just played by one. So when she takes an assignment as road manager for the world famous rock star, Wolf, she's prepared to take him on, full suit of heart-armor intact.

Destined Hearts (A Stolen Melody, #2)

But with stolen dreams, betrayals, and terrifying threats--no one's heart is safe. Not even the ones that may be destined to be together.

To all the Wild Ones out there—the strong women who blaze trails for others to follow. May your beautiful spirits shine bright forever.

AUTHOR'S NOTE

While *A Bridge Between Us* is a work of fiction, this story
was largely inspired by real locations and the attached
history. In an effort to bring you the most authentic story
imaginable, sensitivity was a top priority while creating
this fictional world. I am forever grateful to the people
who contributed their thoughts and experiences. On top
of speaking with these courageous souls, endless hours of
research was conducted in order to respect the
viewpoints of all characters involved in this story. For
specific works, please see Works Cited.

Any resemblance to persons, names, events, and
incidents are either a product of the author's
imagination or purely coincidental.

PROLOGUE

PROLOGUE
CAMILA

I had always known he wasn't mine to keep, but that didn't change the way I loved him—quietly, gently, and from afar.

As the seasons changed, the corn stalks grew strong, and the grapevines flourished with hope. But none of it mattered, not when the soil at our feet bound us in a century-old rivalry. We'd never even had a chance.

They said life flashed before your eyes on the way to death, but on that night, after my final scream burst from my throat and my world started to fade to black, I only thought of him and his sweet chocolate eyes, his desperately cautious stare, and his silence that carried more weight than gold.

I should have died that night. Instead, I crossed the moonlit bridge and never returned. I let rivalry win. If only that had been enough to keep us all safe. If only we didn't have a bridge between us.

1

CAMILA

The dark barrel of the shotgun stared back at me, halting me in my tracks. My heart should have been pounding like a gavel, but I suspected the boy on the other end of the trigger was no threat. He was just scared.

His hands shook, though he was desperately trying to steady the weapon. Beads of sweat formed around his mouth, and his dark-brown hair stuck to his forehead. I was a stranger to him, but even with a scowl and dirt from a long day's work on the farm coating his face, he wasn't a stranger to me.

I'd seen him just the day before when my parents were setting up their wine-tasting booth at the farmer's market in downtown Telluride. I was sitting on the tailgate of our truck, restlessly swinging my legs, when my gaze caught on an older boy carrying crates to one of the produce booths—back and forth, back and forth, like a pendulum. His eyes were cast in front of him, his hair was disheveled, his lips were flattened in a line, and he carried himself in a way that made it all look effortless.

In a small town like ours, it was easy to spot the newcomers because of the clear difference between the residents, the snowbirds, and the tourists. That boy was none of the above.

Curious, I kept my eyes glued to him as he tried to angle the corn bins onto the display and failed miserably as they rolled down and around his feet. I giggled at the show, finding it fascinating how a strong boy could seem so flustered at a simple task. I didn't know why, but I wanted to know everything about him, including why he had come to Telluride, of all places.

A moment later, one of my questions was answered when Harold Cross, an older man with a long, full beard and a plaid button-down shirt over jeans, approached the boy with a disapproving frown and a shake of his head. He mumbled something to the boy, but I couldn't read his lips. Clearly, Harold was displeased, which didn't surprise me. The farmer was known as the town grump, always walking around with a chip on his shoulder.

Two prominent farmlands featured in the red rocky mountain land that bordered the southeastern side of Telluride, Colorado—the Cross Farm and Ranch and the Bell Family Vineyard and Winery. Harold owned the farmland across from our family's vineyard, though we rarely came into contact with him. Our lands were separated by an area of dense woods and a strip of acreage as long as our land was wide, so it felt silly to call ourselves neighbors. In fact, it was forbidden.

When my parents walked back to the tailgate of the

truck, my curiosity grew even more. "Papa, why haven't I seen Farmer Cross at the market before today?"

My papa's eyes widened in surprise as he registered my words, then he took a quick look over his shoulder. The way his back stiffened told me all I needed to know. The surprise wasn't pleasant.

"Must be a mistake," he said, clearly miffed by Farmer Cross's presence. "Cross has been on the vendor wait list for years."

He and Farmer Cross would never be friends. The whole town was privy to the famous Bell and Cross feud that went back over a century. The feud had started with land, became fueled with money, hastened with greed, and ultimately ended in power. My papa held that power, thanks to his prime social standing in the community, and he would do anything to keep it.

I'd just opened my mouth to change the subject when my papa whipped his head toward my mama. "He brought that boy here, Selena. I'm going to say something to Bill."

My mama leaned in and narrowed her eyes. "You will not get the town manager involved in this, Patrick. Harold Cross and his son have just as much right to be here as we do."

"His son?" I asked, the question slipping from my mouth more quickly than I could catch it. "I've never seen him be—"

My papa huffed and gave me a warning look. "That boy is trouble. You're not to go anywhere near him. You understand me, Camila?"

"You're speaking nonsense," my mother hissed. "He's just a fifteen-year-old boy."

Only two years older than me. Hope sparked in my chest.

My papa shook his head. "No. He's a Cross. Therefore, he's trouble. If he's not now, then he will be soon enough. Just you wait." He leaned forward, his face reddening like it always did when he got worked up. "The boy's a Ute, I'll have you know." He whispered that part, telling me it was something bad.

Everyone around there knew the Ute people were the first indigenous inhabitants of Western Colorado. The Ute Mountain reservation was just across the San Juan Mountains, nearly a two-hour drive away. Our teachers talked about it in school, and the various landmarks in and around town pointed to their history. But my knowledge was clearly vague, according to my papa's anger.

"What's wrong with being a Ute, Papa?"

"Those *Indians* think this land is still theirs, and that makes them trouble," he snapped. "My ancestors worked hard to purchase the plots we live and work on, and no one will make me feel different." His indignant huff could be felt for miles. "And that's that."

"You mean *Native American*. And the boy has a name," my mama said, her eyes filled with anger. "It's *Ridge*."

"How do you know?" my papa shot back.

Every time my parents argued, their cultures spewed out like pent-up lava. With my papa's Spanish roots and my mama's Brazilian roots, they shared passionate dynamics that worked for them in love but against them at a crossroads.

"Harold brought him by the country club for a round of golf the other day."

My papa's face twisted in confusion. "Harold *golfs*?"

Mama rolled her eyes. "I don't know, Patrick. Maybe

he was just showing his son around town. The boy seems so quiet and sweet."

"Who wouldn't become a mute if their mother went missing one day and never came home? Doesn't mean the boy's sweet. Don't be so naive, Selena. It's the quiet ones you need to watch out for."

My throat closed at the thought of Ridge losing his mother. *Missing?*

As if detecting my sadness, my mama turned toward me with a sympathetic expression then wrapped an arm around my shoulders and planted a kiss on my cheek. "Don't worry, *mija*. A mother's love never goes away. I'm sure she will turn up."

Then she faced my papa with sharpened daggers in her eyes. "This conversation is over."

I hoped what she'd said was true. Though I hoped Ridge was okay, I didn't know how he could be. To lose a parent in that way and never know if you would ever see them again—I didn't even want to imagine such a thing.

I'd chosen to say nothing more about Ridge or Farmer Cross that day. I'd heard my papa's warning loud and clear. *Stay away or else.* But that didn't mean I had any intentions of listening.

Hence why the boy was standing in front of his property, aiming a shotgun between my eyes.

It was my second time seeing the boy, and I couldn't stop my pulse from racing at just how good looking he actually was. With high cheekbones that kissed the sun, almond-shaped chocolate eyes that looked lost, smooth skin that clearly spent time outdoors, and a strong angled nose that gave him a distinctly different appearance from anyone else I'd ever known, the new boy in town was utterly fascinating, so much that I ignored the flags and whistles that blew with our first meeting.

I propped my hands on my hips and leaned forward so that my small voice would carry over the bridge. "You can put the gun down, Farm Boy. I'm not leaving."

My papa had taught me to stand my ground in the presence of a bully. He told me that in most cases, the one doing the threatening was the real coward. My mama, on the other hand, had warned my papa that he was making me too confident for my own good. I wasn't afraid to test both theories.

The boy clenched his jaw then shook his head before jabbing the gun in my direction.

I tilted my head and squinted, trying to determine whether everything my papa had told me about the boy was true. "You're Ridge Cross," I said finally. I was confident in the statement, but it irked me that the boy didn't even flinch at the fact that I knew who he was.

According to my papa's rant, which had seemed to last the good part of the previous day, the boy didn't speak—ever—but I wasn't convinced it was because he *couldn't*. "Are you really a mute?"

The boy's eyes flashed with anger.

Blood raced through my veins. "It's fine, you know, if you don't want to talk. I don't mind. My parents tell me I talk enough for everyone else, anyway." Daring a step forward, I cautioned him with my eyes. "I just want to come a little closer and introduce myself. Is that okay?"

I didn't wait for his permission again. After a series of long strides over the center of the forty-foot-long bridge, I slowed to assess the situation. Ridge still hadn't moved an inch as he spied me with curious brown eyes and a stiffened frame. And he hadn't taken his barrel off me.

"I'm your neighbor. I live right through there." I pointed behind me at a thick patch of forest that separated a section of landlocked public property from my parents' vineyard. "Where the grapevines grow?" I said the last part as a question to see if I would get any sort of response from him. Even a simple nod would have appeased me.

Again, he didn't shift an inch, causing me to sigh as I took another step forward. Annoyance was starting to twist its way through me. I didn't like to be ignored.

"I'm standing on public property. You shoot me now, you go to jail." I pointed toward a large spruce tree marked with red spray paint by my papa. "Your property is past that red *X*."

That time, the boy looked, following the direction I'd pointed to, and I took it as an opportunity. I marched the rest of the way to him then wrapped my fist around the barrel of his gun and shoved it away from my face.

His head snapped back to mine, and my lips curled into a smile.

I stuck out my other hand. "Camila Bell. Nice to meet you."

His face bunched into a deeper scowl as he glanced at my hand then back to my face. He didn't shake my hand in return or speak. Instead, he blew out a breath and yanked his shotgun from my grip before setting it against a nearby tree. I chose to believe it was a truce of sorts.

I nodded past him again, gesturing to the plot of

land his father owned, where the cornfields grew tall over the summer. "Wanna run with me?"

Confusion replaced his scowl.

"I like to run through the cornfields. It's fun. You'll see." I reached for his hand, but before I could even touch it, he yanked it away.

Shock and annoyance rippling through me, I stumbled back. Not only was I curious, but I was also determined. "Okay, fine. Whatever." Holding up my hands, I rolled my eyes. "I was just trying to be nice."

With a glare, I turned to make it look like I was leaving, but then I pivoted and made a dash for the tree that held his gun and turned the barrel on him.

His eyes flashed with surprise as I started forward, causing him to have to walk backward. "You think you're some tough guy, huh? Pointing this shotgun at me like it gives you power? Well, it doesn't. The most powerful weapon you possess is your tongue, Farm Boy, and it appears you don't like to use yours much. So, tell me, who has the power now?"

I stepped forward one more time, and it was enough. Ridge took a final step back, his foot caught on the edge of the creek, and he fell back into the water. The shock on his face was priceless as water soaked through his white shirt and dark jeans.

I laughed a little too hard and pulled the gun back to check the safety. As soon as I confirmed my suspicions, I grinned. "Surprise, surprise. Safety's on, Farm Boy." Then I inspected the chamber and laughed even harder when I saw that it was empty. "I knew it." I threw the gun to the side and backed toward his land while he pulled himself out of the creek.

He shook his head so adamantly at me that it made me laugh.

"What is it, boy? You don't want me to trespass?"

He nodded just as viciously as he'd shaken his head.

"Well, that's too bad." I took another step back, crossing the red *X* on the tree. "I've been running through the fields for years. Besides, it's the easiest way to get where I'm going." I shrugged. "So come with me or don't. But you sure as heck ain't stoppin' me."

With that, I turned and took off through the woods and into the cornfields.

2

THE HUNTER

Through the scope of his binoculars, the hunter tracked their movements at the bridge and through the woods then lost them when they tore through the cornfields. He didn't bother chasing them there. He'd followed the girl enough to know exactly where they were headed and would take another path.

Twigs snapped and leaves crunched beneath his heavy boots as he worked his way along the creek toward the hilltop, not even bothering to be quiet. No one dared to walk that route. Not only was it inaccessible to the public, but it was dangerous terrain, just a narrow piece of land above a steep slope. The bed of water below widened and rushed faster where it got deeper and colder—which was why the girl preferred the forbidden route through the corn.

With each step, annoyance swirled inside the hunter like it did every time the girl broke the rules. Camila Bell was beginning to become a problem. Her papa was too blind and stupid to see the trouble behind his little girl's eyes, but the hunter saw her for the mischievous little brat she was and would always be. Something would have to be done. A lesson would need to be taught.

The hunter emerged from the woods and stepped into the tall dried grass, which just reached his eyes. His heavy breathing slowed as he paused and scanned his surroundings. A second later, he saw her again, just as he knew he would.

She was trudging across his line of vision a safe distance away from spotting him when she stopped and glanced over her shoulder to see if the boy was still following her. He was, begrudgingly so, but his presence only added to the hunter's frustration. Besides the fact that she had wandered too far, her dad would have her head if he ever found out *who* she was hanging around with.

Camila had only ever traveled to the hilltop alone, and she had already gotten too close for comfort. She had no business traipsing around land she didn't own, especially when her father owned plenty.

That land belonged to the hunter. And he would do whatever it took to keep it.

3

CAMILA

Summers in Telluride had always been beautiful. When the trees were full, the crops were just starting to dry out, and the lakes and creeks were perfect for cooling off. That time of year was also when it felt safest to trespass through Farmer Cross's land, since the corn stalks hid me from view.

I whipped left down a row of corn and moved faster, my dark hair blowing behind me, as I sped down the route I'd run hundreds of times before. Not until I'd reached the end of the path and stopped to turn around did I notice Ridge following not too far behind. He looked breathless and still confused, but the spark in his eyes filled my chest with hope.

"See?" I said around heavy breaths. "No harm. We're on public land again. And now we can go up there." I turned and pointed to the rocky mountain in front of us then swiveled my head back around to catch his reaction.

His eyes were glued to the top of the six-hundred-foot-tall mountain. From the angle he was looking at it from, it looked nearly impossible to climb. I waved him forward. The less time he thought about the arduous climb, the better it would be on his psyche.

"Unless you're going to try to stop me again?" I arched an eyebrow and waited for him to meet my threatening stare.

When he shook his head, I smiled. "C'mon. I'll show you the trail."

I stomped through a section of public land filled with light brush until we reached the other side of the rock, where the incline looked much less intimidating. I hopped into my next step, feeling giddy that I had company on what used to be a solo jaunt to the top of the cliff.

The hike wasn't at all as steep as it looked from the front, and it only took a few minutes to reach the top. Once we were there, I walked Ridge out to the large bristlecone pine tree, its bald branches thick and twisty. The tree was the strangest, most beautiful one I'd ever seen, with its large roots the size of elephant trunks and its only remaining needles visible at the very top. I'd spent hours against the massive trunk.

I spun and raised my arms to the sky, happy to be back in my element. Though I tried to come as often as I could sneak away from the vineyard, I couldn't make it every day, every week, or even every season. My freedom usually came when my parents were busy hosting a wine tasting or giving visitors tours of the vineyard and they left me alone for hours.

"Isn't this amazing?" I asked Ridge when I stopped spinning.

He didn't answer me. His eyes were on the edge of the cliff ahead of us.

When he started to step forward, I wrapped my hand around his wrist and squeezed. "Stop!"

He didn't pull his arm away that time, but he frowned when he looked at me as if to ask, "Why?"

"We can't go any closer to the edge, or someone could spot us."

His eyebrows pinched together even more.

I explained to him that the hilltop and some of the surrounding land was public property that overlooked both Bell and Cross farmland—cornfield and vineyard— with patches of government-owned property around us.

The hilltop was my sanctuary and my favorite spot in all of Telluride. It showcased the beauty of the land below while making me feel like I was on top of the world. But getting a closer view meant risking getting caught.

I searched Ridge's eyes, wondering how much he knew about our families and their ongoing feud. He hadn't been in Telluride long, but his pointing the shotgun at my head back at the bridge showed he already knew how territorial our fathers got about their properties. While they hadn't had a dispute in nearly a decade, the tension was always present.

"Neither of us should be up here. There's no way to get to this hilltop unless one of us is trespassing on land. In this case, it's me. It's too dangerous for me to get here if I go across my land. That's why I go through the cornfields."

I was afraid Ridge would be angry, but I wasn't sure why I cared. He was the boy who'd just held a shotgun to my head like he wanted to kill me. But if anything could make me panic, it was the thought of losing the only freedom I knew of—and Ridge had caught on to my weakness. Something that looked like recognition flashed in his eyes, then acceptance followed as he took a step back from the edge.

We sat down against the tree, letting the sun warm our faces while the clouds moved with the breeze. My arm brushed his accidentally, but when he didn't jump to distance himself from me, I somehow knew that Ridge and I would be friends, even if our parents didn't want us to be. Even if *Ridge* didn't want us to be. I would grow on him like the twisty tree at our backs, until I was so deeply rooted in his life that he couldn't push me away again if he wanted to.

We had our hilltop along with our tree and our land that was spread out below our feet. No one could take any of it away. At least that was what I had convinced myself.

I turned to Ridge, so many questions filling my mind. I hated that he couldn't—or wouldn't—talk to me.

"So you really are a mute, then?"

He slowly turned to meet my stare, then a few moments later, his mouth started to part. Anticipation filled my chest while I waited for words to come. I'd never wanted something so badly.

"I'm not a *mute*. That word is not kind."

His voice surprised and thrilled me in equal measure. His tone was soft, which didn't surprise me at all, but it had a richness that felt significantly his.

"You speak." The wistful words rushed from my throat faster than I could stop them.

"I don't like to waste my words."

His answer hit me like a forceful breeze—powerful yet calm amid the gloom that fated us both. But I was delighted that he'd chosen to speak to me. As hard as it would be, I promised myself I wouldn't take advantage of that gift.

We sat in silence for what felt like hours. As much as I loved to talk, I didn't mind being still. The hilltop was the perfect place to do that. But on that day, my thoughts were consumed by the boy sitting beside me.

"You come here often?"

"As often as I can." My heart kicked at our nearness. "It's my favorite place to think, to dream, and to pray."

His eyebrows knitted, and worry lines formed. "You aren't afraid?" He tossed a glance behind us.

"Of what? Lions and tigers and bears? " I smiled. "What's to be afraid of when humans are the scariest predator?"

"What about hunters? Where I come from, that's all there is."

I smiled again. For an older boy, his innocence was sweet. Sure, my papa had warned me about hunters— quiet men who stalked their prey with sharpshooting rifles or bow and arrows, their aim steady, and never missing a single shot. My papa knew those men well. Over a decade ago, he used to be one of them.

"This hilltop and that bridge we met at might be public land, but everything that surrounds it is owned by our fathers, yours and mine. It's been fenced in for decades. We're sitting on landlocked property with no public access to get here. There are no hunters here."

"How can you be sure?"

"Before taking the vineyard over from his parents, my papa was a hunter. He hunted elk, mostly, but some of the men didn't like to play fair. Designated hunting grounds opened up seasonally, and that was where most of the men would go. A few others would access ground by trespassing onto private property that had been land-locked after the Civil War. Back then, property in Colorado got sold off much like a checkerboard in certain areas. The sold land was used to generate revenue that would support public institutions. Mind you, my papa told me all of this while he was supposed to be reading me *Little Red Riding Hood* one night." I chuckled at the mental picture of my papa holding the children's book while whispering his own stories to me. "Anyway, he told me to think of the black spaces as federally owned public land, while the red spaces are available for purchase."

"That's quite the mental picture."

"Right?" Excitement flitted through me. I'd never forgotten the visual he'd painted for my imagination that night. A map of land ownership would show more of a jigsaw formation, but the Bell and Cross farms were a part of that history. "That checkerboard created a clear problem when it came to accessing hunting grounds that had been landlocked with no available access road to get to it. Hence the fence that has bordered the perimeter of our property for the last few decades."

"Boundaries don't keep people out. They fence you in."

I bit down on my laugh, feeling my physical attraction toward Ridge sprout butterflies in my chest at his quote from Grey's Anatomy. "Shonda Rhimes is a genius."

A hint of a smile lifted Ridge's cheeks.

"While I see what you're getting at, Wise One, our groundskeeper inspects our borderlines often. If anyone was cutting through, he'd know about it."

Ridge looked like he was thinking about my words, so I gave him a minute before changing the subject. "I just have one more question. I hope you don't take offense."

He waited, his expression unchanging.

I swallowed, feeling nervous about intruding for the first time since our introduction, which was ironic, since I'd just trespassed on his land to climb onto the rock. "Why haven't you come to Telluride before now if Farmer Cross is your father? The Ute Mountain reservation is only a couple hours from here."

His slightly upturned lips turned back down, and his jaw hardened. "That's a story for another day." Then he turned his chin up slowly to stare at the sky. "Rain is coming." A rumble of thunder followed. "We should go."

Not even a second later, a raindrop hit my nose, then another one hit my arm. "What are you? Psychic?"

"Not psychic," he said, his tone low. "Nature speaks, but not too many listen."

I blinked as his words sank in, almost forgetting about the storm that was suddenly rolling in. After just a few hours with my mysterious neighbor boy, I became a million times more curious about Ridge Cross and where he'd been for the past thirteen years of my life.

Another crack of thunder finally jolted me into

action. In seconds, Ridge and I were making a mad dash down the hill, through the thick brush of weeds, and back through the cornfields. Instead of heading toward his home, Ridge followed me as I ran down the familiar path, all while the rain soaked into the soil. Mud splashed the backs of my legs and dress while rain coated my dark hair.

I didn't mind the rain or even the mud. The only thing that bothered me in that particular moment was that my time with the strange boy was over.

I looked over my shoulder as I ran. Ridge was smiling as he chased me through the muddy fields. The rain had washed away the dirt that had caked his face earlier, and I couldn't help but take a closer look at the features that had already caught my attention from a distance.

Ridge Cross was unmistakably breathtakingly handsome, and excitement that he was in Telluride to stay overwhelmed me.

Adrenaline licked through me, and we picked up the pace, not stopping until we reached the bridge where we'd met.

When I turned around, the rain was barely noticeable in the surrounding trees. I smiled at him, and he smiled back at me. An ache filled my chest as I wondered when I would see the boy again. I wouldn't allow it to be long. Despite all obstacles, I was determined to make sure Ridge and I stayed friends, no matter the cost.

4

CAMILA, TWO MONTHS LATER

I loved to watch the seasons change, from the white winter blanket that melted away to a promising spring, to the wildflowers that sprang to life under a blazing summer sun, to perhaps my favorite season of all —fall.

In the midst of the summer-to-fall transition was always a sense of uncertainty. One morning, a full spectrum of colors would fill the beautiful landscape of Telluride, and in that same afternoon, everything could change. We never quite knew when our first snow would blow in, but we were always prepared for it.

My friends and I liked to take advantage of our last sunny moments in September. We would ride our bikes through the endless mountain off-roads that would soon become ski trails, then we would take the gondola to Mountain Village, and from there we would ride back down the Village trail. Once back in the box canyon of Telluride, we would stop at one of the many cafes for a snack.

"C'mon, Camila." My friend Trip had just made it to the start of one of the switchbacks.

Like always, I was behind the others but not because I couldn't keep up. On a day like today, when the sun was high and a few clouds brought in the perfect breeze, I loved to stop and watch the vibrant wildflowers dance. Whereas my friends wanted to race through the terrain like we had somewhere to be.

"Go ahead," I yelled, waving them on. I would rather bike the trails at my own pace, anyway. *What's the point in any journey if you don't allow yourself time to stop and breathe?*

Trip gave me a stern look and shook his head. His father, Thomas Bradshaw, was my papa's right-hand man at the vineyard. And since Trip was a couple of years older than me, on outings like that, he always became my unofficial babysitter. As handsome as he was, his arrogance always managed to rub me the wrong way.

I glared at him then turned back to the deep valley of wildflowers and aspen groves, which seemed to stretch for miles. Anger had a way of lighting up inside me whenever I felt forced to follow someone else's trail instead of blazing my own. It was only a matter of time before I erupted. Instead of fighting back, I squeezed the handlebars of my bike as hard as I could and gave in. "Fine."

After hopping back onto the seat, I zoomed past Trip and down the trail, not slowing at the switchback. It only took a few seconds to catch up with the others, who had stopped on the side of the dirt path, waiting for me, no doubt.

Grinning, I flew by them, too, and didn't stop when

they screamed my name. I rode the narrow dirt path over rocks and puddles of rain from the day before, taking each sharp turn like the pro that I'd become in the past couple of years.

If my parents knew what my friends and I meant by "biking the mountain trails," they would lose their minds with rage. While the path was marketed to tourists as "easy," it was anything but. One slip, and the wheel of my bike could skid, throwing me off the thing and straight down a cliff.

The next switchback came and went, and I was nearly down the mountain when I spotted a boy with dark hair hiking with his back to me. Even without seeing his face, I knew exactly who it was.

It had been two months since I'd seen Ridge last. He hadn't tried to stop me at the bridge again, and he hadn't come up to the hilltop when I was there. It had finally occurred to me that he might be avoiding me, which did wonders for my stubborn nature. As adamant as I had been to remain friends with the boy, I was just as determined to avoid him right back. Two could play that game.

Ridge hadn't seen me yet. I would ride right by him without saying a word and with my head held high. But I was so focused on speeding by him that I failed to see a thick stick on the path until moments before my bike hit it. My front wheel jerked to a stop and I lurched forward over my handlebars then landed hard on my back.

Gravel dug into my shoulders before I shot up and tried to breathe. A moan came out instead. Everything felt constricted.

Ridge knelt down in front of me and placed his hand

on my back. "You just had the wind knocked out of you. Try to breathe through your mouth while pushing your stomach out."

My eyes latched on to his as I did as he said or at least I tried like hell to.

"Good. Now exhale while sucking your stomach back in. That will help stretch out your diaphragm."

His presence was so calming that even when I felt like death, I knew everything was going to be okay. Though that wasn't the first time I'd had the wind knocked out of me, it was still terrifying.

Just as I was regaining my breath, the sounds of the other bikes approached. My senses were returning quickly, and I was suddenly aware that tears had stained my face and dirt covered my clothes and exposed skin. I didn't care so much about the dirt, but I didn't like the fact that Ridge had just seen my tears. I never allowed anyone to see my weaknesses, yet I felt prone to them with him.

"Camila!" my friends yelled in near unison.

Josie and Raven were the first ones to me, while Emilio, Brody, and Trip came up behind them.

"Are you okay?" Josie, my best friend, asked, already inspecting me for injuries.

Raven, Trip's younger sister, stood back and stared at Ridge.

"I'm fine now, thanks to Ridge."

Trip's glance bounced off Ridge then back to me like he wasn't even there. "Well, all right," he said without extending an ounce of grace to the boy who'd just helped me breathe.

Ridge picked up my bike, remaining quiet, while

Trip helped me off the dirt. Then everyone looked at each other in awkward silence.

"We should get you home," Trip said soberly. "Are you okay to ride, or should we walk?"

"I said I'm fine." I shot him a glare, angry that my friends couldn't even look at Ridge or thank him for being there to calm me when I fell. I turned back to Ridge, my expression softening. "Thanks again for your help." My words were firm, and I hoped my friends would take a lesson in my kindness. "I don't know what I would have done without you."

Ridge ran a glance over my friends then nodded.

I grabbed my bike from Ridge and hopped on. "Last one down the hill buys the pizza," I called as I took off riding.

My friends all yelled, "Slow down!"

"You are the craziest of the crazies," Josie told me as she reached for a slice of pizza.

"Freaking nuts," Raven chimed in around a mouthful.

"But kind of badass, though," Brody added with a shrug. "You're not afraid of death. I give you that."

He followed his comment up with a hearty laugh, and we all joined in. Well, everyone except Trip, whose narrowed eyes were glued to the door of the pizza joint. When I followed the direction of his stare, heaviness washed over me. Ridge had just walked in, and had stopped at the hostess stand for a menu.

"We should invite him to sit with us."

Trip snapped his head to give me a wide-eyed stare. "Are you crazy? No way, Camila."

He hated my new neighbor, and I blamed our parents for that. Whatever issues Papa had, Thomas Bradshaw had adopted them.

Once upon a time, I'd had a crush on Trip. He'd always seemed so attentive and nice when we were younger. And he was unmistakably gorgeous, with his deep-blue eyes and sandy-blond hair. It seemed every girl in our school had a crush on him. But my crush had ended the moment I found out that he'd only been so attentive because my papa had been paying him to keep a close eye on me. From that point on, I'd felt more resentment toward him than anything else.

"You think the Ute boy can read?" Trip sneered.

Every nerve jolted to attention when I heard the name of Ridge's tribe. *But why does he, like my papa, use the word in such a demeaning way?* It felt wrong and dirty, and I boiled inside because of it.

"It's so strange," Raven said with a contorted expression. "I would never have guessed that Ridge was Native American." She did a double-take then squinted when she looked at him again. "He doesn't look it."

Josie placed a hand on my knee and squeezed, telling me to bite my tongue. Unlike Trip, Raven didn't mean any harm by her words. She just didn't understand.

"His dad is Farmer Cross," Josie said, far more gently than I would have. "It makes sense that he's mixed. But we probably shouldn't worry about someone else's business."

"He's our business now that he moved to town," Trip said with an uptick of his head.

I lifted and eyebrow in a challenge. "You should get to know him, then. Maybe you two will become friends."

Trip's laughter rocked his entire body. He even tossed his head back a little for dramatic effect. I didn't think I could hate my friend any more than I already did. Trip had always been a little bit of a jerk, but I had never seen him react so harshly to someone he didn't even know. Surely, Thomas Bradshaw and my papa had rubbed off on him.

"Me?" he asked, pointing at his chest. "Friends with *Ute Boy* over there? No, thanks. I know you're friendly to everyone, Camila, but you really shouldn't be so naive all the time."

I gripped my glass of water with all my might. "If by naive you mean that I don't judge someone because of their appearance or where they come from, then I guess you chose the right word."

"Oh, come on. You know how the town feels about the Cross family. You of all people should be on my side."

I shook my head. "I've never understood the stupid rivalry. Even if I did, Ridge had nothing to do with it. Just like I had nothing to do with it."

Josie squeezed my knee again. "Okay, time for a subject change. I want to talk about Camila's epic crash on the mountain. Anyone else?"

Emilio, Brody, and Raven joined Josie in a hearty laugh as they recalled me taking off past them only to find me fighting for my breath on the ground. Trip was still glaring at me.

"It's a good thing Ridge was there to save you, right, Camila?"

I didn't even blink before sassing back. "That's right, Trip."

Trip's lips curled up into a smile. "Maybe your papa will give him a reward when he finds out. What do you think?"

"You wouldn't," I said through clenched teeth.

"I would, and I will, if you even think about becoming friends with that boy. I saw the way you were looking at him."

Trip's threat was clear, detonating the anger that had been building in my head and chest. I lifted my glass and threw the contents at his face. Water and ice smacked him, causing his jaw to fall open in surprise. His shirt and hair were soaked, and everyone in the restaurant stared back at us.

I had just imploded, and it felt amazing—until Trip's eyelids snapped open and his gaze landed on me. Fury was all I could see, sending red flags to every nerve ending in my body.

I jolted from my seat and tore out of the establishment, leaving my pizza behind. After yanking my bike off the rack, I hopped on and pedaled away as fast as my legs would take me. My friends didn't have a chance of catching me, but I still rode quickly through town and took the dirt-and-gravel off-road that led to my home.

The last thing I wanted was to make any more trouble for Ridge than he was already dealing with, not that he'd told me much. After his mother's disappearance, moving to a new town, and getting wrapped up in a ridiculous rivalry by default, he hadn't had a welcoming start in Telluride.

Later that night, I called Trip and made him a deal. I wouldn't befriend Ridge if he promised to leave him alone.

I lied. But so did he.

5

RIDGE

I liked to rise before the roosters crowed, when the sun had yet to dawn, and when I still had enough moonlight to guide my way. After dressing for my day on the farm, I pulled my orange notebook from beneath my mattress and quietly closed the door to the ranch house to avoid waking my father.

My father. Such an informal word to use for a man I'd been estranged from for my entire life. I was more surprised than anyone else when Harold Cross requested to take me in following my mother's disappearance six months ago. After I'd moved into the spare bedroom in his ranch house, it immediately made sense. He needed help on his farm. *Who better to help than his fifteen-year-old illegitimate son who he doesn't have to pay?*

And I wasn't exactly sneaking around. Harold didn't mind that I crept out before sunrise. Perhaps the fact that he hadn't been the one to raise me provided me the luxury of loose rules, almost like I was a guest staying in his home for the short term. Or maybe he was afraid of my reactions if he were to be strict after being nonexistent for my entire life.

Either way, I didn't mind, especially since I got to watch the sun rise from the old twisted tree at the top of the hilltop cliff—the one Camila had revealed to me two months ago.

I'd strategically managed to avoid the strange girl until our run-in on the mountain trail the day before. By the time she started her sneaky journey through the cornfields in the late afternoon, I made sure to be long gone. Sometimes I would be tending to my various duties on the farm when I spotted her darting through the field, then when she was out of sight, I would conveniently move to a section of land where she wouldn't be able to spot me from the cliff if she dared to look down.

Avoiding Camila just felt like the right thing to do. While she seemed nice enough, Harold had made it clear numerous times to beware of the Bell family across the creek. He hadn't given too many details, but from what he did say, I got the picture.

I first moved to the farm in springtime, and Harold sowed the seed of fear that quickly grew to my reaction when I'd spotted the young Bell girl crossing the bridge.

"You keep your eye out for any mischief coming from the woods over there, y'hear, son? I don't need any more trouble than I've already got."

At the time, I'd had no clue what Harold was telling me. I just knew I wasn't safe, and I didn't like that feeling one bit.

"You take this just in case." Harold shoved a worn brown hunting shotgun with a scope at me. "Someone comes onto our property, they'll run right back to where they came from."

My hands had started to shake the moment the weapon touched my skin. I was no stranger to guns. As descendants of hunters and gatherers, plenty of men on the reservation carried them, but I'd never held one myself. My mom had never allowed me to go on cattle-hunting trips with my friends and their dads. She said I wasn't old enough, but she was trying to protect me from the shame that came with being the "white-skinned boy" on the reservation. I was forced to navigate that same criticism while growing up on the rez.

Someone from the Ute Mountain Tribe conceiving a baby with an outsider didn't happen every day. Some people considered it a treacherous act. My father owned the land my ancestors were violently driven from in the 1800s. A Telluride settler was the worst kind of an outlander to the Utes and vice versa. Two centuries and two decades later, the wounds were still fresh. And to my peers, I was a reminder of that pain.

I didn't belong on that reservation. And when I held Harold's shotgun, I knew I didn't belong on his farm either.

"No, thank you." My reply was soft, but I tried to give my eyes the conviction buried down deep inside me. My mother wasn't physically there, but her strong values for nature and human life had been ingrained in me.

Harold accepted my response—or so I thought. The next day was a different story.

He took me into the woods, slammed the gun against my chest, and pointed at a thick tree in the distance. "We ain't leavin' 'til you hit that tree."

I definitely couldn't argue with Harold. He saw life one way, with the heart and mind of someone who had to work hard to protect what was his. The instinct to fight to survive was built into his bones. I could see it and feel it in his way of life. He bent for those around him, working hard and following the rules, as unfair as they were. I'd only been on Cross Farm for a short time, but I could see it all so clearly.

In the end, I accepted the shooting lessons to appease my old man. For all I knew, shooting lessons were his way of bonding. And since we'd had a lifetime without it, everything felt awkward, forced, and wrong. But they could never feel right when the one person who had always protected me was gone.

As I sat up on the hilltop, watching the morning sun lift over the horizon, I thought about my mama and the reality of her disappearance. She wasn't the first indigenous woman to go missing without a trace, and the odds of her turning up alive were smaller than any shred of hope I had left. Mama was young, with so much life yet to live, and what a courageous one she lived.

I scribbled some of my thoughts into my journal, wanting to commit her memory to paper in every way I possibly could, from lessons she'd taught me to wisdoms she'd passed on. Her view on life and the challenges we all faced had always breathed so much inspiration into me. She made me feel like I could do anything.

"Living in the moment is not about perfection, my son. Life is meant to be messy and challenging. It is our privilege to free our thoughts, sort through the chaos, and take what survives to bring us closer to our destiny. Our path is never-ending. Imperfections will challenge us, break us, and in the end, make us whole."

I could hear her words like a soft whisper in the wind as I covered the page with inked thoughts and sacred memories.

Moments later, the sound of footsteps approaching jerked me from the depths of my thoughts. I slammed my notebook closed and shoved it into the back pocket of my jeans. With a whip of my head, I turned to find the one person I'd made it my goal to stay away from. She was walking up the path with her eyes pointed down.

Camila was clearly young, yet she was a fierce little thing that knew too much. I pinched my eyebrows together in a glare to warn her to stay away from both me and Harold's farm. She had no business trespassing time and time again. I'd done her a favor by looking the other way, but I wouldn't do it again.

"Go away, Wild One."

My voice must have surprised her, because she stopped in her tracks, and her little eyes widened on me. Wild One was a nickname I'd given her after her mountain-biking incident the day before. The way she didn't even flinch at the gun I'd aimed at her combined with the way she'd hopped back on that bike after falling showed that the girl clearly had no regard for her own life.

Staring back at her, I couldn't help but get caught up in her eyes. They were the color of springtime in the cornfields when the stalks were green and lively, and glimpses of golden kernels peaked through the leaves, just like the golden swirls in her eyes. The caramel tone of her skin only heightened the contrast of them, and after just one meeting with her, I knew better than to fall for the innocence of her expression.

A moment later, a fierce stare transformed her face. "This is public land," she said. "You can't tell me to go away. Besides, I showed you this hilltop. And—" Her expression changed again but to confusion. "I thought we were friends."

I chuckled at her absurd comment. Not only was she bold, but she was also clueless in her assumption. "Friends? Why would you think that?"

"We ran through the fields together, you were laughing, and—" She searched my gaze as if something were missing and she was determined to find it. "You helped me after my fall yesterday."

"What was I going to do? Leave you gasping for air?"

She looked lost, and something in my chest twitched at being the cause of her disappointment. I wasn't a bully, but I sure felt like one.

"You're a Bell," I said finally, as if that would explain it all. I kind of thought it might.

She folded her arms across her chest and glared. "And what about it?"

"Our parents aren't friends."

"Doesn't mean *we* can't be."

I laughed again, adjusting my position on the tree to get a full view of her. She looked taller than I remembered from just the day before as she stood there in her green sundress and worn, dirty white sneakers.

"Why do you want to be my friend so badly, anyway, huh? You don't even know me."

Her jaw hardened, and she jerked her chin up before she spoke. "I dunno. Maybe I don't like keeping enemies. And even if I did, it's better to keep your enemies close. Isn't that what they say?"

I nodded. Her intentions were pure. Just one look at her showed her innocence and curiosity. She might not have been a direct threat to me, but if either of our parents caught us together, that could change really fast. Her friends didn't seem to care for me much either.

"We don't have to be enemies, Camila. But I think you know why friendship is out of the question. Besides, you're just a little girl. You should be watching cartoons at home with your parents."

She stepped closer, releasing her hands as she walked. "I'll be fourteen in two weeks. And I'm not leavin'. If anyone is going anywhere, it's you, Farm Boy."

Camila and I shared the same birthday week. I would be sixteen in two weeks, but if I told her, she would have yet another excuse to want to befriend me. Apparently, my avoidance didn't matter, because a moment later, she plopped onto the root of the tree inches from me.

I let it go for the sake of the peace I'd come up there for. Maybe two people who didn't get along could sit next to each other. Soon enough, it was like she wasn't even there. Each of us was lost in our own thoughts as we stared out at the rising sun.

"How do you know so much about our parents not liking each other?"

Her question came out of nowhere, throwing me off. I thought about what to say, because it wouldn't be much. Ever since I'd gone shooting with Harold, I couldn't get the story of our feuding families off my mind. After an entire century, they should have been able to find peace. Maybe Camila knew more than her innocent eyes revealed.

"Do *you* know the history of our families?"

She was the one who had grown up here. If anyone should be dealing information, it should be her.

Camila scoffed and folded her arms across her chest. "Key word, history."

I shook my head, frustrated, which wasn't part of my makeup. I'd been taught to "go with the flow." Nothing would get solved in anger or frustration. Those emotions only distorted the true problems that lay underneath.

"History doesn't mean it no longer exists, Wild One. The opposite is true. History is more than a time period or an event. It's born into our DNA and embedded in our bones. Without history, there's no future. And the more you know and understand, the more power you have to right the wrongs of our ancestors."

She stretched out her legs and sighed. "My papa doesn't go into detail about what happened, but I know the Cross-Bell feud started over a century ago when *your* family started buying farmland across the creek from mine. Land disputes weren't uncommon back then. But that was nearly one hundred years ago, Ridge. What is the point of dwelling on something that could easily be righted with a simple handshake?"

Camila's attitude toward the subject intrigued me. "Is that really what you believe? That our parents should shake hands and begin to live in peace?"

"I don't understand why it can't be done."

My chest warmed, and I smiled, enamored with her and her goodness. It could so easily be destroyed with some simple truths. I didn't want to be the one to destroy a young girl's optimistic mind, but I felt like I had to.

"For starters, someone would have to apologize. Do you think that should be your father or mine?"

Camila seemed to be at a loss for words until she frowned. "I don't know." Then she turned to me, her eyes still wild, but they held a hint of sadness too. "Did my papa do something to hurt yours?"

"I don't know about that. I don't even know how the feud initially got started, but I do know that while your grandparents were planting their first bare root vines to begin their vineyard venture, my grandparents' farm was filled with livestock. On one side of the land, the Bell family was struggling to keep the animals from the Cross farm off their property. On the other side of the land, the Cross ranch animals were disappearing, one by one. This went on for years until, one day, a horse that had gone missing from the Cross farm showed back up on their property with a gunshot wound in the head, infuriating my ancestors. So the rivalry continued, and a month later, on the first day of the first Bell family harvest, a fire lit a row of vines, nearly destroying the brand-new vineyard."

"You sure know a lot for someone who doesn't talk much."

I turned to her, frowning. "And you're pretty mouthy for someone who speaks more than they listen. You sure you want to be my friend?"

She glared, her small green eyes shooting lasers. "I'm starting to change my mind about that."

"Why don't you, then? We don't belong as friends. Go find some kids your own age."

"What is your *problem*?" she shrieked, and for the first time since I'd met her, I could see her age written all over her. Camila acted tough, wild, and uncaring, but deep down was more than she presented, and that frightened me the most.

I sighed, figuring it was time to end the conversation for good and put it all out there. I'd meant what I told Camila the first time I met her about not wanting to waste my words. And I'd already said too much. In fact, I had never spoken so much to anyone besides my mother in one sitting.

I stood, extending a hand to Camila to help her up, but she ignored it and got up on her own.

"I don't need your help." Then she huffed and started walking down the mountain a different way than she'd come.

"Where are you going?" I called.

"Don't worry about it," she yelled over her shoulder. "I don't need to use your stupid cornfields to get home. I'll make a new path."

Rolling my eyes, I watched her walk away until she faded from view halfway down the red and rocky hills. I wanted to go after her, but that would defeat the purpose of calling an official end to our friendship. Besides, if Camila was going to get to the hilltop again, she would have to find another way. It looked like that problem was solved all on its own.

6

CAMILA

The jagged downhill climb was harder than my stubborn mind had wanted to believe. Getting away from Ridge and anything to do with him had been my number-one goal, but even I could admit that the path I'd chosen to take was the wrong one.

I stepped down on the only rock ledge I could find as my fingers gripped the red rocks above me. The next landing was a four-foot shimmy to my right. I rolled my eyes up to the blue sky and blew out a breath. *Now is not the time to panic, Camila.* It would be fine. I had gotten myself into stickier situations before.

If it hadn't been for Ridge and how rude he'd been, dismissing a friendship with me, then I wouldn't be in the predicament in the first place. It was his fault that I was taking the dangerous route and was one wrong move away from falling to my death. Yet after the way he'd just let me leave, I didn't think he would care much if I fell.

With a final step, I hopped onto a flatter piece of rock, then I looked around while I caught my breath.

The air was chilly, but sweat still beaded above my brow line. My nerves were getting the better of me. I blamed that on Ridge too. I should never have shown him the hilltop. If I hadn't been so stupid, then I would still have access to my favorite hangout. Now, not only did I have to share it, but I also had to find my own way to and from, if I didn't kill myself on the way.

The rocks started to get smaller as I descended farther, making it easier to find leverage. When I saw the main landing up ahead, I sighed with relief. I had never traveled to that section of rock before. I'd seen no point in looking for another route when I'd found the path nearest to the cornfields. With the final slope of hill in front of me, I looked back and said goodbye to the mountain that was once mine. I couldn't come that way again. Even the daredevil in me was smart enough to know when enough was enough.

At the bottom of the final slope, a six-foot drop-off led to a clearing of red rock. I jumped and landed on my feet with my knees bent beneath me, but I miscalculated something. My chin came down hard on my knees, and a howl shot from my throat before I fell back, my eyes opening to the sky.

My ears rang, and the throbbing pain would not let up. A rustle of the tall grass in front of me was like a splash of cold water in my face. *Was that a snake? A bear?* My mind went wild with the possibilities as I forced it away from the pain.

"Camila!" Ridge shouted.

The relief that flooded me at the sound of his voice came with a rush of emotions. He was the last person I'd expected, but he was the first person to arrive minutes later. I hadn't even known he followed me.

Just like after my spill on the mountain the day before, he crouched above me with concern in his warm chocolate eyes, which made me melt in his presence. "Why do I always find you like this?"

Despite the pain that was radiating from my chin and all around my jaw, I couldn't help but laugh. "I never thought I was clumsy before I met you."

"You really are a wild one, aren't you?"

I narrowed my eyes. "You keep calling me that. Why do I feel like it's an insult?"

He stared at me for a moment before shaking his head. "You're fearless. Brave. But you should be more careful. If I hadn't been here——"

"I would have been fine," I cut in, my stubborn bravado back as I lifted myself to a sitting position.

He bent his head and chuckled. "Yes. I'm sure that's true."

Ridge extended his hand, a gesture that sparked a glimmer of hope in my heart. I accepted it, fitting my small hand in his as he helped me from the dirt. He'd been living on Harold's ranch for six months, so I should have expected his rough hands and the dirt beneath his nails. "Your old man keeps you busy, huh?"

He followed my stare and jerked his hand away. "Same way your old man keeps you busy in the vineyard, I suppose."

I searched his eyes, wondering what other assumptions he had made about me. "I choose to work on the vineyard. I want to learn everything about it so that I can take over for my papa one day. It's a great responsibility, and I want to do right by my family's legacy."

Ridge narrowed his eyes. "Those are big dreams, Wild One. You're a little young to be making those kinds of decisions now."

"You're not much older than me. Two years isn't that big of a difference. You're telling me you don't have dreams?"

He chuckled. "Of course I do. They just don't involve taking over a thousand acres of land."

"Maybe you need to dream bigger, Ridge Cross."

His lips tilted into a different kind of smile, one that caught me in the chest. Our age difference clearly bothered Ridge more than it did me. And somehow, in that moment, I didn't care about rules or family feuds or how things were "supposed to be." Something about Ridge Cross made me want to hold on to him, no matter the consequences.

He was the first one to break our eye contact. His gaze lifted to just over my shoulder. Something changed in his expression, causing me to turn to see what had caught his attention.

"Is that what I think it is?"

His question came just as I saw what he was looking at—a worn wood-framed entrance with a rusted steel gate that was closed and padlocked. I had to take a step closer to read the engraved words above the door. "Cornett Creek Mine 1875," I read while my heart pounded. I walked closer to the gate, gripped a section of the bars, and tried to peer inside.

Other than the end of rail tracks at the entrance, I

couldn't see a single thing in the darkness. "This is incredible," I gushed. But with my next breath came a pungent smell that had me gagging. "The smell. There must be a dead animal in there." I waved a hand in front of my nose, as if it would make the smell go away. "I bet this mine was forgotten once the property became landlocked by our fathers." I spoke excitedly as I looked over my shoulder at Ridge. "Speaking of history, this is a big part of it."

He came up beside me and tried to look inside it as well. His nose immediately wrinkled at the smell. "You realize mining in this town is the reason my Ute ancestors were forcibly removed, don't you?"

I frowned. Everyone in Telluride knew the disturbing story of what the European settlers had done to the original inhabitants of that land. All the Ute people wanted was the land they'd been raised on to hunt, fish, and live in peace. Then the Meeker Massacre of 1879 happened, provoking a Ute uprising against a US government agency, which prompted the Ute Removal Act. Twelve Million acres of land that had been guaranteed to the Utes were suddenly denied to them, forcing them into exile.

The horror of our town's past hit me hard, and I swallowed. "We learn about the history of Telluride in school. What happened back then was unfair, and I'm sorry."

A soft smile appeared on his face, surprising me. "Oh no. You had nothing to do with what happened back then. And I can't say much myself, since I'm a bit of a mixed bag."

His ancestry was something I'd yet to ask him about,

though I desperately wanted to understand. Luckily, I didn't have to ask a thing.

"My Cross ancestors were part of the problem and some of the first settlers to own property here."

After one sentence, I started to fill in so many blanks about Ridge's background. No wonder he seemed so fascinating and complex. I wanted to know more. "But your mom took you to live on the reservation. Why?"

His jaw tightened for a second before he released it with a shrug. "I got the impression that we were no longer welcome here. I didn't ask many questions growing up. My mom didn't like to speak about Harold."

I let in a slow breath, trying to stay calm, though my mind was going wild. "That's got to be hard, not knowing."

He released his grip on the gate door. "My mom was a good person. I believe she did what she felt was best, and I'll honor her decision always."

I released my grip on the gate, too, and turned to face him. "Did you enjoy living on the reservation?"

"The rez is all I know, so I suppose I enjoyed it. Never felt like I belonged, though." He raised his arms and looked around. "Just like I don't feel like I belong here."

I started to frown again but found an opportunity to smile instead. "Which is exactly why we should become friends. I'd love to learn more about where you're from. And I can teach you about all the things you missed in Telluride." I grinned, feeling like there was no way he could turn me down. "What do you say, Ridge?" I stuck out my hand. "Friends?"

He twisted his features in hesitation. "Our parents would never allow such a thing."

"They never have to know."

His expression relaxed some. "And your friends? They looked at me like I was an alien yesterday."

I rolled my eyes. "That was Trip. He's just a big jerk. Don't pay him any attention." Then I grinned again. "Just think—one day, it will be you and me running the land. We can end the silly feud then and there. And you know that bridge you tried to threaten me not to cross? One day, that bridge will connect us instead of separate us."

Ridge's gaze froze on mine, like even he could picture our worlds coming together as one. "You think so, huh?"

I nodded, more confident than I'd ever been about anything in my entire life. From that moment forward, it would be my main mission. The day I stepped into my papa's shoes would be the day we ended the stupid feud.

Ridge smiled as his hand met mine for the second time that day. "Okay, Wild One. We can be friends."

I squeezed his hand and popped up on my toes. "Good. Now you can check this mine out with me." I'd just started to release his hand and turn toward the mine when he yanked me back to him.

Ridge's eyes were wide, and he shook his head while letting our hands fall. "Don't even think about it. We don't know what's in there. It's probably not even safe. Besides, it has a lock on it."

I looked around and grabbed a large rock. "Then let's open it."

He ripped the rock from my hand and threw it into

the nearest field. "No way. It's sealed for a reason, whether our parents know about it or not. Before anyone steps into that thing, it should probably get inspected."

His suggestion spiked fear in my chest. "You're not going to tell anyone, are you?"

Ridge sighed without answering and looked behind us toward the tall grass that led to the woods. "C'mon. I'll walk you to the bridge. Then you need to run on home before your papa comes looking for you."

"I can walk myself," I insisted.

Ridge was apparently just as stubborn as I was, because he didn't listen. Instead, he grabbed my hand firmly and started to walk through the tall grass, into the woods, and down to the creek, which we followed. He didn't let go of me until we reached the center of the bridge.

There, he waved me forward and started to walk backward toward his own land. "Hurry home and stop getting into so much trouble."

Though his comment was coming from the right place, all I could think about was what would happen if either of our fathers discovered what we just had. "Don't tell anyone about the mine, okay?"

He halted and tilted his head. "It's dangerous, Camila. Someone should check it out before anyone goes exploring where they shouldn't. They could get hurt."

"No one will get hurt," I insisted.

Ridge shook his head and closed his eyes, silently telling me that I was wrong. "You don't know that for sure."

"I know, but—" I didn't know why I felt so protective over something that didn't belong to me, but it wasn't just about the mine. It was about the hilltop too. "If anyone finds out about the mine, they could have reason to create a public access road to get to it."

"Then you lose the hilltop."

"*We* lose the hilltop, Ridge. It's ours now." I swallowed, praying that he would agree to just leave the mine be. "And I don't want anything to change that."

After a few more moments of silence, he nodded slowly. "Okay, Camila. You have my word, but you have to promise me one thing."

Relief rushed through me, but my heart still pounded furiously. "Anything."

"Don't go near that mine again. Deal?"

"Deal."

"From now on, you'll access the hillside through the cornfields when the stalks are tall, but if Harold catches you—"

I nodded. "I get it, Ridge. If he catches me, it's over."

Ridge tilted his head toward the bridge. "Okay. Now go on, Wild One. Before someone starts looking for you."

7

THE HUNTER

Blood seeped through the hunter's fingers as he hoisted the dead elk over his shoulder. Though it was a heavy son of a bitch, he was no stranger to carrying the load of his livelihood. He'd just started to move through the woods when he heard a howl in the distance. With the same alertness that had made the game on his back grow still before taking the bullet between its eyes, the hunter looked toward where the sound had come from.

When he didn't hear anything out of the ordinary again, he thought he might have imagined the noise. But after he'd replayed it in his mind, an image of the young girl came forward. She was the only one he knew that would be stupid enough to treat the mountain terrain like it was her playground. *Always getting into trouble, that girl.* Someday, she would learn her lesson. *Perhaps that day is today.*

The hunter lifted the elk off his shoulder with a grunt then dropped the sturdy animal to the ground. He couldn't travel quickly with the heavy kill on his back. If he had any chance of investigating the noise, he would have to move fast.

His heavy boots were loud as he stomped over fallen branches and dried yellow leaves. He walked toward the sound of the human howl, which still lingered in his mind while his twisted thoughts worked through all the scenarios he could imagine of the state he would find the young girl in.

Perhaps she'd stumbled into one of his bear traps. But that would be impossible, since the only two bear traps he'd placed were deep in the woods. Even Camila didn't dare to go deep into the woods.

Maybe she'd fallen onto the jagged rocks in the creek. She would be wet and cold and ripe for the beating he dreamed of giving her, since her father didn't have the balls to teach his little girl how to mind her own business.

Thought after disturbing thought of how he would finally find Camila raced through his head before he eventually made it to the clearing. Adrenaline pumped through his veins at the thought of finding her there, helpless and alone.

He emerged at a flat section of land on the back of the mountain then followed his unmarked trail to the side of it, just before the grass grew tall and thick. Nothing appeared out of the ordinary, but a feeling in his gut told him someone had been to the mine—*his* mine.

It couldn't have been the girl. She would never come that way, not when she had those damn cornfields to run through. *But that howl and her damn curiosity. What if she stumbled upon it after all?*

Rage brewed inside the hunter at the thought of the intrusion. He'd had the mine and the surrounding land all to himself for over fifteen years, and he wasn't about to let any of that change.

With adrenaline morphing into anger and boiling through his veins, he trudged toward the padlocked gate and cursed when he saw that the large rock he usually used as a doorstop had been moved. *Did I do that? Or did she?* He wouldn't put it past that little brat to eventually wander too far and stumble upon the ancient landmark.

The hunter picked up the rock and set it back in its rightful place. After slipping his key into the padlock, he unlocked the door and opened it before stomping back into the woods to collect his latest kill.

For years, the young heir had been getting too close to the hunter's grounds than he was comfortable with. The young girl was off-limits and was not to be harmed, and the hunter would obey that sentiment so long as he continued to have access to the land he'd profited from for so long... but he had a lot more to lose than ever before. The moment she became a threat, she would have to go. As simple as that.

CAMILA, ONE AND A HALF YEARS LATER

E very so often, my papa and his old hunting gang gathered in the casita, a detached house on the west side of our villa. The small building held a few offices, including my father's study, where they had their private gatherings. The room filled with smoke and laughter while the men drank too much wine, played poker, cursed every other word, and flung insults back and forth until they either passed out in one of our guest rooms or went home.

Mama always cooked a feast for the men, and I delivered it throughout the night. I'd taken on the job willingly when I was a bold eight-year-old who loved to hide in dark corners to eavesdrop on the men's conversations. Lately, the entire scene gave me chills, and I wished nothing more than to be anywhere else.

"Your daughter is an angel, Patrick," one of the men said as I set down a plate of sandwiches.

My papa looked up from his fanned-out cards. A cigar dangled from his lips, and he beamed at me like I was the equivalent of one of the hunting trophies hanging on his walls. "That she is, Bill. That she is."

I took a few steps back from the table, ready to escape for a night out with my friends, when Thomas Bradshaw snaked an arm around my shoulders. "Trip says he's picking you up to go to Mountain Village tonight."

My papa's attention piqued at the mention of Thomas's son, and suddenly, all the men's eyes were on me. *Awkward.* "Um," I said with a soft laugh. "A bunch of us are going out tonight, Thomas. It's not like a date or anything."

He let out a playful "Ahh" and laughed. "That's too bad. Your dad and I thought we'd be marrying you two off by now."

Heat raced up my neck and spread over my cheeks. That Trip and I would grow up and fall in love one day, have babies, and live happily ever after on the vineyard, had always been the running joke between our families, but it wasn't the case at all. Unfortunately, I was the only person who believed that.

I would only consider dating one boy at my school, not that Papa would ever allow it. I wasn't the only girl who had noticed Ridge either. While he'd received a less-than-welcome reception when he moved to Telluride, he'd managed to turn things around just fine. Our class-mates accepted him like one of their own—except for Trip, of course, who still stuck his nose up whenever Ridge was around.

I knew better than to give Trip any reason to pick on my secret friend, so although Ridge Cross remained off-limits, not a week went by without us meeting. Once fall came and went, snow packed the landscape, and the hilltop became inaccessible. Ridge and I started to meet at the bridge instead. Though we didn't have the bird's-eye view of the land, it was the second-best thing to the mountain. I loved to hear about his life on the reservation, his mom, and the few good friends he had. In turn, I kept him apprised of my hard work on the vineyard.

"Don't listen to them, Camila," the man to my papa's right said. Gus was my friend Brody's dad and had been the vineyard's groundskeeper since my papa took over. "You're too young to be thinkin' about dating. Enjoy your time with your friends."

I smiled at the kind old man. "Thanks for always having my back, Gus."

He nodded, a smile pushing up his rosy cheeks. "You can always count on me, young lady."

The sincerity of his words warmed me, and I left with a sense of relief that felt rare around my papa and Thomas. They were peas in a pod, always playing off each other like two brothers. I often wondered why my papa released so much responsibility to Thomas, but it became obvious as I got older and started to learn more about vineyard and winery operations.

My papa was the brand, while Thomas Bradshaw was the face. And it all seemed to work just fine for them.

I left the casita with a smile and joined Mama in the kitchen to tell her I was leaving. Trip would be picking me up any minute, and I was eager to get going. During the winter months, life in that big home felt like a fancy prison. I couldn't tend to the vines the way I loved to, race to the hilltop when no one was the wiser, or ride my bicycle into town. So a night in the village thrilled me more than it would most kids my age.

When Trip arrived in his loud black truck, I hopped into the backseat to join Josie and squealed as we tore out of the drive. Raven was sitting beside her brother, as quiet as always.

"My dad drunk yet?" Trip asked jokingly.

"Getting there," I said with a smile. "He thought you were taking me on a date tonight, and he was severely disappointed when I told him it wasn't just you and me."

Josie shot me an amused look because she thought Trip might have feelings for me. I chose to ignore her every time she mentioned it. But I couldn't ignore that look or the silence that filled the truck cabin after the words left my mouth.

To the rest of the girls around town, Trip Bradshaw was the cream of the crop—star athlete in literally every sport offered, though competition wasn't tough, since our classes were a quarter of the size of most schools. He already had an in with Columbia University in New York, thanks to his dad, who'd gone to school there back in the day. Since his father was my papa's right-hand man, he had even started volunteering his free time in the vineyard.

It felt ridiculous to think a guy like him could be into a girl like me. I just didn't believe it was possible. Besides, after too many years of him bossing me around, I saw him in a far different light than when I was younger.

"What's happening in town tonight?" I asked.

Trip shrugged. "We can park and figure it out from there."

"Let's go ice skating up at Mountain Village," Josie said with a bounce.

I gasped. "Yes, I'm with you."

"I'll pass," Raven said with a snooty air. "I was thinking about riding the G with Logan and Missy."

"Riding the G" in the context she was speaking was code for "getting wasted in the gondolas." I raised my eyebrows and tried to catch Trip's reaction to his sister's deviance. Raven was in for a verbal lashing.

"No," Trip said, staring at his sister.

Josie squeezed my arm secretly. She was just as humored by their constant bickering as I was. Plus, if Trip was busy worrying about his sister all night, then we could go our separate ways.

"You're not going to ditch us to go hang out in a gondola, smoke pot, and get drunk all night."

"Who said anything about smoking pot?"

Trip shot her another look, and I could have sworn he would have her by her neck if he weren't trying to focus on the road. "The answer is no. You can hang out with us, or I'm taking you home."

A frustrated scream burst from Raven. "I'm so sick and tired of you babysitting me everywhere we go. I'm fifteen. Let me have some fun."

Eventually, their fight started to get old, and Josie and I tuned them out to have a chat. As soon as we parked, Josie and I jumped out of the truck and jogged away.

"Hey! Where are you *going*?" Trip screamed.

Josie and I hooked arms and giggled while calling over our shoulders, "Ice rink."

Trip frowned then waved his hand in the air. "Meet back here at midnight!"

We got to the gondola station and hopped in line. We didn't have to wait long to catch a lift to take us up the mountain. The single cabins, which were attached to a thick cable and carried us up to the small ski resort town, were large enough to fit six people, but Josie and I were lucky enough to get one to ourselves. Inside were two bench seats that faced each other and windows all around us, giving us a three-hundred-sixty-degree view of the San Juan Mountains.

Since I was six years old, the gondolas had been my favorite form of transportation to get up and down the mountain. While driving was an option, they were by far the most scenic way to go.

That night on the town was exactly what my soul needed—an escape into nature from the monotony of life on the vineyard in the winter. As Josie and I strapped on our rented skates, I looked up at the rink, and that happy feeling in my chest transitioned into something darker.

Ridge was there, in the center of the rink, and he was holding hands with a girl his age. She was a pretty girl I recognized from our high school. I could feel my heart in my throat as dread sank into the bottomless pit of my stomach.

The way he smiled down at her, the way he squeezed her hand when she lost her balance, and the way he laughed like he'd never laughed with me before made me feel sick.

"Is that Lucy?" Josie asked.

Lucy was the beautiful golden-haired girl's name. And even though Ridge had never mentioned her to me before, he clearly liked her. I could see it. Everything looked so easy between them. Lucy's father owned the sunflower farm on the other side of town, and their families didn't have a rivalry. She didn't have to sneak around just to keep a friendship with the boy she longed for. Ridge and I had been doing that, and while I cherished every single second, I desperately wanted what he had with Lucy.

"Camila, are you okay?"

I faced Josie, my head and chest swirling with each new emotion. "No. I mean I don't know. It's crazy that I have a crush on him, right? It's not like he and I could ever have that."

My best friend was the only person I would ever trust with that information, and by the look on her face, she had all the sympathy in the world for my feelings. Though it was refreshing, my heart was still breaking.

"I don't know, Camila. I don't think it's crazy at all. Ridge is really cute, and clearly you two have a special friendship. But…" Her eyes slid back to the rink. "Your father would never allow it."

Sadness was a sneaky bastard that snaked around my heart when I wasn't expecting it. The night was supposed to be fun. I couldn't let Ridge and his new girlfriend ruin it for me.

I stood and pushed my shoulders back, treating that icky feeling in my chest like a challenge. "C'mon, Josie. We came here to skate. Let's skate."

I flew onto the ice first with Josie right behind me, and we laughed as we circled the rink at top speed. Maybe I was trying to show off as I pulled out all my tricks, flipping around and skating backward while holding hands with my best friend then twirling back around and crisscrossing my shoes like a speed skater. But whatever I was doing seemed to be working. Every time I snuck a glance at Ridge, my confidence grew when I confirmed that he was watching me.

"Slow down," Josie called with a laugh.

The moment she said it, I realized she was right. I should have slowed down. A little girl stumbling around on skates fell and skidded right in front of me, catching me off guard. I started to brake but knew I didn't have enough time to stop, so I did the only thing I could think of. I leaped toward the center of the ice, which happened to be right where Ridge was standing.

"Are you okay?"

Camila groaned as she lifted her head. Her weight was entirely on me. I held her tightly, hugging her around the waist while my heart hammered. I'd become no stranger to Camila's wild antics, but the worrying never ceased.

"Say something, please, Camila."

Her eyelids opened, revealing her haunting green eyes. The flecks of gold shimmered in the reflection of the white ice. "You caught me." She sounded dazed, then she pulled in a deep breath and smiled. "Of course you caught me."

The way she'd been speeding around the rink with young kids and less advanced skaters near her might have been the most reckless thing I'd ever seen her do. Her fearlessness had always intrigued me, but the stunt she'd just pulled had quickly turned my concern into fury.

"I don't know what you're smiling about. You could have hurt someone. You could have been hurt."

Panic lit her expression, and the regret registered quickly. "Oh no. I didn't mean to go that fast. I just—" She slammed her eyes closed and shook her head. "I was being stupid."

I slid my arms from around her waist almost reluctantly, which was ridiculous. "Are you okay to stand?"

Disappointment flickered in her expression before she nodded and pushed against my chest. "I think so."

She stood slowly as Josie skated to her side and helped to steady her. Then I scrambled to my feet and turned to Lucy with my apologies.

"I'm sorry to cut our skate session short. Want to pick it up again next week?"

I wondered if Lucy's concerned expression was more for me or her missed lesson, but she nodded. "Of course. Next week is fine." Then she hobbled toward the edge of the rink.

I should have helped her exit the ice, but I was too afraid to leave Camila.

Camila's eyes widened as they followed Lucy's exit. She turned to me, looking confused. "You were giving skate lessons? You weren't on a date?"

I could practically hear the clicking of the gears in my brain as I realized what had just happened. As if Camila realized she'd said too much, her face turned bright red. Josie just stood there, looking between us.

"Um," Josie said finally. "I thought I saw Emilio heading toward the G. I think I'm going to join him and catch up with the others. Call me later?"

Camila nodded and watched her friend skate away.

"You thought I was on a date."

Her gaze slid back to mine. "I did."

"And you were jealous?"

Her cheeks reddened. "I can't believe you just asked me that," she hissed before looking around us. "That's not even an option."

Though that wasn't what I'd asked, I didn't correct her. I already knew enough. We were in dangerous territory I wasn't sure how to skirt around. *How long has she felt this way?*

Pushing my newly forming questions away, I focused on the matter at hand. "Is there somewhere I can walk you to?"

She cringed. "You don't have to do that."

Huh? "Do what?"

"You don't have to treat me like a little girl who has a crush on her neighbor. You don't have to protect my feelings."

Is that what I was trying to do? I cared about her more than I should, and I wasn't going to leave her standing in the middle of the ice, crush or not.

"I'm just offering to take you wherever you want to go. Or you can continue skating."

She made a face and pulled up her hand. "To be honest, my wrist is a little sore. I might have sprained it or something."

Sighing, I placed a hand on her back and nudged her forward. "C'mon. I can at least help you find your friends."

Camila didn't move. "Are you headed home now? Maybe you could drop me off at the end of my drive."

I opened my mouth to tell her what we both already

knew. Even if I was headed home, I couldn't be the one to drop her off at hers. I couldn't be seen anywhere near Patrick Bell's property, unless I wanted to make things worse for Harold's farm. The man frustrated me to no end, but he was still my father. And working for him for the little time that I had had showed me how much he loved that damn field.

"I'll get you down into Telluride, then you'll need to go with your friends."

She stared back at me, challenge brimming in her eyes, but for some reason, she gave up the fight and nodded. "All right, then."

We traded our skates in and grabbed the next available gondola car to take us back down into town. Not until we were sitting across from each other on the bench seats did I take a good look at her. A pang hit my chest as I registered what she was wearing—distressed dark jeans with plaid fabric inside the torn parts, tall black boots that gave her a little bit of height for once, and a long cream sweater that did nothing to hide the curves she'd grown into.

My bratty, rebellious neighbor was no longer a little girl, but she was still all sorts of wrong for me, her age being the largest factor in the new dilemma.

"So," I said, attempting to move us into safer territory. "If you weren't here tonight, where would you be?"

She snorted, reminding me of the Camila I'd gotten to know well over the past year and a half. "I'd probably still be serving food and drinks to my papa and his hunting buddies. They have these poker nights once a month, and I've been playing server for years."

"Does your father still hunt with them?"

Camila's face twisted in disapproval. "No, thank god. That's all in his past. Mama made him stop years ago, but I don't know about the other guys." Then she frowned. "I don't think they still do."

"It isn't a terrible thing if they do," I assured her, earning me a smile. "To this day, hunting is the way of life for a lot of my fellow Tribe members."

"But you're not a hunter. You can't even hold a gun properly."

We both chuckled.

"That's because I was raised by my mother. She was more into basket weaving and berry picking."

Camila seemed to be taking that in while she stared out the window to her right. We were passing by a large plot of spruce trees. The snow packed on top of them sparkled like diamonds against the artificial lighting.

"You didn't answer my question earlier. Since when did you become a skating instructor?"

I smiled, knowing what a strange sight that must have been. "I learned my lesson last year on the farm. The ranch house is too small for Harold and me to hang around in all day. Working here gives me something to do, and they pay me. It's nice to make a salary for once."

Camila's face blanched at my confession. Money wasn't something I talked about. It had never been my driving force in life, and it felt so personal. But if I was going to confess that to anyone, it would be her.

"Harold doesn't pay you? But you're working twelve-to-sixteen-hour days sometimes."

I laughed. "Yeah, well, the old man is giving me a place to stay and food to eat. I know it's not ideal, but it's my life."

"My papa pays me minimum wage when I work the vineyard."

"Well, your vineyard pulls in a lot more profit than our cornfield. It's just different. We shouldn't compare it."

Camila frowned. "I don't like that Harold is taking advantage of you. What are you getting out of that labor?"

I shrugged. "He's giving me the farm. One day, it will be mine to run and profit from on my own. Until then, I consider it training."

Her soft smile was like a shot of adrenaline to my veins. She was so beautiful. "You are a good guy, Ridge Cross."

My cheeks heated.

"Then I guess the extra work in the winter not only gives you a break from the farm but also gives you some savings. It's working out."

"Right. And I might pick up some other activities. They always need tour guides around here."

Camila nodded. "That, they do. I guess you and I are alike in that way. We don't like to sit still."

That was true. "It's the Ute way of life, I suppose. My ancestors moved from place to place as they hunted. They created and traveled through trails that crisscrossed the mountain ranges of Colorado. I think that's why I have such a thirst for nature and exploring it all." I raised my chin at her playfully. "What's your excuse?"

She gave me a beautiful smile. Her perfect white teeth beamed back at me between painted red lips. Her skin was naturally tan and looked even darker compared to the white that powdered the earth. Camila was the type of beautiful that made hearts ache and knees weak—classic, timeless, and all things rare. She was wholesome and innocent, like an undisturbed patch of snow at the end of winter.

"I didn't know I needed an excuse to enjoy all that nature has to offer," she said.

"But have you? Have you enjoyed it all?"

She tilted her head and gave me a questioning look.

"There are an endless number of hiking trails around here. You should get out there and see what exists beyond these box canyon walls. Don't get me wrong. The hilltop is great. I understand why that's your sanctuary. I'm just saying don't let that be the end of your journey. Take the bigger hills and harder climbs. I couldn't even tell you about what exists out there. You wouldn't believe the magic, unless you saw it with your own eyes."

"Then take me. Show me."

She was asking me for more than to take her on a hike, and it took all my willpower not to give in the moment I realized it. "You know I can't take you hiking. Even this"—I pointed between her and me—"is pushing the boundaries that have been set for us."

"Screw the boundaries." She glared at me. "They're ridiculous. Look at us, Ridge. What damage are we doing by being friends? I can't see the bad in it. This whole rivalry bullshit doesn't make any sense."

Camila got fired up about injustices often, but never once had I heard her cuss. "It might never make sense to us, but that's not the point."

"*Then what is the point?*" she shouted into the enclosed

cabin, her words bouncing off the walls and pummeling me like little bullets.

"The point is that we don't make the rules." I sounded much calmer than I felt. A wildfire that not even I could contain at that moment burned in my chest. "Not now," I whispered. "Not yet."

She stood, took one step to cross over onto my bench, and sat, wobbling the car as she moved. Her leg pressed into mine as she leaned in. Her chin tilted up, and her lips parted. "Why not now?"

The challenge in her words only added gasoline to the growing fire inside me. I only had one choice. I had to push her away. "You are fifteen." I didn't hide the anger in my voice that time. "You cannot possibly know what you're asking for or whether the risks you're willing to take are worth it."

"You are worth it to me, Ridge." Sadness and fear coated her eyes, tearing up my heart.

"I am *nothing*." My voice boomed. It was the only way she would hear me. "I can offer you nothing. And you mean nothing to me."

She froze, bringing a chill to all the spaces around us. The already-fragile ice crumbled beneath our feet, signaling the explosive end to our friendship.

Before either of us could say another word, we were inside the Oak Street Harbor Plaza, and the gondola car started to slow. The doors slid open, and Camila moved first, hopping out onto the padded mat—where Trip was standing and glaring at me.

10

CAMILA, SIX MONTHS LATER

My first wobbly steps were taken in a large barrel of grapes on my first birthday in 1992 during the Bell Family Vineyard Harvest Festival. My parents loved to retell that fact to anyone who would listen, as if they wanted to ensure that everyone knew I was heir to the invisible throne. And every year, I repeated the tradition, which showcased me as their daughter and future vintner who would one day carry on the family dynasty. I accepted the role with pride.

At sixteen years old, I stood on the wooden platform that wrapped the large barrel of red grapes beside my parents. A smile lit my face as Italian music poured through the outdoor speakers, and a crowd quickly formed around us. Our ceremonial grape stomp had clearly become the highlight of the entire harvest festival. I was thankful that my steps were much less wobbly than my first ones.

I scanned the crowd to find that many of my peers

and their families were already there, while more
continued to pull into the already-crowded parking lot of
the winery. Food, drink, and art vendors were situated on
the red-dirt clearing, offering prepared meals, produce,
and refreshments to consume. From noon to sunset,
people could tour the winery, partake in tastings, and fill
crates of grapes in the vineyard.

Harvest season meant that over the next couple
weeks, the vineyard would be packed with townsfolk who
wanted to help handpick every grape from the vine. But
my parents didn't want to make the festival just about the
vineyard. They wanted it to be an opportunity for other
farm owners in the area to bring their freshly harvested
crops to sell and promote. Well—all farmers except
for one.

The Cross family was strictly forbidden to enter my
parents' land, even at a public event like that one. Not
that Harold or Ridge would try to set foot on my papa's
property. Over the past six months, Harold Cross's name
had officially been removed from the farmer's market
vendor list, and every last business in town that had once
purchased corn from him suddenly cut ties.

My papa was behind it. *Who else could it be?* No one
else in Telluride hated the man enough to meddle in his
business affairs in such a cruel way. Harold was forced to
sell outside of Telluride, and rumor was that Ridge was
the one going off to Ouray and Silverton to chase new
business.

Papa hadn't come right out and said it, but a certain
event at Mountain Village had a lot to do with what was
going on. After Trip saw Ridge and me together, Trip

was brimming with fury. I wouldn't have been surprised if he had gone straight to my papa after we got home.

I hadn't forgotten the agreement Trip and I had made when Ridge first moved to town. Trip promised to be nice to Ridge if I promised to stay away. The timing of it all was too suspicious, and for that, I was riddled with guilt.

For the past six months, Ridge and I had kept our distance. After what he had said to me at Mountain Village, my heart was too broken to see his face. But over time, I started to recognize the power my papa held over his, and my feelings started to change. Ridge was only trying to protect Harold's farm, and he had every right to do so. Once summer came around, the thought of staying mad at him and staying away from the hilltop felt unbearable.

I missed sitting under the crooked tree with him for hours, even when he wouldn't say a word. I missed meeting at the bridge and catching up on everything we'd missed in each other's lives. Most of all, I missed his silence, which always calmed my constant storm, my need for adventure, and my careless search for it. He was the peace in my existence. And even when he did speak, his words were always carefully chosen, respectful, and meaningful. What he'd told me on that first day we met had been true. Ridge didn't like to waste his words, and I loved him for it.

It irked me to the core to know that our families had every opportunity to settle the feud but refused to do so. Three months ago, I'd tried to bring up the feud with my papa again, desperate to put an end to it all.

"There are rumors, Papa. Rumors that you're sabotaging Farmer Cross's business. Is that true?"

My papa had been sitting cross-legged in the vineyard, cutting back the unwieldy vines. He stopped what he was doing and wiped the sweat from his brow before smiling at me. "Don't worry yourself with small-town rumors, mija. Look at us," he said, pointing to his chest and mine. "We're out here working. Does it look like I have time to go around sabotaging businesses? Farmer Cross is doing that all on his own."

A quick flash of a memory brought me back to the first day we'd seen Ridge and Harold at the farmer's market. My papa had been brimming with hatred that day, making me doubt his words.

"Then why can't we all be friends? His family and ours?" I had to be careful with my tone. I wanted him to believe that the intent behind my question was innocent and playful.

My papa cupped my cheek, an adoring look in his eyes. "You are too good and too young to understand, my Camila."

"But I'm *not* too young," I insisted.

"Maybe, but trust me. The history is long and boring, and it's better not to get involved." Then he had turned back to his precious vine, ending our conversation.

My unsettled thoughts were interrupted when my parents nudged me to join them in the barrel of fruit. The grapes immediately squeezed out of their skins and between our toes. While the act of grape stomping was a little gross, I laughed every single time.

I clutched the bottom of my long white dress and bunched it at the top of my thighs, giving me room to move my legs. There was no use trying to avoid getting dirty. I didn't care about stains or getting wet. That was all part of the fun, to dance among the fruit that afforded our family the opportunity to give back to the community in so many ways. I considered it a privilege and an honor to lead the celebration.

As always, my mama was the first one to start moving around the barrel, twisting her shoulders and stomping in time with the folk music, earning the first cheer from the crowd. The wide smile on her face showed that she was filled with pure joy. She was practically exploding with it. And every year that I watched her, I was always mesmerized by her smile, her laugh, and the sheer exuberance as she danced. She was in her element, right where she was meant to be.

I turned to Papa and saw the look on his face as he watched Mama dance. My heart squeezed. He was like a lovesick puppy, grinning and shoving his hands into his pockets while stomping around with much less coordinated movements than Mama.

Those were the moments I lived for and cherished. I would hold them close forever.

I grinned like a fool as I watched my parents, waiting for the perfect moment to jump in and join them.

"Dance, Camila! Dance!" came a familiar voice from the crowd.

My eyes sifted through the people until I found Josie. I stuck my tongue out at her. She was wrapped up in Emilio's arms. They'd been dating since that night I rode the gondola with Ridge. It turned out a love story had been born that night—it just wasn't mine.

Josie's beauty had always been mesmerizing to me.

With her strawberry-blond hair, electric-blue eyes, and freckles that looked like specks of gold in the sun, she was so clearly the reason boys wanted to hang out with us lately. I had always been the tomboy of the bunch—always dirty, always running, and always one of the guys. Josie was so far opposite me on the spectrum that I often had a hard time believing we were friends.

Then something happened over the summer. My hair had grown past my shoulders for the first time in my life, and I suddenly cared what I looked like for school and outings with my friends. I asked Josie to teach me how to do my makeup and style myself in a way that still felt true to me. I became her miniproject, and in turn, the boys had started to look at me differently.

I began flirting and going on one-off dates, but no matter how hard they tried, I wouldn't let them kiss me. Kissing was reserved for something more—something I knew I was waiting for even though I didn't know when it would come.

Josie and Emilio were attending the festival with some classmates of ours, all regulars over the years. Most of us had known each other since we were toddlers. Ridge might have adopted the term Wild One for me, but my preference for living on the edge was no secret. My peers called me a tomboy, a farm girl, and one of the boys. To some, it was an insult. To me, it was a compliment. They knew I wasn't afraid to get a little dirty and that Josie's jeering would be enough to get me to join in on the fun.

I spent most of my days out in the fields with Papa instead of with my mama. While she gathered fresh crops from the garden for supper, I tucked vines in preparation for a storm or chopped wood to be used in the burn bins whenever a cold front was about to come through. Neither of my parents argued with my preferences. In fact, I thought it made my papa realize just how invested I truly was. Since I was the only child, I believed he might have even been relieved, to some extent.

Hiking my skirt a little more, I mimicked my mama's movements. She looked far more graceful than I ever could, not that I was trying to look like a professional grape stomper up there or even a beautiful goddess like my mama. I just wanted to have fun, and that was exactly what I would do.

I exaggerated my steps, kicking up my heels and stomping around while I circled the perimeter. Halfway through the song, I looked around to see how much the crowd had grown in the past two minutes. From the front of the platform that separated the barrel from the crowd, all the way down the first slope of the vineyard, the crowd stood packed in tight.

Everyone clapped in time with the music, causing my chest to swell. I was proud of my family and all they had accomplished over the past century. My papa alone had been managing and operating our ancestors' land and vineyard for nearly three decades. And with the help of his business partner and dozens of workers and volunteers, our vineyard was able to bottle hundreds of thousands of premium bottles of wine each year.

I snapped back to the present when the music transitioned into the next song.

My papa grabbed my hand and spun me under his

arm before bringing me in to dance. "Your dancing gets better every year."

I smiled at the unexpected and sweet compliment. Not many times in my life would I have said that about my papa. After a few spins around the barrel, he released me and took my mama into his arms. Their dance was a slow and romantic one that had the crowd swooning. Apparently, even my mama thought so. She giggled and fell into him while the slow song played on.

When the third song came on, a line had already formed at the bottom of the stairs, and one by one, guests started to climb inside to partake in the stomping fun.

I made eye contact with my parents and saluted them then gestured to my exit. "I'm going to make my rounds!" I shouted then grinned as I climbed out of the barrel and made my way down the stairs.

Trip was waiting for me at the bottom. "Hey, birthday girl. That's quite the mess you got yourself into there."

I laughed when I looked down at my white dress. It was covered with purple stains, just as I had expected. Then I slapped my hands to my sides and looked back at him. "Wouldn't be a proper grape stomp without making a mess of things, now would it, Trip?"

"Well, then get back in there, and I might just follow."

He grinned down at me, triggering the warning bells in my brain. Over the past few months, I had started to see a shift in his attitude toward me. No longer did he act like an older, protective brother but like someone who might like me as more than a friend.

I didn't know what made me feel that way exactly. Maybe it was the extra-long glances, the easy smiles, or the fact that he still tried to go everywhere with me even though his babysitter status had expired. Maybe it was a blend of all the above, but I'd started to believe what everyone else around me had been hinting at for years.

Trip stepped closer. His proximity was stifling. I laughed, trying hard to hide my discomfort. I gently placed a hand on his arm and noticed Josie waving me down from the side of the crowd. "There's something I need to do." I waved an arm at the barrel. Everyone's shrieks of laughter rose as more people were added. "If you're not purple by the time I come back, I'll be terribly disappointed."

With a chuckle, I backed away and darted through the crowd toward Josie, where she was waiting with a devious grin. "You ready to head to the cave and taste some grapes, birthday girl?"

My grin matched hers as I nodded. "I wouldn't miss this for anything."

11

RIDGE

An early morning delivering hay to one of Harold's customers preceded an unexpected and eventful day on the farm. It had rained a few days prior, so our harvest schedule was slightly off. With the sun shining bright and not a cloud in the sky, we had the tractor equipment prepped and were finally ready to go pick some corn.

"Whadda ya say, son? Time to open up these fields or what?"

Harold clapped a heavy hand on my back before giving my neck a squeeze that radiated his excitement. Harvest season was what my papa lived for, apparently. Over the past two and a half years since moving to Telluride, I'd learned a lot about my old man. For one, his smile was as rare as finding an ore of silver from an abandoned mine. I didn't have the heart to argue with Harold when he was in a good mood.

"I'm ready. Let's fuel up."

He nodded and clapped once before putting his

fingers between his lips and whistling. A second later, Bruno, our two-year-old border collie, came running up to join us, his mouth hanging open in a ridiculous smile, like he knew exactly what we were setting out to do.

Harold had picked up Bruno as a puppy soon after I moved to the farm. I suspected he'd bought him for me, but the pup refused to leave Harold's side. They became fast friends, going everywhere together, into town and around the farm. It turned out that Harold was a sucker for furry friends.

We walked over to the tractor, and Harold jumped on to start the engine. When he jumped back down, he pointed at the front of the machine. "Help me attach the chopper to the picker, then meet me on the high field with the bin!" he yelled over the loud engine. "We'll start with the headland. I'll get 'er started, then you can take over for me."

My jaw dropped, and Harold noticed. He winked and clapped me on the back again. "You're eighteen, son. Time to get ya on a real tractor."

My job had always been to follow him out onto the field, basically for the purposes of pulling him out of the mud when he would get stuck. I also drove the bins around to collect and move the husks of corn as we gathered them. But picking the corn and operating the harvester had always been Harold's job. I had never even questioned it.

It took us another hour to get out onto the field. Farming was never as simple as it seemed. Some sort of mechanical issue, a flat tire, or climate issues hindered work that needed to be done. So when we finally made it out onto the field and began plowing the crops, it felt like the hard part was over.

After dumping a few rows of corn, with Bruno happily running after us through the fields, Harold set the tractor to idle and gestured for me to head over to him. He gave me a crash course with the controls, then I was on my way.

We worked through breakfast and lunch, stopping for minutes at a time to scarf down the pile of sandwiches we'd brought with us. In the early evening, I dumped my last load of cobs into the moveable bin, and Harold immediately started hooking up the bin to his tractor.

"You done good, son. Bring the harvester back, and I'll get the bin over to the silos."

I nodded and had just begun to turn when Bruno started growling and barking at the line of trees at our backs. Harold looked over my shoulder and immediately adopted a sour expression. "Happy Harold" was long gone, just like that.

"What is it?" All I could see was the entrance to the woods that reached the bridge over Cornett Creek.

"Damn Bell family, having one of their ritzy festivals again." Harold shook his head and snapped at Bruno to stop yapping. "If I had a party for every harvest that took place on this farm, we'd have no time for work." He let out a huff and took off walking.

Bruno followed, while I lingered a minute longer, staring back at the woods. Camila had told me about the harvest festivals she took part in every year. Knowing that it was yet another event my family wasn't invited to made me understand Harold's frustration. If anyone was keeping up with the ridiculous feud, it was Camila's dad.

I couldn't blame Harold's shift in mood when it came to talking about the Bells. They'd sure done a number on our business operations over the past six months. Before that, Patrick Bell had been less than welcoming, but he hadn't made moves to blackball us. Guilt gnawed at me. The last time I had seen Camila, she'd looked at me like I'd crushed her with my harsh words. Then Trip was right there to take her home like the good Boy Scout he was.

I didn't doubt that Camila and I being together that night had gotten back to her father, either by Trip or by an angry Camila, but I didn't like to dwell on those thoughts. The anger they brought with them had the power of engulfing me in flames. But the guilt had been getting to me. Little by little, day after day, with every passing moment that I avoided Camila and she avoided me, the bubble of the volcano threatened beneath my feet.

Something was about to erupt. Someone was bound to get burned. And my only answer to it all was to finish harvest season, pack my bags, then leave Telluride behind.

12

CAMILA

T he cave Josie and I went to every year was an actual cavity of land on the side of the mountain near the east wing of our home, where we stored our barrels to age. A tunnel connected the cave to the wine cellar where my parents kept their personal wine collection. And "taste some grapes" was our code phrase for sneaking wine from the already fermented barrels.

I matched Josie's wicked stare as I unplugged a red wine barrel. The *pop* made us both giggle. We were up to no good, which was what we did best together. Josie and I often argued about who corrupted who more, and in the end, we always agreed that I was the one.

She grabbed two wineglasses while I searched for a long syringe extractor to suction out the wine. After squirting a glassful for each of us, we crouched in a corner beside the row of barrels, hiding in case anyone decided to pay the cave a surprise visit.

"So, how does it feel to be sixteen? Is it as sweet as they say?"

I smiled and batted my lashes while placing a hand over my heart. "I do declare it's just the sweetest," I said, putting on my deepest Southern belle impression.

Josie giggled and sipped from her glass. "I should have waited a few months to kiss Emilio, then I could have had a sweet sixteen birthday party too."

Grimacing, I said, "Don't remind me. At this rate, I'll never get my first kiss."

"Because you're in love with a stupid boy. That's why. You need to take your mind off him, Camila. He's not worth your time. Not after what he did to you."

After that night on the gondola, I'd confessed everything to Josie while crying my eyes out in her arms. She was such a good friend.

"Technically, he didn't *do* anything to me. He just told me the truth."

Josie's eyelids widened with surprise. "Don't do that. Don't go giving that boy the benefit of the doubt. He told you that you meant nothing to him. He's a liar. Clearly, he didn't mean it, but he hurt you. I hate him for hurting you like that."

Just talking about Ridge made my chest tight, and it became hard to breathe. I should have moved on already, leaving all thoughts and feelings for Ridge behind and opening my eyes to all the other boys around town. Surely, someone else out there could make my heart beat just as fast. And as we sat there in the cave, surrounded by aging barrels, and got drunk on grapes, I decided I would do everything in my power to move on from Ridge Cross.

"Where are you going?" Josie hissed at my back.

We had just stumbled out of the cave after talking and giggling for too many hours. I was getting worried that we had missed the entire festival, but the second we opened the door and the warm evening wind blasted us, merry music and laughter drifted from where the crowd still gathered.

I slammed my pointer finger over my lips to shush her while holding on to her shoulders for support. "Don't judge me."

Her face was flushed and her eyes wild, just like how I imagined mine were after the amount of wine we'd just consumed. "No, Camila. You said you were over him."

"I am," I huffed, feeling indignant as I spoke. I was still furious at Ridge for treating me the way he had, and I was just drunk enough to tell him. "I'm going to tell him what an asshole he is."

She looked doubtful as she turned to the large crowd then back to me and sighed. "Someone could see you."

Josie had no idea how easy it had become for me to sneak away. "No one will even notice I'm gone. You'll see." I started my jaunt down the hill before she could stop me, but I could still hear her final words at my back.

"I know someone who will notice," she warned.

Ignoring the fact that she was right and that Trip had probably been looking for me for hours, I continued on my path, already relaxed at the thought of being shrouded by the vines on either side of me.

Fall was my favorite season in the vineyard, when the grapevines were fully in bloom and perfectly ripe for picking. There was nothing like seeing a year's work spread out for hundreds of acres right before your very eyes. Snipping those grapes from the vines gave me a heaping dose of satisfaction.

But fall was also a bittersweet time. Once winter came along to lay snow on the fields and the vines grew dormant, it would be at least six months before buds began to sprout fresh fruit. That left six months in between for pruning, an act to encourage new growth. In those six months, grape production turned into a plentiful winery season.

While my family lived for our summers and falls, the majority of visitors in Telluride lived for the winter, when the slopes were packed with snow and the entire town shifted into tourist mode. The season was great for our winery, which held tours by the hour every single day. They were always full, bringing in large amounts of our profit while the newly stocked barrels of wine hibernated with their juices fermenting in the cave cellar.

While trying to hold in my drunk giggles, I passed by some guests who were perusing the grapes and made my way down to the first landing. Drunk or not, the vineyard was where I would rather be—getting lost in a sea of purple and green, breathing in the sweet scent around me, and on my way to him.

Once harvest season began, sneaking off to the hilltop always became a lot harder. While the vineyard's branches became bare, the cornfield went through a change of its own. The field slowly flattened to nothing but an empty plot of land with rolling hills and a white ranch-style house off in the distance where Ridge and Harold lived.

"Where are you sneaking off to, young lady?"

My pulse raced, and I snapped my head around to find Gus, our groundskeeper, who was walking the property. I laughed as relief flooded me, then I smiled at him. I'd always suspected he had turned a blind eye when I jaunted off on my adventures. Raising a finger to my lips, I said, "I'll be right back. Please don't say anything to Papa."

He raised his hands, indicating he wasn't about to get involved. "Not my business. I didn't see anything. Just be careful out there."

"I always am."

Once I reached a section of the vineyard where I lost sight of the party above, I started to run faster. I entered the woods and was immediately shrouded in darkness, but I made it all the way to the bridge before stopping. Squeezing my eyelids shut, I took in a deep breath. That was usually the point in my journey when I got my second wind. Something felt different that night.

My heart was just beginning to steady when I caught movement in my peripheral vision. A rustle of branches sharpened my focus as I slowly searched my surroundings. For a second, I thought it might be a deer or bird cutting through the woods. I'd been galivanting around those woods for years, and I'd never seen any wildlife bigger than that near the bridge. Even though the surrounding land had been fenced in decades ago, that didn't stop the occasional creature from wandering in. But something about the icky feeling that entered my chest told me whatever I was hearing was something else.

A crunching noise caused my heart to jolt. I knew what a boot sounded like when it stepped on dry leaves and sticks. I jerked my head up and looked around to find that I was still completely alone. "Gus?" I called, wondering if he had decided to follow me.

No one responded.

All my senses were on high alert. Just because I acted reckless at times didn't make me a novice when it came to the wilderness. If anything, being more adventurous had taught me how to be hyper-aware of my surroundings. And I knew when I was being watched.

13

THE HUNTER

The hunter's lips curved into a wicked grin when he spotted the deer through his night goggles. He had been tracking the beautiful buck for the past ten minutes while it drank from the stream and journeyed slowly through the woods. With his arrow readied and his fingers already pulling the bowstring, he waited for the right moment to release it.

Killing the creature at his first spotting would have been too easy. The hunter craved the adrenaline of the chase. The kills he enjoyed took his patience and aim to a whole other level. The moment the buck caught on to his presence and started to run off—that would be the time to shoot.

The hunter took another step closer. *Crunch* went the branches and twigs beneath his heavy boots, causing the deer's beady eyes to snap toward him. *Got him.* The deer took off, climbed up the side of the creek, then made a break for it through the woods.

Adrenaline shot through the hunter as he prepared

for the kill. His shoulder had just lifted slightly as he reached his arch point and prepared for release when another figure entered his vision, ruining his shot.

He had assumed the section of woods near the bridge would be clear with both fields in harvest mode, festival and all. It should have been the perfect time for him to hunt in a territory he would normally shy away from, considering how close it was to the neighboring fields.

He cursed under his breath before realizing who it was. Dark hair, tanned skin, and a white dress came into view. The girl's eyes were wide, her normally confident demeanor clearly gone. She looked as if she'd been startled by the same footsteps that had spooked the deer.

He hadn't expected Camila to step into his crosshairs, but seeing fear light up her expression made his arousal grow thick and heavy between his legs.

By the looks of her dirty white dress, her wild and knotted hair, and her stained bare feet, she'd already had her fun at the festival—an event the hunter had already left hours ago to hunt on land he should have had free rein of that evening. Of course Camila had to be the one to ruin his fun. Anger blew through him in the next moment when he realized she was off to find the boy.

If Patrick Bell knew where his daughter had run off to, he would kill the boy then probably want to kill his daughter too. As much as the hunter would love to see how that would play out, he couldn't let that happen. If anyone was going to end Camila's life, it would be him—*after* he secured what was rightfully his.

At sixteen years old, she was ripening nicely but not yet ready for the kind of harvest that the hunter had planned for her. A different type of energy coursed through him, then his deep scowl curled into a smile.

Her time was coming, but for the moment, he decided to have a little more fun. It was time to teach the girl a lesson about the dangers of playing in the woods.

14

CAMILA

The flutter and scraping of brush and rocks against the ground came out of nowhere. What sounded like a giant dog scurrying off through the woods, probably running away from me, scared me more than I would ever be willing to admit. I didn't get scared of the woods—or at least, I never had before.

I took a slow step forward then another and another, forcing my breaths to steady even though my pulse was still racing. With the bridge at my back, I started to calm, blaming my paranoia on my drunken state. *So what? An animal ran off. It could have been a cluster of bunnies, for all I know.*

Laughing at myself, I shook my head and picked up my pace, leaving all the tension and fear that had just racked my body behind.

But my relief came too fast. A loud whistling noise zoomed past my head, so close that a breeze hit my face. A *snap* followed, its impact reverberating through the woods. My heart was in my throat, and I couldn't even scream. All I could think to do was run as fast as my feet would carry me.

15

RIGE

Long after Harold had left with Bruno, I was standing in the field, watching the sun start to dip in the sky, when a figure burst from the woods and started running toward me. A jolt shot through my heart at the sight of the vineyard girl, whom I had no business feeling things for. She was dressed in white, her dress and legs were stained purple, and her eyes were wide, like she was frightened. Even then, she was a beautiful sight.

"Whoa!" I said as she slammed into me with her neck turned in the direction she'd come from.

Her breathing was heavy as she hugged me, and my arms instinctively found their way around hers. I searched the field behind me, where Harold had taken off from long ago, and sighed when I verified that he was nowhere in sight.

"For all you knew, I could have been Harold," I scolded her, though my voice was gentler than it would have been if she weren't shivering in my arms.

"I'm glad you're not Harold," she mumbled into my shirt.

I gulped. The feel of her in my arms went against my better judgment. The affection I felt for Camila didn't erase the last six months of destruction her father had caused to Harold's farm. "The party's that bad, huh?" I said sourly.

She peeled herself away from me and shook her head. "No. I mean I don't know, but—there was something in the woods."

I chuckled in surprise, unable to help myself. Camila never feared a thing, especially when it came to nature. A bear could approach her, and she would probably pet it instead of freaking out.

"Seriously, Camila? We're surrounded by the Colorado wilderness. There are millions of critters in those woods."

She shook her head, flustered. "Listen to me," she demanded. "Someone was out there." She shivered, causing a chill to run up my spine. "I could feel it. And I think they shot at an animal, but it had already run off."

I made a face. "I thought you said there were no hunters out here."

"Maybe I was wrong. Maybe someone found a way in and mistook me for a deer."

I cringed, not believing it for a second. "Even so, if there was a gunshot, I would have heard it."

"It wasn't a gun. Or maybe whoever it was had a silencer." Her eyes widened like she'd figured out the mystery. "My papa used to use those."

I shook my head. "No way. I would have heard that too."

She thought for a second. "A bow and arrow, then." She groaned. "Whatever it was went right by me. I could feel it. And it hit something, but it didn't sound like an animal."

"Are you sure?"

"Yes. I just ran. I didn't know what to do."

I didn't want to show her that I was starting to freak out on the inside. While I'd laughed at first at her fear, I started to realize that Camila being genuinely afraid could actually mean that she was terrified for good reason.

Seeing Camila like that, like a deer in the headlights and shaking, made my heart hammer into my throat. "Stay here, okay? I'm going to check it out."

"No!" She grabbed my arm and dug her nails in so hard that I yelped. "What if someone's really out there? I don't want you to be their next target."

I reached into the front compartment of the tractor and pulled out a shotgun Harold kept there. He was always ready to defend his land however he needed to. "I'll be fine."

With a final warning glance telling her to stay put, I walked toward the woods, using the flashlight I'd grabbed to help me see my way through. After a good ten minutes of a thorough search, I walked back to my tractor, where Camila was standing. "Nothing."

She narrowed her eyes when she realized that I was laughing. The way her face turned red and her lips pursed only made me laugh harder.

"You jerk!" she squealed while taking a swat at my arm. "It's not funny. Whatever was out there scared the hell out of me."

I jumped away before she could make contact and laughed again. "Since when are you scared of a few squirrels in the woods?"

She balled her hands into fists and slammed them to her sides. "I didn't say I heard squirrels. I heard footsteps and an animal, then something went by my head so fast that I couldn't see it, but I swear to you, Ridge, some-thing—or some*one* was out there."

I rolled my eyes. Camila was still a wild one, and her constant flair for the dramatics was nothing new. "And where would they have come from, huh? My dad and I have been out here all day." It would take a person days to walk through the land surrounding our properties, and she knew it. I pointed behind her toward her house. "Maybe someone from your party went for a walk and got lost."

Camila's expression changed as she looked back toward the woods, like she was considering my words. "I suppose that could be it." When she exhaled next, she was still close to me, and I got a good whiff of her breath.

My gaze narrowed on her. "Are you drunk?"

Guilt flooded her expression, and her mouth opened before she snapped it shut.

"No wonder you were hearing things out there. Does your papa know?"

Her eyes widened, and she threw herself at me, grip-ping my shirt with both of her small hands. "No, and you can't tell him."

Heat flared in my chest. "Why would I tell Patrick Bell anything? And give him more reason to kill the only business we have left? No, thank you." As much as I didn't want to blame Camila for her father's business dealings, it was hard not to.

"Papa said he hasn't done anything and that he has no reason to cause your family harm. I want to believe him, Ridge. But what's happening to you and Harold isn't fair, no matter who is behind it."

I wanted to believe her, but I also wanted to hate her. She was impossible to argue with or stay mad at for a second. Frustrated, I aimed for a subject change. "What are you doing in the woods, anyway? Don't you have a party to be at?" Then I took another look at her attire. "Looks like you're missing out on all the fun."

Still appearing flushed from the wine, she looked down at her dress and bit down on her lip. When she looked back up, something had changed in her expression. "I hate this feud, Ridge. All I could think about all day was how you and Harold should be there too. Do you think our parents even know why they're fighting anymore?"

"Probably not. Our fathers are proud men. Protective of their land to the point that they'd do practically anything to keep it safe from outsiders. Even if that means fighting each other."

"But why?"

"Why" was Camila's famous question. Why continue to hold onto a grudge that neither of them started? Why continue to fan the flames of hate when everyone had the same goal in mind? I'd resolved that we would never know the depth of our families' war.

I rubbed my thumb across Camila's cheek. I hadn't

meant to care for her the way I did. She was only sixteen, yet she still felt like my only real friend in that town. "I don't know, Wild One." I pulled my hand away, trying to ignore the look she gave me—like she already missed my touch. "We might never know."

I shouldn't have noticed a lot of things about Camila, like how her eyes changed shades of green based on the backdrop around her, the way they sparkled in the sun and lit up when she had something exciting to say, or the way her long, thick lashes fell over her cheeks when she felt relaxed while leaning against the tree. I shouldn't have noticed the way her bratty, know-it-all tone had changed into something more poignant, thoughtful, and introspective. But Camila loved to talk philosophy and history in a way that held my attention like no one else could.

Also, I shouldn't have wanted to protect her in a way that she didn't ever ask for or need. But ever since we'd stumbled upon that mine below the hillside, I hadn't been able to stop worrying about her. She was still wild and reckless, with no regard for her own safety, and while that made her fascinating to me, it also propelled me to think about her far more than was right.

I shoved all those thoughts aside. "You should be getting back."

She nodded, though she looked like she had no desire to go back. Then she faced me with the most heart-breaking stare that made me want to hold her and never let her go. "Did you really mean what you said to me?"

Her words came out in a rush, blowing through me like a winter storm. She didn't have to elaborate on her question. I'd told her that she meant nothing to me when the opposite was true. I didn't deserve her forgiveness, but she was there, offering it to me on a silver platter.

"No, Camila. I didn't mean it. Not at all."

She took a deep breath and smiled. That was all it took to put us back together, but I knew it wouldn't last. It couldn't.

"C'mon, I'll walk you to the bridge." Then I smiled softly and tucked her under my arm. "So the boogeyman doesn't get you."

When she glared up at me, I winked and started forward.

"One day, when the vineyard is mine," Camila said with so much conviction that she almost sounded angry, "you'll get an invite to every event, every harvest, and every farmer's market."

I chuckled. "You're still drunk."

"In fact," she said, ignoring me, "you won't even need an invite. You'll just waltz on over, any time you please. We'll drink wine from the barrel and stroll through the vineyard. We'll pick grapes from the vines then cross that damn bridge to snap corn off your stalks too."

"Whoa, now," I teased. "Getting a little ahead of yourself. Who says I'll still be here?"

The look she gave me next made me regret my words. Even if she didn't know how true they were, the sadness washing over her face twisted me up inside.

"You planning on going somewhere, Ridge?"

"I was thinking about it."

She paused a moment before shaking it off. "You still have the rest of the year left before you graduate to think about it."

We'd talked about the future, but lately, my thoughts had been changing. I could graduate high school from anywhere, and college wasn't something I wanted to pursue. A fancy degree wasn't necessary for farming or going on the adventures I'd been dreaming about. "I was thinking about getting away for a bit after the season's up," I said, waving my arms around me at the field I'd only just made a dent in harvesting. "Harold doesn't really need me here during the off-season, and I'm almost done with school. I can finish anywhere."

"But you *will* come back, right? Harold will need you in the spring, and—"

"I didn't ask for all this." Though I didn't mean to interrupt her, I never knew when she was finished talking. "I'm not like you. I grew up spending my days hiking through the mountain lands, wrangling horses, and catching my dinners in the lake. Part of me will always crave that adventure. Riding a tractor can only fulfill me so much."

"So, then go on an adventure, then come right back home. Or take up more jobs at Mountain Village, like you mentioned. Harold needs you. I need you."

Something caught in my chest with her words, but I ignored it with a quick shake of my head. "You don't need me, Camila." I smiled. "You don't need anyone with that hard head of yours."

She glared, and I sighed. We couldn't start that same conversation again.

"It's not just about me going on an adventure, Camila. This is about me needing to find my own way. I'm eighteen now. I'm free to figure out what's next without being tied to this land just yet."

"Where will you go?" she asked. "Back to the reservation?"

I let out a laugh. "The rez may still hold my roots, but it's not where I belong. I guess I'm still trying to figure out where I do."

Her chin quivered. "After all this time, you still don't know? This is your home. Right here. You're acting like someone's got you tied up in chains, telling you how to live your life. Your problem isn't *where* you belong. It's why you don't believe that you deserve it."

I blew out a breath and looked off in the distance. "You're too young to understand."

My words pissed her off, which was why I had chosen them. I didn't say things by accident, and she knew it.

She righted her shoulder, and the determination I'd come to know so well took over her expression. Then she started to walk away, but she swiveled around just as fast. "Why does everyone think I'm too young to understand? I'm not too young. You're just too scared."

She slammed her hand into my chest, and I caught it, pressing it against me while glaring down at her with just as much intensity as she was aiming at me. Then she growled in frustration before stomping away down the center of the field, back toward the woods.

I wanted to fire back at her. Though I was the calm one between us, that didn't mean I couldn't have a temper when she pushed me, and boy, did Camila Bell push the hell out of me at times. But before I could even open my mouth to call after her, a pair of headlights flashed, causing me to turn in their direction.

The engine of Harold's tractor roared as it drew closer, and the large machine picked up speed until I realized he was headed straight down the corner of the cornfield, right for Camila. Until that moment, she hadn't even turned around to acknowledge the lights coming for her. I always worried that Camila believed she was invincible. She wasn't, and the proof was in the tractor barreling toward her.

16

I shook as I walked away from Ridge.

You're too young to understand.

Repeating his words like a broken record, I grew angrier by the second. Since Ridge and I had become friends two years ago, he had never made me feel "too young to understand." He wasn't the condescending type. Instead, he listened and chose his words carefully, and we always had an unmistakable comfort between us.

Maybe I'd grown too comfortable with Ridge, because his words cut me the deepest. The fact that he'd been thinking about leaving Telluride and possibly never coming back, without bothering to tell me, hurt. Harvest season would be over in six weeks, give or take. That wasn't long enough to get used to the idea of Ridge leaving.

I'd always thought the two of us would be sitting on the hilltop when we got old and wrinkly, admiring the land that belonged to us. We would work as one, because whatever feud had lasted over a century would be over. I was looking forward to that day almost as much as all the days in between. He was about to ruin everything.

I couldn't walk away from him fast enough. When the headlights blasted me from behind, I assumed Ridge had gotten back on his tractor. It wasn't until the machine's engine sounded like it was getting closer to me did I whip around to confront him again. *Does he want a fight?* I definitely had one in me. But the moment I faced the other direction, I had to throw my arms across my face to shield my eyes from the blinding light.

My heart pounded as I realized too late that the tractor was coming at me, like Ridge wanted to run me over with it. Before I could think what to do next, a hard body slammed into me, arms wrapped around me, then we sailed through the air as I screamed at the top of my lungs. We landed hard, and I realized that Ridge was beneath me. From the way his eyes were squeezed shut and the sound of his moans, I knew he'd taken the brunt of the impact.

"What the—?" *If Ridge is the one who grabbed me, then who was driving toward me in the tractor?*

A door slammed, and I rolled off Ridge to sit up. It was too dark to make out much, but a pair of dirty-jean-covered legs walked toward me. Harold Cross leaned down, a furious scowl twisting his sunburned face, then he grabbed me under the arm and yanked me to my feet.

My heart was in my throat. I'd never been so scared in my life. Harold wore his natural scowl, but his gaze held something darker that frightened me to the core.

"Well, well, well, look who we have here. I should

stick a stake in the ground of your daddy's vineyard and tie you to it by your neck, after all your family has done to mine."

His breath reeked like an ashtray, and his tone was nearly too gravelly to make sense of. Harold's eyes were dark brown, almost black, not nearly as beautiful as the chocolate brown and golden hues in his son's eyes. But his violent threat scared me most of all.

I tried to shake him off me, but he held on too tight. "Let me go," I demanded.

He let out a coughing laugh. "Your daddy know you're here? Did he send you to spy on me? To poison my harvest?" He jerked my arm, bringing me closer to him. "Tell me."

"I—" My vocal cords wouldn't act normal, with my nerves getting in the way. "I mean no harm. Truly. I came by to ask if you wanted any table grapes from our harvest." My lie rolled like butter off my tongue, but my voice pitched an octave higher. "And no, sir, my papa doesn't know I'm here." I gulped. "I was hoping we could keep that between us." A silent prayer whispered through my thoughts as I let out another breath.

"And why on God's earth should we do that?"

Ridge stepped forward and pressed his hand to his father's chest. "Let her go. Like she said, she means no harm."

Harold's head snapped toward Ridge. "And you know this how?"

Ridge bowed his head. "Look at her. She looks innocent enough to me."

My heart, still beating a mile a minute, sank. It seemed like he wanted to make no claim to the fact that we'd become friends. Right then was the perfect time to admit that he knew me and my intentions were good.

"That right, Miss Bell?" Harold asked, narrowing his accusing eyes at me. "Are you as innocent as my son here claims? You mean no harm?"

I whipped my head from left to right. "No, sir. No harm at all."

The grip on my arm tightened like he was planning to rip it right off. "That why you sneak through my fields when you think no one's lookin'?"

My eyes shot open wide.

"I've seen you galivanting through my corn like it's your personal playground. Guess I was hopin' my son here would shoot you before I ever had to." He let out a low chuckle as he shrugged his free shoulder. Then I saw the shotgun in his grip.

I narrowed my eyes at him. "Why don't you ask Ridge what happened the one and only time he was stupid enough to point a gun at me. It didn't go his way. I'll tell you that much."

Harold tossed Ridge a questioning glance, but I could feel Ridge's eyes on me while mine remained on Harold's.

"You should know the laws if you're going to be threatening me, sir. You'll go straight to jail, and my papa will have every right to buy your land the moment the state condemns it. That your plan?"

"Not if you just threatened my son's life and I shot you to defend him."

"Did I threaten your life, Ridge?"

Ridge took a step forward. "No, you did not. Let her go, Harold."

Harold tilted his head at me, surprise written clearly on his face. "Maybe it's not your daddy I need to be cautious of after all. Maybe it's you, darlin'. Seems you've got more balls than a pit at Chuck-e-Cheese."

"That, I do. Now, I suggest you let me go before you leave a bruise that I can tell my papa about. Trust me— he'd love to hear all about it."

Ridge stepped closer to Harold, his hand still pressed against his chest. "C'mon, Harold. Leave the girl alone."

Harold tightened his mouth and looked between Ridge and me. Then he released me and took a step back with a growl. *"Your daddy would love that, wouldn't he?"* he roared. "It's not enough that your old man ripped my family apart years ago or killed off my business. He'd gladly do all of it again. But this time, he won't stop there, will he? He'll take my land and bury us all in it before he ever makes things right."

I rubbed my arm where he'd grabbed me and shook my head. "I don't know what you're talking about. My papa says he never did a thing to your family."

Harold scoffed. "Your *papa* is a liar, Miss Bell. Now go on. Get out of here before I change my mind and it's you who gets buried in the cornfields you love so much."

I didn't wait to see who could win the staring contest, and I didn't give Ridge another glance. Instead, I let my bare feet carry me as fast as they could.

"And don't come back!" Harold shouted.

I darted through the darkened woods, over the bridge, and back into my vineyard without stopping to catch my breath.

17

"**A**re you fucking crazy? You could have *killed* her!" I roared. As soon as Camila was out of earshot, I stomped off after Harold, ready to let him have it.

Harold whipped around, pointing the butt of his shotgun at me. "I was just scaring her a little," he grumbled. "You should be wishing I had killed that little brat. She's a nuisance. And soon to be the heir to the Bell throne. She'll be your problem one day, not mine. Good to set her straight now."

"You're not helping the problem, you know. This goddamn feud between you and Patrick Bell only hurts you both."

"No, son." Harold faced me and pointed between us. "It only hurts us. The Bells have the upper hand in this town, always keeping us on the defensive—what business they let us have and what land we get approved to purchase. If it were up to that greedy asshole, he would own the entire city. What I did back there—" He gestured to the spot where Camila had almost been mowed over. "That was for you. For your future on this farm."

"Well, then I don't want it. Not like this. We're not the Wild West."

"That's where you're wrong. Our guns may have changed shape. Our strategies may have changed. But there's no escaping where you came from. Not here."

"Then I don't want to be here anymore." I took a step back and watched Harold's eyes grow wide with surprise. "You said it was Patrick Bell who tore our family apart, but it was you who gave him the power, wasn't it?"

Harold shook his head, his face red with frustration. "You don't know what you're talking about, son."

"Then tell me," I demanded. "For two and a half years, I've worked with you on this farm and lived in your home, and I've never asked a single prying question about what happened back then. I figured you'd tell me in due time and that none of it was important, anyway. But now I want to know. I'm demanding to know it. What happened between you and Patrick Bell?"

Seconds, maybe even minutes, passed. He just blinked like he was working through his words in his mind. Then he spoke. "Your mother was a runaway, son. At seventeen years old, she showed up on our farm, with bruises and cuts all over her body, asking to work for nothing except a barn to sleep in without question. My parents agreed. At that time, we were a cattle ranch, and she proved herself when it came to wrangling, so she was hired. Over the next six years, we fell in love. When she got pregnant, we couldn't hide her anymore, but we thought maybe the reservation—her family and everyone —would have given up the search by then. What we didn't expect was for Patrick Bell to tell the tribe where to find one of the girls he'd long ago added to the rapidly growing list of *missing.* If we didn't give her up, we could have all been arrested for harboring the missing girl. So we let Molly go with my baby inside her. I thought she would come back, but she never did."

I gulped, taking in the load of information that had just been dumped on me. "You haven't said anything before today."

"You haven't asked, boy. I thought you knew."

Then I realized Harold was right. I'd always thought the past was as good as buried, and I would never get the details of the whys that had become my life.

"But she wasn't safe. She went missing again, only this time, she won't be turning up alive. And you can thank Patrick Bell for that."

The firmness of his words and the certainty of his tone felt like two hands clasped around my throat. "What did you say?"

A breeze blew in with the next few beats of uncomfortable silence, whistling through the air and whipping the remaining stalks halfway to the soil. The scene was as eerie as the moment felt, with darkness at every turn and only the headlights of the tractor illuminating us both.

"Ah, son, I'm sorry. I didn't mean for it to come out like that."

I could feel the blood draining from my face. "What did you say?" I repeated the words slowly and quietly, with all the venom I could muster. I knew what he'd said, but I needed to hear him confirm it.

While the number of women that had gone missing from the rez was unbelievably high, I'd still held on to a glimmer of hope. And after hearing his story about how she'd come to Telluride and conceived me in the beginning, my glimmer of hope only grew, and I'd wondered if she found a new safe haven and was still alive.

But the truth was that no one had followed up with me regarding my mother's missing status after I moved. I didn't know of any investigation, and we had no family left there. At just fifteen years old, I'd been alone, trying to cope with the fact that my mother might never come home and that I might never see her again. Harold's words had destroyed any hope I had, and I felt more broken than ever.

"They found your mom. They found her dead. I'm sorry, son. She's not coming home."

Like a dagger, his final words plunged through me. My chest and neck tightened as emotion tried to claw its way out. Stinging heat rushed to my eyes.

Harold Cross hated Patrick Bell because of the life that had been stolen from him. Patrick Bell was the reason I'd grown up without a father. Instead, I was raised by a single mom who could barely hold down a job and could barely feed us without bringing home leftovers from her bar dates with random men. In the end, she'd paid the ultimate price for it all.

"When the harvest season is done, I will leave Telluride." My voice shook with every syllable. "And I won't be coming back."

18

CAMILA, ONE AND A HALF YEARS LATER

I'd just finished cleaning the kitchen after an early family dinner when I looked up to find the older version of me swirling her wine with a frown. Her eyes were on the liquid sloshing around in her glass, and a pang hit my chest as I pondered canceling my plans to stay home. Papa had already retired to his casita for some late-night work. He probably wouldn't come out of there until morning. I hated the thought of leaving her by herself.

After a minute of internal debate, I set the rag I'd been holding on the counter. "Do you want to watch a movie tonight, Mama? We can find something on TV or pick out an old DVD."

She let out a short laugh and shook her head. "No, sweetie. I'm going to call it an early night."

I bit my tongue, wanting to ask her why—and why it felt like my parents had been bickering a lot lately. But she would never give me the answers. If anything, the fact that I'd picked up on it would only sadden her more, and that was the last thing I wanted to do.

Mama worked hard, not just as the vineyard's book-keeper and winery host but also at the country club where she volunteered her time. From the looks of her when she came home, I'd assumed the country club was where she was the happiest. Getting time to socialize with her friends and get away from the exhaustive pressures my papa set for himself and everyone around us was probably refreshing.

Papa was all about production, timelines, and perfection. A simple concept, but perfection became a laborious benchmark that was impossible to reach. Patrick Bell wasn't happy unless he'd succeeded in all things, and no one wanted to bear the wrath of my papa's unhappiness.

"I thought you were heading out to go camping with your friends," she said before checking the time on the clock above my head. "You'd better get going if you want to beat nightfall."

I waved a hand. "My friends are already checking us into the campsite. I just need to park and plop myself down by the fire when I get there." I grinned but couldn't hold it for long. Something just felt off, and I hated leaving, even if just for a few days, without knowing she would be okay. "Seriously, Mama. I'm happy to stay if you want company."

Mama walked over, giving a soft and completely genuine smile. She held my face and kissed my cheek before staring me dead in the eyes. "Go. Have fun with your friends. You deserve a fun spring break away. Just be careful out there."

She was referring to the snow patches that still packed sections of terrain, making an overnight hiking trip in the mountains a risky one. It was late April, just past the end of ski season in Telluride, but the unpredictable weather patterns in the mountains remained. I dreaded winter, purely for the fact that the "white gold," as locals called it, blanketed everything I loved most in the world—the vineyard, the cornfield, the hilltop, and the wildflowers that always came alive in the late spring and summer. I always entered a state of hibernation in the wintertime, locking me in place until the cold melted away. So the spring break my friends and I had been planning felt much like an awakening of sorts.

I hugged her tight and nodded. "I promise to be careful. Please don't worry."

The "You don't know how to be careful, Camila" look plainly written in her eyes made me laugh.

"Don't look at me like that. I'm going on an entirely guided trip with well-trained staff."

"Where is this place you're going again?"

"Some private campsite near Camp Bird in Ouray."

My mama shuddered. "Don't they call that place a ghost town?"

I laughed. "You can call most of the towns around here ghost towns, Mama."

Telluride and the surrounding areas had been big on silver mining back in the day. In the 1950s, a final mining bust had shut down all the mines in the area, causing families to leave town in droves. Business on Bell Family Vineyard suffered right along with it. Not until the area slowly started to become a ski resort area in the 1970s did life begin again.

"Raven set the whole thing up, so blame her. But you know Trip will be there to report back on my behavior, as always. In fact, this whole spring break thing is starting to sound like a drag if you ask me." I winked at my mama. "But Josie insisted, since there's this boy, Ryker, she likes, and you know I can't refuse the girl."

Her face twisted with confusion. "What happened to Emilio?"

I smiled back at her adoringly, knowing she always had a hard time keeping up with the gossip. "They broke up months ago. She doesn't think he liked her as much as she liked him. Can you believe that? I just—"

"Yes, yes." She waved me off, as she always did when she recognized I'd started on a tangent. "I know you'll be just fine, mija." She squeezed my hands.

My mama knew me too well, and while she feared for my adventurous nature, she honored it as well, never wanting to get in the way of what lit life inside me. So she stayed quiet when most mothers would ground and lecture. She let me be, but I had a feeling she sometimes knew more than she let on, like my old weekly trips to the hilltop.

"Well, if you're going to go, then *go*. Before I change my mind." Her words, though an effort to shoo me away, were playful and encouraging. "Oh, and don't forget your bear spray."

I chuckled. "Already got it covered, Mama. I'll text you when I get to the base camp."

I arrived in Ouray, a city less than an hour outside of Telluride, just as the sun was starting to set. The two cities were separated by the rugged Sneffels Range, where my friends and I would be hiking for the next few days. The Victorian-era mining town of Ouray was nestled in the thirteen-thousand-foot peaks of the San Juan Mountains. Many referred to it fondly as the Switzerland of America, and with its surrounding mountainous backdrop of never-ending hillsides and natural beauty, it was easy to see why.

Raven had booked us a private hiking tour through a campground where we all would spend our first night and meet our hiking guide. A sign on a wood post read Camp Lachey, signaling where I should turn in. The spacious area was an open clearing complete with yurts, trailers, and tiny homes where visitors could stay without having to worry about their own setup or equipment. From there, my friends and I would partake in a three-day hiking adventure through the Mount Sneffels wilderness that would end back at the camp with a send-off party.

I parked my Jeep in the gravel lot and followed the trail toward the line of yurts that were set up against an old wooden fence overlooking a large ranch. It was already dark out, but beyond the open field, I could just make out the stacked skylines of the mountain. The stars shone brighter than anything I'd ever seen in my life.

"You looking for your friends?"

I jumped and whipped my head toward the deep voice. He was just a shadow, sitting there in his black jacket, until he stepped into the dim lighting from a nearby lamppost. Silver glittered in his long dark hair, and age lines ran across his forehead. He wasn't tall, by any means, but his build made up for it. He smiled when he caught a look at my startled expression.

"Name's Jason Lachey. You're in my camp."

I hadn't even realized how much tension had been building in me until it all came out in a *whoosh* I hoped he didn't hear. "Oh, I'm Camila. My friends and I are taking a guided hike."

"Well, I appreciate your business." He pointed at the skyline I'd just been staring at. "You've got the best view in all of Colorado this week. I hope you enjoy it."

I smiled back at him. "I'm sure I will."

Jason nodded in the direction I'd started walking. "Camp's down that way. Your friends are at the fire."

Eager to find them, I slung my backpack around my shoulders and gave a final wave. "Great. Thank you." I made my way to the tent site. About halfway down the row, I spotted the yurt I would be sharing with Josie for the night. She had gotten there earlier in the afternoon with Trip and Raven, since I'd been tied up at the vineyard all day. The cloth doors were tied open, and it looked like my best friend had already made herself right at home.

Josie's backpack was lying on the side of the bed she'd already claimed, and a bottle of stolen Bell Family Vineyard vintage red wine sat open at her bedside with a note for me to pour myself a glass and stay awhile. I laughed and tossed my backpack onto my bed, and then did as she asked.

The crackle of the fire and my friends' laughter made finding them easy.

"Finally!" Trip's voice boomed from across the campfire as I approached. "The straggler has arrived."

Laughing, I curtsied while sneaking my middle finger up, a gesture directed at the bane of my existence. My peers chuckled at my boldness, and even from a distance, I could see the broad smile that had popped onto his face.

Trip had graduated from Telluride High School the previous year, but he never stopped being an overprotective older brother to Raven when he was home from Columbia University. I still saw him every now and then when he stopped by to help Papa and Thomas distribute wine to all the restaurants, grocery stores, and resorts around town.

I plopped onto a log as I greeted my friends and hugged Josie. My insides danced at the thought of the days to come—campfires, camping in the woods, and a challenging hike through the melting white and green mountains. Hiking and camping in the wilderness were things I'd been craving for as long as Ridge had made the suggestion, which was before he had vanished without a trace, running a tractor over my already-shattered heart.

The spring break trip was meant to be a rite of passage for my friends and me—a shared adventure we would remember forever—and I couldn't wait for it to begin.

"It's like a reunion." Trip's deep voice forced my eyes onto his. A translucent flame from the fire waved between us. I didn't miss the significance. Fire had always danced between us and not in a good way. I'd seen Trip's future long before he knew what was happening. His father always brought him by the vineyard, even before he'd gone off to college, and taught him the ropes, molding him into the future of everything Thomas Bradshaw had grown to be at Bell Family Vineyard. So far, his plan was panning out just right.

I laughed. "A reunion? For whom? I just saw everyone else on Friday. You're the one that can't stay away from high schoolers."

Trip glared at me. His red cup was filled to the brim with what I assumed was beer. "That's not what I'm talking about."

Something in Trip's tone chilled me to my core. Then he nodded in the direction of the fire. A man in a dark-blue hoodie and black jeans had just poked a long stick into the flames. I could only see the man's build, thanks to the silhouette created by the fire, but it was enough to make my heart squeeze tight.

At the same moment I realized who the man was, he turned his head slowly and locked his gaze directly on me. My entire body, inside and out, froze. The fire blazing between us was of no help. I was shocked to the root. Hard and cold on the outside but a pile of messed-up emotions on the inside, I didn't know how to thaw a single ligament in order to save myself.

19

CAMILA

Ridge Cross had left Telluride a year and a half ago, without even saying goodbye. It had taken weeks for me to realize that the whispered rumors through the school halls were true. I didn't want to believe them. Harold Cross's boy was gone, leaving the mean old farmer alone once again.

I had given up hope that he would come home and had stopped trying to search for him in all the places I knew he wasn't. He'd broken every important piece of me that had existed before him, and I swore I would never forgive him for it.

My eyes flicked over the man standing in front of the fire, and I wondered if he was just a mirage. I didn't know whether I was happy or mad about seeing him again. The dull knocking on the hollow shell of my ribcage could mean either.

He wore a badge on his jacket with Camp Lachey's branding, which confirmed several important facts. He had moved away and gotten a new job. But he hadn't gone far.

Ouray was nearly an hour from Telluride, only a quick winding drive around the mountains. He could have easily come home to say hello or said goodbye in the first place. Instead, he remained gone, apparently with zero intention of seeing me again.

My chest felt heavier with each compounding thought. I'd never allowed myself to feel upset because I'd refused to believe that Ridge *had chosen* to leave after how that night ended. But as I looked at him, the truth was a slap in the face. Clearly, he'd chose his fate and shunned me in the process.

"What are *you* doing here?" My tone was meant to be uncaring, but the moment the harsh words touched the crisp air, I wanted to take them back. I missed my friend —my comfort and my shelter—but anger was all I could express.

Everyone around us besides Josie wouldn't bat an eyelash at my tone. My peers would assume that my feelings for Ridge mirrored Papa's and that I had forgotten him as soon as he'd left town. But I hadn't forgotten. I wouldn't. And I was slightly colder for it.

Ridge didn't respond. Instead, he turned back to the flames and poked at it with the stick. That was it. Not even a hello. After all the time we had spent together, sneaking around and hiking up to our personal heaven, he had nothing to say to me. My heart, which he'd already stomped on and left buried in the cornfields that fall evening, felt like it was finally breaking.

Josie nudged my side to get my attention. "Ridge will be our hiking guide." She stared wide-eyed at me and seemed just as surprised as I had been. "I tried to warn you," she whispered. "But your phone was off."

"Shitty service," I said without having to look at my call log. That was the one thing I hated about venturing out of town. While I was perfectly fit to hike the trails in even the roughest conditions, it wouldn't be easy to call for help if I was lost or had an emergency. And I would have definitely deemed seeing Ridge as an emergency. A warning would have been nice.

I focused on Ridge again. He was still standing in the same spot, his jaw set hard like he was grinding his teeth. *Is he upset to see me?* Perhaps he was angry that he was surrounded by everyone who had bullied him when he'd moved to Telluride.

With one sweep of my eyes, I could tell that Ridge's days of being the victim were over. He'd grown in every visible way. His face had lost its boyish softness and was cut like the mountains, with sharp peaks and valleys defining his bold cheekbones, and rugged jaw. He had cliffs for eyebrows and sweet chocolate pools for his eyes. And his quiet nature no longer screamed shy new boy but of a lethal weapon ready to strike at any moment. Time had made him colder, darker, and more on edge than ever before.

As if seeing Ridge again wasn't bad enough, Raven's gaze made my stomach churn. She stared at him, completely oblivious to the rest of us as she practically drooled at his every movement. I'd always suspected that she had a crush on Ridge, but I'd never imagined it would go anywhere. Trip would never have allowed it. *But now...*

My gaze flicked to Trip, who sat beside her, studying

me. If anyone knew more than Josie, Trip would. He'd probably made a small fortune in high school, watching after me. Trip had slowly made his feelings for me known, despite my deflection of his advances, and for whatever reason, he'd hated Harold Cross's son with his every waking breath.

If Trip is busy watching me, then who will watch Raven? I swallowed at the mental image of Ridge and Raven hiking through the emerging wildflowers, snuggling, and giggling the entire way. My heart started to beat faster, and my mind raced with thoughts that didn't belong in my head. Though it was an awful fantasy, I couldn't seem to let go of it.

The last thing I should be thinking about was Raven and Ridge together. But Raven was really pretty, with her long bleached-blond hair that nearly reached her waist, her always-ready smile that could light up a dark room, and her deep-blue eyes that had the potential to hypnotize a wild coyote. And the mental image of them together made my stomach roll.

If tonight was any indication, the next three days were bound to be torture, as I watched Raven eye fuck Ridge while he gave me the silent treatment. I wouldn't survive.

Luckily, tonight would be a short night. With our plans to wake up early to start hiking in the morning, we knew not to get stupid.

Not long after I arrived, my peers started to excuse themselves from the fire to make their way to their tents. Eventually, the last of our group trailed off, leaving Josie and me with Ridge.

Josie stood next, without my having to give her a hint. "I'm heading to bed. See you soon?"

Her look was pointed and held a tinge of warning that I should heed. I nodded and watched her walk off before raising my gaze to Ridge. He'd already been looking at me, waiting. And I hated that something so small could give me so much hope.

"So, that's it, huh? Not even a hello?"

He sat there, stoic, for another minute before blowing out a breath and looking at the sky. "How are you, Camila?"

His question, while it was a start, only angered me. "I'm great, Ridge." I could practically feel the sarcasm dripping off my tone. "How about you?"

His laugh floated on a single breath that twisted into my chest. "I'm doing well."

Despite the tension between us, I believed his words. I felt his calmness. He was so perfectly paired with nature. Maybe he'd finally found his home after all. Even in my anger, I could be happy for him, if that was the case. But I didn't know what to say, so I allowed another minute or two to pass as our eyes shared a conversation our hearts had yet to catch up with.

"Have you hiked around here before?"

My chest pounded, not from his question but because he'd asked a question at all and such a casual one. His voice was deep and rich, but the velvety softness that I remembered from our past remained. He could still lull me into a calm just by a simple sentence.

"No." I swallowed, hoping to steady my nerves. "I hear it's beautiful."

"That, it is." He twisted the stick he'd been holding

into the dirt. "Especially in the spring. Just wait until you see the stars from up there. There's nothing like it."

My heart beat fast at the mental picture he provoked. In all the years we'd met on the hilltop, never once had we met up at night. I'd always dreamed of looking up at the stars with Ridge. And while I was younger than he was, it didn't stop me from wanting our first kiss to be among them.

He stood, ending our conversation, and I couldn't help but notice just how different his body looked. Even through the flickering flame of the campfire, he was obviously no longer a boy. He was tall, thick with muscle, and had features that made my insides ache. Ridge Cross was becoming a man.

"It's dark. Can I walk you?"

The tent I was staying in with Josie was only a few sites away, but I didn't care. Ridge had offered, and I would steal every precious moment with him. So I got up, dusted my leggings off, and met him at the dirt walkway. There, I could really see how much Ridge had filled out since I'd last seen him. *Who would have known a year and a half would turn such a baby face into a rugged cowboy?*

I led the way down the path slowly, and he matched my pace. "So, this is where you call home now, huh?"

He shrugged. "Nowhere has ever felt like home to me. You know that, Camila." He glanced at me. "But I suppose this is the closest I've come to feeling settled."

I shouldn't ask questions I wouldn't like the answers to, but I was a glutton for punishment. "I guess I can see why." Even in the dark, I could make out the shapes of the mountains and the contrast of each peak as they lay staggered in the distance. "Everything feels bigger than life here. Have you been back to the farm at all?"

"Nah, I think Harold and I needed a little break."

Something about his statement infuriated me to no end. My pulse throbbed in my throat. "Did you need a break from me too?"

Ridge stopped in his tracks and bowed his head. "Camila…"

I stopped walking too and turned to face him. "No." I stepped closer to him so that I was right under his nose, inescapable. "I asked you a question, and I deserve an answer."

He gave me a blistering stare. "You want to do this now? Fine, Camila. Let's do this now. Let's get it out of the way."

"Do what now? I just asked you a question."

His jaw ticked. "Get all of your punches out of the way. Tell me how mean I was to leave the farm, leave Telluride… leave *you*. Make it all about you, and send me groveling on my knees. Go ahead."

My jaw dropped. "It was a shitty thing you did, leaving like that. After everything we—I thought I meant more to you than that."

He let out a cruel laugh. "Always so dramatic."

His words were bite marks on my soul, and I feared the next attack more than I'd feared anything else in my life. Little by little, the small amount of history Ridge and I shared felt like it was crumbling into ash and floating in the wind. Soon, it would be as if it didn't exist at all.

"I'm not being dramatic. You left, Ridge. Without even saying goodbye."

"And what would have been the point of that?"

My thoughts stumbled over the hurt in my heart but kept fueling my mouth, anyway. Even the sting behind my eyes didn't stop me. "Maybe it's not so much the fact that you left so abruptly. Deep down, I think I knew you wouldn't last on that farm. But—after Harold tried to run me over with his tractor, you acted like I was nothing to you."

He said nothing after that, just stared at me with his dark eyes while pressing his lips together. His mind was churning, but he allowed me a chance to speak.

"Maybe I meant nothing to you at first, but I'd thought we moved past that. I thought—" I couldn't say any more, afraid to bring up my feelings for him again.

A moment of silence passed while his dark eyes scanned over me, like he was finally taking me in. Maybe he was noticing how much I had changed too.

"You thought what, Camila?" Ridge asked, his tone gentler. "What do you think would have happened if I had stayed? If we had continued our silly little charade of climbing to that hilltop?"

My pulse raced as I let his question consume me. All the possibilities flooded my mind, and I desperately swam through them, trying to sort out the good from the bad and hold on to one scenario that could have benefited us both. I found none.

When I looked back at him, defeated, he nodded.

"Harold would have dragged you right on over to your papa and told him about all the times he knew of you running through our fields. I omitted the truth from Harold to protect you. That night was the first night I realized what our friendship could do if exposed. This feud between our families, it's bigger than us."

I folded my arms across my chest and tried to keep my lip from quivering. "That's where you and I disagree, Ridge. Nothing is bigger than you and me. Not even a century-old feud. We're the ones who are supposed to end it. But we can't do that now, can we? Not with you here."

For a time, I'd considered Ridge one of my best friends. He had gotten to know a side of me that no one else knew, not even Josie. I'd trusted him with my silly fantasies of life after gaining the keys to my papa's kingdom. He knew that I trusted him and that our friendship was important to me. And I never pushed him to say more than he felt the need to say. With Ridge, I found stillness—a calm state where my rampant thoughts grew quiet to make room for so much more. I'd never imagined finding that.

Ridge hadn't just stripped me of a friendship. He'd stripped me of my better self when I was with him. And for that, I couldn't forgive him.

I took a step back toward my tent and let out a laugh while my insides cried painful tears. "This week should be interesting." Sarcasm crept back into my voice, and I didn't even try to stop it. "We can go right back to how it used to be. Pretending we aren't friends. Only this time, we won't be pretending." With another backward step, I smiled. "Good night, Ridge."

20

RIDGE

I still liked to wake up before sunrise, and today was no exception. After peeling my eyes open, I carried my shower bag and a change of clothes to the communal bathhouse, stuck some quarters into the machine, and rinsed myself off. I was used to the routine. A year and a half ago, after packing my bags and driving in a random direction away from Telluride, Ouray had been my first stop. Named after the old Ute Tribe's chief back in 1876, it seemed like a safe middle ground between the rez and Harold's Farm. I could get lost without completely losing sight of where I came from.

One of Harold's clients we dropped hay off to, Jason Lachey, had a plot of flat land he wasn't sure what to do with. The plot lay beside the livestock ranch he owned with his brother. The guided tours had been my idea, and he ran with it with my help. I quickly got acquainted with the numerous hiking trails around town and part- nered with the mine owners and other businesses to cross-promote to tourists. And it all just evolved from there. For the first time ever, I felt like I finally had a purpose in a way that gave back to the community and the surrounding nature on equal footing. Running a corn farm didn't fulfill me in that way. I couldn't imagine ever going back to that farm, but I would be lying to myself if I didn't admit that seeing Camila again altered something in me. I'd felt a shift in my heart, though I'd yet to fully grasp its meaning. All I knew was that I wanted to see her again.

After dressing in a pair of charcoal hiking pants and a light-gray thermal shirt, I slipped on my hiking boots and a red knit cap. When I stepped back outside, the cool air stung a little, but the sun would warm us considerably during our trek up the mountain. The plan was to take twelve campers on a hike on the Blue Lakes trail, starting with the lower Blue Lakes, past the middle lake to Upper Blue Lake, then finally to Blue Lakes Pass—camping in between destinations.

My job that week was to guide the group and help them camp safely in the wilderness. Jason would hang back at base camp, like he preferred, to watch over the other campers who were just there to party.

I stopped by each campsite to tap on the tents and remind everyone that we would be leaving in an hour. When I got to Camila's tent, I hesitated for a second before climbing the two steps to get to the top of the deck. After sucking in my next breath, I placed my fist on a wood plank above my head. I was about to knock when the tent doors fluttered open, and out walked Camila.

She was a storm, always bringing unpredictable weather with her. A person never knew how to prepare for her presence. I could never get a grasp on it. It seemed not much had changed, even with time and distance between us.

Her hair was a disheveled mess that bounced around her shoulders in loose curls. Her eyes, while still filled with sleep, looked hopeful as she gazed at the new light of day.

She was oblivious to me as she pushed her hands above her head and stretched, revealing an inch of caramel skin around her navel. Even though I'd seen her the night before, nothing prepared me for what daylight revealed. Camila might not have been a little girl anymore, but she was still in high school. I shouldn't have been looking at her the way I was, noticing her beauty, or the way her pajama pants hung below her soft stomach.

Her boyish shape seemed to have filled out, complete with a deep curve of her hips that accentuated her small waist and perfectly formed backside. She was wearing a thin white tank top that had me averting my eyes the moment I noticed her hard nipples staring back at me. Clearly, she wasn't wearing a bra, and I cursed myself for noticing.

I didn't normally think so vulgarly about a woman. I'd seen all shapes and sizes come through the base camp, and I appreciated them all just fine. But no one could light a candle to Camila. She'd always been strong and feisty, keeping up with the boys just as well as any. *But now…* I swallowed back my thoughts, which were so carelessly rolling through my mind like an approaching storm.

Feeling suddenly stalkerish, I cleared my throat to let her know I was there.

Her lids widened as she snapped her head around.

Our eyes met, and I was instantaneously transported back in time, to a place I swore I would never go again. I was right back in that cornfield, swimming in a sea of green and specks of gold. Memories of chasing her through tall stalks of our future harvest overwhelmed me like a flash flood, drowning me before I even had a chance.

How has Camila Grace Bell always had that effect on me? I laughed while trying desperately to hold back my affection for a girl two years younger than me. I combatted feelings that felt like more than friendship or lust, and I harbored guilt for years for thoughts and feelings I couldn't control. Even that morning, my thoughts were dangerous and wrong.

"Good morning," she said, not masking her surprise at the sight of me at her tent.

A ping-pong match started in my chest from just the sound of her voice, and I didn't know how to stop it. "Just coming by to give everyone a wake-up call." I dared another look at her, which was a mistake.

"Oh," she said slowly, her eyes dimming some. "I see."

Ignoring the guilt that was compiling in all the empty spaces of my head and heart, I continued, "We're heading to the trailhead in an hour."

Something flickered in her expression before everything hardened. "Great." She stepped past me. "Then I have time for a shower."

She walked away, toward the bathhouse, and I couldn't stop watching her leave.

My favorite part of leading various hikes was the reactions of our guests as we navigated the incline between Mount Sneffels and Wolcott Mountain. Bear sightings were frequent, the wildflowers were aplenty, and the crystal-blue lakes made the hike one of the most scenic and rewarding one could possibly experience in their lifetime.

While I guided the tour, that didn't always mean that I led it. A few of the more ambitious hikers always liked to walk a little faster than the rest of the pack, which was fine by me. My job was to give everyone stopping points so that we didn't get too spread out, and ensure that the stragglers didn't get too far behind. Camila, of course, had taken the lead. Trip, unsurprisingly, was right behind her, while Trip's sister, Raven, was trying desperately to keep up with me.

Josie and the rest of the hikers were taking up the tail of our group as we ascended over the craggy peaks and endless mountain valleys. I wouldn't alter anyone's pace, though, even if I did want to secretly corner Camila somewhere on an uncharted path and take a truly good look at her. But to be attracted to a girl still in high school —a Bell, no less—was wrong, and I would keep reminding myself of that.

I'd left Telluride for a reason. It had been a decision I'd been weighing, but after everything that had happened and everything I'd learned that night, I couldn't stay. But seeing Camila again reminded me just how innocent she was in all of it and that the ticking time bomb hadn't just started. It had been ticking since I'd first met the feisty vineyard girl, and it was getting louder, threatening to go off when none of us were ready.

Though it was mean of me to purposely try to out-walk Raven, when it came to the steeper inclines, she slowed down slightly, and I picked up the pace. I'd never had anything against Raven. She was nice, pretty, and sweet. But she also reeked of a desperation I didn't understand. I'd never gotten to know her the way I had with Camila. I wouldn't even have considered Raven and me friends, but she seemed to have some other ideas about us.

I took the crumbling rock stairs two at a time and reached the next section of flat land to find Camila in the distance. She was at the first jaw-dropping scenic point, standing right at the tip of a cliff that over-looked an open valley with wildflowers surrounding us. Only she would find comfort at the edge of a steep ravine.

Taking a deep inhalation, I moved toward her. Trip was nowhere in sight when I climbed the rocks to stand beside her. Maybe he'd gone on ahead. All that mattered was that for a moment, we were alone again.

Neither of us said a word as we stood there, basking in the tranquil sounds of nature all around us—from the water flowing over the creek rocks that marked 1.5 miles into our journey, to the susurrus of fir trees as they blew in the wind, and to the wildlife singing their familiar songs.

Crisp air filled our lungs as our gazes panned from one end of the valley to the other. Birds fluttered past us and soared through the endless blue sky.

"Look at that," she whispered.

I searched above us to find whatever she was seeing just as her hand clutched mine.

"An eagle." She gasped. "Wait, two eagles." She pointed at the sky with her free hand and traced the path of the birds as they flew low overhead. One of them swept the valley below before rising again into the sky to soar with the other. Their wings were rounded in shape and short in size.

"Those are red-tailed hawks," I corrected her without thinking twice about it.

Her head snapped to me. "They're what?"

"Red-tailed hawks."

"How do you know that? They just look like big white birds to me."

The annoyance in her voice over the fact that I knew something she didn't made me smile. "I used to go bird watching with my mom on the reservation. She was fascinated by these guys, in particular. Their feathers are actually brown on top, but their underbellies are pale, almost white." I squinted at the sky, where the hawks had risen to soar again in a wide circle overhead. "They love open spaces like this."

We watched them duck into the valley before they rose back up into the sky.

"Are they—together?"

I smiled again. "Pairs who are courting usually soar together like that." I nodded at where the male bird was parting ways with the female. "Watch."

Her eyes faced forward completely, and she gasped as the hawk climbed high into the air and dove as if in a free fall with half-closed wings. When it rose again, it spiraled in its ascent until he was joined with the female again, and they locked their talons together and spun each other in midair.

"Wow," Camila gushed, her small eyes wider than I'd ever seen them. "What was that?"

"A courtship flight. It's a territorial ritual they engage in before breeding."

We watched quietly as the hawks danced through the air then finally swooped down toward the thick with woods beneath us and disappeared.

Long after the birds had left our sight, I could feel Camila's eyes on me. I met her stare. Unspoken words drifted between us, and for the first time in my life, I felt like I had so much to say. My reasons for leaving were so much more than what I'd confessed to her, and my feelings for her were somehow stronger than they ever had been. Years apart had done nothing to erase the forbidden ache I felt for my Wild One. And I wanted to tell her all of that.

"Oh shit, oh shit, oh shit."

Camila and I snapped our heads toward the voice coming from the other side of the trail. Trip stood there among the weeds, looking in the other direction. He was frozen still, and I knew he'd spotted a bear before I saw its black fur rippling as the silent beast crept toward him.

"Shit," I muttered.

Camila turned her head sharply to me. She'd never heard me cuss, because I'd never found a use for such words until my move to Ouray. Being around so many different campers since working there had changed me. I'd become more outspoken and less worried about what anyone else's agendas were. I lived for me and for the mountains, and my vocabulary had grown more colorful for it.

"Don't move a muscle," I called to Trip. "He's more afraid of you than you are of him. Remember that. Got any bear spray on you?"

Trip shook his head, looking completely panicked and helpless as the bear continued to stare him down.

"I do," Camila said, taking a step forward.

My hand gripped her arm so fast that her eyes shot to me in surprise.

"Give it to me."

She searched my eyes until she realized she couldn't fight me on this. "Here," Camila said quietly, handing me her can.

I took a slow step forward, feeling her hand squeeze around my wrist.

"Be careful."

I scanned her before nodding in thanks and ducking into the tall grass to make my way toward the field.

Just then, more of our group started to come into view as they climbed the hill. I held my hand out, catching Josie's eye, in a gesture that made her stop immediately and direct the others behind her to do the same. I turned my attention back to Trip just as the black bear took several quick steps forward then stopped.

"Jesus," Trip cursed, making me cringe.

"Stay calm," I warned him. "Don't move. That was just a bluff charge. He's not going to attack. He's just letting you know you're too close."

Taking a deep breath to calm my nerves, I tried to remember everything Jason had taught me. "Hey, bear," I called, causing Trip to stare at me with wide eyes. I ignored him and waved my hands in the air. "Hey, bear. Hey. Go on."

I darted a glance at Trip, who had started to take a quick step back to the trail, causing the bear to grunt.

"Slowly, Trip. Any sudden movement, and he'll make you his dinner."

Trip paused and turned back around to view the bear, who was grunting as if questioning what his next move should be. I took another slow step forward.

By the time I reached Trip's side, the bear had already stopped his ascent, but I released a spray from the can for good measure. I didn't even know if the stuff worked, since I'd never used it before, but after a final grunt from the beast, he started his retreat.

Several minutes later, the bear was completely out of sight, and we made our way back to the trail just as the rest of the group met up with us.

Camila still stood on her rock, while Raven threw her arms around her brother and gazed up at me. "Thank you, Ridge. You saved my brother's life." Her eyes were wide and tear-filled.

I waved it off. "Nah, but that brings me to my first important lesson of this hike. If you see a black bear, do not run away. Stay calm. And please, whatever you do, do not make direct eye contact. If a bear does charge you like that one did with Trip, stand your ground. The odds of them retreating are far better than you outrunning them."

The tension seemed to roll off of some of their backs, while the others nodded to tell me they were listening.

I shrugged and grinned. "What's a hike in the wilderness without a bear encounter?"

Nervous laughter flitted through the group.

"Shake it off, hikers. Take a breath, grab some water, pee on a tree, or whatever. Take a buddy if you're heading into the woods, but don't go far. We've got another two miles to go until we make camp, and I'd like to do it well before sunset." I checked my watch. "We'll take off in fifteen minutes."

Camila stepped down from the rock and locked arms with Josie. Together, they started off into a section of woods, making my instinct kick in. I wanted to go after them and watch them, to ensure they would be okay. If anything happened to Camila on the trip, I would never forgive myself. Selfishly, I was glad Trip was the one who'd come face-to-face with the bear instead of her.

Without another glance in Camila's direction, I took off toward the small stream, hoping for a reset. We'd been on the hike less than a day, and all I could think about was finding a way to get her alone. And those were dangerous thoughts to entertain.

21

R idge kept in front of the pack for the rest of the hike, and it had everything to do with Trip's bear encounter. In return, Trip didn't fight him on the lead. Instead, he hung back with his sister at the tail of our group. I managed to stay near Ridge, but he never allowed me to get too close, making it obvious in his quick steps whenever I did manage to bridge our gap.

I wanted to hike with him and talk more, but I wasn't about to fight whatever demons had taken root in his mind. That was how it always seemed to be with him. He always cared about the "what-ifs," and I was willing to take any risk imaginable, if it meant being close to him. In a way, I was tired of the bullshit excuses, the fears, and the never-ending retreat to stay far, far away from me. If that was how he wanted it to be, then fine. I wouldn't push him anymore.

The trail began to widen and diverge into multiple directions, so I made sure to follow Ridge's lead. A large body of water started to come into view, and while I'd heard of the place and seen photos online, nothing could compare to seeing it in person. My heart began to beat fast as I looked out at the turquoise water that sat nestled in the glacial basin, glittering beneath the sun.

I stopped walking, wanting to take in the entire view, which was currently unoccupied with campers and hikers. Ridge stood off to my side, taking in the same exact view. He must have hiked that trail dozens of times, but nothing in his expression told me that he was any less amazed than his first time.

Emotion caught in my throat, and I didn't know why. I'd climbed mountains, biked down steep hills, and thrown caution to the wind more times than I could count, but being here felt different somehow. I felt liberated and like anything I ever wanted to do beyond today was within reach. All I had to do was climb the damn mountain.

"Holy shit." Trip stepped past me and jogged toward the water. Raven followed, then came the rest of the group, and one by one, they entered our campsite for the night.

"Get a load of this," Josie said as she took up a spot beside me. "We're skinny dipping in that."

She said it with so much confidence that I had to laugh. "Are we, now? We might freeze to death, but sure."

Josie threw me a wink. "Actually, I was talking to Ryker on the hike. He says he knows where there's a hot spring near one of the upper lakes."

"A real hot spring?"

I'd swum in hot springs before but never one that I'd

found in nature. The ones I'd been to had pool walls around them and a cost of admission.

"Yup." She grinned and twisted her shoulders a little.

I narrowed my eyes at her then followed her gaze to Ryker before letting out a laugh. "So, you're really into Ryker now, huh? You just broke up with Emilio."

She made a face. "That was months ago. Besides, Emilio refused to go past second base. Totally over him."

My jaw dropped at her confession. "Josie Parker."

She blushed. Josie had always been boy crazy, hopping from one boyfriend to the next without a break in between until she and Emilio became a thing. But Josie was the type of girl who knew what she wanted. If she said she was over her ex-boyfriend, then I believed her.

"What? It's not like Emilio and I were going to get married or anything. We dated for over a year, and I just wasn't feeling it anymore."

I laughed. "But you told me Emilio was the most handsome boy you'd ever seen." I fluttered my lashes to mock her.

She whacked my chest with the back of her hand. "He's cute," she said defensively before sighing like someone in la-la land. "But Ryker is cuter *and* funny and strong and smart…"

I had to stop listening to her. My best friend was moving on. *Noted.* As beautiful as she was, with her strawberry-blond hair, electric-blue eyes, and outgoing nature, when she set her sights on a guy, it was a done deal. Josie didn't have to play games or be played. She let a guy know when she liked him, and it was up to them to return the sentiment or not. By the way Ryker continued to sneak glances back at Josie, it seemed he was playing right into her hands.

"C'mon, let's check out this lake," she said. She grabbed my arm and carted me forward with a jump in her step, down the hill to where the blue water sat calmly, teasing us to jump in.

We took selfies and group pics to celebrate our first leg of our journey until we eventually went off in our own directions to set up tents and to scour our surroundings.

Josie picked our tent spot, which was conveniently placed near Ryker's. After shoveling all my gear into the small space, I walked back out to the water to take it all in. Never had I seen water so blue or felt that kind of peace among nature. It was the best natural high I would ever experience, and it didn't cost a penny.

"In all my time hiking around these parts, I don't think any view has come close to the ones this lake brings."

I hadn't even heard Ridge approach. "Well," I said, trying to find my voice. "You were always looking for your purpose. I guess you found it here."

When I turned to look at him, his expression didn't give me much. His eyes were set forward and his features were still hard all over, like nothing would break him. I'd always found Ridge something of a mystery, but I'd enjoyed unlocking layers of him as time went on. I fooled myself into thinking that he'd opened up to me and we'd become friends, and maybe we could one day be more. When he'd left, the reality of our time together hit hard, because I knew so much of what I felt came from fantasies of an alternate reality.

I paused, holding an internal debate on whether or not I should ask my real question. Then it just slipped out. "You could have gone anywhere. Why here? Why Ouray?"

I didn't know what to expect in his response. Ridge was the master of speaking through his silence, so I almost imagined that would be his approach. I didn't expect total and complete honesty.

"People don't question who I am or why I'm here."

His words struck a chord. Back in Telluride, all anyone had done when he first arrived was question his very existence. He was hated without being known, ignored while still being seen, and seen but not under-stood. No one even tried.

"Here, I'm not the farmer's son or the Ute boy. My skin color isn't questioned, and my history isn't examined with a fine-tooth comb. I'm just me. And I get to live here. Blanketed by all this." He waved his hand, gesturing to the sky.

I nodded, hating that it was so hard to hate him. He was too good, too pure, and too innocent. And the life he'd left behind hadn't been fair to him. Still, I had bitterness in my heart at the fact that he'd left me behind.

"I'm happy here."

His voice still managed to hit me like the softest breeze, enveloping me in its power and sinking deep into my pores to where I knew it would never leave me, even after it had faded away.

"Good." Staring forward again, I nodded as I ran the bottom of my shoe along the pebbles. "Then I'm happy for you." I hated how my heart cried out with my words.

My chest felt heavy in a loss that felt as close to death as I'd ever felt. *Why? Why has Ridge always had the power to hurt me in the deepest of ways without ever trying at all?*

Maybe that week signified the end of all that and I could move on. I made a silent vow that I would do just that—move on and truly be happy for Ridge and for whatever the future held for him. I twisted my nose at a familiar scent wafting over from the campground. One glance behind me told me exactly where it was coming from. Four of the campers were passing a joint around a rock pit, with a fire growing between them.

"I thought we weren't allowed to build fires out here."

Ridge blew out a breath and shook his head. "We aren't. Doesn't mean everyone follows the rules." He stretched his neck to get a better view of the boys. "Guess that's my cue to do my job and be the bad guy."

I laughed as he walked away. "You could never be the bad guy, Ridge. Not even if you tried."

I'd thought I'd spoken quietly enough that he was already out of earshot, but when his body tensed for a millisecond too long, I knew he'd heard me. Then he kept walking.

The rest of the afternoon passed by slowly. Josie had dipped one toe into the lake and decided against her threat to skinny dip. Instead, we warmed ourselves by our propane stove, heated some quesadillas, and killed time asking Trip all about college, like what it was like to live in New York, how he liked his classes at Columbia, and whether he missed high school. His responses, though predictable, only made me ache for my own after-high-school adventure.

"What are you planning to do after graduation, Camila?"

I was so deep into dreaming about my future that I almost missed Trip's question. When I looked up to answer, I noticed that we weren't alone. Raven and Ridge were sharing a log not too far away, and Ridge was looking at me, waiting, like he cared to know about my future.

"I'm moving to California." I shrugged and leaned back, propping my body up with my palms. "My getting a degree is important to Papa. My getting out of Telluride to do it is important to my mama. They've drilled it into me since I was little, and it just kind of stuck. But I'm excited to get out of town for a bit, scope out the Napa vineyards, and learn more about the business end of things."

Raven narrowed her eyes at me. "Really? I would think all the schooling you need is right there in your backyard. Why leave?"

I took her question as a challenge, but I didn't know why. Perhaps it was because her shoulder was brushing against Ridge's. Or maybe it was because her father had always felt somewhat like a threat to my future at the farm. I didn't want to tell her that while Thomas Bradshaw was a huge advocate of me going off to school, he was also one of my biggest motivations to get out of Telluride. Because I truly believed there was more to the life we'd all been living for so long.

My papa was old-fashioned, stuck in his ways, and

stubborn as all hell, which worked for him, for his way of life, and for how he wanted to run things. But the fact that he wasn't the face of his own business had always been troublesome to me. And he wouldn't last long putting in all that labor.

When the keys to the palace got handed to me, I wanted to have a plan for a new future, one that could evolve with the times. Climate change, for instance, was something my papa dismissed almost as if it would all magically work out if we were greeted with an early winter or tested with the quickly intensifying heat. I wanted to bring back preventative solutions for anything that could threaten what I loved most in the world.

"My parents have always wanted me to have a good education first before I finally take over the vineyard." A smile lifted my cheeks. "Besides, I'll be in California. What's not to love? Beaches, cute guys, movie stars. It sounds like a dream." Excitement must have been lighting up my face. "It won't hurt to get away for a bit and experience new cultures."

Trip coughed out a laugh, though his expression appeared far from amused. "I'd hardly call cute boys something you can add to your resume under the topic of Cultural Experiences."

Josie laughed before I even said another word. "Good thing I won't be needing that resume, then, huh?"

Trip almost looked as annoyed as Raven, and I couldn't entirely grasp why. Their family very much had a stake in our family business, since my papa held Trip's father to such high standards. I'd often sworn that if I weren't the promised heir, then Thomas Bradshaw would be at the helm and set for taking over the Bells' lives' work. It made me sick to think that if anything were to happen to me, that was exactly what would happen.

The conversation shifted to Raven and her post-graduation dreams, and I wasn't surprised to hear that she wanted to do something in event planning or hospitality. She was always the social director of our little group, setting up parties and outings just like the hike.

I stared back at her as she laughed about how awesome it was that Ridge worked where he did, since the other camps around town were booked, and it hit me like a blow to the stomach.

"Wait. You knew Ridge worked here?"

Raven's eyes widened because I failed to keep the shock out of my voice. My mind was officially blown, and the shrapnel was freely attacking my heart.

"Well, yeah." She shot a look at him then turned back to me with a soft smile. "We've kept in contact."

My stomach churned, and it wasn't from lack of food. The tortillas had done their job of filling me up, but I wasn't sure how long dinner would stay down. Ridge had left without even a goodbye to me, yet he'd stayed in contact with Raven—of all people. She was the one he'd allowed into his life. I was happy that the sun was in the midst of setting, because it was the perfect excuse to retreat to my tent for an early bedtime.

Tomorrow was a new day, and I was intent on moving forward, metaphorically and physically. I was going to hike the next leg of the trail up the mountain to our second camping destination. And I would do it while leaving my past right where it belonged.

22

RIDGE

Camila and Josie's tent was already packed up by the time I started making rounds the next morning. I, on the other hand, was in no hurry to leave the comfort of my tent after a night of restless sleep. After seeing the look on Camila's face when she realized how she'd ended up on my tour, I tossed and turned. She looked as if I'd betrayed her, and in a way, I had.

A group of campers was already suited in hiking gear with their bags strapped to their backs, waiting for me near the water's edge. We would take the next uphill hike up to the middle lake and camp out there for the night before making our way to the very top. The entire point of the backpacking trip wasn't the strenuous hike but the quiet experience of staying still, getting lost inside a world that didn't consist of deadlines and watching the clock, and posting everything you ate on social media. The stillness was our destination and where we learned to live.

I scoped out the empty campsite behind me as I approached the group at the water. "Well, this is a first. Usually, I'm the one waiting on everyone else." I scanned their faces to see if Camila and Josie were among them and quickly confirmed that they were not. "I see we have a couple of ambitious hikers. Camila and Josie already took off?" I looked straight at Trip.

"Yup. Left before dawn. I told them to wait, but of course they didn't listen to me." Trip's jaw hardened as he looked up the hill at his back. "That's a steep incline."

"The girls will be fine." I waved off Trip's worry. He knew just as well as I did that Camila was more than capable of venturing off on her own. He just didn't like that he couldn't watch her like a hawk. "Let's get going, shall we?"

The group all agreed, and with me in the lead, we took off toward on the next leg of the hike. It consisted mostly of small rocks and a narrower trail, one I'd always managed to navigate with no problem. Unfortunately, I'd figured out the day before that the majority of the group with me wasn't experienced enough to manage the trails with the same confidence.

When I heard a high-pitched scream and the sound of sliding rocks, I flipped around to find Raven on the ground, her face twisted in pain and a howl bursting from her throat. *Shit.*

I walked down the hill, careful to not make the same mistake as Raven, and got to her at the same time as her brother. She was holding out her leg and clutching it as she stared at it in shock. "I heard it pop." She looked more terrified than in pain. "I swear, I heard it break."

"Are you fucking kidding me, Raven? How could you be so clumsy?"

I ignored Trip while internalizing the fact that he hadn't changed, not even after graduating from high school. He was still the prick he'd always been. "Where did you hear it break? Where does it hurt?"

Raven pointed at her ankle while tears sprang to her eyes. "It hurts so much. I'm afraid to move anything."

"Don't move it," I warned her. "I'm going to slowly remove your boot so that I can take a look, okay?"

She nodded, her lids pinching together.

After her boot and sock were off, her quickly swelling ankle showed that she'd broken it somehow. I didn't know whether it was a non-weight-bearing break, but she wouldn't be able to walk on it for at least a few weeks. I'd seen injuries just as small before, but though it was a little bone that wouldn't cause any long-term damage, it was a break no less, and it probably hurt like hell.

After doing everything I knew how to do for her— helping her stand to test her ability to walk then taping up her ankle—I sighed and looked up at Trip. "She won't be able to walk on it, but she needs to get back to Camp Lachey. I can have Jason send someone to meet you on the trail with a stretcher, but you'll need to help her back."

"Are you kidding me? We've walked like three miles!"

I shrugged, letting him know there no other choice.

Trip's expression was a mix between crestfallen and furious as he assessed his sister's ankle, then he cursed under his breath.

"W-Why can't you take me?" Raven asked, looking up at me while batting her lashes.

"I've got to stay with the group. I'll alert Jason to meet you, but you might want to take some of your friends with you to help." I nodded to the four pot smokers, who were taking up the tail end of the group and looked miserable. "Maybe them."

After Trip talked to the guys, he hauled Raven up into his arms, then they started down the hill, successfully cutting my hiking group in half.

It definitely felt like I was carrying a lighter load for the rest of the hike up. The hikers with me kept up easily, and they reined in their chatter. When we reached the top, I waved them over to the edge of the cliff, where they would get a view of why we'd really came on the trip.

"Unreal," one camper said breathily.

"Holy shit, this is beautiful," another said.

I smiled.

The lake below us looked better than any filter on any image I'd ever seen in my life. The water was a crisp turquoise, its surface smooth, and patches of snow were still evident in sections of the land and hills around it. I backed away from the edge to give the group some space and made my way over to the campsite, where Camila's tent was already set up. The girls were nowhere to be found.

I trekked around the outskirts of the woods to see if I could spot any sign of them, when I heard a faint giggle past the woods and in another clearing private from where hikers traveled. Never in the hundreds of hiking groups I'd taken up there had any of them found that clearing. Of course, Camila and Josie had. Jason had told me about it the first time we went up there but warned me that if I told one person about it, the beauty would be ruined fast. After seeing it, I knew he was right.

Shaking my head, I walked down the unmarked trail and circled a section of the mountain that was all rock. I reached a small landing that led to a natural hot spring that overlooked another section of the mountains. It could almost be mistaken for a hot tub, from the way someone had built up the rock formation. The girls were there, only their heads visible from where I stood.

"Why does it not surprise me that you found this place?"

Camila and Josie's heads snapped in my direction, their eyes wide, and I laughed. Their expressions eased, and they started to laugh too.

"Jesus, Ridge, you almost gave us a heart attack."

"But I didn't."

They giggled.

"Is this some sort of secret or something?" Josie grinned at me.

"It is. Top secret. Think we can keep it between us?" I was responding to Josie's question, but my eyes were on Camila, who seemed to be avoiding eye contact. She was still pissed at me for our conversation from the previous night.

"No can do," Josie said with a shrug. "Franklin was the one who told us, and I'm sure we weren't the only ones he spouted off to."

Franklin was one of the guys who'd walked back with Raven and Trip. "Franklin took off, so maybe he took his secret with him."

The girls eyed me, confused.

"Raven broke her ankle on the way up here. At least, I think she broke it. Trip, Franklin, Ryker, and one other guy helped take her back to base camp so that she could get it looked at."

Josie's jaw dropped. "You're shitting me."

"I am not shitting you."

Camila appeared relieved until she looked over at her best friend and noticed how sad she was. "Aw, I'm sorry, Jo. Maybe Ryker will come back once they get Raven settled."

Josie shook her head and stood up in the water. "I'm going to see if I have any cell reception."

"You won't," Camila and I said at the same time.

Josie shrugged us off and stepped out of the hot springs, looking dejected. When I noticed what she was wearing—a black bikini—I averted my eyes to give her some privacy. I waited until she walked off to turn back to the water, where Camila was already looking at me.

"It was just a bikini, Ridge. It's not like she was naked."

Camila giggled, bringing me back to the days of us running through the fields with her laughter enveloping me in all the ways I knew were bad. I had resisted my growing feelings for her for so long that I hadn't even recognized them until it was too late. Seeing her again was like being blasted with a hose that had been pinched off for so long that its bursting was inevitable. After I tossed and turned in anguish last night at how hurt Camila had looked, my thoughts had betrayed me and drifted to less innocent destinations. I'd failed to fight off the most inappropriate erection stemming from thoughts that far surpassed what our friendship had entailed. I had even tried to picture someone else, but it was useless. I wanted Camila. And the image of her, soft and strong and beautiful, had greeted me at my climax.

"You're staring at me."

I blinked, clearing my mind of the memories, which were making my heart race—another inappropriate reaction to the girl I'd vowed to stay away from. Clearly, her presence had effects on me that were impossible to ignore.

"I was just thinking."

She smiled, but even the tilt of her lips couldn't erase the pain that was so clearly written in her eyes. I'd hurt her, when I was only trying to protect us both.

"Always thinking, aren't you, Ridge? You must have been sad to see Raven go. What with your close friendship and all."

I ground my teeth to combat the beast inside me that wanted to unleash at her. There was so much she didn't know and I would never dare say. "You know that's not what we share." My voice was quiet, but Camila could hear me.

Hurt flashed across her features again. "Do I? I'm afraid I don't know as much as I thought I did."

"You know more than anyone."

She let out a sarcastic laugh. "But I'm too young to understand. Isn't that right? That was why it was so easy for you to leave while I waited for you to come home. While I waited for you to miss me the way I missed you."

Her tone, her expression, and her deep, impenetrable innocence combined lashed angrily against my heart. I deserved it, but I didn't know of any other way after what Harold had told me that night.

"I didn't leave you, Camila. I was saving you. From my father, from yours…"

"Oh yeah? Well, who's going to save me from myself?"

She stood from the water, and I could have sworn my heart jolted so strongly that I could feel my demise. My Wild One, untamed and boldly herself, unlike anyone I'd ever known, was naked before me. Her breasts were full and heaving with each breath. Water rolled down her skin, beading on dark nipples that were firmly pointed from the cold, and goose bumps rose on her caramel skin. She walked forward, focused on me, while I struggled to pull my eyes away.

Camila had always been a rare beauty, even when disguised with dirt and scratches from her cravings for adventure. I'd always seen her, but the beauty walking toward me with the water steaming around her and rippling as she moved was a sort of beauty that owned me at the very root of my soul. Camila Bell was a figment of my every desire, both past and present, and I knew hell existed wherever she didn't. I'd been living in it since I left her.

She reached the edge of the water and started to pull herself over the rocks. After catching a glimpse of her light-pink underwear, I looked away, cursing myself for not averting my eyes sooner the way I'd done with Josie. The girls were my responsibility to look after, not gawk at while fighting off the urge to jerk off at the first pair of breasts that caught my eye.

I was deeply punishing myself when I felt Camila's

presence mere inches from mine. The crisp air had to be biting into her skin after she'd stepped out of the hot water, but she still didn't reach for a towel.

"Look at me."

I rolled my eyes up to the blue early-afternoon sky and blew out a breath. "I refuse."

"I demand."

Shaking my head, I squeezed my lids together and felt for the rock to my right to find her towel. I grasped the fabric and wrapped it around her shoulders without even looking. "You need to cover up."

"Not until you look at me." Her voice was quieter, but the firmness was still there. "It's not wrong, you know. To want me." She stepped closer so that her head was right under my chin while her hand slid up my chest. "I'm not a little girl anymore, Ridge. Look at me and you'll see."

"I saw enough," I bit out, keeping my eyes on the sky.

She let out a light laugh. "So much willpower. It's admirable, really." Her hand slid back down my abdomen as it rose and deflated with each quickened breath. When she reached the waistband of my shorts, she froze. "Or maybe not so much willpower."

My eyes snapped open, and I looked down to find her staring at the bulge in my shorts.

"I'll take that as a compliment."

I followed a bead of water as it fell down the center of her chest, between her perfect breasts, to her soft stomach, and finally dipping into her belly button. At nineteen years old, I'd never seen a naked woman in person. I didn't know how I'd expected to feel about it—

excited, sure, but Camila had so much more to her than the way she looked. She was boldly confident and thirsty for knowledge, and the way she stood her ground had captured me from the beginning. But I couldn't deny her natural beauty in all ways that surpassed innocent thought or intention. The fact that she knew she was beautiful made everything harder—*everything*.

I greedily drank her in a second longer before our eyes locked again. Sucking in a deep, controlled breath, I pulled the towel tighter around her shoulders and closed it in the front. "Get dressed. Now is not the time to be daring, Wild One."

"Daring with my body or my truth?" she challenged me. "You seem to be frightened by all of it."

A flame licked through me as I frowned. "You don't scare me."

"That's a lie."

"It's not. You don't scare me, Camila. You have never scared me. I scare myself when I'm with you. These thoughts—" I shook my head to try to clear every vision that had entered my mind. "They're wrong."

Her eyebrows knitted as she glared back let me. "What's so wrong about me? It's not like you're living on Harold's farm anymore. No one's telling you to stay away from me."

"*I* am telling *me* to stay away from you. You're beautiful, Camila. I'd be lying to us both if I denied it. And you may not be a little girl anymore, but you're still too young."

"And Raven isn't? I'm the same age as her, but you had no trouble staying in contact with her."

The accusation in her tone was too much. The same

flame that had lashed me earlier started spreading at a ferocious speed. "That's because I have no interest in Raven. With you, it's different. With you, I lose every battle of will, as you seem to have noticed."

She searched my face like she was trying to grasp something while confusion danced across hers. "My papa wants me to be with Trip. Trip's father too. He's the same age as you, so obviously, age doesn't matter."

Her words were a punch in the gut. Trip was interested in Camila, and he had never tried to hide it. That their fathers were cheering them on from the sidelines stung. I ignored the comment about her age.

"Well, then maybe you should be with Trip." I took a step back, away from the temptress with the devil in her eyes, and turned around before I changed my mind. "Get dressed, Camila. See you at the campsite."

23

CAMILA

I wish I could hate him.

His rejection was brutal, more so than the year and a half he'd stayed away. As adventurous as I liked to believe I was, handling disappointment wasn't one of my strong suits. It ate at me, gnawing away on my fragile core like venom through an apple. I didn't normally sulk, but after lunch, when Ryker had returned to the campsite, Josie ran to him, and I was left in her dust.

Okay, so it didn't happen as cruelly as it had played out on endless repeat in my mind, but she was in swoonland, gaga over a new man. Everyone else had paired off, and I was alone.

The sun had nearly set when I parked my butt on the edge of a rock cliff that overlooked the lower blue lake basin. *How can I exist in such a beautiful world and feel the sadness that aches in my chest?* It was the same sense of loneliness I'd felt over the past year and a half. It came in waves. Some moments, I missed Ridge intensely, and other times, I allowed myself to get lost in my present world, one where he didn't physically exist. In my mind, the loss of him had consumed me, and I coped without him and our hilltop the only way I knew how.

It had felt like a miracle when I spotted Ridge by that fire that first night in Ouray. As angry as I had been with him for leaving me, I'd thought we'd been given a second chance. *Why did I ever think he might want the same?*

I remained at the cliff's edge long after the sun fell below the horizon, with my legs hanging dangerously over the edge, until nothing was visible save for a perfect moon and a canopy of stars.

I felt Ridge's presence before the beam of his flashlight presented itself. Then he sat by my side.

"I won't tell you how dangerous it is to be out here in the dark. You already know." He switched off his light and leaned back on his hands.

He was barely visible by the glow of the moon, but I could see him looking at me before I turned my gaze back up to the endless night.

"I never did see the stars last night."

Silence followed, but I could almost hear his unspoken apology for hurting me before his voice broke through the invisible barrier that stretched between us. "They're far more beautiful up here than they would have been last night, anyway."

"I guess five hundred feet makes a big difference, huh?"

"Proximity is important, yes. Without the distractions all around us competing for our attention, everything becomes clearer. It's like the sky is naked out here.

Exposed for only those who wander to see it in all its glory."

Something inside me stirred. "Is that a subtle reference to me exposing myself to you earlier?"

He chuckled, and my heart swelled.

"Because if so, it's not funny."

He looked at me then. He was just a faint outline, thanks to nature's light, but I could have sworn I could see him clearer in that moment. "You didn't have to show me your body for me to see you, Camila. I see you. I've always seen you. You've got to know that's the problem. It's why I left. It's why I've stayed away. But when Raven contacted me about the tour, I only agreed to be the guide because I saw your name on that list. I was weak. I wanted to see you again, even though I know I shouldn't."

"But why?" My voice was pleading. "Our parents, my age? None of that matters. Not when we share what we do. And don't tell me that this is all in my head, because I saw the way you looked at me back there. You want me just as much as I want you."

Adrenaline soared through me at my admission. My boldness had always been part of me, but I'd never begged for a man's attention before, probably because I had never felt anything so intensely in my life.

"You're a beautiful woman, Camila." His voice was husky with unmistakable desire, and my heart raced because of it. "And maybe your age is no longer a factor, but there's a lot to say about our families."

"So what if our fathers hate each other. They'll get over it. We've never done anything wrong."

"Except trespassing."

Fury swirled through me. "It wasn't trespassing after you invited me onto your land to use as my passing route. I was your guest."

"You know what I mean. You know it's deeper than that. What do you think would happen if we did get together? Sneak around like we did to get to the hillside? Go on dates and pray your father isn't waiting on the front porch with his shotgun?"

"You seem to forget I'm a risk-taker."

Ridge blew out a breath and laughed. "Trust me, Wild One. I will never forget just how far you've tested me in the past. Seems nothing has changed."

I couldn't help my smile.

"I'm not saying your feelings are wrong." His voice was softer. "I'm saying this isn't our time to explore those feelings."

Another ache penetrated my heart. "You talk as if it's just me with these feelings."

"It's not. You know that."

Disappointment and relief combined to create an elixir of confusing emotions. Not even wild horses could outrun the way my heart was galloping. Blood pumped through my veins so quickly that I had to take a deep breath to try to steady my nerves. "Tell me how you feel about me."

"You know how I feel about you."

"You keep telling me I know, and maybe I do, but sometimes it's important to use your words, Ridge. Sometimes you should tell people how you feel."

"Words mean nothing when I can't show you."

"Your words mean everything to me. And I want to

hear you now. What would you do differently if our families weren't at war? Would you want me then?"

"Camila," he pleaded.

I sucked in a breath, not ready to give up. "Please, Ridge. I need to know."

An eternity stretched between us before Ridge finally spoke. "I care about you more than I deserve."

The shame in his tone was as crushing as it was liberating.

"More than a friend," he continued. "More than time and distance can ever erase. If anything, seeing you again was a reminder of what I left behind. But I had to leave." A beat of silence followed. "The night that Harold threatened your life in that cornfield was—" He paused again, like he was struggling to find his words. "They found my mom, Camila. She was nothing but a pile of bones on the outskirts of the rez."

My hands shook as I brought them to my mouth, and my insides squeezed at the thought of all the unimaginable pain Ridge had to have been feeling when he found out.

"Deep down, I already knew, but hope is a strange thing. It acts like a net, keeping us from our darkest thoughts. That night, I felt like I'd been cut loose and had nowhere to go but down. I've been digging myself out of that hole ever since."

I scooted toward him and placed a hand on his knee. "I'm so sorry. I wish I'd known."

He shook his head. "I didn't want anyone to know, especially not you. Things were already at a breaking point that night, and I would have only taken it out on you."

A tear slipped from my eye, and I wiped it away before he could see it. "I would have been your punching bag, if that was what you needed. I would do anything for you, Ridge Cross."

He looked at me, that time with all barriers down, like he saw me and wanted me to know that he did. "I know," he whispered. Then he wrapped an arm around me and pulled me close. "I know."

We sat there in silence for the longest time, staring up at the sky while I soaked in what he'd just told me. *Why is life so unfair?* And why does it feel like Ridge got the brunt of it all? He was the best person I knew—the kindest and gentlest. Yet life continued to deal him shitty hands.

"Don't cry, Wild One." He slid his arm down my back as he leaned into me until I could feel his breath in my ear. "Don't cry for me."

"I hate this. All of it. Our families, what happened to your mom. I still hate that you left, even though I understand now. And I hate that I'm so selfish that I want you to come back despite it all. I don't want to lose you again."

"And I don't want to lose you," he whispered.

I swiped at another tear. "You were right to keep your feelings from me. I think knowing only makes it all so much harder. What's the point when we can't change a damn thing? What does that leave us?"

His lips brushed my ear. "It leaves us right now."

I shivered as his whispered words flooded me, filling my every exposed pore with the life I could only wish to keep.

He moved a section of hair from my shoulders and pressed his mouth to my ear again. "We have tonight."

He gently cupped my chin as he turned me to face him. "We have the stars."

Our lips were closer than they'd ever been. Our forbidden confessions had brought more clarity to my heart and mind than I'd ever had before, and I thanked the stars while I cursed the land that divided us.

"And this can be our secret." He ran a finger across my lips as his eyes drank me in under the moonlight. I started to lean in but stopped myself. For once in my life, I wanted someone else to take the lead. And I didn't have to wait long. He pressed his lips to mine, and our exhalations tumbled from our chests in unison. We became one —one breath, one heart, and one mind.

There, under the starry sky, we shared our first kiss and what I feared down to the depths of my soul would be our last.

24

CAMILA, THREE MONTHS LATER

While fall in the vineyard brought a year's worth of hard work to life, the most crucial work to prepare for a successful harvest happened during the summer months. Grapevines got rather unwieldy during our hottest season, and the only anticipation I could liken it to was waiting for paint to dry. Not knowing whether the buds would flower to give signs of life for sprouting grapes was torture beyond belief, especially for my papa.

"Papa, you need to take it easy." I approached him with a tray of homemade lemonade Mama had prepared and set it on the tractor he was currently hard at work fixing. The machine was an ancient one that he chose to use to cart around the grapes from deep in the field.

He stood and wiped the sweat from his dirty brow before picking up the glass and guzzling it down to the bottom. He swallowed one last time and shook his head. "No time, Camila. Not if we want to use the sunlight to our advantage. We do that by cutting down the shade. Remember, every step of the process can affect your grape production, from how they grow, to the way they look, to the way they ferment. Pay careful attention."

As always, a quick visit to him in the field turned into a work-study session in which I got down and dirty with the rest of the field workers.

"This one here," he said, pulling out one of the longer green vines. "You want to cut that back to give these healthy vines access to sunlight."

After my lesson was complete and my papa felt like I'd mastered the art of pinpointing the vines with no signs of bearing fruit for the season, he sent me on my way to work my own row.

I always got lost in the process of tending to the vines. Every year, I only grew more careful in the missions my papa afforded me and more excited for a time when I would be a master at the art of winemaking like he had become. The job wasn't always easy—my papa would be the first to admit that—but it was in our blood. It ran through our veins and pumped us with adrenaline-induced joy that couldn't be matched. And I was my papa's daughter, dedicated to the mission and overcome with accomplishment at the end of a day's work, so much so that I didn't realize I'd made it to the very bottom of the hill until I ran out of vines to trim back.

I slipped my hand shears into my dress pocket and smiled up at the row I'd just finished pruning, before a rustle from somewhere nearby made the hairs on my neck rise. I glanced right toward a small opening in the woods, a place I no longer dared to go or felt welcome.

The last time I had heard noises in those woods, things had ended very badly.

Heaviness rested on my chest. The first year and a half without Ridge hadn't been easy, but the last three months had been worse after knowing Ridge returned my feelings and having felt it in that first kiss and the million kisses that came after it. Even if it was just one night, it was a night that spoke volumes.

Chills still swept over my skin when I thought about that night on the mountain. We had kissed like it was our first, last, and only. We didn't speak much in between. And instead of returning to my tent, Ridge had brought me to his, where we lay together all night. Our inexperience was revealed as we explored each other's mouths and our hands wandered in all the safe places. Neither of us tried for more. Not that night or the next. More would have been too much and turned the night into something completely different that risked tainting a beautiful memory I would never forget. But one beautiful night didn't erase the ache in my heart from missing him.

The startling sound in the woods had nearly vanished from my mind when it picked up again, that time followed by what sounded like a chain clinking. Something about it was familiar, but I couldn't place the sound until a black-and-white border collie made a dash from the woods, straight to me.

I gasped in surprise before laughing when Bruno jumped at me playfully. Back when Ridge had lived there, we would often take Bruno with us to our hilltop. He loved the hike, always wandering a safe distance away to race through the weeds or tumble around in the dirt.

I sank to my knees to pet my old friend before looking up toward the woods with a frown. "What are you doing over here, Bruno? You know my papa will lose his mind if he sees you, huh?" I whispered, even though my papa was nowhere near us.

When Bruno still didn't budge to go home, I laughed and stood. "Go on, boy. Go home."

Bruno just stayed there, looking up at me with his big brown eyes as his mouth hung open and his tail wagged.

"Oh, fine." I clapped my leg and started for the woods, knowing he would follow.

He ran up beside me and paced me on my trek.

It felt weird to head back in the direction of the bridge after so long. I hoped Bruno would take off as soon as he saw it. Maybe he'd followed a squirrel or a rabbit and got turned around. Who knew. I was just happy to get him off our property and keep him safe. My papa would never hurt a dog, but the last thing either of our families needed was ammo to restart a feud that lay as dormant as the grapevines during winter.

The moment the bridge started to come into view, Bruno took off running. When I saw the reason why, I froze in my tracks and blinked harder than I'd ever blinked in my life. Standing at the center of the bridge, with a hand gripping the rail and his chocolate eyes on me, stood a man I didn't think I would ever see again, at least not without me tracking him down, which I had most certainly thought about doing.

Ridge was home. At least, I thought he was home. It looked like him. He was even wearing the same old white-and-red flannel he often wore after a long day on the farm.

I blinked again, certain the image before me was a figment of my very vivid imagination. It wouldn't have been the first time that I'd conjured up a memory of Ridge and wished that he would return to me.

"Don't tell me I rendered you speechless, Wild One. I would be terribly disappointed."

And just like that, my wishes and prayers and wildest fantasies were confirmed. My heart exploded, and a smile broke out wide on my face. I bolted from my frozen stance toward him. My cheeks hurt from smiling so hard, and my lungs already felt like they were going to combust.

Emotion swept over me, and I could have sworn it was the force of my love for Ridge that carried me straight into his arms until I burst into a puddle of happy and relieved tears. I didn't know why he was back or for how long he was staying. But it didn't matter at that moment. All that mattered was that he was there, wrapping his strong arms around me in an embrace I would never forget for as long as I lived. Even his scent wrapped around me, a rich blend that reminded me of blooming orchards and a woodsy meadow.

"You're here." I whispered the words into his shirt, my eyelids shut tight in an effort to never awake from that moment. It felt like Ridge was home—not the home he'd been searching for as long as I'd known him but the home that had always been waiting for him, as long as he was ready.

Ridge chuckled as he practically peeled me off of him so that he could get a good look at me. His eyes swept over my dress, my dirt-caked hands, and my flushed face then met mine and softened as my body melted back into him. I clung to him, desperate to keep him. Even better, he didn't let me go.

"I'm here."

I searched his eyes, swallowing over the emotion built up in my throat. "For good?"

Doubt flickered in his gaze.

"Ridge," I pleaded. "Does this mean what I think it means? Are you back to stay?"

He cupped my chin and shook his head. "The truth is I don't know. I wanted to see you. And I don't plan on leaving anytime soon."

My face burst into a smile. No words could have made me happier, and just the fact that Ridge was back pried open all the doorways to my heart.

He smiled back as he took me in again. "That's a pretty dress you've got on."

I already felt warm all over, and it wasn't from the summer sun. Before Papa had put me to work on the field, I'd put on my Sunday best, a red sundress that fell just below my knees. I stepped back and pushed my hands into the pockets before twisting left and right. "Thank you."

Ridge nodded behind him. "I've gotta get back to work." When I frowned, he chuckled. "The corn isn't going to detassel itself." Then he winked. "Meet me here at three?"

"We'll go to the hilltop?"

He nodded, and my world righted once more.

At three o'clock on the dot, we met again. Ridge was already there when I arrived, and he had changed into a white shirt and jeans, while I still wore my red dress that he had complimented earlier. I couldn't keep the smile from my face as I approached. Several times over the last few hours, I'd questioned whether I would actually see him.

We walked toward the center of the bridge. I had always viewed our meeting spot as a symbolic representation of what Ridge and I could be—the end of our families' lifelong feud, as a connection rather than the divide that had always stood between us. Maybe that day would come sooner than I'd imagined.

I hugged him just as tightly as when I'd first spotted him earlier, and his warmth thawed me from what had felt like an endless winter. Everything was good and right. I chose to ignore the fact that Ridge couldn't give me a solid answer on how long he would stay. Instead, I chose to cling to the present as hard as I possibly could.

Peering up at him, I smiled. "First one to the tree is the winner?"

Ridge narrowed his eyelids at my challenge. "You're on."

I laughed as I zoomed past him, his arms slipping from around me as I went. He took off behind me and quickly closed the distance, which made me giggle even harder. When we got to the cornfield, I flew down one row, while he went down another. All I could see around me were bright-green stalks and the soft brown soil. *Who knew one could find heaven in a cornfield?*

By the time I reached the end, Ridge was already running through the weeds up ahead. I followed, my calves burning as I tried to keep up, but he was so fast that when I got to the bottom of the hill, he'd completely vanished from sight. He'd already made it to the top, and I was exhausted.

I slowed my pace, trying to regain my breath before reaching the top, but when I got there, Ridge was still nowhere to be seen. Swiveling around in a circle, I searched for him, my heartbeat beginning to quicken with panic. I found the edge of the hilltop where I knew Ridge liked to sit after it got dark.

"Ridge!" I called as I raced forward.

I'd barely reached the bristlecone pine when arms shot out from the other side of the tree and pulled me in. I slammed against a hard body and looked up to find Ridge laughing.

With adrenaline still racing through my body and my fears of something happening to him quickly dissolving, I smacked his chest while glaring up at him. "You scared me."

The corners of his mouth tilted up as he gripped me firmly at my waist, then he moved me so that my back was pressed against the tree. He stepped into my space and leaned in, touching his forehead to mine. "I didn't mean to scare you," he whispered. "I just wanted to do this."

When he opened his eyes again, his gaze fell to my mouth. Energy buzzed between us as I anticipated the feel of his lips. I'd memorized them three months ago and longed for them every moment since. Then he brushed his lips to mine so softly that I questioned once more whether I was just dreaming.

I rested my hands on his chest, reacclimating myself

to the firmness of his body, while he gently pressed his mouth to mine. With my senses heightened, I could feel everything physical and emotional between us—everything lost, everything found, and how perfectly right it felt to be back in his arms.

Our kiss made me remember everything that had been sweet and innocent about our first, but our mutual intensity was growing by the second. The desperation in our hearts was rising to the surface with each sacred moment as the acceptance of our shared passion was finally exposed between us.

With every subtle move I made, he made one too. I clutched the fabric of his shirt, and he deepened the kiss. When I slid my tongue along his bottom lip, and he bit down on it gently. I ran my hands up and through his hair, and he parted my lips with his. When I gripped his hair and tugged just slightly, he groaned and pulled my body closer.

As time ticked on, our bodies molded into one as the heat burned between us with an intensity I hadn't known existed. We were finally speaking our truth, and our friendship was exploding into so much more. Our tangled tongues, our exploring hands, and our heated bodies were all part of a distinct language only Ridge and I understood. It conveyed feelings that had rooted into our souls when we were just kids.

Just like the unwieldy vines I'd been busy pruning all day and the corn stalks in need of detasseling, Ridge and I were an unkempt field that had been shaded for too long, giving us zero chance to grow. The time had finally come to let the sunshine in.

25

THE HUNTER

At the familiar sound of her laughter, the Hunter's focus snapped up from the creek where he had been resting. He was far enough away from the bridge for anyone to spot him, but with his binoculars he could see them far too clearly. Not even the quickly mounting fury in his chest could blur the charade taking place before him.

The Cross boy was back, and him and Camila were off to frolic through the damn cornfields and up to the hillside just like old times.

The hunter cursed out his disgrace. It had been nearly two years since he'd spotted the girl in territory that felt more like his today than ever before. He thought she'd learned her lesson the last time the arrow whizzed straight past her head, aimed perfectly to frighten her in a warning to stay away. He had even watched as a spooked Camila ran straight into the arms of the Cross boy, leading to a fight. He'd hoped it was Camila's demise when Harold charged toward her in his tractor.

It had all played out better than he could have ever imagined. The hunter's problems would have been solved right then and there if the old man had stuck to his drunk guns and ran the girl over. Even then, the outcome of that night had still worked out in his favor. Ridge had left town and Camila had no reason to venture back into the woods.

Well, apparently until now.

The hunter reached for his bow, squeezing the grip while deciding on his next move. He could track the two friends through the woods. He could get rid of the problem with two shots through the heart and kill them both like he'd always wanted to. But he knew that was too risky. Having them both go missing would certainly lead to too many eyes poking around the hunter's land. He couldn't have that.

If the hunter was going to get rid of the problem, then he would have to wait. Timing was everything and getting Camila alone in the woods was key. He released the grip of the bow and let his binoculars hang around his neck before cupping his dirty hands through the creek water and then drinking from it in one slow slurp.

26

RIDGE

I leaned over the fabric bench seat of my truck and tugged the latch to open the passenger door. "You get the goods?"

Camila beamed and held up a cloth bag from the market she'd just walked out of. "Sandwiches, salads, waters, and fruit. Did I forget anything?"

"Nope. That's perfect." I took the bag from her and set it on the floor as she started to pull herself into my truck.

I'd already taken a good look at her once I spotted her rounding the side of the store, but I was gawking like a fool now. She leaned over to shut the door, and my gaze immediately fell to where the fabric of her dress rode up her thigh. The golden-yellow V-neck sundress was shorter than the ones she liked to wear on the farm. A thick ruffle wrapped around the bottom of her skirt, matching the pair of ruffles that went around each of her shoulders. Three thick brown buttons trailed down to her waist, where the material gathered and was tied by a thin string bow.

She looked at me as she started to fasten her seat belt, and I felt a kick of guilt in my chest for the way I'd been staring at her. I focused on her bright eyes and flushed expression. Camila always got exhilarated by our sneaking around, but today, we were taking our adventures to a whole new level.

We'd met at the market nearest to our homes, where she would leave her car for the day. Since we couldn't go inside together, she'd grabbed lunch for us and met me at the side lot to sneak into my truck.

Summer had already ended, and the weather pattern was becoming more unpredictable as the days went on. The darkening nights were becoming colder, and the mountain peaks in the distance were beginning to fill with snow. Camila had already started her senior year of school, and our time together had shortened significantly, especially with her working extra hours in the vineyard to keep up with the season's demand.

Before school had started, we managed to see each other every day, even just for a quick meetup at the bridge. But today, I had something extra special planned. At least, I hoped Camila would think it was extra special.

"You ready to go?"

Her green eyes shone back at me. "Yes. Where to?"

I shook my head. "I told you. It's a surprise." Frowning, I looked toward the busy parking lot. "You might want to duck until we get onto the main road."

Without question, she lay down sideways and rested her head in my lap. For a second, I was hypnotized by her pretty gaze of bold green and swirls of gold. After breaking away from her stare, I put the truck in drive and turned right out of the parking lot.

For the most part, we tried not to dwell on the things we couldn't control. We knew what we were getting ourselves into by sneaking around, but that didn't make it easier. If anything, each day felt like it was getting harder to keep up the charade. It seemed like we were living parallel lives, hers in the vineyard, mine in the cornfield, and our only connection was the bridge that was meant to separate us. In a way, it still did.

Camila had her friends, school, church, and her dreams to one day run the vineyard. I had my father, who barely spoke to me, a job that felt like it had no end, and my only friend back in Ouray, cursing me out for leaving him in a bind. But the moment Camila and I were together, it felt like we were lifted above the clouds, and all that mattered was us.

"Okay," I said when I was finally on the mountain road, leading toward our surprise destination. "You can sit up now."

She righted herself and looked around. "Can I at least have a clue as to where you're taking me?"

"You'll see soon enough."

Camila didn't argue. She liked surprises, and the fact that I'd planned an entire day for her made her happy enough. It didn't matter where we were headed, just that we were together.

"Have you talked to Jason at all recently?"

"Not lately. I keep thinking about how I left him the way I did. Maybe I should have stayed long enough to help him find a better replacement for me. He's already got that big ranch to worry about."

She frowned. "You're still feeling bad about that?"

"Well, yeah. This was his dream, but we never talked about me working for him forever. He understands. Still, I'd feel better knowing he had someone permanent that he can rely on. Someone other than his brother."

"Jason has a brother?"

"Yeah, Dave Lachey. Owns a plot of land near Jason's camp. They inherited the livestock ranch together, but the guy's not all there. I never met him, but Jason told me that he got into some trouble a while back for poaching, so Jason does most of the heavy lifting."

"Damn."

Damn was right. I had given Jason a few months' warning to replace me, but finding a hiking guide he could trust had turned out to be a harder mission than we'd thought. Between the camp and the ranch, he had to be drowning.

"I thought he found someone to help."

"Didn't last. Jason's kind of an old grump. No patience. He found someone else since then, but the time it takes away for him to train them is cutting into his profits." A beat later, I blurted out what I'd been hesitant to tell her. "I was thinking about splitting my time between here and Ouray to help him out." My eyes were on the winding mountain road, but I could feel the heat of her stare with the silence that followed.

"You want to leave again?"

My chest tightened at the hurt in her tone. "No, Camila. It would just be temporary. Just for the winter season until he's able to find someone he can trust." I rested my hand on her knee and gently squeezed. "I told you. I'm not going anywhere, but you know I don't have much going on in Telluride during the winter."

She frowned. "I know, but—"

"I haven't worked out the details yet. I haven't even talked to Jason about it yet. But I figure Harold doesn't need me after the harvest is over, anyway. Maybe I could spend a few days at the camp then come back here to see you."

She let out a sigh, and I could tell she was slowly accepting the idea. "You really hate that cornfield, don't you?"

I chuckled. "I don't hate it. But I don't like staying still for too long, not with all that's out there. Life on the tractor isn't my dream."

Camila shifted to get a better look at me. "What *is* your dream, Ridge? You know all about my dreams, but we never talk about yours."

She'd asked that question before, and every time she did, I felt closer to knowing the answer. "I'm not sure, but working at the camp with Jason has given me a few ideas. I loved those hiking tours, but there are all sorts of activities around here that could use a guide. I just need some certifications. All I know is that whatever I end up doing will be based on preserving the land. That's important to me. Who knows—maybe Harold will make good on his promise, and the farm will be mine one day. If it is, I'd rather give access to others who can enjoy it rather than dedicating my life to a failing crop."

"That's harsh."

I shrugged. "It is, but it's also true. Climate change is

killing us. We're already seeing the effects, with the hotter summers and early winters. In forty years, our land will be nothing but a wasteland if I don't do something about it early on." I paused as I went through a roundabout to continue on the road toward Ridgway. "I used to be so against this town because of what it stood for, but that was before I really started to see what Jason did with his land. My people fought against land development and unnecessary digging. When they lost every battle, they clung to the only land that the government allowed them to have."

I felt excited just talking about everything I'd been thinking lately. "When I think about the farm, I think of the unique opportunity I have to take back stolen land and do something to make my people proud."

"Wow." It was a simple word but enough for me to know that Camila was on board with my line of thinking. "That's huge, Ridge. I mean, talk about acknowledging history and rewriting the future."

"Exactly."

Camila and I had had a million discussions regarding where I'd come from, what we stood for, and the stereotypes that still existed. She knew how important it was for me to find my own way and make a home for myself when no other existed, at least not in my heart.

I was happy when the conversation transitioned to her day at the vineyard where she'd been in charge of labeling the new shipment of vintage bottles. And she was happy to tell me all about it until ten minutes later, when she started to realize where we were.

She gasped. "No way."

Pride filled my chest. "Last Dollar Road. You said you've never been. Surprised?"

Her mouth gaped, and her eyes were bright. "Yes! Why didn't you tell me? I would have brought my good camera."

"Ah, I'm sorry. I wanted it to be a surprise. We can come back, and you can bring your camera then."

She grinned. "Look at you, being so thoughtful about our date."

I shook my head, fighting the blush I could feel creeping up my cheeks. A date was something I couldn't take Camila on, and she knew it. Not unless we were to go somewhere hours away from home. Even then, a quick stop at a fast food joint would be all I could afford after the gas money it would take to get there. "It's a ride in my truck into the middle of nowhere, but if you want to call it a date, go for it."

She hummed. "You did make me buy picnic food. If you have a blanket in the back of your truck, I'm going to have to rule this a date."

I squeezed her leg and pulled my hand back to the steering wheel to focus on the bumpy drive ahead. "All right, you win, then. It's a date." I nodded to the stereo, which I'd recently added a CD player to. "I made us something for the drive. Can you get it?"

She shuffled through my plastic folder of the short selection of CDs I owned until she got to one marked Last Dollar Road and pushed it into the slot just as I turned onto the main gravel road that marked the beginning of the thirteen-mile scenic drive through the San Juan Mountains. Tom Petty's "You Don't Know How It Feels" started up, and a smile bloomed on her face. Instantly, a different sort of energy—calm, peaceful freedom—entered the cabin as the music enveloped us.

While we always enjoyed our time together, no matter where we were, an underlying line of tension always seemed to radiate between us while we were in our hometown. The anxiety of possibly getting caught and knowing it would be enough to end whatever it was we'd yet to define was enough to lose sleep over.

As we started down the off-road, we passed open pastures and numerous caution signs warning us of mud, rocks, and fallen trees. Historic farmland was marked off by rotted fence posts that surrounded us, and mountain bikers zoomed by us on their way back from where we were headed. Every now and then, I stopped the truck to force us both to breathe and take our time on our way across the mountain.

Beauty enveloped us as we passed by enchanting aspen groves and open wildflower meadows by the plenty. We made our way through the curvy drive slowly and with care. Steep drop-offs met us at every turn while beautiful valleys stretched for miles below us. Open sky and mountain peaks met us at every turn. And once we reached a higher elevation and farmland was still stretching around us, we stopped to watch a herd of sheep slowly walking across the land.

Finally, we slowed at the end of what had seemed like an endless gravel drive. After one last cliff and a round-about, we went back downhill and exited the truck for one final pitstop before we would find a place to eat lunch. I helped Camila out of the passenger side and wrapped my arm around her in a close hug. As exhilarating as it was to reach the high elevation, my anxiety hit its peak when she wanted to sit at the edge of the cliff.

Something about that girl, who took every situation to the extreme, made me want to hold on to her and never let go. Pushing limits and seeing how far she could go were in her nature. Allowing her that freedom, while being more than ready to catch her when she fell, was in mine. We'd already been walking that fine line for years. I loved her wild spirit as much as I loved protecting her from it. It was just who we were.

We returned to the truck a few minutes later, and I started the engine again. "Hungry?"

Her eyes lit up. "Starved."

My lips curled into a small smile I hoped she didn't see. "Good." I had one more surprise in store for her.

I circled the roundabout and headed back down the path we'd come from then didn't stop again for a few miles until I found a private off-road that led to the real reason I'd brought her there. "Hang on," I said as I passed the drive, then I stopped and backed onto the private road. The short drive backward ended at a wide, open meadow of wildflowers that looked like it went on for endless miles.

Camila's expression said it all as she stared through the back windshield, her mouth open and her eyes wide. "Wow. Ridge, this place is beautiful. But how in the world did you find it?"

I parked the truck before shutting off the engine. "I met a lot of people on those hikes. Come to find out there are a million little treasures around this area that very few know about. Like the one you found at Blue Lakes."

Her blush made me chuckle. The memory of finding her and Josie at the hot spring in Ouray was one I would never forget. "C'mon," I said while sliding open the back window that led to the tailgate. "Let's eat." I grabbed the food then climbed through the window before turning around to hold out my hand to her.

Camila's fingers slid through mine, and she followed my lead without asking questions as to why we hadn't just gotten out and walked to the back. She was smart enough to understand that meadows like these required all standards of preservation. Neither of us wanted to be responsible for destroying the beauty spread out before us. Instead, I laid out a large blanket, then we pulled out the food and ate until satisfied while sharing the most beautiful visual of the open field.

I started to clean up our food. After passing the empty bag through the window and setting it on the seat, I looked over at her to find her bottom lip still glistening from the sip of water she'd just taken.

"What?" she asked, eyeing me with amusement.

"Nothing."

She sat up straight and tilted her head. "Really? Because you're looking at me like there's something on my face."

I chuckled before sliding a finger across her bottom lip. "Your face is perfect."

Her expression grew serious. "Do you really think so?"

I tilted my head. "Do you question my words?"

"No, it's just… that was a sweet thing to say. You don't compliment me very often."

Camila was as crazy as she was wild, and I loved it. "I don't?"

She shook her head. "You don't. I mean, I think I know how you feel, but it's nice to hear sometimes, you know? You should speak up when you're thinking nice things about me."

I'd learned to keep my thoughts private when it came to Camila. For years, I'd built up a sort of filter to speaking my true thoughts when it came to her physical attributes—mostly out of respect for her age, but it also felt wrong to have those feelings. "But I'm always thinking nice things about you."

When she looked surprised again, I leaned against the back of the truck, pulled her to me, and brushed her cheek with my thumb. I turned her face so that we both stared out at the meadow. "What do you see, Camila?"

She hesitated for a second, looking confused. "I see a meadow of wildflowers and a backdrop of the San Juan Mountains. Why? What do you see?"

My eyes flicked between hers for a second before I turned to the explosion of color in the picturesque scene before us. "I see the very essence of nature as we should understand it. I see the heart of the land that we've lost sight of over decades of fighting a war we're all losing but won't realize until it's too late. But I also see our potential. The land has been preserved with love, and that means something."

I panned the landscape slowly, taking it all in as I continued. "I see untamed beauty living in a world of chaos with roots so strong that the changing seasons don't matter. A wildflower always comes back stronger in the end, more beautiful than the year before and only that much more precious to those fortunate enough to bask in its presence."

As I turned to Camila again, my heart beat fast. "What do I see when I'm staring at that meadow of wildflowers?" The truth of my words shone in her eyes before I even spoke them. I leaned in so that my forehead met hers while I sucked in a deep breath. "I see you."

Though I didn't mean to make Camila cry, a tear slipped from her eye, and my chest ached. I was worried that I had caused her pain, and my heart was already breaking for it. But when she shifted her position and pulled one leg over both of mine to straddle me, the ache in my chest exploded into a galaxy of stars.

Her mouth met mine as her small hands gathered the fabric of my plaid shirt. Her position brought her that much closer to the erection I'd always been careful to hide when we were together. But I had no possible way of hiding it at that moment with the way she was moving against me, making me grow, while her hot tongue dove into my mouth.

I was defenseless against her advances, prey to her sweet lips and luscious body, which fit perfectly against mine. I timidly moved my hands to her thighs and nearly had a heart attack when I felt nothing but bare skin. I'd never dared to touch her like this, so close to crossing a line we could never return from, but I no longer lived by the rules that had always kept us apart. All I had now was desperation to be as close to Camila as possible.

My hands skated up her thighs to where I finally felt the fabric of her ruffled dress that bunched at her waist, then they slid to her ass and squeezed. When a tiny moan escaped her mouth and her clothed center pushed down firmly on my hard-on, panic seized in my chest.

I tore my mouth from hers. Our heaving chests pressed into each other's, and I cursed under my breath before locking eyes with her. She glared, her anger with me for breaking our kiss written in her expression. I should have known she would find a way to up the ante.

She was still staring at me when I noticed movement at her waist. I looked down. Camila was unknotting the tie of her dress, loosening the fabric. A beat later, she gripped the bottom of the skirt and started to lift it away from her skin.

I slammed my hands onto hers to stop her from undressing. "Camila, no."

"Why do I feel like you're always rejecting me?"

"I am not trying to reject you. I'm trying to be careful with you. It's complicated between us."

"No, it's not. We are the opposite of complicated. We aren't our parents, and we never will be."

I took another heavy breath, desperately trying to calm my racing heart. "This isn't why I brought you here." I searched her eyes. "I just—don't want you to think I brought you here to sleep with you."

Camila frowned. "You don't think I know that?" She sighed and leaned in to kiss me before pulling back slightly to whisper, "I know what we are, Ridge. We've never needed words to communicate that. But it doesn't make me want you less. And I can feel that you want me too."

With another glare, she pursed her lips, and defiance radiated from her core. She pushed my hands away and lifted her dress over her head. A lace bra the same color as her dress covered her breasts, and her matching panties moved slowly over my hard length. She wouldn't give up the fight, and I was quickly running out of reasons to hold either of us back from what we wanted.

"It's been six months since you looked at me," she said as she reached behind her. "You want to see me again, don't you, Ridge?"

I squeezed my eyelids together for a second before nodding. When I finally peeled them open, Camila's bare breasts were exposed in front of me. My head fell back onto the window so hard that I thought I might have left a mark, but she didn't give me a chance to check the damage. She pressed her lips to my neck, kissing, sucking, and greedily stealing my breath as she explored. I hadn't even noticed that she'd been working the buttons of my shirt until I felt the warm air kiss my chest as she spread the fabric wide.

Gasping, I looked down to find her hips moving against me at a rhythmic pace as she ran a hand down my chest. Camila had always scared the living hell out of me but in ways completely different from that one. She was stealing every last ounce of resistance I'd built up over the years, and I was starting to lose sight of why I hadn't tried to go further with her.

I slowly moved my hand up from her ribcage until her breast was in my palm. "You are excruciatingly beautiful, Camila Bell." My gaze fell to where she continued to rub her core against me, and curiosity won out. I slid my free hand to her panties and traced the delicate material across the top.

"Touch me," she whispered. "I need you to touch me."

I slipped the lace fabric to the side, exposing her glistening pink lips, before I ran my finger between them. She was so wet, from her clit to her ass. It felt as if I were having an out-of-body experience as I glided my finger back and forth, slowly memorizing the naked parts of her and reveling in the intimacy of my touch as she purred against my mouth.

"I've only ever done that to myself."

Her confession brought a guttural moan past my lips. I'd already known that I was her first kiss, so my being the first to touch her in that way didn't surprise me. But the fact that she'd touched herself before did something to me. I stretched the material of her panties farther to the side and pushed a finger against her entrance then let it hover there for a second to give her a chance to object. When she didn't, I slipped it into her, and my eyes rolled to the back of my head at the soft and wet sensation that wrapped tightly around my finger.

She shivered as I moved deeper and deeper until my finger fluttered inside her so fast that my head was spinning, her breaths became shallow, and our mouths were back together. Her release started in a gasp as my finger relentlessly worked her to her brink. I'd never touched another girl like that, so I didn't know what to expect. When she squeezed around my finger and shivered out her release, I could have sworn it was the most beautiful sight I'd ever seen in my life.

Camila began to unzip my pants. By that point, I knew better than to try to stop her. So I watched her free me and wrap her palm around my length. I let her stroke me a few times before showing her with my own hands how to grip me in just the right way. Like everything

Camila attempted, she mastered her mission with ease, bringing on an orgasm so explosive that I felt a meadow of wildflowers burst to life behind my eyelids. And when we lay together after, our mouths intertwined and our hands still exploring, I knew that was the beginning of something.

I just didn't realize that it was the beginning of the end.

27

CAMILA, SIX MONTHS LATER

Almost one year exactly had passed since the spring break trip to Ouray where Ridge and I had reunited, and we continued to survive every single season. He had spent his winter working for Jason, just as we had discussed, and joy radiated from him when he'd recapped one of his trips.

Ridge was the type of man who needed not only adventure but also a purpose. So once the winter season blew in, powdering the earth with its cold white blanket, and while there wasn't much to do on the Cross farm, Ridge found his purpose in the nearby mountains of Ouray. Meanwhile, I had my own purpose to pursue in Telluride.

I was in my senior year of high school, and while I eagerly awaited news from the colleges I'd submitted applications to, I was dedicated to spending the last moments of my high school experience with my close friends. My heart was still set on attending UC Davis, though the thought of leaving Telluride was beginning to weigh heavily on my heart.

California was a fifteen-hour drive from home. I might get to come back for the major holidays, but I worried about all the days in between. Ridge and I had yet to discuss the topic, but we couldn't wait much longer. I could feel the ticking of the clock as our time together ran down.

While Ridge had planned to pick up more work with Jason in the springtime, he wasn't needed there anymore. Ridge had fulfilled his obligation to find Jason a replacement. So Ridge drove up to Mountain Village, the ski town above Telluride, and got a job working the gondola for the rest of the snow season. He worked there during the days while I went to school, then we met at the hilltop until suppertime.

Ridge and my eagerness to see him was on my mind when the final bell chimed at school that day. After grabbing what I needed for the night's homework at my locker, I slammed the door and slid my backpack over my shoulders, then I met up with Josie and Raven near the front of the school. They were giving each other strange looks, and I couldn't figure out why until Raven drove off and Josie stopped me outside of my Jeep.

Josie looked around before stepping closer to me. "Trip is going to ask you to the prom."

Her words didn't sink in right away, but when they did, a laugh burst from my throat. "Funny, Josie. Trip doesn't even go here anymore."

"He doesn't have to go here for him to come as your date."

I scoffed, still finding the humor in what she was telling me. A college boy wanting to go to a high school dance was ridiculous. My chest ached as I remembered that Ridge was the same age as Trip, and if I could have it my way, Ridge would be the one asking me to go to senior prom. "Trip is in New York, remember?"

"Actually, he's already home and taking the rest of his courses virtually."

I just stared at her for the next string of seconds, hoping she would burst into laughter and tell me it was all a sick joke. When the laughter never came, my heart started sinking fast. "Okay, Josie. I'm having a little trouble grasping this."

"Look," she said. "This isn't a rumor or a hunch. Apparently, Thomas put some pressure on Trip to make a move last night at dinner."

"*What?*" I shrieked. "How do you know that?"

Josie frowned and looked around us, like she was worried someone would hear. "Raven vented to me in science class. She feels like Thomas doesn't give a shit about her. He never once asked who she's taking to the dance."

Raven and I had never been the best of friends, but I hated that she felt that way. "That's sad."

Josie sighed. "Yeah, well, I just wanted to give you a heads-up."

I shook my head, trying to clear the clutter from what Josie had just told me. "If Trip wants to go to prom that badly, then he'll have to find another date. He can take Raven, for all I care."

Josie burst into laughter. "His sister?"

I shrugged.

Sympathy shone from her eyes. "I don't know how you don't see this for yourself yet, but Trip is madly in love with you. Always has been. And you giving him the cold shoulder at the vineyard when he comes home from school has only made him more adamant to get your attention."

Her words began to sink in, the weight of them crushing me. Trip had always been a friend, even as annoyingly protective as he had always been. Sure, he was smart, wealthy, and handsome, but he wasn't Ridge. And that last fact was enough to tangle my insides with dread. I'd thought if I ignored his advances, he would go away. I'd thought he *had* gone away.

Groaning, I leaned against my Jeep. "What am I going to do? If I tell him no, Papa won't be happy. But if I say yes…" I wanted to cry at the thought of having to tell Ridge I was going to a dance with another boy.

"Why can't you just talk to your parents? You and Ridge shouldn't have to keep your relationship a secret because of a stupid old feud that no one even knows what it's about anymore. You're eighteen. Almost in college. This is your life, Camila. I can't believe your papa still thinks he can control you."

I shook my head. "It's not that simple. I can't even go there right now. You know my papa. Everything's a business negotiation to him. Thomas is in his ear all the damn time. My parents and Thomas have been planning my wedding to Trip since my birth. Turning Trip down isn't even an option."

"I'm sorry. I wish there were an easy way around

this. I don't know why Trip hasn't moved on by now, but you need to deal with it. Either by talking to your father about Trip or talking to him about Ridge."

She was right, and I knew what I wanted to do. When it came to adventure, I was never too intimidated to look fear in the face and barrel through it at full speed. But talking to my papa about Ridge was different— bigger than taking a risk that could lead to a broken bone or a scrape on the knee. Ridge and I had the power to end a century-old rivalry… or start a brand-new one.

"Papa, I need to—" I skidded down the hall to my papa's office and froze at the doorway.

Thomas was sitting at my papa's desk, his fingers resting on the keyboard, and he peered at me over his glasses.

"Your *papa* is working." Thomas looked at his screen and typed something else before looking back at me. "In the vineyard."

His pointed response caused heat to rise in my chest. "Isn't that where you should be? Does my papa even know you're in here?"

Thomas's laugh boomed before he set his glasses down and pushed back against the chair. "And what is it you think I do around here, Camila?" He raised an eyebrow and waited a whole second before continuing. "As future heir to this beautiful palace, I sure hope you know."

I narrowed my eyes, more annoyed by his presence

than with his tone. Thomas was the business development manager for Bell Family Vineyards, but he didn't just create marketing strategies. He was our greatest salesman, too, giving him far too much power, in my opinion. And while my papa loved to work in the vineyard, hand in hand with our grounds supervisor, cellar worker, and winemaker, it strangely felt like Thomas was the one in charge lately.

"Don't you have your own office down the hall?" I made a purposeful sweeping gaze in dramatic fashion. Everything felt and looked wrong, from who was sitting at my papa's desk to the closed blue-framed windows behind him. My papa loved to keep them open when the weather permitted so that he could breathe in the same air as his grapes, especially at that time of year, when they began to sprout from new buds.

"Don't you have a vineyard to frolic through?"

I glared at the older version of Trip, wondering what my papa saw in Thomas Bradshaw that he couldn't find in someone else. I also started to question the validity of what Raven had told Josie. Thomas wasn't acting like a man who wanted to see me date his son. He sounded like someone who thought I was a nuisance and an obstacle he wouldn't mind doing away with.

My thoughts were interrupted by a shuffling of feet stepping into the office. "Camila," my papa boomed. "You're home from school early today. Is something wrong?"

With a final squeeze of my eyelids in an attempt to dissolve my blatant hatred for the man behind the desk, I turned to face my papa with a smile. "Nothing's wrong.

It was a half day today." I walked toward him and embraced him before kissing him on the cheek. "I hoped we could talk for a minute." I kept my voice quiet as I dared a glance behind me to Thomas, who was getting up from the desk. When I turned back to my papa, I tilted my head. "Please."

He pulled away and squeezed my hands before looking over at Thomas. "All set?"

Thomas walked forward with a slimy grin. "All set. I left the marketing folder open on your desktop so that you could go through each piece. You'll find all the new branding on the menus, flyers, and signage proposals. It's all there. Just holler if you need me." He winked at me before walking past us. "I'll be in *my* office for the rest of the day."

The moment he was gone, I closed the door behind us and followed my papa to a small living room setup in front of a fireplace. That was where he sat to talk to anyone who joined him in his office, even informal visits like mine.

"Do we need your mom for this?"

"I asked her to pop in." I looked at the door. "She should be here soon."

Not a minute later, my mama opened the door and breezed in with a smile. Her bright-yellow dress was a clear indication that she'd just come back from an outing with her friends. She shut the door behind her, sat down beside Papa, and bent to kiss him on his cheek.

After thirty-eight years of marriage, they still loved and respected each other most days. Though there'd been a clear tension between them lately, it warmed my heart to see them together.

"It's about Ridge Cross."

Papa's entire demeanor shifted. "What did the boy do now?"

Mama cut him a glare but remained silent.

Heat licked through me. The start of the conversation was a clear indication of the disaster that would happen if I didn't word things in just the right way. "Nothing at all, Papa. That's what I wanted to talk about. Ridge has been nothing but kind to me since he moved here."

Surprise appeared on both of my parents' faces.

"I wasn't aware you knew the boy," Papa said dryly.

"We live in a small town, Papa. Of course I know him."

Papa shifted in his seat, while Mama stared back at me with knowing eyes. "What are you getting at, mija?" she prompted cautiously.

I took in a deep breath before letting it out slowly as my heart beat rapidly. "Don't you think it's time that the Bell family and the Cross family come to a truce? Don't you want this rivalry to be over, Papa?"

He laughed heartily, as if my suggestion were a ridiculous one. "Don't be absurd."

"Just hear me out, please." I waited for my papa's laughter to die down. "Harold is a grumpy old man. Everyone in town knows that, but if that's all he is, then it doesn't make him any different from half of the old farmers in this town. And just like I'm heir to this vineyard, Ridge Cross is heir to that farm. Shouldn't we end this feud now, before yet another generation is forced to suffer through it? Isn't enough enough?"

My papa shook his head, sighing. "You have a good

heart, mija, but that boy is troubled beyond repair. He comes from a broken home. His mama died, and his father never even wanted the boy."

Rage swirled in my chest at the mention of Ridge's mom. "His father didn't want him? Or *you* didn't want him and his mother living next door?"

Shock lit up my papa's face, but I wouldn't let up.

"I know what you did, Papa. I know you're the one who had her removed from the farm. You're the reason Ridge never had his father in his life, and now you look down on him for it?"

Papa's face turned red as he sat up. "Now hold on a damn minute, Camila. I don't know where you're getting your facts, but I don't appreciate the accusation."

He blew out a breath and darted a glance at my mama, who was looking down at her hands before launching into his own version of the truth. "When Molly suddenly appeared on the Cross farm, she had been badly beaten. She had bruises all over, and they even paid the town doctor to come see her in private. The story was fishy from the get-go, so I kept my eyes on them. Years later, imagine my surprise when an official from the reservation paid us a visit with a list a mile long of all the indigenous women and girls who had gone missing over the years. Then I saw a photo of young Molly. Of course I told the man where he could find the girl. I didn't know she was pregnant. The Crosses could have been the reason she went missing, for all I knew. But if I did such a bad thing, then answer this." My papa leaned forward. "If Molly had been unjustly taken from Harold Cross, then why didn't she ever come back,

Camila? Why did she stay away and raise that boy on her own?"

I shook while taking in my papa's version of the story. "And you never thought to talk to Harold? To ask?"

Mama was wringing the fabric of her dress, still not looking at me. Clearly, she wanted nothing to do with the conversation. Meanwhile, Papa coughed out a laugh and sat back against the couch. "Every damn time I tried talking to Farmer Cross, he raised a shotgun to my head and threatened to shoot me dead if I didn't get off his property." Papa pointed at me like he was driving his point home. "You want to talk about Ridge Cross? Apples don't fall far from their trees, mija."

I hated how insensitive my papa had always been to Ridge without ever taking the time to know him. Since the day Ridge had moved to Telluride, he hadn't so much as gotten a parking ticket, but my papa would never see Harold Cross's son as anything different from what had been ingrained in his head all those years ago.

"He's never done anything to you."

His eyes softened. "You're a good girl, Camila. Always seeing the best in people. And maybe the boy has never done anything to me, but that doesn't mean he won't."

I let out a heavy sigh. "You've been saying that for years."

"And I will for as long as I live. History travels in the bloodlines, my Camila. He's a Cross. There's no stepping around that fact. Learned behavior doesn't carry to the root. Learned behavior is a clever mask to all who want to believe. I assure you. The longer Ridge chooses to stand on ancient soil, his mask will crumble, slowly if not all at once."

"I don't believe that for a second. I won't let this feud carry on. When I'm in your position, I will make things right."

A laugh burst from my papa. "When you're in my position, you'll understand. It's business, Camila. Plain and simple."

I tilted my head, confusion bursting through me. "This is about business now? You treat the Cross family as if they're competition. Harold Cross sells corn, alfalfa, and hay. None of which has an impact on the vineyard business. This isn't business, Papa. It's unsubstantiated cruelty, and I'd like to see it end. Harold Cross as our ally can only benefit us."

My papa grew rigid in his seat. "That man can never be an ally. Not after he bought every last piece of land that should have been mine."

"Is that what this is about? The size of your land? You have plenty, Papa. Business for you is better than ever. Meanwhile, the Crosses are drowning."

"Why on Earth do you care if they're drowning or not?"

"Because—" I had to be careful with my words. "I don't think it's fair to punish Ridge and me for the anger you two have carried."

"No, Camila. End of discussion."

I wanted to push harder and tell him that Ridge was nothing like his papa and never would be. Though I believed it to my core, I couldn't argue with a man whose opinions had been ingrained in him since birth.

Hatred was a choice. So was love. And while my

choice between the two had been set the moment I laid eyes on Ridge Cross, right now wasn't the time to confess that to my papa. He needed to see what I saw. Unfortunately, while Harold Cross was in the picture, there was no chance of that happening.

Mama hadn't said a word in a while, and she clearly already knew more than she would ever speak aloud.

"Are we done here?" Papa stood before I'd even answered. "I have a new hire I need to train today. I can't be late."

"Sure, Papa."

Though I allowed our conversation to end, fire still burned through me as he stomped out of the room.

Mama followed him, but instead of walking out, she shut the door and sat back down across from me. She leveled a gaze at me and sighed. "What were you thinking, Camila?" she hissed.

My throat burned, and any second, tears would spring to my eyes. "Why is it so impossible to talk to him about this?"

"Your papa is passionate, as are you. But you cannot argue with him about the Cross family. Trust me. I've tried. You won't win that war, Camila. Not for as long as your papa is alive."

I bowed my head with defeat. It was burying me alive. "So, I guess this means I shouldn't ask Ridge to take me to my prom."

My mama's eyes widened, and she shook her head emphatically. "No, Camila, please. Don't make things worse than they already are. I beg of you."

Something in her expression lacked the shock I

expected. I searched her eyes as something clicked. "You knew?"

She pulled in a deep breath, her eyes fluttering closed, and nodded. "I did. I've known for a while now."

I frowned, thoroughly confused as to why she hadn't ripped me a new one. "How?"

"Did you really think Gus would let you waltz into the woods without saying anything to me or your papa? I spared you your papa's wrath by making Gus promise to talk to me."

Hot tears threatened to spring from my eyes. "And you were okay with it?"

"It made you happy, and happiness is all I want for you. But I didn't think it would go this far."

"Well, it did." I gripped the fabric of the couch and squeezed my eyelids shut. "Trip is going to ask me to prom, and I'm afraid if I say yes, I'll lead him on and hurt Ridge. I don't want to do either of those things."

Her eyes softened in understanding. "But you know you cannot turn him down. Thomas means too much to your father, and Trip has a future here too."

"Yeah, a future with me that I don't want. Thomas doesn't even like me, yet he's encouraging me to be with his son. It makes no sense."

"You know your father, and you know Thomas. They're businessmen. No one is asking you to marry Trip, but if he asks you to that dance…"

I nodded, blinking back the tears that were threatening to leak down my face. "I know," I whispered.

"Oh, mija." She walked over to sit beside me and wrapped her arms around my shoulders. "I'm so sorry."

She was still holding me tightly minutes later when

the main door to the casita closed and Trip's voice boomed down the hall. "Camila, you in here?"

I looked up, eyes wide on the door, praying that Trip wouldn't find me. Not that it would make a difference. He would find me, then he would ask the dreaded question, and I would say yes, because this was yet another battle that I was fated to lose.

28

"Where are you goin', boy? It's gettin' late."

Harold was drunk and nearly passed out on the couch with the television blaring when he stopped me on my way out the back door. I was surprised he knew what time it was.

"Out," I said before pulling on my cap and reaching for the door.

"Again? You were out all day."

"I told you I was going to work the gondola up at Mountain Village earlier."

"You left me high and dry to deliver all that hay by my lonesome. You've already got a job. Workin' here."

"Yeah, well, the pay is shit here."

That last comment earned me a glare, but he was too drunk to do anything more than that.

"Your payment will be this here land when I croak."

We'd had the same argument often. Nothing ever changed. "Yeah, Pop. I know." I sighed and rolled my eyes. "I'll be here all day tomorrow to work the baler. If we've got deliveries, then I can take those too. We'll get it all done."

I turned the knob and pulled the door open, eager to escape into the cool evening air.

Harold slurred, "It's not going to end well, son."

I froze. I'd been back on the farm for nine months, and Harold had never let on that he knew about Camila and me. We'd been careful, only sneaking up to the hilltop when the crop was taller than us or meeting somewhere secluded outside of town and keeping our daily meetups at the bridge short enough that no one would suspect we were ever gone. But Harold somehow knew. I could feel it in the looks he gave me every time I left the house or the cold silence that followed my late returns.

"I know what love looks like, young man. It's written all over your pathetic face."

"I don't know what you're talking about."

He barked out a laugh, and his eyes drooped closed as he continued to speak. "You think I'm dumb, boy? You think I didn't know why you came back here last year? Patrick Bell's daughter sure did a number on you. After everything that man did to us too."

"For all the business we lost, I've been gaining it elsewhere. I've worked hard for you, so you can stop blaming the Bells for your lack of networking skills. His dealings are crooked, but so is your mean streak. Now, if you don't mind, I've got somewhere to be."

Harold grumbled something while struggling to stand.

A chill raced up my spine, and I spun around to face him. "What did you say?"

"Said I should make good on my threat and hang your girlfriend to that post in the vineyard. See just how precious she is to that daddy of hers. Bet he doesn't even notice her tied up there."

My gut churned, my heart rate spiked, and I tore across the short distance before the final words were out of his mouth. I delivered a punch so hard that I could hear the cracking of his nose before he flew back and crashed into the glass coffee table.

Harold moaned and picked himself off the floor while gripping his bloody nose. "What the fuck?"

With a glare, I stomped off to the kitchen to soak a towel and wrap it around my hand. Then I walked back to the door and gripped the knob with my good hand, wanting nothing more than to rip the door off the hinges and leave my asshole father in the cold. "Don't ever talk about Camila like that again. I don't care that your threats are empty. You know nothing about her. She's not her father, just like I'm not you." With that, I slammed the door behind me and took off.

If Harold knew about Camila this entire time, why didn't he say anything to me? Why didn't he try to stop us from seeing each other sooner?

I wasn't going to get any answers that night. Instead, I jumped in the tractor and drove it down the field toward the entrance to the bridge.

With a hop onto the soft soil, I dusted the tractor's dirt from my jeans and started walking. A minute later, I spotted Camila sitting on the rail of the bridge, her head ducked. She wore white jeans and a long burnt-orange sweater. Her hair was swept up into a ponytail, and her lips shone with a thick layer of gloss. God, she was beautiful.

"You're early."

She looked up sharply, like she hadn't heard me coming. The moment she saw me, she visibly relaxed. "I am." Her eyes darted to my wrapped hand next then widened in shock. "What happened to you?"

"Just a little accident on the farm. Nothing an aspirin won't fix."

When her smile didn't reach her eyes, I quickened my steps until my arms were wrapped around her. I pressed my lips to hers, wanting to make whatever sadness she was feeling go away. She returned my kiss hungrily, tugging me closer by the collar and delving her tongue into my mouth until we were both breathless. When we parted, her head fell onto my shoulder, and she took a deep, slow breath.

"Is everything okay?" I whispered, afraid of the answer.

She groaned and pulled away to look at me. "No, and I don't know how to fix it."

Camila thought she could hold the entire world on her shoulders. I'd never seen her look so defeated.

"And what is it you want to fix?"

Emotion welled in her eyes, and her chin quivered. Something had broken through that tough shell of hers, and it damn near shattered me too.

"I tried to talk to my papa about the stupid feud. I just wanted him to see it my way and to realize this will be my problem to deal with one day, not his." She looked at me with wide eyes, like she was pleading for me not to be upset. "And I love being with you, Ridge, but all this

213

sneaking around is getting to me. I thought that if I talked to my papa, then maybe—"

"That maybe things could be different?"

She cast her eyes down and nodded. My heart was starting to pound violently. I didn't know where the conversation was heading, but I also didn't know if I wanted to find out. "C'mon, Camila," I said, taking a step closer to her and tightening my hold around her waist. "This isn't something we need to figure out today. I'm not even sure that's possible."

She furrowed her eyebrows as she glared at me. "Then what are we doing together, Ridge? Just killing time before I go off to college? Time's running out, you know. Or do you even care?"

"Whoa." My chest puffed, and tension radiated in my neck. "Why are you picking a fight with me?"

"Why are you making it so easy?"

Camila was a spitfire, but I hated it when she used that fire against me. I put my good hand on her face to force her to look at me. "You know I want to be with you. I came back here for you. And when you go off to college, I'll wait for you to come home. Don't you think it will be much easier to deal with our fathers once you're out of high school and working at the vineyard full-time? Either way, we'll cross that bridge when we come to it." I squeezed my eyelids shut, realizing the significance of those words. When Camila's giggle left her throat, I opened my eyes and smiled. "We'll deal with whatever obstacles are in front of us then. And one day, when the vineyard is yours and the corn farm is mine, then we won't have to worry about what anyone else thinks. We'll be the ones making the rules."

A tear fell from Camila's eye, and she swiped it. "That could be thirty years from now."

"No way," I said gently. "Four years, tops. We'll be more equipped to deal with our fathers then. Plus, they'll be too old to argue with us anymore."

She smiled, a challenge in her eyes. "You'll really wait for me? Four years is a long time, you know."

"Not as long as the lifetime I've already waited. And I'll wait forever more if it means we get to exist in this world together. We're going to change the future together, Wild One. Four years isn't going to stand in our way."

She looked at me for several seconds before tugging me by my collar and smashing her lips to mine. We kissed until the moon hung brightly above us through the treetops and the stars twinkled boldly in the dark night's sky. We kissed slowly then feverishly, saying all the words we wanted to say but couldn't.

Camila and I had only explored each other the way we had on Last Dollar Road, and I ached to touch her like that again. "I've missed you," I said before planting a soft kiss between her neck and shoulder.

Her body relaxed into me. "I've missed you too."

When the next few seconds filled with awkward silence, worry crept into my chest. I was so used to Camila always driving the conversations with her intense enthusiasm. "Is something else wrong?"

She searched my eyes, and the extra stretch of silence worried me more. "Um." She looked down, like she was guilty for something. "There's this dance thing at my school…"

"Senior prom?" I asked.

Camila nodded.

"Okay, what about it?"

"I haven't decided whether I'm going yet."

"I never went to mine." I was still confused but also trying to make her feel better about whatever had upset her.

Her eyes were cast down, at the top button of my shirt, which she'd undone. "Why didn't you go?"

I chuckled. "Probably because the only girl I would have taken was a sophomore at the time."

A smile tilted her lips. "I wish you could come with me."

I frowned, wishing all the things that she did. *Is that what's upsetting her?* "Be careful what you wish for. I might just show up with a dozen stalks of corn instead of flowers and wearing a flannel instead of a suit." I winked, trying to lighten the mood, but she didn't laugh. Closing my eyes, I let my forehead rest on hers. "I wish I could take you to your prom, Camila. You'll be the most beautiful girl there."

"What's the point in going if I can't go with you?"

Something yanked at my chest. A selfish part of me wanted to tell her not to go, but I couldn't ask her to do that. "The point," I said, cupping her chin with my fingers, "is to have one last hurrah with your friends. Dance until your heels hurt. Laugh until you cry. Make memories that you'll never forget. Then when it's all over, save me your last dance and meet me at the bridge so that we can make a memory of our own."

Camila's eyes welled with emotion. She took my hand and squeezed it. "I love that plan."

Good, because I love you.

29

RIDGE

A sleek black Mustang pulled down the gravel drive to my ranch house when I came back from the hilltop. The Saturday of the dance had arrived, and I'd been keeping myself occupied all day. The last thing I expected was for Raven Bradshaw to pay a visit, especially when she should be at her prom with Camila. Harold was working on one of the old tractors in the garage, and I wondered what he would think of our visitor. A Bradshaw was almost as bad as a Bell in his mind.

Raven stepped out of her car, revealing the gown she'd picked for the evening. It was a long, beaded gold dress with a high slit that revealed an overly tanned thigh. Her makeup was bold, painted in just the right spots to make her appear older than her eighteen years. I would be a liar if I didn't recognize my attraction to my old friend, but I'd had many reasons for not exploring that attraction. Lord knew Raven had given me plenty of opportunities. The way she was looking at me on her approach told me she might be there to offer me another one.

"Lost on your way to the dance?" My joke was a lame attempt at trying to ignore the real reason as to why Raven had chosen that night of all nights to show up in her prom dress.

Her blush was still visible on her highlighted cheeks. "Something like that." When she stopped in front of me, her height was almost a shock compared to Camila's. "I'm here to ask you to my prom, actually." Her blush deepened. "I should have asked you sooner, but I had some trouble getting up the nerve. I know you graduated two years ago, and the last thing you probably want to do is go to a silly high school dance, but—" She laughed quietly then looked me boldly in the eyes. "I think it could be fun. You know, to go together. You already know a lot of people going, since they were at the camp last year, and…"

She just kept talking, and I just kept listening. At one point during her run-on, I opened my mouth then snapped it shut. Raven had always been nice to me, despite her brother's feelings toward me. The last thing I wanted to do was hurt her.

"You're not saying anything." Her eyes froze on me, and her nervous mood dissipated into darkness.

"I'm sorry, Raven. I guess I'm just confused. We've been friends for a long time, and your brother isn't exactly my biggest fan."

She waved her hand. "Don't worry about Trip. He'll be there tonight, but he won't bother you."

I let out a laugh. "He'll be at your prom? Who'd he sucker into taking him tonight?"

Raven smiled at my amusement. "Camila Bell, of course."

The air left my chest as soon as I heard her name. Raven didn't seem to notice.

"Trip's had his eyes locked on that girl for as long as I can remember."

Not a person in town could have missed that, but to hear those feelings might suddenly be reciprocated had me fuming. Just the previous week, we'd met at the bridge, and she'd been so distraught over the fact that we couldn't go to the dance together. She failed to mention that she'd agreed to go with someone else. Even if she had told me she was going with someone else, I wouldn't have been upset about it, or at least no more upset than I naturally was that we couldn't go together. *But why did she feel the need to lie?* I could only think of one reason—that she had feelings for him back.

Camila Bell, of course. Raven's words went around and around in my mind.

"So," Raven said, her expression still hopeful. "Will you be my date tonight? I mean, you're already dressed up and everything."

She'd noted my crisp black slacks and white button-down. I didn't dare tell her why I was dressed up, and I cringed internally and let out a slow breath before responding. As pissed as I was at Camila for lying, I couldn't accompany Raven to a dance, knowing she had feelings for me. Not only would it lead her on, but I would have to stare at Camila with Trip all night. Imagining them together was bad enough.

"I can't go with you, Raven. I'm sorry."

Her eyes widened slightly. Surely, men didn't turn

Raven down—especially outcasts with zero events on their social calendar. I had to give her a reason.

"It's just that… I'm seeing someone, and it wouldn't be fair to them."

"Oh, I didn't realize. I'm the one who's sorry. I put you on the spot like that. It's just—" She let out a laugh and waved at her car. "All my friends are going with someone else, and the only guy who asked me to go is a freshman. Sometimes I really hate living in such a small town."

I smiled back at her sympathetically. "Trust me. I get it. Maybe you'll meet someone at the dance. Any guy would be crazy not to want to dance with you."

She shrugged then took a step back. "Yeah, well. Consider yourself crazy then." She winked, making me feel a little better that I hadn't completely crushed her.

Not until after she'd driven off did I allow myself to think about Camila again and the fact that everything I'd planned for that night, everything I'd planned to do and say, was a complete waste.

30

CAMILA

Loud pop music blared from the giant limousine when I climbed in to greet my friends. I was the final stop on the way to dinner before the dance, and as soon as I stepped inside, I laughed at the setup. Someone had gone all out with our transportation. Not only was the limo large enough to fit thirteen of my closest friends comfortably, but it was also lined with neon-blue lights that reflected off the wood floor. It felt like I'd just stepped into a club, complete with two poles and a bar. Undoubtedly, some of my friends had sneaked alcohol into those cabinets.

"There's my date!" Trip's voice boomed from the other side of the limo.

I waved at him and smiled before squeezing in between Josie and our friend April. Calling Trip my "date" would be a stretch. He'd asked me to accompany him, and I'd said okay but with conditions—we would go with a large group of friends, we would go as friends and nothing more, and no slow dancing.

He'd tried to argue that last one, but I put my foot down. If he wanted to come to the dance so badly, then he had to play by my rules, which ensured he wouldn't get the wrong idea about our going together.

"You'll never believe what Raven did," Josie whispered to me while everyone was shuffling out of the limo for dinner. She waited until everyone was out of the vehicle before she turned to me fully, her eyes wide. "Raven went to Ridge's house and asked him to be her date to prom."

"What?" The word came out as a shriek. "She did *what*?" I hissed.

Josie looked uneasy. "Carla and I were getting our nails done, and I kind of accidentally overheard their phone conversation. I don't think Carla even realized I heard, but I did, and you should know he turned her down." She giggled. "Obviously, since he's not here. He told Raven that he's seeing someone."

I glared at the window, suddenly feeling an overwhelming desire to skip dinner and the dance and head home to find Ridge. "Of course he turned her down. On what planet does she think she has any chance with Ridge Cross?"

Josie squeezed my hand. "We already know Raven lost her marbles a long time ago. But that brings me to the other thing I wanted to talk to you about. Are you sure Ridge is okay with you being out tonight with Trip? Seems a little double-standardish on your part."

Guilt shot through me faster than I could stop it. "Double-standardish? I didn't realize that was a word."

She rolled her eyes. "You know what I'm saying."

"I'm not out with Trip," I corrected her. "I'm here

with my friends. All of you. Trip just happens to be one of them."

Josie frowned. "But he asked you to come *as his date*, and you agreed."

"What was I supposed to do with our parents standing by like he'd just proposed?" I hissed. "What matters is that I don't have feelings for Trip. At all."

"And you're sure Ridge will see it that way?"

I wanted to cry. I hated her questions because they brought all my anguish about the night to the surface. "He doesn't have to see it any way, because I didn't tell him Trip asked me to prom."

She glared at me. "So you lied."

I pulled in a deep, painful breath and shook my head. "I might have omitted the total truth. But this isn't a date. I won't let Trip pay for a thing."

"He purchased this limo we're in right now."

I groaned, the urge to cry strong. "We're not even going to slow dance together," I mumbled. "I made him agree to the rules, and he did."

"Oh my god, Camila. You're in denial."

I covered my face with my hands and leaned down until my elbows were resting on my knees. Everything felt tight—my chest, my throat, and even my freaking dress. I was suffocating, and it was all my own doing. "What do I do?"

Josie's warm hand landed on my back and started circling it. "That's completely up to you, Camila. What do you want to do?"

It wasn't even a debate. "I want to be with Ridge."

"Then you should be with Ridge."

Josie had always been the one warning me to be

careful. She knew just as well as I did that it could all lead to disaster. But she also loved me and knew that if I saw that night through with another man, I would never forgive myself.

I looked up, feeling a deep whoosh of relief pass through me, and felt love for my friend for the sharp slap of reality. "I need to go."

Josie smiled then turned to the driver, who was waiting for us by the door. "Sir, do you mind running my friend home? She's not feeling well."

31

RIDGE

The scent of stale beer wafted around me as I lay the blanket over Harold's passed-out body. He'd been drinking a lot more ever since I'd punched him in the nose, and he hadn't spoken a word to me since either. I was half-shocked that he hadn't met me at the door with a shotgun when I returned that same night. Whether it was loneliness or the need for help on the farm, he'd let me stay.

I picked up the bottle that had rolled beneath the coffee table, tossed it into the garbage in the kitchen, and reached into the refrigerator to pull out another one. After opening it, I walked out to the front porch and sat down.

Passing the bottle from one hand to the other, I glared at it like it was peer pressuring me to drink it. I'd never had a sip of alcohol in my life, but the past year had seemed all about firsts—first kiss, first love, first potential heartbreak. A beer couldn't possibly make things worse.

"Here goes nothing." I moved the bottle to my lips and let it linger for a second, taking in the bitter scent with a wrinkled nose and closed eyes. "Jesus, who drinks this shit," I mumbled against the rim. But just as I was going to suck it up and take a swig, the sound of tires rolling over the gravel drive had my eyelids popping open. "Oh no."

Dread rolled through me as the limo came into view. My only thought was that it was Raven, back to haul me to that dance. That time, I wasn't sure if I would have the strength to say no, not because I wanted to go with her but because it would give me the perfect opportunity to shove my fist into Trip's face once and for all.

I set the beer down on the top stair and stood. The driver exited the limo and walked around the car. When the back passenger door opened and fabric from a red dress was all I could see through the cracks, my heart began to pound like crazy.

Before Camila even stepped past the driver and smiled at him in thanks, I knew it was her. She looked up at me, a timid smile on her lips, and walked forward a few steps, like she was too nervous to come any closer. Red was my favorite color on Camila. She wore it well, especially that night. The fluffy fabric fell just above her knees in front and dipped a few inches lower in the back. A sheer layer draped over the solid fabric of the skirt, and the neckline left her shoulders completely bare.

After blinking a few times, I finally felt like I could speak. "Won't you be late for your prom?"

"I'm not going," she called back.

The driver shut the door, walked around the limo, and got back into the driver's seat.

I watched him drive away, confused. "What are you doing here, Camila?"

She shook her head, and as I stared back into her wide, beautiful eyes, I could see the fear she'd carried with her. "I'm here to apologize. Because I lied to you," she said.

Not trusting my anger, I didn't say a word. Instead, I kept my stare firm as I waited for her to continue.

"You already know, don't you?"

I remained silent.

"You're angry with me."

Again, I remained silent.

Camila took a small step forward then stopped. Instead of my feisty Camila, in that moment, she was hesitant and afraid. Camila was never afraid.

She cast her eyes down. "Trip asked me to the dance. And I agreed to go with him." She looked back up, that same look of guilt and fear swimming in her gaze. "But I insisted to him that we only go as friends," she said. "There were fourteen of us riding in that limo, and I left before we even sat down for dinner."

I grinded my teeth. "Why? Why leave? You already lied."

Her chest puffed out with her breath, accentuating the tightness of the bodice of her dress. "Because prom means nothing if you aren't there with me. And maybe I'll be sad one day because I didn't get to have that experience with my friends, but if I have to choose, Ridge, then I choose you."

She took another step then stopped, and her expression morphed into anger when too much silence passed between us. "Please say something."

I swallowed past the tightening of my throat and took the two steps down to where she stood. "The fact that you're standing in front of Harold's front porch after he tried to run you over with a tractor tells me I should probably give you the benefit of the doubt."

She let out a laugh and threw her arms around me. "I was so afraid I'd messed this up."

Another wave of anger passed through me when I thought about her lie. "I wish I hadn't found out about you and Trip from Raven. That really hurt, Camila."

Her eyes shot open. "I'm so sorry."

"I know."

Camila's eyebrows furrowed. "Did Raven really ask you to prom?" Then she took in my attire for the first time. "Oh my god, were you going to go with her?"

I glared and shook my head. "No. I wasn't going to the dance with Raven. I couldn't." I clenched my jaw, suddenly feeling embarrassed about what I had planned for the evening. "I wore this for you. For our last dance." Heat rushed to my cheeks. "It was a ridiculous thought, I know."

Camila gripped my shirt and held me as close to her as possible. "No, it wasn't. Don't say that. I'm here now. We can have that dance. I want to."

So many thoughts rushed through my mind in that next minute. I contemplated right and wrong and what I wanted versus what I shouldn't want. I reminded myself that Camila could be at her prom right that moment, but she'd chosen to come to me on her own. She'd done the right thing in the end, and that was what I should be focusing on.

"I don't know. It just feels stupid now. I had all these

plans for when you got back from the dance…" I ran a hand through my hair, frustration still tumbling around inside me.

"What plans?"

I looked down to find her eyes searching mine desperately, as if she were begging me to let her back into my heart.

"Ridge, please. Tell me what you had planned tonight."

The emotion in her tone clawed at my heart. Denying her was impossible, especially when I knew I was the one who could break her. I couldn't do it.

"All right, then," I said before stuffing my hands into my pockets and rocking back on my heels. "But you'll have to come with me."

"Where to?"

"To our prom."

A smile bloomed on her face. "Then let's go."

"Your chariot awaits."

I laughed at the green tractor Ridge was gesturing to. It was completely dark out, save for the surrounding house lights and the high beams on the tractor. He hopped on first and started the engine before reaching out to help me up. He placed me on his lap, fastened his grip around my waist, and took off down the side road of his house.

Even while I was strapped to him, I could sense the tension that still existed between us because of my lie. It hadn't been forgotten. His rigid body and his silence spoke volumes. He was too quiet, even for Ridge.

I'd really hurt him, and I hated myself for it. He would have understood if I'd just told him the truth about Trip from the beginning. But while I could stare a shotgun in the eye and dare him to shoot me without flinching, losing Ridge was something that scared me beyond words. Our time together was already so fragile.

Knowing that, I'd allowed for all logic and common sense to go out the window.

We couldn't have been going faster than five miles an hour, but with the wind blowing in my face and the loud engine engulfing us in its roar, I couldn't help but feel a sense of relief as we moved along. No matter how Ridge felt at the moment, we were still together. I could make it right. He would forgive me.

I finally took in the white ranch house I'd only ever caught glimpses of from afar. While it was small, paint chips covered its aged exterior, and dark-blue shutters dangled off its hinges, its imperfect nature was charming. A matching white barn sat on the other side of the home.

The barn was where they stored extra bushels of hay, grain, tractors, and other equipment used in their day-to-day. While Ridge and Harold didn't raise livestock to sell, they cared for their share of animals—horses, chickens, and dairy cows—and they were kept near the barn. Harold believed in living a fully sustainable life on the farm, and Ridge had adopted that lifestyle just fine. They ate what they cooked and cooked what they grew.

I rested my hand on Ridge's arm, which still wrapped around my waist, in a silent apology I wouldn't stop giving. Over the next few minutes, we rode to the edge of the field. There, he parked near the overgrowth of weeds that separated the one-thousand-acre property from public land then helped me down from the tractor.

After removing my heels, I placed them on the seat behind me and let Ridge lead the way. I had walked the surrounding land hundreds of times while barefoot, and that night was no different. Aware of my shoeless feet, Ridge stopped every now and then and carried me over a puddle or a pile of rocks. My heart swelled more each time.

If that was the closest Ridge would ever come to showing me romance, then I would take it without a second thought. I would take the barefoot walks up rugged terrain to whatever he had planned instead of a fancy dinner any day.

Ridge was so different from my male peers I had grown up with. I had always known that. And maybe that was what kept drawing me to him time and time again. He wasn't affected by social media and didn't even know what it was. The mobile phone he owned had the barest minimum of functions. He used it to send quick text messages or make work calls, but other than that, you'd never even know he had a phone. I loved so much about Ridge, but that was a definite highlight. And the fact that he was walking me up our hillside with nothing but a flashlight to guide our way was another. Ridge had something up his sleeve, and I couldn't wait to find out what it was.

We were halfway up the mountain with his hand firmly wrapped around mine when I decided to try to break the silence. "I hate to be the one to tell you," I teased, "but proms usually consist of dancing, spiking punch, and sneaking boob grabs. Hiking is usually saved for the morning-after walk-of-shame."

To my surprise, Ridge laughed. "You might be out of luck on the spiked punch, but I think I've got the rest of that covered."

Joy flittered through my chest. "Even the boob grab, huh?"

He nodded. "Admittedly, it wasn't on my list until you just suggested it. I would hate to disappoint."

I was smiling like crazy when we finally made it to the top of the hill.

"Wait here," he said before running off into the darkness.

I could barely make out the outline of a dome-shaped object next to our tree, but soon enough, all my questions were answered. One second, all was dark, then the next, a string of lights lit the scene.

Butterflies danced in my belly, fluttered up to my chest, and squeezed my throat with emotion as I took in what Ridge had done. From the lights, to the giant flannel blanket filled with a picnic basket and scattered pink roses, to the tent we'd slept in together in Ouray, it was like I'd just walked into our own private prom.

When Tom Petty's "Wildflowers" started playing through the wireless speaker hanging from the tree, emotion swept through me, and I realized how differently the night could have turned out. I hated the thought of the additional hurt I could have caused if I had gone through with attending prom with Trip after hiding it from Ridge. Just thinking about the what-ifs could easily ruin the night. I couldn't let that happen.

With the dim light, I could barely see Ridge's face as I walked toward him. After I'd closed the distance, the look I found in his eyes hit me hard. Fear, uncertainty, hope—the mixture fed me the confidence I needed to show him just how sorry I was.

I touched his cheek. "You made us our own prom?"

He nodded, his jaw firmly locked in place.

I stepped closer so that I was right under his nose,

locking my gaze to his. "You asked me to save my last dance for you, but now you get to have all of them."

His eyes softened, causing my insides to melt into a puddle at my feet.

I placed my hand in his. "All my dances are yours, Ridge Cross." I molded my front to his. "And so am I." Pushing myself onto my toes, I found his mouth with a gentle brush of my lips and kissed him until his mouth started to move against mine.

He picked me up easily, and I wrapped my legs around his waist while deepening our kiss.

"I'm sorry," I whispered against his mouth. A tear slipped from my eye. "Please forgive me."

"Don't cry, Wild One." His voice was gentle and pleading. "I forgive you." His lips found mine again as he walked us to where the majority of light shone around the blanket, which acted as our dance floor. He set me back on my feet and moved his hands to my waist while I positioned my arms around his neck. Then we danced.

I followed his lead, but he didn't move all that much, just slight steps from side to side, before I looked up to see a bashful smile spreading across his face. "I think the last time I danced was when I was small enough for my mom to carry me around on her toes. I'm not sure how to do any of that fancy stuff. Like twirl you or dip you."

Biting down on my bottom lip to contain my smile, I rested my cheek on his shoulder and closed my eyes. "I think we're doing just fine like this."

He held me close as we swayed, his minty-pine scent engulfing me in his spell. I loved holding Ridge like that and could almost believe we were on a dance floor, surrounded by my closest friends, and no one batted an eye at seeing us together.

I understood why he had gone all out, even if it had all only been meant for our one promised dance. A night like tonight might never come again. We could almost pretend that we existed in a world where we could be together without worrying about the thoughts and feelings of everyone around us.

The music transitioned to another slow song, and Ridge's hand started to move in circles over my bare back. "Did Trip see you in that dress before you left?"

I cringed before looking up to find amusement in his eyes. "Yes. Why?"

The corners of his mouth lifted into a smile. "He's probably crying into his spiked punch about now, if that's the case."

Relief and amusement rushed through me all at once. I laughed and slapped Ridge on the shoulder. "You're horrible."

He nodded. "Maybe. But it's your fault. You look beautiful, Camila."

My heart skipped a beat, or at least it felt that way when he looked at me with adoring eyes. "Thank you."

We danced for a few songs more before sitting down to snack on what Ridge had prepared. Since he'd figured I would have had dinner, he brought just a small selection of fruits, and cheese, and some crackers, but it was enough to settle my growling stomach.

When we set the food aside, he pulled me between his legs and handed me a small white box with only a string wrapped around it. My eyes opened in surprise as I took it. "You bought me something?"

"I made it, actually."

I smiled back at him before I unknotted the tie, and when I pulled open the lid, I gasped. "Ridge, this is—" I swallowed back the emotion in my throat and reached for the wire-wrapped arrowhead necklace. A small silver plate hung beside it with the words Wild One etched into it.

"You made this?"

He nodded slowly, and his expression showed that he was waiting to see if I liked it.

"I love it, Ridge. This is the sweetest, most thoughtful gift anyone has ever given to me."

He smiled, melting my heart.

"Can you put it on me?"

He wrapped the dainty chain around my neck and fastened it so that the arrowhead was resting above my throat.

"It's perfect. Thank you." Leaning back on him, I looked up at the stars. "I can't believe you did all this for me." I felt so happy that I thought I might burst. "It's perfect. The lights, the music, the necklace." I paused, my smile growing. "The tent."

I turned to catch Ridge smile.

"Okay, that looks bad," he said. "I don't know what came over me, really. I was thinking about that night we spent together in the Mount Sneffels wilderness, and I guess I wanted to recreate it." He shook his head, looking flustered, before locking eyes with me again. "Do you ever think about that night?"

A shiver snaked through my body. "All the time. Every night, I go to bed thinking about how you held me and didn't try to take things further when you could have. I practically mauled you that night."

He chuckled. "I wanted to." He dropped his head to my shoulder while letting out a low groan. "You have no idea how badly I wanted to."

"But you were a gentleman."

"I wouldn't go that far." He looked up again. "I may be a virgin, but the things that go through my mind sometimes, especially when it comes to you, prove that I'm no saint. I'm very attracted to you, Camila." His gaze dropped to my chest. "I'm especially attracted to you in that dress."

I sucked in a deep breath and started to stand.

"Where are you going?"

The terror in his eyes made me bite down on my smile. "I'm not going anywhere." I continued to stand until I was tall above him, then I reached behind me to the back of my dress.

Ridge's expression darkened, and he scrambled to his feet. "What are you doing?" I had only started unzipping myself when his hand moved to my back to stop me.

"I'm making sure you know that you don't have to be a gentleman tonight."

His throat bobbed, making me wonder if he was nervous. "Well, then at least let me do the honors of taking that dress off you."

Stunned and thrilled all at once, I dropped my hand, letting Ridge take over. Cool air skated across my back before my entire dress was pooled around my feet. I stood before him, wearing nothing but a red bra and panties that did little to cover me in all the places that counted. But by the way he stared back at me, I might as well have been naked.

His gaze roamed over me slowly, like he was committing my every dip and curve to memory. His touch was gentle as he traced a finger from my neck, over my shoulder, and down my arm. I unbuttoned his white dress shirt, and as soon as it came loose, my hands started to shake.

I drew in a slow breath and pushed open his shirt, reveling in the sight of his body. How the young, awkward boy from the farmer's market five years ago had turned into such a beautiful man was beyond my comprehension. His shirt joined my dress on the blanket, and my breaths immediately felt shallow.

As if he could sense my nervousness, he leaned in and pressed his firm lips to my ear. "You are so beautiful, Camila. Every single part of you, inside and out." His hand grazed over my breast and up my neck then cupped my cheek.

He always knew just what to say to remind me of just how safe I was with him. Squeezing my eyes shut, I moved to undo his slacks. They fell easily to the ground, joining the rest of our clothes.

We stood there, our chests pressing against each other while our eyes were locked in silent conversation. He was doing what he always did, giving me time to commit to the decision we both would make, but for once, I wished he would take the lead, demand the things he wanted, and lose just an ounce of that control he held on to so dearly.

As if he could read my thoughts, he took my hand and pulled me toward the open flaps of the tent. When he gestured for me to enter first, I ducked inside, smiling at the simple setup. Blankets and pillows cushioned the floor, while a propane lamp that hung from the corner cast a flickering yellow light.

When I heard the zip of the tent behind me, my head started to spin as my heart beat rapidly. I'd wanted to be with Ridge for so long that I couldn't believe it was actually happening.

He wrapped his strong arms around my middle and buried his mouth in my neck, sending a wave of shivers over my body. Then he trailed kisses down to my shoulder while working the clasp of my bra and freeing my breasts.

His palm rested on my belly before his fingers drew light circles over my skin. "You do things to me," he rasped, pressing himself against me to show me what he meant.

I gasped at the feel of him, hard between my ass cheeks.

"You make me want you in a way that drives me insane. I can't see straight. I can't think. I can't breathe. I just crave you and want you and love you so damn much."

I swiveled to face him. His words were a shock. We'd never spoken about love or just how deeply our feelings ran, but I'd known for years that I loved him—I'd just never truly believed I would receive that love back. Emotion clogged my throat as I blinked back at him.

"What did you say?"

A soft smile tilted his lips. "I love you, Camila."

Relief and happiness swirled through me, and my heart swelled so much that I thought I might float straight up to the sky. "I love you too, Ridge. I've loved you for such a long time."

Our lips melded in a kiss that sealed our words with a silent promise of forever.

I pulled away, feeling an ounce of fear that came with such powerful sentiments. "You need to make me one promise." I cast my eyes down before sucking in a breath and locking them back on his. "You can't disappear on me again. That almost broke me, Ridge, and I can't lose you again. I'm terrified of it, more than anything I've ever feared in my life."

He nodded, cupping my cheeks, and his warm brown eyes melted me into a pool of love at his feet. "I'm not going anywhere, Camila. Not now, not ever. I meant what I said about waiting for you while you went off to college. I will. Okay?"

I nodded back, and my chest felt like it could explode with happiness.

"And you should know that I didn't have any expectations for tonight, but I'd be lying if I told you I didn't want you. I want you in a way I've never wanted anyone before."

I drew in a deep breath and closed my eyes before pressing my lips to his. We kissed slowly at first, almost like it was our very first time, but nothing could ever replace that night on the mountain when all our feelings had been revealed to the stars. That night had been magical, surreal almost, and brought him back to me.

Tonight was something different. Something more. Something that transcended space and time and planted us in an entirely different galaxy. He deepened the kiss first as his hunger for me grew with every single one of our tangled heartbeats.

"I could kiss you for eternity," he whispered.

"Then do it." My words were a challenge, a plea, and a wish. "Kiss me everywhere."

He tightened his hold, hugging me while devouring my mouth with his. Then he lifted me in his arms. My legs wrapped around his waist, and our bodies pressed together with our hearts beating like one. Two steps later, he'd backed me to the middle of the blankets and laid me down.

He dipped his head, hovering over my breast with his hot breath blowing against me, making my already-aching nipples harden. I spread my legs, allowing him room to fit between them, then I arched my back and pushed my chest up, feeling needy everywhere.

I wanted his touch from his mouth and his hands, all over my body. But Ridge took his time, exploring me in all the places he'd never ventured before, running his hands gently over my breasts, exploring the sensitive skin with his finger, and breathing me in while stealing every last ounce of control from me.

The moment his mouth finally landed on the peak of one of my breasts and circled it with his tongue, my gasp was so loud that any lurking critter would surely have run off. My head spun as my heart raced as Ridge's first timid taste quickly transitioned into more. I could feel his confidence growing when he sucked me into his mouth and moaned with satisfaction then moved to my other breast to give it equal attention.

He sat up, his breaths heavy as he stared down at me. The flickering light revealed a new side of Ridge, one I'd only dreamed of. He stared at me like I was the most beautiful treasure in the world. And when his fingers moved to the only scrap of fabric that still remained, he treated it like a perfectly wrapped package that he didn't want to ruin.

My red panties slid down my legs, off my feet, and to the tent floor. With a deep breath, he placed his hands on my knees and pushed them open, exposing me. A curse left his lips, and slowly, my legs began to widen further until he dipped down and ran his tongue along my slit at an achingly slow pace.

My body jerked at the initial contact, but his strong arms held me firmly in place while he continued to gain more confidence with each stroke. His hair felt thick and wild beneath my fingers, and while he was one hundred percent in command, I couldn't help but writhe against his mouth, creating even more friction as time went on.

"I could breathe you in forever," he rasped, his mouth never leaving me.

He was relentless, taking his time to figure out what made me react, then he homed in for the kill. Heat built from my core and spread like wildfire to every pore of my body until I exploded on his tongue and cried out with my release.

My entire body shook, and I didn't know how to stop it. Ridge stood, pushing down his black briefs. I watched him while I came down off the highest of highs. I was just regaining my breath when Ridge tore apart a condom wrapper and pushed it over his length. Then he returned to his knees. My legs were still spread for him, and he inched his way to my entrance.

He was no longer second-guessing or trying to be the

cautious Ridge I'd always known. I could see it in his eyes. He was a different man, one who knew exactly what he wanted, and nothing in the world could stop him.

With a hand wrapped around his length, he leaned over me, planting a kiss on my lips. "Tell me if I hurt you, okay?"

I hadn't even noticed how tense I was until that moment. I nodded, too afraid to speak.

He took in a shaky breath before kissing me again. And as he parted my mouth with his, he pushed into me, spreading me, filling me, and embedding himself in my core in a way no other man ever could.

33

THE HUNTER

The hunter stalked through the mine, following the tracks of the underground railroad beneath the string of flickering overhead lights. The sound of dripping water echoed off the red rock and stalagmite walls as he gripped the edge of the old rail car. The high-pitched groan of its wheels lasted the entire mile-long journey in the resistance against the tracks.

Daylight was just breaking over the horizon when he approached the steel-padlocked gate. With a quick shove, he shifted through the baggy material of his coat to find the key, then he grunted when he realized he didn't have it. Frustration tore through him, and he leaned forward, gripping the bars of the gate. He was trapped, a prisoner of his own making.

As he started to contemplate his options—breaking the lock with one hit of a rock at the top of his list—the sound of footsteps above him piqued his awareness. He wasn't the only one out there.

He released his grip on the bars, careful not to make a noise, as he strained to hear a pair of muddled voices.

"I can't believe we slept until morning. Papa is going to kill me if he sees me coming home like this."

"This route is dangerous," the boy argued. "And you're barefoot. If you're too stubborn to let me give you a ride to the bridge, then at least let me walk you."

"Are you sure *I'm* the stubborn one?" A laugh flitted through her. "Sometimes I wonder about that."

The hunter picked up on whom the voices belonged to easily.

A second later, Camila dropped onto the gravel, her puffy red dress bouncing around her. She should have been at prom last night, not with the Cross boy, especially not with her breasts practically ready to burst from her top. Obviously, from the way her dark hair was tangled around her head, the flushed nature of her skin, and the flirtatious smile set on her face, she'd worn that pretty little dress for him.

The hunter took two slow steps backward, knowing exactly where he needed to stand not to be seen. And when the girl's gaze dropped to the steel bars between them, a thrill rushed through him at their proximity.

For years, he'd left the future heir alone. He'd watched her age and change from her innocent tomboy ways into a little vixen. Always a daredevil, that one, sneaking around behind her father's back. Soon enough, her betrayal was bound to catch up with her. Maybe today was that day.

She stood and smiled at where she'd fallen from. "You coming?"

"I should get back before Harold comes looking for me."

She nodded, but her big, bold green eyes stayed on him. "Meet me at the bridge tonight?"

"I'll be there," he called back. "Please be careful, Wild One."

She grinned. "I promise. I'll be careful."

She started to dash away, then she turned to look up at the boy again with a smile. "I love you."

"I love you too."

The hunter remembered something and slipped his hand into his pants pocket, retrieving the key he'd thought he'd left behind. A thrill rushed through him as he looked up again.

Before Camila turned to run off again, her gaze slid in the direction of the mine. Something flickered across her expression—worry or curiosity, maybe—but only for a second. While the hunter couldn't be sure of exactly what she was thinking, one thing was certain. She didn't realize it, but in that moment, with her eyes locked on the steel gates of the mine, she was staring directly into the eyes of the hunter.

34

CAMILA

The journey back to the bridge was a slow one. I couldn't run barefoot through the tall grass or hop and skip over the rocks near the creek. I couldn't travel quickly through the woods or stop for a quick twirl around a tree branch. My feet ached, my entire bottom half was caked in dirt and mud, and sweat coated my face. If anyone saw me, I was done for.

When I finally reached the bridge, I collapsed against one of the wooden beams and rested for what felt like days. If I was going to make a mad dash through the vineyard, into the villa, and up to my room, then I would need all the energy I could muster. Besides, I wasn't ready to let the previous night go. I replayed each memory over and over like a priceless vintage record that I would hold on to forever.

The last thing I'd expected to see when I snuck through the front door of my home hours later was a welcoming committee. My already-buzzing heart took a flying leap off a cliff I didn't see coming. No safety net or pool would greet me at the bottom. As I stared into the faces of my parents and Thomas Bradshaw, the rocky pit of my fate glared back at me.

Thomas spoke first. "Good morning, Camila. I hear prom was quite the turn of events last night."

My throat felt so constricted with fear that I couldn't even offer a retort to his cold greeting. It felt like the end of everything I'd ever loved. All I could do was clutch my ribcage to try to quell the blinding ache.

I waited and waited for what felt like minutes as the angry eyes of my parents and Thomas stared back at me. Whether they were examining me or sizing me up, I didn't know. They just stared, and I could only imagine what they were seeing—the hickeys on my neck, which I had planned to hide, my disheveled hair from a long night of lovemaking, my bare and dirty feet since I'd never retrieved my heels, and smeared lipstick from bruising kisses that had marked my heart and soul for eternity.

No matter what happened, I would never regret the previous night. We'd been reckless and wild, but we weren't wrong. And that was how I would fight the war, with a determination to make them all see it my way.

"I know who you were with last night, young lady."

The menace behind my papa's words chilled me to the bone.

"What I don't know," he continued, "is why."

Fear slithered through me as I wondered what lengths they would go to from then on to keep Ridge and me away from each other and turned to Mama for help. I hoped she would at least beg Papa to be kind, but as soon as our eyes met, she turned away, angling her gaze down. My chest squeezed at the knowledge that I had disappointed her too.

"Papa," I started, willing my voice to stop shaking. "Papa, let me explain."

"*Explain?*" The question burst from my papa's mouth so fiercely that it felt like a slap in the face. "Explain why you burst through the door at nine in the morning, expecting no one to notice that you've been gone?" He gestured to me with a disgusted expression. "Looking like that?"

His booming voice lingered in the air before finally dying off, only to be followed by another terrifying roar. "There is no explaining this, young lady! You went off to a prom last night that you never attended. Then you ditched poor Trip, leaving him to fend for himself."

"Trip hardly had to fend for himse—"

"Stop!" My papa's voice hit a decibel I'd never heard him hit in my entire lifetime. His face was red and darkening by the second. "You're missing the point." Even with my mama's firm hand clutching his, he balled it up into a fist and pushed himself off the couch.

I'd seen and heard how angry my papa could get with the vineyard workers over the years, but I'd never imagined that I would be the one in his direct line of fire.

Feeling desperate for support, I turned to my mama again. If anyone in the room would give it to me, she would. "Mama, please. I'm eighteen. I'm not a child anymore. I didn't want to go to prom with Trip. I never did. I only said okay because I knew it was what you all wanted. But I can't bend to your will anymore. This is my life. And last night was my choice."

She stood next to my papa while Thomas continued

to sit idly by, watching us, for whatever reason. Our discussion wasn't his business, but somehow, he'd always made it so.

"Camila Grace Bell." Her voice was much too quiet for my comfort. "I'm afraid there is nothing you can say right now to make this right."

"But, Mama!" I cried.

"Stop with the begging!" my papa roared. "You may be eighteen years old, but you are still our child. And no child of ours will go galivanting around until all hours of the night with a Cross."

"You cannot control who I love." My voice was firm despite the nerves that were rattling through me.

A dramatic hush fell over the room. Even if they had all gathered that Ridge and I were more than friends, hearing me say the words aloud was the confirmation they'd never wanted.

Papa's narrowed eyes shot darts back at me. "*Love?* You're living in my home, eating food that came from my hard-earned money, and are all set up to go to your dream college with the tuition I am providing, and you have the nerve to tell me what I can and cannot control?"

"Then don't send me to college. I don't need to go to college. I can stay right here and work. And if you don't want me to live here, then I'll take the salary you pay me and get a place of my own." My whole body shook.

Thomas looked bewildered at my suggestion. "That wasn't what you and your father agreed to. If you're going to run this vineyard one day, then the proper schooling is critical, not just for your experience, but also for our clients and investors."

Papa nodded. "Absolutely. As my daughter and future heir to Bell Family Farm and Vineyard, you have a reputation to uphold and responsibilities to adhere to. If I'm to entrust this land to you, then I'm afraid there are steps you must follow in order to claim it."

I glared at them, hating what their relationship had become, then my eyes zoned in on my papa. "What are you? His puppet? All Thomas does is order you around, and you believe every word of his gibberish. This vineyard is yours, not his. You make the rules, not him. Those clients are yours, not his. But you're so tucked away between the vines that no one even knows you still exist!"

"That's enough, Camila!" Mama took two steps forward, coming between us and pointing at me. "You disrespected this family by sneaking off all night long. Do not turn this around on your father." Her eyes were as wild as the fire in my chest.

"I'm sorry my staying out all night upset you all, but I am not sorry that I did it. Your hatred for the Cross family is completely unjust. Even the Hatfield and McCoys sit back and laugh about the days of their crazy ancestors. The rivalry needs to end. Ridge and I are determined to make that happen."

Thomas barked a laugh, causing all attention to turn to him as he stood. "You think you and your crush on the boy next door is going to end a century-old rivalry? The Crosses have disrespected your father and his land and his ancestors' land for as long as they have existed. Don't you see that by you befriending the boy, you're betraying your own family?"

My papa nodded, his eyes focused on my reaction.

Disgusted that Thomas even had a say in the fight, I ignored him and took a step closer to my parents.

"Papa," I said, trying to dull the quiver in my voice, "I'm just asking for you to listen and trust me when I tell you that Ridge is a good person. A good friend. And I do love him."

Thomas scoffed. "The only thing you know about love is the feeling you have inside when you're getting yourself into trouble. And *trouble* is exactly what Ridge Cross is. Just like his father."

Thomas's words were so similar to words Papa had said the first time I asked him about Ridge at the farmer's market that it was eerie, as if their opinion had been tattooed to their brains and no one could erase or make them change their minds. No logic could ease their fears about who Ridge Cross truly was. They didn't care. All they cared about was maintaining the feud.

My chest heated with anger. "Ridge is nothing like Harold. You would know that if you gave him a chance. Just because you have a problem with Harold shouldn't make Ridge a target. He's innocent in all of this, just like I am."

My papa scoffed. "Innocent isn't at all how he looks right now. Keeping my daughter through all hours of the night. Returning her like a used bag of potatoes." He threw his hand up, gesturing to me with disgust. "He treated my daughter like a whore. Is that what you are to him?"

I gasped, the blows becoming more painful with each shot.

"Patrick!" my mama snapped before stepping in front

of him. "Don't speak to our daughter like that. Sit and calm down. We can discuss this like adults."

My papa screamed something back at her until the two of them started bickering. I was too stunned by his words to hear anything they had to say to each other, stricken with the pain of what had come from the happiest night of my life, and my eyes were too blurry with tears to see clearly.

In those moments of silence that followed, Thomas Bradshaw saw himself out of our home, but not until his all-too-knowing eyes met mine and his whisper left a chill in his wake. "Whore."

35

RIDGE

Harold was already far out in the field, on a tractor, when I finally strolled up the drive, whistling old tunes that next morning. I had a smile on my face and a buzz in my heart, and for once, I didn't feel like I had anything to hide and I had everything to celebrate.

Friendship with Camila had always felt so impossible —if not for her wild behavior or her nonstop chatter on the hillside, then for my growing attraction to her over the years. She endeared me in a way I didn't think possible, with her insane curiosity for the land at our feet and the dreams she held so close to her heart. Those dreams had started to become mine too. Last night had felt like everything we'd ever been through or talked about had become one—one mind, one heart, and one soul. Not only did friendship feel possible now, but a deep love had bloomed from it.

I had confidence in what we had—confidence that ran so deep that I didn't care about the battles we would have to fight to make Harold, the Bells, or anyone else see it our way. When the time was right, everyone would know. Camila and I had made it so far, through numerous seasons, a secret friendship, distance, and time. We could make it through anything.

After my shower, I dressed in my farming clothes, old jeans and a flannel. I'd started to head out the kitchen door, across from the barn, when a figure stepped around the side of the house.

I froze in midstep at the sight of Thomas Bradshaw, someone who would never normally pay us a surprise visit—unless something was terribly wrong. Thomas was loyal to the Bells, which meant we were just as much his enemies as we were to his employer.

Before his appearance, nothing could have brought me down from the high I was on. But for some reason, standing in front of a man rumored around town to be as shady as a slow-moving storm cloud, I felt my sense of cool start to fade. Whatever he'd come to say wouldn't be pleasant. We weren't his clients. He had no schmoozing to do with us.

The timing of it all sent my nerves into a frenzy, spiking the fear that I'd buried down deep in my chest.

Thomas had a menacing calm that surrounded him like a block of ice. "Hello, Ridge. Hope I didn't catch you at a bad time."

I locked my stance, like I was preparing for a fight. "What do you want, Bradshaw?"

A smile curled the corners of his mouth. "I think we need to have a little chat."

"A chat?" I challenged, meeting his stare with a cold one of my own.

"Afraid so. You see, we have a little problem regarding a certain girl we both know."

I narrowed my eyelids while blood started to pump furiously through my veins. "If this is about me turning down your daughter's invite to the prom, well, then I'm sorry, sir, but Raven's just not my type. I do hope you understand."

Thomas barely flinched, but his hands responded as they balled into fists. "We both know I'm here about Camila Bell and your all-night rendezvous last night."

"I don't know what you're talking about."

His eye caught on the tractor parked near where he was standing, the same one I'd taken out with Camila. I cringed at the sight of her heels hanging off the edge.

"I see. Well, let's pretend you *were* with Camila all night long while she should have been at her prom with my son, shall we?" When I said nothing, he continued. "She's currently getting reamed by her father, thanks to you." He took another step forward. "She says she loves you, which must be true, considering she just suggested she skip college and stay in town to work in the vineyard. Because of you."

"You're lying. She's going to California. That's the plan."

"Not after her daddy told her she'd lose her school funding if she carried on with you."

Thomas must have been ten feet away, but it felt like he'd just socked me in the gut. "I don't know why you're having this discussion with me. Camila is a big girl, and she can make her own decisions. Whatever those are, I'll support them."

"I don't think I've made myself clear, so let me try

again. If Camila doesn't go to college, then she forfeits the vineyard."

I rolled my eyes and shook my head. "You honestly think I'll believe that Patrick Bell is going to refuse passing down the family business? Nice try."

He raised his eyebrows. "Call my bluff if you'd like, but when you're heir to an award-winning vineyard, those decisions aren't made alone. A family legacy is at stake, investors are involved, and those investors believe strongly in the value of a good education."

The more I thought about Thomas's words, the more sense they made. "Then there's no way she'll refuse to go to school. All she's ever talked about is following in her father's footsteps."

Thomas nodded. "She loves the vineyard very much. She also loves you. Unfortunately, she can only have one. Do you really want to be responsible for tarnishing her dreams if she chooses you?" He scoffed. "Well, you *are* a Cross. Perhaps that's been your plan all along—to be the undoing of your rival—and you'll do whatever it takes to see that plan out, including using Camila's affection for you to your advantage."

An inferno raged in my chest, and I was two seconds away from unleashing it. "I want nothing to do with the stupid rivalry. Neither does Camila. All we want is for our families to live in peace once and for all. To carry on business without meddling in each other's affairs. It's simple to us. The cornfield doesn't pose a threat to the vineyard, just like the vineyard poses no threat to our corn. Do I hate Patrick Bell for what he did to my family? Without a doubt. But it would be pointless to transfer that blame to Camila just because of where one property line ends and another begins."

Too much silence followed, creating an eerie calm between us. Then Thomas spoke again, saying the most shocking thing of all. "What if I told you I could help you end the rivalry?"

My heart pounded. "I'd call you on your bluff."

Thomas smiled. "Not surprising, but you should consider what I'm about to offer, because I think it could be the answer to all things."

Swallowing, I let an internal battle ensue. Part of me wanted nothing more than to trust Thomas Bradshaw. The rest of me knew better.

"Go ahead." My words were quiet and tentative, but the desperation woven into my tone was evident.

"Sure, I'm the one who cut your business ties and worked with the Bureau of Land Management to cut off future purchases of land. But I'm also the one who can undo it. All you have to do is agree to stay away from Camila."

"You said this deal would be the answer to all things." My heart was breaking with my words. I'd already lost the battle. The only thing left to do was salvage what I could.

"Well, I guess it's important to put a few things into perspective. What is Camila to you without her vineyard and without her dreams? Because all of it could be stripped away if she chooses you. Or, she could go off to college as planned and come home to have everything she's ever wanted. Without you."

My body shook. "Either way, I lose."

Thomas' eyes widened, and he shook his head. "No,

son. You'll have your farm, and I can assure your profit will be extraordinary compared to the losses you and your father have suffered over the years." Then his expression eased back into a smile that told me he knew he'd already won. "The only thing you'll lose in all of this is Camila." He adopted a mocking frown. "But she was never really yours to begin with, was she?"

As evil as Thomas Bradshaw was, he was right. Falling for Camila had never been the hard part. Pushing her away had always seemed to cause the problems. But I had nothing left to do. No matter what I decided, someone lost. What Thomas had offered would at least serve the people I loved.

I looked straight into the eyes of the devil and gritted my teeth. "Fine. I'll give you what you want. I'll end things."

His boastful laughter made his body shake. He stepped forward, leaving only a few feet of distance between us, so close that I could see the way his dark eyes swam with an evil gleam I would never forget. "You'll need to do more than end things. You'll need to break her heart. It's the only way to ensure it's the end. If you love her as much as you say you do, then you'll know just the thing that will break her. Whatever *that* thing is, I suggest you do it."

My entire body quaked, and I couldn't stop it. I'd done nothing to the evil men who had it out for me and my father. And the fact that Patrick Bell would treat his own daughter with such disregard was manipulative and wrong.

"She'll never forgive her father for this." I narrowed my eyes, feeling my entire world imploding in my chest.

Thomas took another step toward me. "Didn't you hear what I said? Camila's father won't be the one to break his daughter's heart. *You* will be."

We stood there for several minutes in a staring contest fit for an old Western. If a revolver were hanging from a holster around my hips, I would probably have found great use for it in that moment.

"What the hell is going on here?" Harold grumbled as he tore around the back of the house.

Thomas looked at me coldly before shifting his gaze to my father. "Just doing a little business with your son, Harold. Good to see you too."

Harold took another few steps before lifting the shotgun from his side and aiming it over my shoulder at Thomas. "Get your sorry ass off my land before I shoot you dead right here."

Thomas lifted his hands, smiling and seemingly not at all phased. Then he took a few steps to the side and reached out to grab Camila's heels off my tractor. "I'll just take these and be on my way."

I wanted to scream and lunge for the man who'd just stolen my future. But more than anything, I wanted revenge.

"Oh," Thomas said with one final glance at me over his shoulder. "You have until midnight tonight."

36

CAMILA

After the confrontation with my parents, I locked myself in my room and stayed there for hours. I cried, I screamed, then I called Josie and told her everything. Ridge and I had plans to meet soon, and I knew I had to tell him everything. If I was going to make a decision about the rest of my life, I wanted him to be part of that conversation. If anything, he would at least bring me the calm I desperately needed.

After showering and finally putting on a fresh change of clothes, I laced up my sneakers and raced through the vineyard. My cheeks were streaked with newly dried tears, and my lungs felt as if they would burst from lack of oxygen. I could barely see straight. I had to see Ridge.

I got to the bridge early and waited, sending urgent messages to Ridge to let him know I was there early and needed to see him.

Sitting there at the center of the bridge, my feet dangling over the water, I waited and thought about how years of secrecy had ended because Trip Bradshaw had to cry to his daddy about my ditching him at the dance. At least, that was what I had assumed the moment I saw his sour face staring back at me along with my parents. *How else would my father have known to wait for me?* I would never forgive Trip for that betrayal.

But I couldn't just be mad at Trip or Thomas. My parents had been just as cruel with their conditions, threatening my future as heir of the vineyard and telling me who to and who not to love. They should have known I would walk away after such ultimatums. But I didn't know where to go. I couldn't afford college on my own, and I wouldn't be awarded any type of financial aid. Without the vineyard or any other experiences, I didn't have much.

I looked desperately off into the distance of the cornfield, wishing Ridge would call or message me back. He never checked his phone and never even had it on him when he was out in the field, but it wasn't like him to be late.

After wiping the last fallen tear, I reached for my necklace, as if it had the magical ability to steady my nerves. Last night with Ridge, when my heart started beating out of control, I latched on to the beautiful gift and felt an instant calm wash over me. The same calm washed over me whenever I was near Ridge.

The desire in his eyes when he'd pushed into me, the extraordinary strength of him as he'd rocked mercilessly into me, and the way he'd stretched me as if molding me to him while he filled me with every inch of his love—it was all so surreal, and I found my hand often brushing the space below my neck to find my way back to center.

I felt around my neck for the piece of him I would

cherish forever and gasped when I realized it was no longer there.

"Oh no!" I cried and turned in a circle, hoping to spot the necklace somewhere at the bridge.

Without thinking twice about it, I raced toward the cornfield, not caring whether Harold tried to run me over with that damn tractor of his again. Nothing could make the day any worse than it already was.

I continued down the field, through the tall grass, over muddy land, and quickened my pace when I saw the hilltop up ahead. My necklace had to be there. I must have dropped it in the midst of all the excitement. But the moment I reached the top and noticed that Ridge had cleaned up all the evidence from our special night, my heart sank.

Ignoring the steadily brewing clouds, I got down on my hands and knees and started to crawl over the sparse grass. I tried hard not to panic when, after one false alarm after another, I came up empty.

Not ready to give up, I decided to retrace my steps back to the bridge and moved down the side of the hill we'd hiked down earlier that day, not stopping until I reached the foot of the mine. My eyes were on the red rocks at my feet when I finally spotted something that gave me hope. One of the roses that I'd been holding when I jumped was lying on the ground.

I reached down to pick it up, hoping to find my necklace beside it. No luck, but when I got closer to the rose, I noticed that the petals had been crushed. It wasn't the end of the world, but the disappointment weighed heavily. The previous night had been everything and more, and I hated that a piece of the night was ruined.

I stood and spun in a slow circle, noticing all too well the eerie silence that surrounded me. The sky was still darkening, and the gray clouds loomed, but the breeze that had shaken the trees minutes earlier was gone. Even the birds had stopped chirping. Everything was eerily still, like the calm before the storm.

A sudden flash of a memory of the night I'd gotten spooked in the woods entered my mind. I felt that same sense of unease that had crawled through me then, but I didn't know why. I took a slow, sweeping gaze at my surroundings but didn't see a single thing out of place.

My eyes landed on the steel bars of the mine. The door was closed, just as I remembered it from earlier that day, the padlock still hanging locked on the door, I swallowed over the quickly growing lump in my throat.

With my curiosity awakened at my discovery, I wrapped my fingers around the bars and peered inside. I'd expected to see nothing but a dark sea of nothingness, just like the first day Ridge and I had discovered the mysterious mine. Instead, an old ore-mining cart sat positioned on the rail tracks near the entrance. How had I missed that before?

Confusion and chills swept over me, causing all the hair on my body to stand on end. Fear shook through me as I swiveled around. It felt as if someone were watching my back but one thousand times stronger than before.

Nothing was out there save for an empty clearing before the section of tall grass and woods that met up with the creek. Taking a small step forward, I breathed in slowly and frantically tried to regain my wits. I had absolutely nothing to fear. But when my entire body locked up and I held my breath, I heard it—the squish of soft soil beneath heavy feet, tall brush swaying like it was being pushed aside, then stillness.

I looked in the direction of the noises with my senses on high alert. I had nowhere to run. Forward was my only choice unless I wanted to climb back up the mountain, which I could do, but I couldn't outrun whatever was out there.

Then I saw the tip of an arrow aimed straight for my head. Behind it, there was a man holding onto a bow. He wore gray camo from head to toe, and a skull mask covered his entire face.

I didn't have time to react.

He released his grip, letting the arrow fly, and my life flashed before my eyes.

37

THE HUNTER

The shot was too easy. At the precise moment the hunter released his grip on the arrow, he switched his aim, and the arrow pinned the old wood structure around the opening of the mine rather than Camila's head.

The arrow served its purpose. Camila took off running, moving so quickly that even he missed her first step. A thrill rushed through him. The chase was what he lived for. And Camila Bell had just become his next target.

He had no choice now that she'd gotten a good look at the mine. She'd seen too much, and the risk was too great. If there was ever a sound excuse to kill the girl, then that was it. She would tell someone what she'd seen, and they would investigate and find his mine tunnel and the private land it led to. They would see the years' worth of trophies from the game he'd illegally hunted, then they would arrest him and find out that he hadn't committed all that crime alone.

He'd come to the woods tonight to let off some steam. Maybe it was fate that put Camila in his path. Now that plan A had clearly failed him, killing the girl seemed like a great plan B. After all, hunting accidents happened all the time. Camila's long dark hair could easily be mistaken for an animal.

The hunter slid another arrow from the suede quiver that rested over his shoulders. And as the girl rushed by him, not more than one hundred feet away, he watched her go. He tried to stay calm, though adrenaline—which he craved more than venison—rushed through his veins.

Ten, nine, eight, seven... he counted silently, giving the girl enough time to gain somewhat of an advantage. Then the hunt began.

38

Running had always been a form of meditation for me. I'd never done it for the exercise or for the conditioning, and I'd never once competed in a school sport. I didn't have any desire to do so. But I had energy.

Over the years, I'd noticed that all the energy I dispersed thanks to my runs had been exactly what I needed. By the time I reached the hilltop, I would be so relaxed that despite whatever had sent me there in the first place, like a bad day or a fight with my parents, I had a clear mind to deal with my emotions. And without even trying, I'd earned the endurance of a lion.

I was fast. When my adrenaline fueled me, I ran even faster. But when a psychopath decided to chase me with a bow and arrow through the woods, fear stoked that adrenaline, and I flew.

Trees zoomed past my peripheral as I zig-zagged around every obstacle that could block me from the madman chasing me. Even if I was faster than he was, I couldn't outrun his arrow.

My calves screamed, and my throat burned, but my confidence, my speed, and my determination were futile. Once that second arrow whizzed straight past my head and splintered into the tree right in front of me, I knew I'd already lost.

A dark laugh boomed from deep in the woods, causing a sob to burst out of me. I couldn't have helped it if I'd tried. The terror running through my veins was far too much for me to take. But I was so close to the bridge. I couldn't give up.

Whoosh.

After another arrow came another menacing laugh.

I dug my heels into the ground, beating the life out of the soil in my escape. Though I had just a partial view through the break in the trees, I wanted to cry tears of happiness at the sight of the bridge up ahead.

The run was wearing on me, and my energy was spent. When I got a better view of the bridge, my happy tears turned to sad ones. Ridge still wasn't there. *Where is he?* He never kept me waiting for long, especially not at nighttime.

Fear twisted through me, and desperation emerged. The man in the mask was still behind me. I could hear his feet pounding against the earth. "Help!" Another sob burst from my lips. "Help!" I yelled louder while I darted toward the cornfield, on a desperate mission to find Ridge. At least there, I could hide among the corn stalks instead of running uphill through the vines.

I pushed on, though my steps slowed. But before I could clear the woods to burst into the field of corn, another arrow whizzed by me, grazing my side at my waistline before sliding through debris. My skin ripped open, and I grimaced with pain. Heat flooded my eyes as I reached for my wound, still continuing to run.

Distraction was a devil. My focus was no longer on my path ahead or weaving in creative patterns to avoid another arrow but on where Ridge could be. And that was a grave mistake.

On my next step forward, my foot caught on a giant log that I saw too late, launching me forward toward the ground just in front of the cornfield. A scream burst from my throat and pierced my lungs, and I only stopped when my head slammed to the ground.

The faint sound of a gunshot rang through the air.

I sank, oozing and dissolving into the night. Then my world started to fade to black.

39

CAMILA

A siren wailed in the distance, but somehow, I knew it was approaching.

"She's over here!"

The panicked voice confused me. It didn't belong to Ridge, and he was who I wanted to hear. At least, that was what I remembered through the fog clouding my head.

But why does everything hurt? The pain in my side stung like no other. Every single muscle in my body ached, and my calves burned, like I'd run too fast for too long. I groaned as I homed in on my splintering headache, which made my head feel like it was going to explode.

Don't cry, Wild One.

I could practically hear Ridge's words like a whisper in the wind.

Hands grabbed me and rolled me onto my back. I groaned, but in my mind, I was screaming bloody murder. I just wanted the pain to stop.

"She's breathing!" the person cried, then I felt his face get closer. "Camila, can you hear me?"

Cries of relief and footsteps approached, then bodies started to crowd around me. My eyes fluttered open, and I tried to ignore the pain to see who was by my side. Dark hair and age lines came into view.

"Gus." My words were barely a whisper. "What's going on?" Even with my mind shouting at my body to move, I couldn't.

Gus nodded. "You're going to be fine. You're safe now." His friendly eyes searched mine. "What were you doing in Harold's cornfields, Camila? After that awful fight with your father, you should have known better."

"Mija, what were you thinking?"

I turned to see Mama's knees falling into the dirt on the other side of me. She grabbed my hand and squeezed. My eyes panned to directly above me, where my papa stood with his hands on his hips and head bowed, like he was ready to cry. I couldn't process their worry. Shaking my head, I tried to sit up again and felt my strength starting to return.

Gus added pressure, keeping me down. "Don't try to move too fast," he scolded me. "You hit your head pretty badly, and you're bleeding at your waist. Help is on the way, but you need to take it easy until it arrives."

I fought through my swimming headache to try to regain some semblance of clarity. For me to feel the way I did, what had happened must have been bad. Slowly, bits and pieces began to come back to me—the fight with my parents, the bridge, and the missing necklace.

One by one, I retraced my steps, which brought me down the wrong side of the mountain, where I'd seen the

272

gated mine. My heartbeat started to quicken as a flash of camo and a matching skull mask visible through the weeds came to mind. And as I pictured the arrowhead flying through the air, I could almost believe it was happening all over again.

Like a bullet, I shot up, ignoring Gus's hold and the pain that lanced through my body. My breaths quickened as I panned the space around us. All I saw was a vision of a gray camouflage skull mask and a mad hunter on the prowl for my blood.

"Where is he? Where's the man in the mask?" Panic flooded through me until the fog that had drowned me before I'd passed out returned.

I started to stand, but Gus held me down. "Take it easy, Camila. You're going to be okay."

"*What?*" I shrieked, not understanding how he could be so calm. "There was a man who was chasing me through the woods with a bow and arrow." My breaths came too fast, and my words had become muddled. "He shot at me. He was trying to kill me!" Tears flowed down my cheeks.

Gus grabbed my shoulders and squeezed. "He's dead, Camila."

I didn't think I'd heard him right. I blinked hard, trying to steady his face in my gaze. "What?"

"He's dead. You're going to be okay. And that… man…" Gus spit out the word like he'd just chewed up garbage. "Will never hurt you again."

I finally registered his words. "But how?" I panned the space again. "Where is he?"

Gus lifted his flashlight and revealed a lifeless body lying on the ground about a hundred feet away. Then he panned up, revealing another man, one with a shotgun hanging by his side. Bruno was there, too, sharp teeth bared, and his growl was low and constant as he stared down at the masked man. My body started to shake again at the sight of Harold Cross, who had a sullen look on his face.

"*Y-You* killed him?"

Harold glared back at me. "Bruno here was growling like a lunatic before he took off toward the woods. Went after him, and that's when I saw the son of a bitch with his weapon aimed at you. Didn't even think. I just shot him. But I didn't mean to kill him. Would have liked to see the bastard behind bars for trespassing."

The fact that the man who'd tried to run me over with a tractor had just saved my life gave me a shock. Shaking it off, I looked at Gus. "Please help me up."

"Camila—"

"Gus, help me up. I need to see the face of the man who tried to kill me." I stared firmly into his eyes. "Please."

He sighed and finally helped me to my feet. With his arms around me, we limped over to the body at Harold's feet. His skull mask had already been removed, and it rested eerily on his chest. Trip aimed his flashlight at the man, and the moment I got a good look at him, I shuddered.

"Do you recognize him, Camila?"

I looked between Gus and Harold, confused. "No." I looked down at the man again. "I've never seen him before. Should I recognize him?"

Harold shrugged then cleared his throat. "This here is Dave Lachey, a livestock farmer from Ouray."

Lachey, Lachey, Lachey. The familiar last name repeated in my mind as I tried to place it. Then it hit me, and my eyes shot back up to Harold's. "Jason's brother? From Camp Lachey?" If anything, I only felt more confused. "But why? Why would he want to hurt me? I've never even met him."

Harold's permanent scowl deepened. "Jason's a client of mine, so I knew of his brother. Crazy Dave, they call him. Disturbed fella. My guess is he was out here huntin', and when he saw you, he must have thought you were a deer or somethin'."

I frowned, still trying to piece together the events of the day. Anxiety at the fact that anyone would think of what had just happened as an accident gripped me. I'd looked directly into that man's eyes. He'd laughed as he was chasing me, like I was part of some sick game he was playing.

"No," I said finally with an adamant shake of my head. "He was toying with me. Letting me gain distance so that he could hunt me." I shivered. "At one point, I ran right by him, and he didn't even try to take a shot."

Harold cringed. "I don't know, Camila. Like I said, the man was disturbed. Been in and out of jail for poachin' crimes. But I don't think he would ever hurt a human."

Unable to look at the dead man anymore, I took a wobbly step back. With my energy depleted, my entire body started to give out, but I didn't want to leave. Even though Harold had saved my life, and Gus had been there when I awoke, something felt wrong. The pit of my stomach hardened when I realized exactly where that feeling was coming from. The loss in my heart was too strong to ignore.

"Harold, where's Ridge?" For a second, I panicked that someone would get angry with me, but then I realized I didn't care. I needed to see him. I needed to know that he was okay.

Gus and my parents averted their eyes, and Harold cleared his throat again. "He's gone, darlin'. Left town. Said for you not to look for him neither."

My lips parted, but my heart didn't believe a single word. "No." I shook my head. "He wouldn't do that to me. He wouldn't just leave."

He promised. Ridge promised he wouldn't leave me again. But even as I tried to deny the inevitable, deep down, I knew the truth. Ridge hadn't been at the bridge when he should have been, and Harold had still been out in the field late at night, when he usually wasn't. "He sent you to the bridge to talk to me?"

Harold nodded. "Yes, darlin', he did."

Fresh tears stung the backs of my eyes, and my heart squeezed with every last shred of hope I'd had left for him.

"Camila," my mama said gently. "Let's get you back to the house, where you can rest. I'm sure the authorities will be here soon, and they're going to have a lot of questions."

After another moment of silence and a nod to Harold Cross, I squeezed Gus tight and let him walk me toward the vineyard. And with one final backward glance, I said goodbye to my past.

I had always known he wasn't mine to keep, but that didn't change the way I loved him—quietly, gently, and from afar.

As the seasons changed, the corn stalks grew strong, and the grapevines flourished with hope. But none of it mattered, not when the soil at our feet bound us in a century-old rivalry. We'd never even had a chance.

They said life flashed before your eyes on the way to death, but on that night, after my final scream burst from my throat and my world started to fade to black, I only thought of him and his sweet chocolate eyes, his desperately cautious stare, and his silence that carried more weight than gold.

I should have died that night. Instead, I crossed the moonlit bridge and never returned. I let rivalry win. If only that had been enough to keep us all safe. If only we didn't have a bridge between us.

CHAPTER 40

CAMILA

Nothing could have prepared my heart for the nostalgia that swept over me the moment I stepped back onto the vineyard grounds earlier today.

It seems like a lifetime has passed since the days when my world felt as endless and wild as the fields I used to run through, when life was nothing but one big adventure, bountiful and there for the taking. But things have changed, and life has changed us all.

A cold breeze blows in as I push open the French doors to the balcony of my old bedroom. After locking them in place, I quickly zip my puffy white jacket up as far as it will go.

I often used to stare out at the vineyard from this very spot. Beyond the gentle slope of land are trees with a craggy creek and a wooden bridge. But the purpose of the bridge is useless. The symbolism is futile. It doesn't connect us. Instead, it separates the two things I once loved most in the world, rendering me helpless.

Panning slowly, I take in the familiar view, which provides a much different perspective from when I was younger. When I was a child, the winter months were never my favorite. I couldn't see the beauty in the white gold that powdered the earth or appreciate the crisp freshness in the air. When everything lay calm and quiet, the chaos in me brewed like a deadly storm threatening to strike. Winter always felt like my personal prison.

Maybe the simple fact that I'm older now is why I find peace in what used to be my chaos. I can look at the iced-over vines and see life in what I used to believe lay dormant for six months out of the year. Now, I know better. While the buds won't blossom and the leaves won't spring to life, a much different story lies beneath the surface, where the roots still grow, soaking up nutrients while preparing for spring.

The root system of a grapevine is a phenomenon I've come to understand in a way that feels parallel to my life for the past ten years. Perhaps, in a way, I've been lying dormant too. While I've spent time away from the family vines, I never stopped growing, learning, and readying myself for the future I've always dreamed of. I just wasn't sure that dream was what I wanted anymore—after I lost him that night.

I suck in a deep breath then release it in a slow, steady stream. Ready or not, I'm home.

Home is such a strange word for a place that has felt like my worst nightmare for more than a decade. But the long-lasting effects of that night did more than break my heart. My family never recovered, torn apart by the rivalry that started it all. I left for college, and my mama moved into the guest villa. Three months ago, Papa died from a stroke while snipping grapes from the vines he loved so much. As promised, he left the Bell Family Vineyard and all its business operations to me—if I chose to accept.

As a college graduate with various degrees from UC Davis, all in the fields of viticulture and enology, and with numerous international studies under my belt, I can say I've put in the work. Now it's time to pay my dues where they matter most.

With a quick turn, I enter my old room and toss my jacket onto the vintage four-post bed before making my way into the bathroom to get ready for dinner. As I switch on the sink faucet, I can already smell the rich aroma of a home-cooked paella. It's just a scent from my favorite rice-and-seafood dish, but it envelops me just the same as my memories do every time I visit home. Only this time, its powerful fragrance has a different effect on me, one that churns in my gut and fires off every nerve ending in my body.

After Papa's death, Mama moved back into her old bedroom to grieve for him. Though their marriage had been broken for years, she never gave up hope that he would come back around. Neither of them gave me any intimate details, but I always assumed the fact that they never separated completely was a silent promise to each other that they would never find another love like they shared.

I cup my hands under the warm running water and lean down to wash my chilled face. I'll have to get used to the frigid winter again. Living in northern California, not having to be in icy conditions or worry about the tips of my hair freezing together, spoiled me.

After turning off the faucet, I grab a rolled-up hand towel from the small basket on the sink to dry off and look at myself in the mirror.

My dark-brown hair is gently tousled from traveling, though it's nothing a quick finger-comb can't fix. My face, on the other hand, is going to need something more. I have dark circles under my eyes from the lack of sleep last night, and the permanent ache in my side intensifies by the moment.

Anxious feelings have always had the habit of keeping me awake, but the thought of returning home permanently has been twisting me up inside for weeks. Now that I'm actually here, I'm in knots.

My eyes flutter closed as I pull in a deep breath and focus on steadying my heart rate. Combatting the memories of my past was much easier when I stopped by for weekends a few times a year before flying back to California. I holed myself up in the house, visited with family and friends who swung by, then went on my way. As tempting as it was to trace the roots of my past and run through the vines to the bridge and beyond, going back there, either physically or mentally, was too painful to bear.

Nightmares from that night haunt me often. They feel so real sometimes that I wake up in a cold sweat, screaming at the top of my lungs. When I finally snap out of it and realize it's all a dream, I think of Ridge. His face is the only memory that regulates my breathing. Despite how it all ended, thoughts of him still manage to bring me peace, even when he isn't with me.

Well, except for now, when seeing him again is more of a reality than ever. I can't stop thinking about how I'll react or what I'll say, and I can't imagine the reunion will be anything but uncomfortable. While I have so many questions, I'm too hardened from the pain to ask them and too broken to care about the answers.

Unfortunately, growing up in the small town of Telluride, I learned that there is no such thing as "avoiding your problems." Everybody knows your business, and those who want you to fail will be the first to announce the news the moment you do. Good folks exist, too, but weeds grow in even the greenest grass, and snakes find a way to slither through it all.

Leaving my bathroom, I focus on the here and now —namely tonight's festivities. Most of my wardrobe boxes are still sealed, but I still have a closet full of old clothes. Something should still fit me. I head to a back corner of my closet and spy an old yellow sundress that is absolutely wrong for tonight, considering it was my favorite summer dress when I was fourteen. I run my fingers over the worn cotton fabric and shiver, remembering the exact reason it was my favorite.

"A little girl could get lost in these cornfields, dressed like that."

Ridge's quiet voice is just a memory, but it's as clear as the day he said the words. My chest squeezes, and my next deep breath fights through my tightened airways. Every thought of him always brings the bad with the good, and there's no getting around it, going back, or forgetting. I'm alone with my thoughts, which threaten to suffocate me whenever they come. And as I always do, I stuff all thoughts of him to the back of my mind and try to cope with whatever task is at hand.

Red fabric catches my eye, and I immediately go to it. I purchased the dress on a whim in high school with

Ridge in mind, but the moment I brought it home and Mama took one look at it, she ordered me to put it back in the closet. It has stayed here all these years, and though it's not exactly weather appropriate, I have no plans to escape into the chilly night.

I slip on the flowy robe-like fabric and pull the long sheer sleeves over my arms. The dress has a slit up the right side that reaches midthigh and a plunging neckline that stops just above my belly button. For a last-minute wardrobe find, it works pretty well.

After curling my hair and pulling it up into a half ponytail, I choose some simple silver jewelry for my neck and ears then pluck a pair of heeled black boots from my closet. The whole ensemble is a bit too elegant for my taste, but tonight's affair isn't meant to be simple. The soiree awaiting me is a celebration of sorts, one where I'm the guest of honor. Everyone is trying desperately to move on after my papa's death, and they're looking to me to lead the way.

As soon as I begin to descend the mahogany staircase, not only does the scent of what's in the kitchen bring my senses to life, but the hearty laughter of my mom, the vineyard workers, and our close friends reels me into the present.

This is real. This is happening.

As heir to the Bell Family Vineyard and Winery, I've come to take what's mine—what used to always feel like mine. And I'll feel that way again.

My first order of business: to right the wrongs that have cursed my family for over a century and rewrite the future before it's too late.

CHAPTER 41

RIDGE

Flickering lights dance on the Mediterranean villa as the party lives on. I never expected to be invited to the homecoming celebration, though I would not have gone if I had been. While a truce exists between farms now, an underlying tension remains.

Still, my curiosity got the better of me, and I hiked up the snow-covered mountain to reach the hilltop in the dark. Being sheathed in darkness is a benefit when you want to remain invisible to the only person in your life who has ever truly seen you. But that was a long time ago.

For the past three months, word has spread like wildfire about Camila Bell coming back to town. "Roll out the red carpets. Patrick Bell's heir is coming home." Those might not have been the locals' exact words, but they spoke of her coming home as if she's royalty. With the Bell Family Vineyard being an agricultural staple for our small town, I guess I can understand why. But emotions are definitely mixed among the townsfolk, since most of them remember the incident that took place before she moved away.

So many different versions of what happened that night have circulated, but Harold was there, and he told me what he saw—that a hunter trespassed and mistook Camila for an animal. Bruno took off toward the commotion in the woods, putting Harold on alert. Camila ran in the direction of the cornfields, fear on her face, and Harold spotted a man holding a bow and arrow behind her. He pointed his shotgun right at the man's chest. Camila tripped, and Harold fired, killing the hunter on the spot. Not until he ripped away the man's hunting mask did he recognize him as Jason Lachey's brother, Dave.

I still get chills when I imagine the events as Harold explained them. The other stories floating around, the ones in which Camila thought Dave Lachey was purposely chasing her through the woods, are too disturbing to believe. I took comfort in knowing that Camila was alive and well and ready to live out her dreams.

Camila always knew she would run her papa's vineyard. She was so proud to one day contribute to her family's legacy, and I knew her well enough not to second-guess her. Once Camila's mind was set on something, her determination won out every single time. I assume nothing has changed in that regard, even if it did take her papa's death for her to come back to Telluride.

I don't know what I expected to see or feel when I made the late-night trek up the cold hillside, but the heavy weight on my chest tells me I'm not going to figure it out tonight. Too many hearts have been broken.

Hatred has won. And while Camila will carry on her father's legacy, I'm still trying to salvage what I can of mine.

Camila and I may be neighbors again, but we are right back to where we started—enemies with a bridge between us.

Pressing my palms into the snow behind me, I make a move to stand, then something in the upper story of the villa catches my eye. I recognize the balcony to Camila's bedroom and the French doors that open onto it.

Until this moment, no one from the party has stepped outside. I assume their attire leaves them much too cold to dare catch a chill. But when a puffy white jacket, dark-brown hair, and a face that often haunts my dreams appear on the balcony, my heart stops midbeat.

I breathe out slowly, releasing a sheer curtain over a sight I can't quite believe. It's as if I've been punched with the reality I should have been prepared for. But no one can feel prepared when facing the ghost of their past.

A vision of Camila from the last time I held her in my arms invades my mind. Her long beautiful hair that hung over her shoulders and brushed my naked chest as she rode me. Her anger at what she felt was my betrayal, exhibited in the quick jerk of her hips as she took me deeper. Her long white fingernails that dug into my chest, clinging to me as if I were going to vanish at any moment. Camila's gorgeous green eyes that were focused on mine, daring me to look away with that same ferocity that had intrigued me from the start. Her long lashes that fell to the tops of her cheeks as her dark-pink lips parted just enough to let a high-pitched moan escape at the first sign of another orgasm.

She was in command that secret night we found our way back together, taking the reins and pleasuring me in all the ways I had been dreaming about. I didn't deserve it. I didn't deserve *her* after what I had done and where I had been. If Camila Bell had a chance in hell of following her dreams, then it would have to be without the weight of our families' history.

So I walked away from her again, hating myself more and more every step I took in the wrong direction, knowing she would never forgive me for it.

I watch now as she grips the balcony rail while she looks out across the downward slope of the vineyard. Even from here, I can see the longing for what once was on her face. She looks toward the entrance to the woods and the bridge that brought her to me in the beginning. I can tell she's thinking of the dreams we once shared before they all turned to nightmares.

Or maybe she isn't thinking about any of that at all. Maybe I'm the one who feels the longing in my gut, in my soul, and in every single beat of my heart. That would explain the ache in my chest, which intensifies every time I think of my Wild One.

As if she can hear me saying her name, she looks up in my direction. For a second, I can imagine our eyes meeting again and that same spark in me fighting the same fire we shared when we were younger. I think of the taste of her lips as I gave in to feelings that couldn't be hidden any longer.

We were a wildfire, and together, we made a

firestorm—a tornado of heat and wind—with our families' hollow pasts driving a wedge between us.

But life is so much different now. Our pasts have been cruel. Our time together was over before it ever truly began. And just as our ancestors have taught us, there is no such thing as rewriting the past. If anything, history will repeat itself.

CHAPTER 42

CAMILA

"Camila, come help me in the kitchen."

Mama's voice sounds chipper, carrying well over the crowd noise coming mostly from the living room.

"Coming, Mama." I take a glance around the grand entrance hall. It seems everyone was invited tonight, from my papa's old poker buddies, to the vineyard workers, to long-time customers. My old acquaintances from school are here, too, which is strange, since I haven't spoken to many of them since I moved away. But that's the thing about small towns. No one ever becomes a stranger.

I sneak the rest of the way down the staircase and into the kitchen. When I spot Mama hard at work, I laugh. She doesn't need my help at all. The paella is already done, warming in a big pot on the stove, while a few men and women are bustling around her, preparing the bread, dessert, and appetizers.

"Looks like you have it covered, Mama."

She smiles at me over her shoulder, the skin around her eyes crinkling around the edges. At first glance, it appears that she has barely aged. Her caramel skin is still smooth, save for the deep frown lines around her mouth and the gray streaks through her dark-brown hair. She might be fifty-five, but she's just as beautiful as she ever was.

Mama reaches out a hand, and when I take it, she pulls me to her. "It doesn't feel that way. I haven't cooked a feast for this many people in years."

Joy lights up her eyes, causing a pang to hit my heart. "You miss it, don't you?"

She nods, her smile slipping. "I miss him too, mija. He was a hard worker, your papa. Despite our differences, I loved how much he loved this place. His passion kept us together for so long."

"And his passion broke you both too. I know, Mama." I frown, and my heart feels heavy. I hate the reminder of how my parents fell apart. Sometimes I blame myself for what became of them. If I had never fallen in love with Ridge, I wouldn't have betrayed my papa's wishes. I wouldn't have left Trip on the night of the dance, my papa wouldn't have become so infuriated with me, I wouldn't have taken off that night in search of a necklace I never found, and I wouldn't have ended up alone in the woods with a masked man who still haunts my dreams. Maybe then my parents wouldn't have had a constant reason to argue after I moved out of the house. When Papa buried himself in his work more than ever before, my mama felt left behind and alone.

My hand moves to the spot on my neck where my

necklace once hung. I know better than to wish for a different fate than I was handed. As badly as I want to, there's no use dwelling in the past. I will never regret loving Ridge Cross. I hope my mama doesn't have regrets either.

"He loved you so much," I offer softly.

Her expression changes again, to a hardened one she adopted from having to stand up to her stubborn husband. "All that man had to do while I prepared for events like this was drink his bourbon and light up cigars with his boys in the casita."

I laugh and wrap an arm around Mama while letting my cheek rest on her shoulder. "You were always so good to us. Thank you for helping out tonight. I know it's hard for you."

She slips a cautious look my way. "For you, too, mija. Don't think you can fool me with that painted-on smile and this big, fancy party. It's been ten years since you've lived here. In a lifetime, that's not that long."

"I'm fine." I repeat the words in my mind, like I might eventually believe them.

Mama's eyes search mine before she lets out a sigh and squeezes the arm I have wrapped around her shoulders. "Well, for what it's worth, your papa would have been so proud to know you've chosen to carry out the family legacy. He was already thrilled about your schooling and all your travel. In a way, I think he always lived vicariously through you."

Her expression grows wistful. She's spoken to me about her many wishes, and convincing Papa to take her away on vacations was one of them. He dedicated his life to the vineyard, and Mama was along for the ride, whether she was unhappy or not. She's unquestionably loyal, patient, and the kindest person I'll ever know, which is why she never felt the need to divorce him. She always held out hope that he would see what he'd lost.

"You think?"

"Oh, yes. Patrick always wanted to travel, but he never made time for it. He always said he wanted something different for you—something more than he would have ever allowed for himself. Hence the reason he pushed you so hard to leave."

A dark cloud passes through my thoughts. "Sometimes I got the sense that he wanted me out of the way."

Mama purses her lips, and she shakes her head. "No, mija. How could you ever think that? He loved you very much. He always lit up at the thought of giving you this place, and he always believed you would do great things with it." She frowns. "I will say this, though. I think there were things he didn't want you to see over the past ten years. Bad business deals he made, the financial hardship he underwent, and the quality he sacrificed to bottle more wine more often. It just all started to go downhill. He barely spoke of it, but it was impossible to ignore that he'd lost sight of why he loved this place."

I hate to think about my papa losing his grip on this vineyard. *How could this place possibly come up against financial hardship?* It doesn't make sense, but I'm sure I'll find out more than I ever wanted to know soon enough.

My throat becomes thick with emotion. "Well. He made his choices."

She nods. "He did. And he was very happy once. I think he was always fighting to get back to that happy place.

But in the process, he missed out on so much." A beat of heavy silence falls over us, then she squeezes my hand again. "Promise me, mija. Promise me that you will never stop doing whatever it is that makes you happy. Whether it be travel or taking more classes." She looks out the long window above the sink toward the fields. "These vines have a tricky way of digging deep into your soul and entangling you with their roots. And let me tell you, Camila. Feeling trapped is a curse I would never dream for you to bear."

For a second, I think of the haunting truth of her words. Papa's behavior and his need for revenge based on an ancient family feud was out of control. The rage that overcame him when he found out about Ridge and me is still a haunting memory. Being torn from the person you love feels very much the same as being trapped. But he never tried to see my side of things.

After we finish preparing the rest of dinner and stick some side dishes into the oven, I help Mama out to the party to find her a seat. She has been in the kitchen all day, and I insist that she take it easy. We have staff to do the serving.

"Welcome home, Camila. I think a congratulations is in order."

I look up to find Thomas Bradshaw, whose smile is failing to meet his eyes. My stomach churns at the phony congratulations, and I know this encounter is only the first of many to come.

"Thank you, Thomas. It's nice to be back."

He nods, assessing me with his eyes. "No one is more excited to have you back than your mother, of course, but I know my son is eager to get reacquainted as well.

You and Trip were quite chummy back in the day. Perhaps you will be again."

I push out a laugh, trying to hide my discomfort. Even after ten years, Thomas is still hinting for us to become more. "Surely Trip has found a wife by now." I know he hasn't, but I hope my comment is enough to keep Thomas at bay.

"You know my son. He's a picky one, that boy. Trust me. I've been putting the pressure on for years. I'm ready for grandbabies by now."

Though I've always thrown up caution flags around Thomas Bradshaw, he's certainly throwing me off tonight. His hearty tone almost gives me the belief that he wants to work around any animosity we've shared in the past, and maybe that's not such a bad thing, seeing as we'll be working together.

"Trip was going to come tonight, but a client dinner pulled him away."

I don't care enough to question what Thomas means by "client dinner," so I allow the rush of relief to wash over me, knowing that an awkward reunion has been avoided. During my short visits, Trip and his sister, Raven, were two people I tried to avoid at all costs.

"Well," I say, pushing out a smile, "I'll be happy to see him when we run into each other again. I hope he's doing well."

The confused look Thomas gives me next and the questionable glance at mama cause a stirring in my gut.

"What is it?" I look between Mama and Thomas with a laugh. "What am I missing here?"

My mama pats my leg while shooting Thomas a warning glare. "Nothing that needs to be discussed tonight, Camila. Drink wine. Be merry. Tomorrow will be a day for business."

For the next hour, while I mingle with old friends and family, my mama's words continue to shake me. Josie finally snaps me out of it with a pointed look before grabbing my hand and pulling me around the foyer and down the back hallway.

When we reach the arched wooden door that leads down to the wine cellar, she throws me a grin over her shoulder, and I laugh. She and I, sneaking downstairs into the cave to sip from the barrels of all the blended wines my parents have recently been sampling, feels all too familiar. We always giggled too much and shared all our secrets.

Plenty of barrels are ready, but we're older now, so sneaking wine is no longer necessary. She quickly scans the section of vintage wine on the far wall, grabs one, and sets it on an old wooden table that has tree stumps for legs. "Sit," she says, her tone warning me that a lecture is to come.

I sit slowly as a sense of warning swirls through me. "What is this about, Josie? You realize we have practically an entire vineyard of wine upstairs at the party."

She makes a face and starts to uncork the bottle. "That doesn't sound nearly as much fun as it is to open a dusty old bottle. It's your fault, you know. Abner hates my taste for rich vintage." She grins as the cork pops.

Abner is her husband, a stockbroker in downtown Telluride. They live in a quaint section of town that overlooks the box canyon. They're madly in love. I like to believe it's only a matter of time before they start popping out kids. I'm happy for my best friend, though I would give anything to go back in time and spend the day together, free of all responsibility and with our one main concern in life being the boys we chose to give our hearts to.

"Are you sure it's not your own fault? I happen to remember you being a very strong influence on my disobedience."

She lets out a laugh. "Influence? More like accomplice. I wasn't *Wild One*." She winks, and my stomach turns at the old nickname. "You very much did as you pleased and couldn't be peer pressured by anyone."

Okay, maybe Josie is right about that. I may have been the one to encourage her to join me on numerous adventures, all of which our parents would have throttled us over. But I can't say I have a single regret after all we had the chance to experience.

Josie holds up a glass, gesturing for me to pick up mine. "To you, for finally coming home to stay. It's where you belong, friend, as hard as it is for you to admit."

I bow my head, accepting her toast. "To home." I pinch out a smile and clink my glass with hers. She holds my eyes while we sip, and I know she's got a follow-up brewing. I can feel it, thickening the air like a fog hovering over our heads.

"I was going to wait to bring this up if I could help it, but I simply can't. There's a giant elephant in the room, and I think we need to talk about him."

Even I thought Josie would wait to broach the subject. She knows we don't talk about him. I *can't* talk about him. "It's pointless, Josie. He's in my past, buried there six feet deep, and that's where he'll stay."

Lies. Blatant, transparent, phony, lies. But love means that

I've gotten great at keeping secrets, even from my best friend.

"I don't believe you."

I shrug, knowing my response is stubborn and immature, but the way my insides feel like they want to crawl out of my skin tells me this isn't the time or the place for this conversation. "I don't need you to believe me. Even if I did want to see him, I wasn't the one who left. Twice." Just saying the words causes my throat to tighten and anger to brew in my chest. "I'm not having this conversation," I whisper.

She stares at me before she settles back in her seat and takes a gulp of her drink. When she pulls the glass away, she pinches the stem between the pads of her fingers. "I'm not asking you to tell me what happened between you two after that awful night."

"Good," I snap.

"But you're back," she says, ignoring my harsh tone. "And while you've been able to avoid Ridge all this time, the question isn't whether you'll see him again but when. It's just a matter of time."

I open my mouth to cut her off, but she's too fast.

"And when you do see him again, you'd better be careful, Camila." Josie's eyes widen, fear burning bright around her irises and making my heart beat faster.

"Things have changed a lot around here since you moved away. You're back for good now, so you're going to see that. But you know better than most that history repeats itself. This town doesn't need another Bell-Cross feud rising from the ashes."

I swallow and straighten my shoulders so that she can see how serious I am. "Ridge broke my heart, Josie. It was over then. It's still over. And if I see him again—*when* I see him again—I'll be cordial. But I'll never forget."

Josie seems like she wants to trust my words but isn't confident that she can. "Okay," she says finally. Then she nods, as if finally accepting my answer. "Okay."

CHAPTER 43

CAMILA

The party lasts for too many hours. I feel drunk and worn out from a night of laughing with people I barely know while masking a longing for someone I know all too well. A decade is long enough for feelings for a long-lost love to fade. For my family and peers, ten years is long enough to forget completely.

But I know something that no one else in this room does. It's been five years since I last saw Ridge Cross, not ten.

Four years after leaving Telluride marked the significance of many things. Ridge and I were supposed to reunite and be together again, but that was before he decided to break my heart. Another was my first college graduation at UC Davis. The last was Harold Cross's death.

Word quickly spread around town then to me about the old corn farmer's freak accident. Harold had been breaking up crusted grain in a silo bin when he slipped into it. Seconds later, the kernels sucked him under like quicksand, and he died.

Upon hearing the news, I didn't think twice. I caught the first flight to Telluride Regional Airport and went to Ridge. I drove right up to the Crosses' farmhouse and pounded on the front door. Hours later, I found out I was already too late.

According to the court docs, on that same dry summer night of his father's death, Ridge got drunk and took Harold's tractor out to the middle of the field, where he started a fire, burning every last bit of the crop to the ground. The Cross Farm failed to produce corn that year, and Ridge Cross went to San Miguel County Jail for fourth-degree arson.

One year after his sentence, I found myself back in Telluride, in front of the jail, awaiting his release. I will never forget seeing him again after all that time, nor will I forget the way his newly cold eyes found mine, stopping my heart completely. I hated him, but I loved him just the same.

At that point, it had been five years since I'd laid eyes on Ridge. He was twenty-five, and if I had to guess by the looks of him, jail hadn't treated him kindly.

He'd broken my heart into a million pieces, he'd lost his last living parent, and he was a convicted arsonist. Yet my heart still rattled my ribcage like it wanted to break free at the sight of him.

Ridge looked like a true rebel that day, wearing a pair of khakis, a black T-shirt, and black boots. His hair looked like it had recently been cut, and his face still carried the strength it always had, but I couldn't get over the coldness of his stare. What used to remind me of melting chocolate had hardened to blocks of ice. If I had thought they would thaw with one glance at me, I was very wrong.

I gestured for him to come forward, staying put in my rental car while my heart thrummed like a hummingbird. I hadn't dared go home to get my Jeep for fear that someone would know the reason for my visit. While a truce existed between families, that truce didn't apply to me and Ridge. I'd caught on long ago to the reason for Ridge's disappearance that night. I was the bargaining chip, and Ridge had obeyed to protect his father's land. He ended a century-old feud just like that, as if I were collateral damage that didn't deserve a second thought.

Outside the jail, Ridge looked as if he was contemplating his next move. His head moved one way then the other, like he wanted to make a quick exit. I wouldn't try to stop him. I wasn't setting a trap. He'd just gotten out of jail, and the last thing I wanted to do was to put him back behind a different set of bars. He was free. All I could do was put the offer out there.

Minutes passed, but when Ridge started to move toward me, my heartbeat quickened. It felt like he'd just jolted me back to life. As stubborn as I had been over the past five years, promising myself I would never forgive him, I realized that feelings and forgiveness were two separate things. I could hate him for what he did while still loving the man I remembered. The conflict was beyond my skills of processing, and in that moment, I chose not to try.

Every step toward me was like an unveiling of the new Ridge Cross, who was a product of the unkind world. He was still the innocent boy who had lost his mother, yet the mask he wore appeared impenetrable. He didn't crack a smile, his eyes didn't light up at the sight of me, and each step toward me was at the same stoic pace as the one before it.

Ridge got into the passenger seat of my car. Neither of us spoke a word as I drove, and he didn't question my direction when I passed the entrance to his ranch. He didn't ask me to slow down when I took the mountain turns too fast. Instead, he rolled down his window and faced the fresh air while we cruised through the San Juan Mountains. His silence was enough. It had always been enough.

I pulled into a quaint plot of land with log cabins, tents, and hot springs and took a deep breath. It felt like my first. Then I looked at Ridge, who was slowly turning his neck to face me.

I swallowed, suddenly feeling nervous. When I'd made the decision to pick him up from the jail, I didn't have a plan, just a need. I *needed* to see him and know he would be okay. But I was starting to realize that Ridge wasn't the one I had to worry about. I would break yet again when it was all over.

"I'm going to get us a room."

His eyes narrowed slightly. "Why?" His voice was deeper than I remembered, and the softness was lost.

I blew out a breath. "I-I don't know."

"For how long?"

Annoyance shot through me. "Why? Is there somewhere you need to be?"

His glare darkened. "How long, Camila?"

Our history was far too fragile to test the waters. Despite all we'd been through and all he'd done, I'd wanted to be the first person he saw out of jail. And I wanted for us to be alone. Beyond that, I didn't think. I just acted.

"I don't know. I didn't plan this. I just wanted to make sure you were okay, and I—I thought we could talk."

He shook his head. "No talking."

My heart sank, which was unfair to Ridge. I was the one who'd brought him there, and I'd told myself over and over again that I had no expectations, but maybe I had. Maybe in the pile of rubble that was my heart, I'd hoped for Ridge to want to put those pieces back together and honor the promise he'd made to me long ago. *Four years, tops.* Apparently, none of that mattered to him anymore.

The only room left was what the owner called his "well house," which was just a small log cabin with a king bed, a wood-burning stove, a bathroom, and a private hot spring. I wished the beautiful details of the elegant, authentic-looking cabin had stolen my attention when we walked in. It had a lot to take in, if it weren't for the man who entered the cabin behind me.

He showered before putting back on the clothes he'd come with—I cursed myself for not thinking to bring him a new shirt and pants, which wouldn't remind us both of where he'd been for the past year—then he walked toward the front door and opened it.

My heartrate quickened with fear that he was leaving me.

"I'm going for a walk," he growled without looking back at me, then he let himself out and shut the door behind him.

He was gone for hours, leaving me to my dark, unhappy thoughts. Regret wasn't something I often felt, but I was starting to wonder if picking Ridge up had been a bad idea. The fact that he'd gotten into my car was all I had to hold on to. But with every second he was gone, I became unglued.

I was sitting outside by the campfire I'd made when he returned, and I followed him into the cabin, my insides shaking with anger. I slammed the door behind me, causing him to whip around and stare wide-eyed back at me.

Finally, a reaction.

"I get it, Ridge. You don't want to talk. I can respect that, but at least *be with me.*"

He glared. "Forgive me for not wanting to be holed up any more than I already have been. I just went for a walk. You could have gone too."

My jaw dropped. "You didn't ask me to come. You left, just like you always do."

His jaw ticked. "When did you start needing permission to do what you wanted to? If you'd wanted to walk with me, then you would have walked."

With a frustrated growl, I turned away and headed out to the fire to put it out. *What was I thinking, bringing him here? What was he thinking by coming if all he wants to do is get away from me?*

I beat myself up in my thoughts, having an internal debate about whether I should call an end to whatever my misguided intentions were. *Why be here if he truly doesn't want to be?*

By the time the flames were smothered and nothing but smoke remained, it was dark out. I walked back into the cabin, ready to give Ridge the option to leave and be done with it.

"Do you always talk to yourself when you're alone?"

I jumped and looked toward his voice. Ridge was standing by the window, wearing nothing but the pair of khakis I'd picked him up in. His arm leaning against the frame, he was looking out to where the fire pit was. The stove fire was lit beside him, its shadows licking at his skin.

Though I wasn't sure how long he'd been watching me, the fact that he had been at all was enough to warm my chest. Ignoring his question, I walked toward him—through fear, nerves, and second-guessing. And when I stopped in front of him, I gently placed a hand on his chest. He was built in a way that no farmer should be, cut with muscles I didn't even know existed. Each peak of stone led to the next valley. And each valley carried a river that created an eight-piece grid that made up his abdomen. I traced each line with steadiness that took willpower to maintain. My heart pounded furiously. Ridge Cross was a beautiful man, and despite it all, I wanted nothing more than make him mine again.

"When Harold told me you left town that night, I swore I would never forgive you," I whispered. "You knew that leaving would break my heart, and you did it anyway. But the timing of it all—" I shuddered. "At first, I didn't try to figure out why you left. I was too full of rage to care. You must have heard what happened to me that night, yet you never reached out to see if I was okay."

"I couldn't." His voice sounded shredded with

anguish and guilt. He started to reach for me but stopped. "I did what I had to do."

"You did what you had to do?" My voice quivered as it rose another decibel. "I could have died that night, and you didn't even care."

His jaw hardened. "If you think for a single second that I didn't—" He squeezed his eyelids shut and turned his head to face the window.

My heartrate quickened. "What were you going to say?"

He shook his head. "Nothing. I told you I didn't want to talk."

I glared and breathed in through my nose. "I know you're the one who ended the rivalry."

The way his body went completely still, not even a breath racking his body, was a major tell that I was right.

"It's okay. You don't have to confirm with your words what your body just told me. You made a deal with the devil, and you scarified my heart in the process. Don't worry, Ridge. I won't tell anyone. It can be our little secret. My papa made you choose, and you chose your cornfield over being with me. Isn't that right?"

His chest swelled as he leaned forward. "That's not —" But whatever he wanted to say didn't come out. Instead, his Adam's apple bobbed, and he leaned back on his heels. "It was the only way."

Just like that, his confirmation broke all the remaining fragments of my heart. "So then why did you get into my car, if it was so easy for you to give me up? Why are you still here?" I dropped my hand from his chest, drawing his eyes back to mine. "Why were you watching me out that window just now?" My entire body shook.

Ridge's eyes flashed angrily before they dimmed again. "You know why."

His words should have made me happy. His confession should have been enough to make me believe that he still could love me.

"But you made your choice, and you can never take it back. We've lost years because of it."

"Don't you think I know that?" His angry growl shook through me. "I'm dying a slow death inside because of what I lost. I have nothing left. Nothing! And even though we're standing here now, it doesn't change where we come from. But *you* brought me here, Camila. Why? What's the point, if you already knew why I left?"

I shook my head in frustration. The war in my head created casualties of my hopeful thoughts, killing them off one by one. Finally, I couldn't stand it anymore. I let out a growl. "I tried to forget you, but I couldn't. I shouldn't still love you, but I still do. What I should do right now is walk straight out that door and never look back, but I won't—unless you want me to."

When he didn't make a move or say another word, I slipped my fitted gray dress over my head and dropped it to the floor. All I could hear was my heart crashing against my ribcage, all I could see was a man I couldn't stop loving as hard as I tried, and all I could feel was our energy, which had always connected us, sparking in the air and encircling us with its flames.

Pushing my hair over one shoulder, I waited for him to make the next move. If we were going to make this mistake, then we were going to make it together, both of us knowing it was wrong but wanting it just the same. I wouldn't touch him again, until he made it clear he wanted me too.

I waited what felt like an eternity, but he didn't move. He didn't even drop his gaze to look at my nearly naked body. Instead, he stood there with a firmness in his expression telling me he wouldn't break.

I didn't believe him. Stepping away from the pile of fabric at my feet, I walked backward until the backs of my knees hit the bed, and I sat. His head finally started to turn, his eyes locking on every part of me save for my probing stare. He remained expressionless throughout his perusal, making me shifty and eager beneath my skin.

All I wanted was for him to react to me and crave me again. Maybe then he would remember what we'd once shared.

I pushed myself back until I rested on the center of the mattress. My heart beat a mile a minute as I lay down and slipped off my panties. Opening myself to him, I reached between my legs and pressed a finger to my clit, sucking in a breath at that first touch of my sensitive bud.

Over the crackling fire, I couldn't hear him react, but I could feel his heated gaze right where I wanted it—on me as I pleasured myself, circling my clit until I was close enough to make myself come. I didn't let up, refusing to feel shame. I let Ridge see that I'd become a desperate woman in need of a man's touch, and he was the only one I would accept it from. My fingers had been all I'd had since prom night with Ridge. I'd gotten good at pretending that my self-induced orgasms were enough, and I wasn't afraid to show him just how skilled I'd become.

I slipped two fingers into my entrance, gasping at my wetness and groaning at the pleasure that would soon follow. Rolling my eyes to the back of my head, I pushed my fingers in deeper and started to work myself to the brink.

My breaths came quickly as I pumped myself full, and I cried out at the image of Ridge on top of me that first time, injecting himself into me without realizing the long-term effects. Then I felt him—the real him. I was in the midst of coming down from my high when I opened my eyes to find him standing at the edge of the bed, a look of torment etched into every line of his face.

I scrambled to sit up and reached for his pants, then I popped off the button and yanked down the zipper before I gazed up at his angst-ridden face. His fingers were in his hair, and his eyes were squeezed shut like he was doing everything to keep his erection at bay. But when I looked down at his pants, which I'd just slipped down his legs, I knew he had never even stood a chance against what hung thick and heavy between his legs. It seemed that every part of Ridge had grown over the past five years.

I wrapped my hand around him, just as he'd shown me how to in the meadow of wildflowers. Reveling at the feel of him, I applied pressure then rolled the skin over his thick and veiny shaft. His lips parted, and he took a shaky breath that seemed to rack his entire body, and I warmed at knowing I was doing it right. My confidence grew quickly. I was the master of his pleasure and the conductor to his pending release, and I would do everything in my power to make sure he never forgot it.

When I snuck a look at his face and his hooded gaze locked on mine, it was all the encouragement I needed to fuel that adventurous spark within me. I slid off the bed and sank to my knees, then I did something I'd never had the courage or time to do before. I wrapped my hand around his base, opened my mouth, and tasted him. He jerked in my hold, like the shock of my tongue was too much, but I didn't let up. I ran circles around the tip while rolling his skin toward my mouth. With each stroke, I fit more of him into my mouth as my jaw stretched around him.

Soon, I started to feel the impenetrable man before me quiver. His fingers slid through my hair as my lips firmed around him, then he pushed his hips toward me. I could feel the intensity of his need with each thrust. He continued to greedily rock into my mouth until he grunted out a release, filling me with every inch of warm stickiness, then he pulled himself away and fell onto the bed beside me.

His breaths came hard, but I didn't give him time to think before I stood. His eyelids flew open as I reached behind me to unclasp my bra, then I climbed on top of him, straddling his legs.

Ridge moved his hands eagerly to my breasts and hungrily took in every inch of me with his eyes. He wasn't the gentle Ridge I knew, the one who had treated our first time like we were both made of the most fragile glass. He was lion and bear, ferocious only if provoked, and I was doing all I could to stoke the flames that would ignite him.

He was already growing hard again beneath me, and it wouldn't be long until I felt him inside me once again. I shivered at the ache between my thighs, which pulsed with want and need, thanks to every memory I'd tortured myself with over the years.

Leaning down, I brought my mouth to his ear and released a breath before sucking one in. I loved how he reacted beneath me, tensing and shuddering all at once. "I'm going to fuck you, Ridge Cross. No matter how hard you try to fight what we are, you'll never get away from me. Not then, not now, not ever."

He blew out a breath as he grew even harder at my entrance. "I don't have condoms. Even if I wanted you, I couldn't have you."

I rubbed my center against his length and bit down on his ear lobe. "I'm on the pill, and I haven't been with anyone since you." I swallowed my nerves at what I would find out next. "Have you—?"

"No." Anger filled his tone as he growled out the word.

Trying to hold back the sob of elation that wanted to climb my throat, I reached between our bodies and placed him at my entrance. As I moved my hand away, Ridge dug into my hips, and before I could ease onto him gently to reacquaint myself with that feeling once again, he slammed me down to him. The all-consuming sensation that ripped through me was such a surprise that stars burst behind my eyelids.

It was deep-seated pleasure.

It was overwhelming fullness and joy.

It was aggression and love.

It was a wildfire rising from the ashes.

It was us.

Once I started moving over him, the shock quickly dissolved. All I could feel was our connection, electric and sparking hot at the base. We didn't talk or even kiss. Abiding by my word, I fucked him as recklessly and as wildly as our love we pretended didn't exist. I fucked him mercilessly until he came inside me. And when he got hard again, I fucked him until we came together, just like we would always be.

When I woke up the next morning to cold sheets beside me, I knew Ridge had left me once again. At least that time, I wasn't surprised. And I was done chasing my past.

CHAPTER 44

RIDGE

I had watched Camila until she went back inside her bedroom, closing the doors behind her. A long while later, I stood and went back down the mountain, to the white ranch house Harold and I spent four years renovating before his tragic death.

What used to be a small two-bedroom home that made up a dot on the one thousand acres of Cross land is now double the size. "Perfect for a family," my father had told me near his end, nudging me toward a better life than the one that had been stripped from him.

In the four years leading to my father's untimely death, our relationship had strengthened. After Camila had left for California, I returned to the ranch to help Harold with all the new business. We had a new understanding that stemmed from heartbreak and the loyalty he had shown me when I needed it most. For the first time in my life, I felt like I had a father. Then I lost him. Other than my losing Camila, that was the biggest tragedy of all.

On that same dry summer night after my father's death, I got drunk and hopped on Harold's old tractor. All was fine until the target practice against the big rubber wheel ended in disaster. Sparks flew, and a row of corn stock caught fire. I got away to avoid danger, but the field wasn't as lucky.

That night, I managed to accidentally burn every last bit of the crop to the ground. Then I went to San Miguel County Jail for fourth-degree arson. It didn't matter that it was an accidental fire. I was drunk and reckless, and it's a miracle no one was injured because of my poor decisions.

I follow the wrap-around porch to the front of my home and freeze when I see a figure sitting on the top step with her chin propped on her knees.

"Raven?" I don't know why I said her name like it was a question. I know it's her, but I wasn't expecting to see her tonight. "I thought you would still be at the party."

She's even dressed for an evening at the Bells', in a sparkly blue gown, and her blond hair is pinned in some fancy updo. A flashback to prom hits me. But when her head lifts and her sad eyes meet mine, I know this isn't one of her casual visits. At least, her visits have been casual in my mind. I've recently learned that they mean something more to her.

She lifts her quivering chin. "When are we going to tell people about us?"

I squeeze my eyelids shut and swallow past the dread consuming my insides. Raven's great, but when we started hanging out five years ago, it was just fun and casual. Both of us knew that was all it could be. But I've noticed that she's become needy in the past couple of months—calling me every day, stopping by unannounced if I don't get to her calls or messages soon enough, and bringing me presents. It's all sweet, but the timing of it all tells me that the change in her has everything to do with Camila returning home.

Raven's feelings for me finally became clear a few weeks ago when we'd both had too much to drink and she kissed me. I should have pulled away faster and reminded her that we were friends and only that. But I also owed Raven a debt of gratitude for the friendship she'd provided when I needed it most.

"There's nothing to tell, Raven. It was one kiss, and it should never have happened."

Moisture coats her eyes as she stares back at me, and her jaw falls open. "Really? After all the times we've hung out, your feelings for me haven't changed?" She pauses, waiting for my reaction. When I don't give her one, she stands, her face beet red with anger. "Not even a little?"

A breath rushes out of me, and I take a step forward, desperately wanting to find a way to end the conversation before she gets more upset. "I'm sorry you expected more from me, but—"

"Don't." Her voice is lower than I've ever heard it. Raven and I never get angry with each other. We never get into fights. That has been the entire point of not making our friendship anything more. It's been easy and noncommittal, and it's freed her from expecting something more from me that will never come. At least, that was my intention when this all began.

She narrows her eyes to slits and balls her hands into

tight fists beside her thighs. "This is because of Camila, isn't it? That's why you've been distant ever since you found out she was coming back. That's why your feelings have changed."

I can't believe what I'm hearing. *How is it possible that two people see the world so differently?* "My feelings haven't changed. It's always been this way, Raven. And if I'd known that you were hoping for more, then…" I try to find the right way to say what I need to convey. I don't want to hurt her.

Her chin quivers. "Then you would never have started hanging out with me. Is that what you were going to say?"

I bow my head. My response is cowardly at best. Then I nod before lifting my gaze to meet hers. "I'm sorry."

"You're *sorry?*" she shrieks. "That's all I get from you? Don't you think I deserve a little more than that? After all this time, I thought you would eventually come around. That you'd finally give up waiting for *her* and see what's standing right in front of you."

"Stop making this about Camila." Somehow, despite the anger forming in my chest, I manage to keep my voice calm and quiet. "This isn't about her."

"Then why, Ridge? Why don't you want to be with me? Don't you want love and a big ole family to help you with this land?" She gestures to the ranch house like she's flipping it off. "That's what the remodel was for, wasn't it? Harold wanted you to start a family, since he never got to. He'd be rolling around in his grave right now, if he could hear you."

"Don't talk about my father like you knew what he wanted for me."

Her mouth hardens, like she's stopping herself from saying something she'll regret. "I thought it was you and me 'til the end."

The shock of her words swirls around my mind rapidly. "Until the end? C'mon, Raven, listen to yourself. What would your brother think about that?"

"I don't give a fuck what Trip thinks. I love you, Ridge. I've loved you ever since I laid eyes on you, and I never gave up hoping for something to come of us. Not even when you fell in love with Camila, and you two were keeping secrets from all of us. Not even when you got sent to jail." She swiped her eyes. "I waited for you. Then I waited for you years after you came home while you kept everyone away."

"Well, you need to stop waiting for me. It's just not that way between us, and I'm sorry."

"Stop telling me you're sorry." She picked up the bottom of her dress, stomped forward, and jabbed her pointer finger into my chest. "I hope you're being honest when you tell me that you aren't still pining over Camila. If you are, you're in for a rude awakening."

"What are you talking about?"

A small smile lifts her cheeks. "Things aren't the way they were ten years ago. A lot has changed, and something tells me that when Camila figures it out, she won't stick around for long."

CHAPTER 45

CAMILA

As a young child, I thought I lived in a castle. With a tall, ornate gated entrance and a long paved drive lined with trees that open to a large countryside villa, it is unquestionably one of the most beautiful homes in all of Telluride. Everywhere you look, you see intricate details—from the texture in the painted walls, the handcrafted accents, and even in some of the ceilings, reminiscent of the Sistine Chapel.

Wonderment filled me to the brim whenever I dashed through the halls, my mama hot on my tail in a game of chase. She often ended up winded, and we would both fall onto the nearest surface and laugh.

"Soon," she said. "You'll have a brother or sister to keep you company." She always wore a hopeful smile when she said those words, and I never questioned them. A few times, I caught her rubbing her belly like there was a baby inside it. But that hopeful smile grew dimmer as the days went on, until eventually, she stopped making the promise entirely.

I was fifteen when I finally felt brave enough to ask her why they'd never delivered on that promise. I still remember the darkness that blanketed my mama's features and the chill that swept over us, even though it was the middle of summer. I shouldn't have asked, but I couldn't take the question back.

"Your father and I would have liked that very much, mija. Sometimes, parents only meant to have one child, sometimes two, sometimes three, or sometimes none. Your papa and I were blessed beyond our wildest dreams to have one." She held my chin between the tips of her fingers, a sad smile lifting her cheeks. "That's why God made you so strong and so brave. Your papa needs you, Camila. You and you alone will need to carry on the Bell family legacy."

My mama wasn't normally so cryptic and dark, but I held tight to her words like they were her dying wish. I was so used to her passion, her constant movement, and her smile, which seemed to be a permanent fixture. Around the time of my question, I noticed things with her start to change. She kept to herself a lot more, no longer dabbling in the affairs of the business unless called upon by my papa. Meanwhile, Papa worked closer with Thomas, and Mama's tasks were given to him.

Now, it's all coming full circle, and the feelings are surreal and overwhelming. As ready as I've always been for this opportunity to transition into more of a leadership role on the vineyard, standing here, getting ready to take the plunge, is a whole other thing.

As I enter the casita and walk down the narrow hallway to papa's old office for my first day of work, I have trouble believing this castle is all mine. It feels like just yesterday when I excitedly charged into this very room to tell him that I'd just spotted the first flowering bud of the season. But when I enter the office now, and my eyes register that I'm not alone, the reality of it all sinks in fast.

Thomas Bradshaw is sitting on the couch, in the same spot where Papa used to sit, and Mama is sitting across from him. I freeze in the threshold, taking in their serious faces. Their chatter is low, and they're leaning toward each other almost intimately, and a deep sense of betrayal swirls in my gut.

At some point in the conversation, Thomas looks over at me and waves. "Hello again, Camila." He stands and holds out a hand to squeeze mine, which I accept with an internal cringe. "You look lovely this morning."

My insides tense at the compliment.

"Yes, you look beautiful, mija," my mama adds.

I'm wearing nothing special, just gray leggings, a bright-white sweater, and snow boots. "Thank you." My smile is pinched. "Figured I'd take a stroll through the vineyard later to reacquaint myself with the vines and say hello to the crew."

Thomas nods. "That sounds like a great plan. I can introduce you to some of the new staff I brought on board for the winter season."

He gestures for me to take a seat across from him, but I take my papa's old seat instead. His shock registers quickly before his salesman charm returns, and he sits across from me.

I quirk an eyebrow, confused, as mama gets up and sits next to me. "New staff?"

He frowns. "That's right. To make up for the loss of production after your father's passing."

"But it's winter." I tilt my head, trying to understand. "The vines are dormant. Pruning season doesn't require a lot of labor right now."

"Not a lot. But we need some," Thomas says. "Pruning is an arduous job, I'm sure you remember. But I suppose I should have run the new staff budget by you first."

I open my mouth but snap it shut just as quickly, forcing my instinctual retort to the back of my mind. Thomas did the right thing, and if I had gotten to the vineyard three months earlier, then the decision would have been ours and not just his.

"Right, well, thank you for taking the charge on that. I'm sure our buyers will be happy with the seamless transition." Since we're on the topic of operational changes, I suddenly have so many more questions. "Speaking of our buyers. Do you have a list of our clients—active, pending, and former?"

Thomas squints, confusion painted all over his face. "I do. Of course I do. I *am* the head of Business Development."

I give him my best syrupy smile. "You're the head of a lot of things, aren't you, Thomas?"

He chuckles, and I'm not clueless to the worried glances Mama is throwing my way.

"I suppose I am, yes. Operations, business development, marketing…"

I have no desire to continue listening to the long list of roles Thomas has acquired over the years. While I promised myself that I would go into this meeting with a clear head and all preconceived notions aside, I find it hard to look past the feeling that has always twisted in my gut while I'm around him. "I'd love to take a look at that client list as well as all the business documents you can muster up. Operations handbooks, updated business plan, employee logs, you name it."

Thomas nods toward the desk. "Everything you need to know is in your father's desk drawers. Everything else is in a shared cloud drive on his desktop. I've left the logins and passwords for you, and if there's anything I can help you find, just let me know."

"I definitely will." I snap my fingers, remembering something. "Speaking of passwords." I open my organizer, where I stored my notes and questions and checklists. My one and only goal for today is to hit the ground running. "I thought I could take a look at the website and our mail lists. I'll need access to those as well as our domain and hosting sites."

"Of course." He tilts his head, looking reluctant. "But you realize those are all things your father left up to me?" Thomas's smile is restored. "He had approval over everything before it got published, of course, but he never bothered himself with the marketing details."

"I don't doubt that you'll continue to manage all of the same things, but I would still like access to everything."

"Of course. No problem." Thomas jots a note in his notepad and looks back at me.

I rattle off a list of to-dos regarding all the different departments—set up meetings, tours, demonstrations with the staff, and on and on—until Thomas looks back at me with annoyance on his face.

"I'm your partner, Ms. Bell, not your assistant. While I'm more than happy to help you get up to speed, this—" He rips the paper out of his notebook and slides it on the coffee table between us. "Can be done by you or someone you employ. I do not set up meetings. Frankly, I don't have the time, since I'm pounding the pavement every day to ensure our assets are locked in."

My jaw drops, and I wish I'd been able to contain it. It's too early to let Thomas Bradshaw know that he has the ability to get under my skin. He never failed to do that before, but working together in a business setting means something different.

As if she detects the tension, Mama leans over and slides the paper into her lap. "I can take care of this while you look for someone, Camila. Hiring an assistant isn't a bad idea. It's something I wish your papa had done long ago." She turns to me, and I know the warning look all too well. *Keep your cool, mija.* "Patrick was always doing way more than he should when it came to operations. Someone else would be more than happy to take on the smaller tasks."

"Do we have the budget for that?" I ask Thomas. And as the questions continue to come to me, I realize just how in the dark I've been all these years.

He tilts his head and purses his lips in thought. "I believe we're well-equipped to add on, but financials, payroll, and accounting were your father's responsibility. The budget documents are on your desktop as well." He reaches for his notebook. "How about you review them, and we can discuss things in the morning with the new business manager?"

Why do I get the feeling that Thomas is calling an abrupt end to our meeting? "We have a new business manager?"

"Yes," Thomas says, rising to his feet. "And he's been a dedicated full-time employee for eight years."

One by one, I silently think about all the vineyard workers I'd gotten to know and love over the years while growing up, and not one of them is coming to my mind as a likely candidate.

My mama touches my leg to get my attention. "He's talking about Trip. Trip is the new operations manager."

"Oh." I widen my eyes. "I didn't see that coming."

Thomas smiles, pride appearing to puff out his chest. "That's right. Trip will take over my old job as business manager as well. He already knows our clients and has had his hand in vineyard operations. And Raven will continue to manage the winery and all event planning."

My chest feels tight with anger. "Again, Thomas, those are some major decisions you made without even speaking with me."

"With all due respect, Ms. Bell, you weren't here. The vineyard couldn't wait three months for you to tie up your affairs back in California. I still had a business to run."

I stew inside, wondering how I'm going to manage to work alongside this prick like my papa did for over thirty years.

"I had to sell my house, give notice at my job, and pack an entire decade's worth of stuff within three months. The least you could have done was pick up the phone and call me."

Thomas shrugs. "I suppose I could have done that.

But what's the point? You should trust that I know what I'm doing by now."

"And what is it that you're doing, exactly?" I ask, condescension in my tone. "Since you're giving all your jobs away, what will yours be?"

Thomas shoots a look at mama then back to me, like they're in on the same secret. "You don't know?"

I squint at him in confusion. "Know what?" Then I look at my mama, who has her head bent low, just like she would do when Papa used to scold me.

"My title is vineyard owner," he says. "Just like you."

A laugh bubbles in my chest. I can't believe the nerve of him to invite himself into my office, sit down in my papa's old seat, then claim that he has the same title as the heir to the vineyard. I stand, leveling him with my gaze. "I hope you didn't print that on your new business cards, because that is a decision that will not get my approval."

He smiles back at me. It's the same creepy smile I remember from when I was a teen. The man called me a whore with those same twisted lips.

"I don't need your approval. Once you brush up on some of that homework you desperately want to do, you'll see for yourself. You've been gone for a long time, Camila. This isn't the same vineyard you left. In fact, you may want to consider whether your being back here is the best decision after all." He nods at me. "It's been a pleasure, but I have work to do. I'll be back tomorrow."

"He's part-owner?" I half growl, half scream the words once I find Papa's ownership papers, which clearly states that Thomas Bradshaw owns fifty percent of the business along with me. As an only child, I've never had to share anything in my entire life. *What would have made Papa believe I'd want to share this?* It was supposed to be mine.

I hold it up to Mama, who hasn't moved from the couch. She knew all along. I can see it written all over her guilt-ridden face. "Why didn't you warn me about this? How the hell did this happen?

Mama sighs and looks up at me with sad eyes. "Your papa never included me in these business discussions. I knew something was wrong, but no one ever consulted me. But to be honest, I feared something like this would happen."

"What?" I can't even comprehend what's going on. "Why? How?"

"Your father was getting himself into trouble. I've told you that much. Before you walked in, I was trying to get Thomas to explain to me exactly what happened, but that man is impossible. I warned your father repeatedly that he'd been giving Thomas too much control, but it got to the point that Patrick couldn't make any business decisions without him."

"And Papa cut you out of every single decision?"

She frowns. "He omitted a lot. I got the sense he was drowning, but you know your papa and his pride. I knew things were bad. I just didn't know they were this bad."

I look back down at the documents, feeling a tornado of emotions whirl through me. "This can't be happening. How are we just finding out about this?"

As I flip through the documents page by page, I start

to catch on to a pattern. And it all started the summer after I left for college, after my parents separated. Each year, Papa gave up his shares five percent at a time, until it added up to what it is today, and Thomas Bradshaw paid a mint for each of those shares.

What I can't figure out is why. *Why sell? And why keep it from everyone?* It's all too much to process.

Ten years ago, I would probably have shed a tear or two at my papa's betrayal, but I refuse to shed a single tear today. I don't care how Thomas managed to get my papa to give up ownership of his company. I will find a way to get it back.

CHAPTER 46

CAMILA

I let out a growl as I stomp around Mountain Village well into the evening. I can't enjoy a damn thing, the way my mind is circling the conversation I had with Thomas Bradshaw this morning. This used to be my favorite place to get away and stroll by the plazas, ice skate on the Village Pond, or dine outside at one of the scenic restaurants. Something about knowing I was over nine thousand feet above sea level made me truly feel like I was on top of the world. But no matter how far I walk, how many familiar sights I take in, or how much joy I can hear in the laughing voices around me, nothing can restore my mood.

After I pored over business and legal documents all damn day, so many things started to make sense, including why Thomas Bradshaw encouraged me to go away to school. Having the future heir gone made it easier for him to manipulate Papa. And my papa's last will and testament was shared with me, but the actual property share documents were not. Clearly, no one wanted me to know what was going on. I'd been living on a false sense of security my entire life, while Thomas slowly chipped away pieces of my future and stole them for himself and his family.

Well, I suppose *stole* is the wrong word. Thomas evidently paid for everything that's now his. But all I can think about is *how. How did a full-time vineyard worker rake in the millions and millions of dollars it took to pay my papa off? Why did Papa even consider accepting?* And it isn't just the vineyard he's been purchasing.

He now owns half of the land, the villa, and the freaking llamas, for heaven's sake.

I don't know what I'm angrier about—that I'm to operate the vineyard with Thomas, as if we could actually agree on anything, or that my papa decided all of this without remotely consulting with me. Surely he realized the risk he put our family legacy in by handing over so much power to another family. *Did he ever care what I thought about any of it?* A sinking feeling enters my gut when I realize that it's possible he didn't care at all.

Papa and I never fully reconciled after our big blowup about Ridge, but we were still family. I visited him and Mama, he sent me wine, and I called home often. We never talked business, and perhaps that was a mistake. I should have been asking the hard questions, but I never expected him to leave this world as early as he did. I thought when I was finally ready to come home, I would have training, then we would have a transition of power. I would be in the fields while Papa smoked cigars and drank crates of wine until the last of his days.

This wasn't the plan. This wasn't why I went away to

school for a slew of degrees, all to benefit the Bell family name, for a freaking decade.

My brain hurts, and my body feels sore from too much walking. So when I spot the outdoor dining area at Poacher's Pub, I grab a seat and begin to order a few too many glasses of wine.

None of them make me feel better, but my buzz is strong when Josie calls.

"Sorry," she says. "We just parked." She's breathing heavily, like she's walking fast. "Where are you?"

I drain the last of my wine and set it down. "I'm up at Mountain Village, trying to clear my head."

When I talked to Josie earlier today, I vented to her about what was going on, and she suggested we meet up for dinner and drinks tonight.

"Is it working?"

"Nope."

She laughs, but I can hear sympathy there too. "Well, come down and meet us at High Pie. If the best pizza in the world doesn't cheer you up, then I will."

I smile. "I'll start heading there now."

"Great. We'll grab a table."

After hanging up, I pay my bill and head back to the gondola station to wait for the next cabin. I look up to the sky and exhale, trying to ease my anxiety with slow, deep breaths. As I watch the fog from my breathing fade from view, I focus on the present. Dozens of people are in line, and even more are still perusing the sights around Mountain Village. Laughter and joyful shrieks fill the air. Blades cut through ice as skaters circle the ring. Heavy boots crunch through thick snow. Ski equipment gets placed on the racks of the gondolas.

So much noise and activity is around me, but somehow, I'm able to filter that out as I trace the constellations with my eyes.

"Next!"

I jump at the operator's deep voice and lurch into action. I jog toward the slow-moving cabin and take a step up to get in. But when my left boot catches on something, my first wine-induced instinct is to tug it harder— big mistake. My boots are loosely tied, enough to cause the bow of one lace to catch on the metal edge. The moment my boot slips off my foot, I lose my balance and stumble into the car, landing on my knees and palms just as it begins to move.

"Oh no!" I scramble across the floor on my hands and knees to get to the door before it closes.

I make a move to stand so that I can jump out as one of the workers swoops down and grabs my boot. When the gondola stops, relief floods me, sobering me enough to thank my savior and retrieve my shoe. But when the doors open completely, and I see who's standing on the other side, my buzz comes right back, slamming me hard in the chest.

His chocolate-brown eyes meet mine, and his face has the same hard look as the first time we met. Only this time, he isn't holding a gun. He's holding my boot, and he's handing it to me.

CHAPTER 47

RIDGE

Camila's boot isn't the first personal item I've rescued while operating the gondola station in Mountain Village, especially on nights after the alcohol sets in. I just never expected for those cornfield-green eyes to be the ones staring back at me when the doors opened this time.

The moment our eyes meet, it's like a jolt of electricity, firing up my every nerve ending and putting me on high alert. She's every bit the Camila I remember and so much more. Her hair is longer and even appears darker against the snowy backdrop. Her white sweater sets off the deep caramel of her skin, showcasing her Spanish-Brazilian roots. And her eyelashes seem bolder—thicker and longer—transfixing me.

"Ridge."

She says my name with wide eyes, like she can't believe it's really me. Maybe if I walk away, she'll convince herself it was all a mirage. That would be far easier than engaging in the reality of who we are today —opposites and enemies.

"What are you doing here?" she asks, her eyebrows knitting.

"Working." My response is gruff, but even with all the thoughts about Camila circling my mind, I never once planned how I would react to coming into contact with her again.

People are waiting, staring at us and wondering. If Camila were any other passenger, she would have grabbed her shoe, thanked me, and been on her way. Even I'm starting to get a little uncomfortable, standing here while the shock settles between us both.

I lift her boot, trying to get her attention. "I believe this is yours, Ms. Bell."

She seems startled by my voice and looks down at her shoe. Swallowing, she reaches for it, and her hand brushes mine as she glances back at me. "Thank you."

Her voice sounds so small and unlike her. My heart squeezes at the loss of the strong, determined, and stubborn Camila I once knew. Nothing ever made her voice small, which was one of the things that drew me to her then and one of the many things I still miss.

She clutches her shoe against her chest as her shocked expression quickly dissolves into something colder and harder. It resembles the look she gave me the last time I saw her.

Time has been cruel to me, and in turn, I've been cruel to her. I will never forgive myself for the decisions I made, but I also know they were all the right ones. Unfortunately, the damage has been done, and it appears Camila feels the same.

She takes a step backward into the cabin, and I mirror her, stepping away from the car. A second later, the gondola starts to move, and the door to Camila's cabin slides shut, creating yet another wall between us. But it doesn't matter when every wall built before it is more impenetrable than the next.

Over the next hour, I continue my shift at the gondola station, inspecting and cleaning as cabins come through, assisting passengers with mounting their ski equipment onto the outside of the rides, and making sure everyone leaves with their articles of clothing intact.

By the time my shift ends and I jump into a cabin to head down the mountain, I'm exhausted. Not physically or even because of lack of sleep, but I'm mentally drained from the constant cycle of thoughts about Camila. I go from past to present, from good to bad, and from fantasy to reality. My mind just keeps spinning and hurling memories at me like tiny grenades, exploding in my heart.

We got the hard part out of the way. We saw each other again. *Is that how it's going to be from now on? We run into each other in town and share an awkward glance?* It feels wrong, but not much feels right anymore.

As I'm carried down the mountain, I look out the window at a view I will never take for granted. The surrounding land appears to be painted right into my vision. Peaks and valleys spread out over hundreds of miles, all white with fresh snow. A box canyon sits below, snuggled between the mountain walls. From where I sit at nine thousand feet up, the buildings scattered below resemble a picturesque Christmas village, like the kind one would put on display in their house every winter.

As the buildings at the bottom of the box canyon grow, tension in my body mounts right along with it as Camila's words from earlier pop into my head.

"What are you doing here?"

Apparently, the ten years Camila spent away from this place resulted in some memory loss. She must have forgotten that I love to pick up extra work during the winter. While my time at the farm is now busier than ever, no matter the season, I still love to be where the action is in the cold months. If jail time taught me anything, it's the importance of making every moment count. But the purpose isn't to relieve boredom or to earn some extra money anymore. If anything, I thoroughly enjoy the time I spend out in the community.

After Harold passed away, I made a commitment to do more with my life than just tend to corn stalks six months out of the year. Whether that be by picking up tour guide jobs in Mountain Village, hand-making furniture in my garage, or hiking one of the winter trails, not a day goes by when I'm not doing something.

My father was undoubtedly a hard, dedicated worker who loved his land, but it is clear to me now that his relationship skills were lacking. If he had spent any time at all getting to know his buyers, then Patrick Bell and Thomas Bradshaw could never have hurt his business. I've spent the last five years rebuilding my reputation after the fire as well as Harold's old business relationships. I've hired a few local residents, who have been helping me on the farm to give me the time I need to work on a new venture—an idea that sparked thanks to Camila, of all people. I can't wait to unleash the news to the town.

Camila has missed so much. Thanks to the so-called truce between Harold Cross and Patrick Bell ten years ago, life has actually been quite peaceful. The city opened its arms up to my father's business, accepting deals that had been pending for decades. Cross Farms finally got a permanent spot at the farmer's market, and we were no longer dependent on someone canceling their appearance. We started sponsoring events and truly became a part of the town my father had tried to produce in for decades. Nothing makes me happier than knowing he left this world after finally getting his shot. At the time of his death, he was finally a respected man in the community.

The gondola cabin enters the Telluride station, and I jump out, nodding my thanks to the attendant standing by. Shoving my hands into the pockets of my jeans, I stride forward to where I parked the truck. I trudge through a blocked-off Main Street, keeping my eyes pointed forward. The crowds are out tonight after a long day of skiing and shopping, and they drink merrily while live music plays from a side stage.

I'm nearing the street where I parked earlier today when the rich Italian scent of stone-oven pizza turns my head. My eyes catch on Josie, who's sitting at a high-top table inside of High Pie. The windows are open, as they usually are to let the cool breeze through.

My natural reaction is to pull up a stool and join her for some drinks, but after my run-in with Camila earlier today, I debate it. Josie and I have always gotten along, especially more so lately. While she used to be a strong advocate for Camila and me to push through all the external struggles to be together, her opinion has drastically changed. The moment Camila's life got put at risk and I broke her heart, yet again, she promised never to forgive me for all the hurt I caused her best friend. Eventually, we became civil again, but I'm not so sure she feels the same way now that Camila is back.

After a moment of hesitation, I veer left to enter the pizza place then walk toward Josie to join her.

Her eyes widen in surprise when she sees me. "Hey, Ridge." Then she squints, like she can read exactly what's on my mind. "Um." She seems jittery as she looks around us.

"What's your problem? Afraid to be seen with me?"

She tilts her head, her eyes softening. "No, of course not. But you should know I'm not alone."

I make a face. *Why is she acting all weird?* "Yeah, I've met your husband. Don't worry. He's not going to think I'm hitting on you." I chuckle, amused by her reaction. "I'm going to go grab a beer."

"Wait." She jumps, her eyes opening wide. "Take this one. I didn't like it, so Abner's getting me a new one." She slides a full beer over to me.

I slide the beer back to her. "You don't need to give me yours, Josie. I'll get my own."

Then I notice a few empty glasses on the table along with a few half-eaten pizzas. I stop in my tracks and turn back to her. "You and Abner eat all that?"

A look of concern flashes across her face "Camila's with him now. They're grabbing another pitcher at the bar."

I blow out a breath and roll my eyes to the sky. "Ah, shit, Josie. I should go."

"I agree, but let's be real. You two are going to be seeing a lot of each other. Might as well get the reunion over with now, don't you think? *In public.*"

Her intentions are clear. Josie has always been a good friend to Camila, so I know she's keeping her friend's best interests in mind.

"She didn't tell you? We ran into each other in Mountain Village at the gondola station. She lost her boot when she was getting into a cabin, and I retrieved it for her."

Josie shakes her head, appearing annoyed. "She didn't tell me." Then she rolls her eyes and smiles. "Only you two would have a reunion that resembles a fucking fairy tale. Did you place the boot on her foot too?" Josie bats her eyelashes sarcastically at me. "Did it fit?"

I chuckle, though the Cinderella reference bothers me more than I let on. Camila has never been the rags-to-riches sort of girl. The opposite was true, in the sense that she has never been afraid to get her hands dirty, and that was what had intrigued me from the beginning. "Not quite. But we didn't exactly become best friends either." I take a step back from the table. "I changed my mind on that beer. I should be getting back to the ranch, anyway. I've got an early morning."

Josie eyes me with a challenge. "Sure ya do." She relaxes. "But all right, I'll let you off the hook. Go on. Run off before she sees you. That's probably for the best, anyway."

I don't like the sound of that, but I agree that it probably is for the best. After I wink at Josie, I turn away, only to stop in my tracks when I come face-to-face with Trip and Raven.

Raven looks just as pissed at me as she did the night before, and Trip eyes me with the same disdain he's carried for me for nearly two decades. He was and always will be a bully. And I've always found pleasure in the fact that he can't get under my skin the way he wants to. But then I think of what Raven told me last night, and my blood immediately begins to boil all over again.

"Things aren't the way they were ten years ago. A lot has changed, and something tells me that when Camila figures it out, she won't stick around for long."

Clearly, Raven doesn't know Camila very well. Camila would never allow anything to come between her and that vineyard. But just the tease that she could leave again drives me insane. Trip never shied away from his affection toward her, even when he was busy bossing her around. He was the guy at school who threatened anyone who even considered asking Camila Bell out, and he was also the guy who ratted her out after she left him before prom that night.

If Trip doesn't feel at least a twinge of guilt for what happened to her that night, then he is even worse of a human than I thought. The guilt I still carry for not being at the bridge when Dave hunted her as if she were a deer is something I know I will never live down.

"Running off somewhere?" Trip asks with a quirked eyebrow.

I stifle the flames of hate. He's about to hang out with Camila, when I could be doing the same.

"Nah." I shake my head and spin back around to rejoin Josie. "Think I'll have that beer after all."

I try not to look at Josie, but I see her worried expression in my peripheral vision. She seems just as surprised by Trip and Raven's arrival as I am. And I swear I hear a mumbled curse. She's worried, and maybe she has every reason to be. But perhaps I'm not the villain this time.

CHAPTER 48

CAMILA

A bner and I wait for the bartender to acknowledge us for ten minutes before he finally strolls over and does a double take when he sees me. "Well, well, well. Who do we have here?" The man leans on the counter and flicks his eyes up and down in a quick perusal. "Camila Bell. It really is you, ain't it?"

I smile uneasily then tilt my head and squint to get a better look at the stout man in a beanie cap. He doesn't appear to be much older than me, but I can't seem to place him right away.

He narrows his eyes in response and tosses the rag he was holding onto the counter. "You don't remember me, do you?

I smile at the man, guilt radiating through me. "I'm sorry. No."

He shrugs. "That's all right. Must not've given you much to remember." He grabs hold of his long beard and tugs. "Besides, I look a little different now."

"Don't we all?" I laugh, hoping to ease the tension floating between us. "I'm so sorry for my bad memory."

"Name's Brody," he says gruffly. "Brody McAllistor. My dad worked with your dad at the vineyard. We used to go mountain biking together in the summer."

That's all it takes for my memory of him to return. Gus McAllistor was the groundskeeper at the vineyard for nearly three decades. Brody and I were in the same grade. I can't believe I didn't recognize him sooner. "Oh, I do remember you now. I just couldn't see you behind all that beard." I smile fondly at my old friend. "I'm sorry. I've been away for so long."

He waves a hand to tell me my apology isn't necessary. "Heard you moved back. Hope it works out for you this time."

As genuine as Brody sounds, a pang hits my gut when I think about his father. "I'm sorry about Gus. I heard that he got fired all those years ago for what happened to me. I tried to fight for him. It wasn't his fault, but my papa could sure be stubborn."

Papa was furious with Gus after finding out that Dave Lachey had cut the fences for his hunting missions. Dave let the wildlife in and illegally hunted on our grounds, and when Dave spotted me in the dark, he thought I was a deer. When I tried to tell the cops what I believed really happened that night—that Dave Lachey knew exactly who he was hunting down—they searched the surrounding land. They looked for any evidence to account for my story, but they came up empty in that regard and ultimately ruled what happened to me a hunting accident.

"It's old news now." Brody waves a hand, but I can't

shake the annoyance still buried in his expression. "We're all just glad you're okay, Camila." He gestures with an uptick of his chin. "What can I get ya to drink?"

I order a glass of pinot grigio, and Abner orders a pitcher of beer. When Brody walks away, I cringe, and Abner laughs.

"I wish I could have helped you out there. But I'm not from here. I don't know many people."

I grin. "You don't know how lucky you are."

Brody isn't the first person in town to recognize me. It seems I have the worst memory of all time, because I don't remember many faces in return. I blame it on my obsession with a certain neighbor boy who stole all my time and attention back then—and most of my good memories too.

After Brody hands us our drinks, we back away from the bar and start off toward the direction where we left Josie. I'm nearly there when the crowd parts, and I see that she is no longer alone.

Over the past couple of hours, Josie, Abner, and I have been catching up on everything we've missed since we last saw each other, all while drinking slowly, devouring the best pizza in the world, and sharing a few laughs. It's been cathartic. But when I see Ridge standing at the table with Josie, the night almost begins to feel like a cruel joke.

I freeze so fast that wine sloshes onto my hand, and I genuinely debate whether to walk away or continue forward. One run-in with Ridge today is enough. I don't need another awkward encounter.

Then as if things couldn't get more awkward, I spot Trip and Raven at the table too. *What the—?*

Before I can make any decisions on what to do next, Ridge's gaze finds mine, sending a jolt of electricity straight to my heart. Abner rushes off toward Josie, surely oblivious to what is happening inside my head.

Then Trip's voice booms over the noise of the crowd. "Well, holy shit, there she is."

I'm not looking at Trip when he says it, but I could never mistake his intonation for anyone else's. His voice sounds so much like his father's—loud, arrogant, and annoying.

Before I can blink, Trip is in front of me and scooping me up in his arms, and he doesn't seem to care about the wine that's spilling down his slick black jacket. He's taller than I remember, and he lifts my feet off the ground as he squeezes me tight.

Josie, Abner, and Raven laugh at Trip's greeting, and I can't help but laugh too. Ridge, on the other hand, looks shifty as he stares off to his left, like he's trying to find the fastest escape route.

Trip finally lets me down, but he doesn't let go of my waist. He grins, his broad smile even bigger and brighter than I remember. "God, it's good to have you back for good, Camila. Telluride has not been the same."

"It's nice to see you again, too, Trip." I smile up at my friend, putting Ridge out of my mind for a second. "It's a bit strange to be home, but it'll grow on me again."

Trip squeezes my waist, and I try to hide my wince. "If there's anything I can do to help, I'm here."

"I appreciate that."

He removes his hands, slips an arm around my neck and leads me to our table, where the others are waiting.

My encounter with Ridge at the top of the mountain was awkward, but it doesn't compare to this scenario. Never in my wildest dreams did I think that Ridge and Trip would be standing at the same table. It's actually confusing me so much that I laugh.

"Okay, I have to ask. Is this a thing now? Do you guys hang out like this often? Because it's kind of weird."

Complete silence follows as they all exchange glances. Something about the look Raven gives Ridge in particular heats my chest for a reason I don't quite understand. But it eerily resembles the time we all went on that hiking trip in Ouray. Then they laugh starting with Josie, then Trip joins in, and Raven is next. Ridge still doesn't smile.

"I told you things were different now," Josie says with a wink. "We're all one big happy family. Right, guys?"

"Well, I wouldn't go that far," Trip says, flipping a glance at Ridge. "But things aren't like they were when we were teens, Camila. The Bell-Cross truce shifted dynamics for the entire town."

The Bell-Cross truce. Ending the feud after over a century of conflict should make me happy. In a way, of course I am. To know Ridge and Harold struggled less because my papa stopped putting roadblocks up to hinder their success is a great thing. Unfortunately, Ridge and I suffered the consequences.

"Well, okay then," I say, sinking onto my stool.

Trip takes the stool beside me. Ridge hesitates for a second before sitting down next to Raven.

Then Josie does what Josie does best and starts talking to distract everyone from their discomfort.

"Sorry I missed the big party last night," Trip says,

leaning closer to me. "I had a client dinner, and it ran too late, but I'd love to make it up to you sometime. I'll take you out for dinner this week, and we can catch up."

High Pie is bustling, so even at our small table, the odds of any of our friends hearing us is slim. But the fact that Trip is dipped down to my ear to ask me on what sounds like a date has me squirming under my skin for all the wrong reasons. I find Ridge's dark eyes, and I swear he can hear every word that rolls off Trip's smooth tongue. Ridge always had some sort of superpower when it came to his senses—and me.

I look away and reach for my drink, suddenly feeling parched. When I notice it's practically empty already, I set it back down and answer Trip. "We'll see," I say. "I've got a lot of work ahead of me at the vineyard." *Since your daddy is trying to steal it away from me.*

At my mention the vineyard, Trip's eyes light up. Then he launches into a brag fest about all of the great work he's done over the years. I listen, pretending to be impressed while I bite my tongue. I wouldn't be surprised if Thomas has been keeping all of his slimy business dealings to himself and using his kids as his pawns without them even knowing it.

"My papa appreciated all the work you put in. And so do I. I can't wait to see everyone in action. Working in Napa was a definite eye opener. I have some ideas I can't wait to implement here."

"Like?"

I'm almost surprised to hear Raven speak up. For a second, I feel like her question is an attempt to challenge my intentions, but I shake the feeling away. She's curious, and she has every right to be.

"Well, for one, I hear you've been running operations at the winery. I can't wait to talk with you more about how we can improve our hospitality efforts." I look at Trip, excitement bubbling deep in my chest. "And I know you're heading up the business-development front. What are our clients saying? Are they happy? Are they looking for something different? More variety, maybe? I want to take a hard look at the diversity in our grape varietals. It's been a long time since we produced a vintage like our 1998 Bell Red."

Raven snorts. "C'mon, Camila. You know we have no control over which varietals we use, considering we live in Colorado."

I raise an eyebrow, meeting her challenge head-on. "There are plenty of opportunities, if we work with the soils and elevations. You'll see."

When Raven doesn't say anything in return, I smile and look at Josie. "Then there's blending or cofermentation to bring out unbelievable flavors that wouldn't otherwise exist. I learned all about the techniques in Napa, and the options are endless. I thought maybe you could help me taste test those." I wink.

Josie grins. "Now that's a job I'll volunteer for."

My eyes dart to Ridge, who looks uncomfortable and stands, leaving his full beer on the table. He whispers something to Josie before walking off. The fact that I'm not instantly ecstatic at his exit tells me I'm in a world of trouble from here on out.

Raven's expression remains cold and unimpressed. "Well, you'll have all the time in the world to put all the knowledge into action now that you're back. Once we move into the villa—"

She stops abruptly when Trip cuts a look at her, but I don't miss the shake of his head and the warning in his gaze.

"What's going on?" Apparently, Raven and Trip know a hell of a lot more than I do. "What do you mean, once you 'move into the villa'?" I let out a laugh. "You can't just invite yourself to move into my home."

Raven scrunches her face in confusion and looks at Trip.

He lets out a heavy sigh. "Our dad was supposed to talk to you first." He gives Raven another look. "Obviously, there are things to discuss. You just got home and need time to settle in, but with our investment in the business, it's the right thing to do."

My mouth hangs open. The surprises just don't stop coming. "No, it is not. That is my home." I search their faces, grasping for hope that this is all one big joke.

Trip frowns. "I know this is a lot right now, Camila, but you need to look at it from a business perspective."

"But this is my life we're talking about. I just find out today that your father has somehow managed to wrangle his way into a fifty-fifty partnership in my family business. And now you all want to move in too?"

"I'm at the winery for sixteen hours a day," Raven says sharply. "Between events, wine tastings, and tours. This is all in the best interests of Bell Family Farms."

I look between them, wanting to scream, and bite my tongue so that I don't react with emotion. I'm already worried my tone is coming off all wrong. "Look, no disrespect to your family, but—I just got here, and suddenly there are all these changes. It's—I'm still trying to process it all, and I wasn't even given a say."

Raven lets out a laugh. "With all due respect, Camila, the only reason your *papa* was able to keep the vineyard afloat is because of our father. We're dealing with a hostile climate and the harshest of critics. Our fathers worked together for thirty years for a reason. And while you've been off getting all your fancy degrees, we've been here. Working."

Her words burn me straight through my chest. Everyone at the table has fallen silent and is looking at me. The old Camila would have told Raven that she didn't have a clue as to what she was talking about. She's giving her family credit for far too much. My grandfather planted the first bare root vines, and he did so against all odds.

I'm getting too worked up over something I don't quite understand yet, so I give them all a forced smile. "I think it's time I head home."

"Camila, don't go," Josie begs.

I ignore her and stand. "It was nice seeing you all." I nod to the table without making eye contact with any of them. Then I grab my purse and head for the door.

In my rush to leave my friends, this night, and this entire homecoming behind, I don't pay attention to my path ahead. I've just rounded the corner of the taproom when I feel my shoe catch on the metal gate surrounding the perimeter of the bar, and I fall forward onto the snow-packed sidewalk. My palms break my fall. Immediately, I feel the cold burn of the impact and moan.

Rolling over onto my back, I ignore the snow that melts into my hair and the crowds that pass me by while laughing or giving me strange looks. I don't care. I'm done with today and with the avalanche of news that hasn't stopped pummeling me since I arrived home.

My head is starting to hurt, the cold soaks through my skin, and the backs of my eyes sting. When a figure leans over me and extends his hand, my throat closes up with emotion.

I think I fell in love with Ridge's eyes before I fell in love with his soul, his heart, or his mind. But I can't be sure since my feelings for him developed so fast. Within months, I went from meeting the strange neighbor boy to anticipating the feeling in my chest that awakened at a single glance. I lived for those glances and for those precious moments when we got to be alone on our hilltop.

Just looking at him now brings back all of those feelings and more. I could cry. I should let the dam burst and have my emotion pour down my cheeks. It would probably feel good. But the salty water will freeze before I allow a single tear to fall. Crying won't solve a damn thing.

"I'm okay," I tell him without reaching for his hand.

His square jaw tenses, and his eyes narrow to slits. He always hated how stubborn I was, which only made me want to exaggerate my performance.

Instead of arguing with me, he grabs me under both arms and lifts me like I weigh nothing, then he sets me down and releases his hands almost as fast as he'd grabbed me.

Ridge would never have been able to lift me like that when we were younger. I can't help the way my gaze scans over his broad shoulders and his tall body. Even under the layers of clothing he's wearing, I can tell that

Ridge has grown in more ways than I ever imagined. He's thicker and taller, and everything appears to be as hard as stone, just like his damn heart proved to be years ago.

"I thought you left."

"I went to the bathroom. Came back, and I saw you fall. I wanted to help."

"That wasn't necessary."

Without wasting another second, I lean down to check my boot laces then brush by him with a nudge of my shoulder into his side.

"You can at least say thank you," he calls after me.

Choosing to ignore him, I walk faster, until I've rounded the corner to where my Jeep is parked. Footsteps follow. The crunch of each step seems to echo in my chest until I've had enough.

I swing around and throw my hands onto my hips. "Stop following me, Ridge."

"I'm just making sure you get to your car."

Incredulous, I let out a laugh. "What a fucking gentleman you are. Newsflash. I've been walking fine on my own since I left this damn place. I didn't need your help then, and I definitely don't need it now."

"That's not how it looks to me, Wild One."

I blink a couple of times. My vision begins to fade to black as my heart hammers away. Then I take three steps forward, until I'm directly under his nose, glaring up at him with what I hope he can read as a warning look. "You lost the right to call me that a long fucking time ago." I keep my voice quiet and steady but firm. "Don't say it again, you hear me?"

Something flashes in his eyes, but he blinks it away

before I can know for sure what it means. Maybe it's anger, hurt, or annoyance. I don't know, and I really wish I didn't care.

"Sure thing, *Camila.*"

Ignoring the ache in my chest that comes from him saying my name, I turn and walk the rest of the way to my Jeep and leave.

CHAPTER 49

CAMILA

Early Friday morning, I step into my office and shut the door behind me. No other lights are on in the casita, and I won't be disturbed for the next few hours. I sit behind my desk, unlock the file-cabinet drawer, and pull out a month's worth of financial documents to peruse.

For the past few months, I've been working with an attorney to look into the shared partnership. One of his suggestions was for me to go through every single transaction, big and small, over the past ten years and make note of anything suspicious. I found out that Papa was selling off his personal assets left and right over the years to invest in more machinery—destemmers, fermenters, and bottling equipment, and the list just goes on.

As of now, I can do nothing to stop the Bradshaws from moving into the villa. Thanks to our shared partnership, Thomas and his family have just as much right to be here as I do. At least they are being civil enough to agree to take the guest villa rather than the main house. They are now situated with their own kitchen, four bedrooms, a living room, and access to their own private garden, so hopefully we can all keep our distance until I can figure out how to take back what should be mine.

"They're going to take over this place," I said to Mama after I found out the Bradshaws were moving in. "And you're letting them."

Mama sighed, showing her age as she eased into her favorite oversized chair in the living room. "I don't have a say, mija. I wish I did. But I've never had a say in how this place is run."

"Because Thomas Bradshaw made sure of that."

Mama nodded. "I believe that's true."

I fumed. "So, while I was going to school to get all these fancy degrees, certifications, and work-study experiences, Trip and his father were making all the local connections and establishing relationships with Papa's clients. I'm sure Papa's intentions were good, but how could he give so much of this place away to another family? It makes no sense." I raised my arms in defeat. "Now the Bradshaws are moving into the guest house. How long before they make their move into the main house? This is our *home*. I will not share it with them."

"Camila, when are you going to stop worrying about all the things you cannot control? Stop worrying so much about all the things that are wrong and think about the things that are right. Live for today, mija. You can't rewrite the past, but you can do something about right now."

Mama was always right. So over the last few months,

I've put all my focus and energy into overseeing operations with laser focus. I am everywhere, all day, every day. I refuse to rest, for fear of missing a single thing. My eye is on the prize and will be until I find a way to take back majority ownership of what should already be mine.

I've been pounding the pavement, getting to know our clients as intimately as possible, establishing friendships and hoping to earn their trust, just as the Bradshaws have. I have routine meetings with everyone on the staff to keep up with their concerns, and I've been fully immersing myself in marketing, wanting to understand the strategies. I give my input, and I've won a few battles along the way. And I've also been working with our winemaker to come up with a new seasonal blend that we can release by summer.

Trip, with his dad as his ongoing mentor, is often busy schmoozing new and old clients. And Raven keeps up with all the winery activities, a skill she's always been great at. As much as she rubs me the wrong way, even I can admit that she's exceptional at her job. For the most part, I leave her be, knowing any confrontation will result in a snooty bickering match I have no time for. A part of me also has never forgotten the way her eyes searched Ridge's at High Pie, like she knows him better than most.

I don't want to believe my suspicions, but she's always liked Ridge. With me gone, maybe Raven finally got her shot. They've always been friends, even when Ridge was working in Ouray. But she's Trip's sister, and I can't imagine him being okay with the two of them together.

Ugh, why am I distracting myself with thoughts about Ridge?

I haven't seen or talked to him since our fight outside of High Pie.

Pruning season has kept us all busier than ever. Sustainability was always the focus of the Bell Family Vineyard. Due to the harsh weather conditions and the long winter, we focus on cane and spur pruning during those months. So as the snow began to melt off the vines and new growth started to blossom from the healthy buds that had been dormant all season, not only did the vineyard have an awakening, but so did my soul.

I shouldn't have stayed away so long.

As soon as the thought enters my mind, I push it away. Beating myself up for choices I otherwise wouldn't be regretting is useless. The truth is that I loved school. After Ridge landed himself in jail and my parents were on the outs, the last thing I wanted to do was move back to Telluride. So I went back to school. After Ridge walked away from me again when we were in Dunton, I finished my master's program but was in no rush to return home, especially when I had the opportunity to travel to Italy for a work-study program. Then, upon my return to Napa, I was offered a job at one of the vineyards. In my mind, all of those years were benefiting my future. *How could I have ever seen what was coming?*

Sighing, I set aside the financials and reach for the vendor list. I've almost made it down our long list of potential clients, and today I plan to visit one more. But when I spot the next name on the list, my heartrate triples its speed.

The short description beside the business name of Wild One Ranch says that it's a vacation rental property with log cabins and wood-framed tents, reminding me a hell of a lot of Dunton Hot Springs and Camp Lachey combined. I continue to the right of the spreadsheet to find the address of the property along with the owner's name. *Ridge Cross.*

CHAPTER 50

RIDGE

Wild One Ranch is what's chiseled into the wooden plaque I had made for the main lodge. What started as a conversation with Camila in Ouray will soon be a reality. Over the past five years, I've worked with architects, builders, and the county to create the type of resort that reminds me of the ghost town Camila took me to in Dunton.

I still remember how wild my imagination became when we arrived and I took a walk around the property. My mind exploded with visions of creating the exact same thing in the woodland areas of the ranch. Harold had never done anything with the surrounding property, and I always loved that he'd wanted to preserve as much nature as possible. But to think that it could be preserved while allowing others to enjoy its natural beauty sparked something in me that I'd never felt before. I had a dream for the first time in my life, and nothing would stop me from living it out.

Fitting strategically into the outskirts of the property,

all spaced apart for privacy, now sit log cabins, luxury teepees, and tiny homes. I received my final approvals from the county just last week, which confirmed construction was done and Wild One was an official business. All that's left to do now is furnish each of the vacation homes and start booking stays.

I step back and take a look at the sign now fastened to the main cabin, which I'll use as an office, and smile.

"Clever name."

I spin around to face Camila. When my eyes lock on hers, I feel a jolt in my chest that reminds me of when we were younger. Something about her beauty always seems to shock my senses. That feeling has only intensified by all the time and distance between us.

Her hair is longer than how she wore it in the past. Her eyes are bigger and brighter than ever. Her green button-down dress is similar to the ones she used to wear, save for the mud and dirt that used to cake to the back of her legs.

She's carrying a giant basket filled with cheese, crackers, chocolate, and a bottle of Merlot from the Bell vintage collection. But it's the gentle smile she wears that strikes me most of all. It's free of anger and resentment from the hurt I've caused her. Instead, it's filled with surprise and pride for what I've created.

I glance at the sign and can't help but smile. "Yeah, well, you can say this place was inspired by someone of the same name."

Her eyes glaze over for a second before her smile widens, and she walks forward. She pushes the gift basket toward me. "I had to stop by and congratulate you. This is incredible, Ridge."

"Thank you." I take the basket from her, and our fingers brush. Words have never been my strong suit, but being this close to Camila makes me speechless in the most unbecoming way. Not a day goes by when I don't beat myself up over the way I lost her. Though my intentions were good, that doesn't change the fact that I was terrible to her. I broke her heart, and I will never forgive myself for it.

She spins in a slow circle, taking in the long trails that lead into the woods, where some of the cabins are vaguely visible through the trees

"Want a tour?" I finally ask after a quick internal debate.

"Yes, I would love that."

I turn to enter the main cabin. It's set up like a living room, with a couch, a large fireplace, and a big-screen television. It also has a check-in counter and a back room for storage and cleaning supplies. "This is the only cabin I've furnished, so be warned. It's a whole lot of nothing out there right now."

"I highly doubt that," she says, sounding amazed. "I can't wait to see it."

Nodding, I grab the ring of keys to unlock the doors, then we take off down the nearest trail marked with a wooden post that reads Honey Bee. I bite my bottom lip when she gives me a curious look, but she doesn't say anything about it.

Each of the dirt trails leads to a grassy clearing with stone steps that are pushed into the ground and wind toward each cabin. The cabin we get to first is somewhat crooked, with one roof sloping at more of an angle than the other. The unmatched wood is knotted and rough. It was made from all types of fallen trees, and I kept the exposed wood as natural as possible.

While she walks into the small one-bedroom, one-bathroom space, I can picture it fitted with a queen bed, some rugs, and local art to help tell the story of the area. While interior decorating isn't my expertise, I've had plenty of offers from local furniture stores to help me gain the look and feel I'm trying to achieve.

"No shower?" she asks, stepping back out of the bathroom.

I grin and point to the door on the back side of the cabin. "Out that way."

She pushes her way outside and straight into a secluded shower complete with a tall fence to give the feel of privacy. "Wow." She laughs. "Did you build this yourself?"

I nod. "It's taken me five years for good reason, but the reality so far is better than I could have ever imagined. Want to see the next one?"

She follows me eagerly then walks slightly ahead of me on the trail. "What ever happened to Bruno? I miss the little guy."

My chest squeezes. Her question brings to light just how long Camila was gone. "Raven took him when I went to jail. She loved him and probably would have kept him, but Bruno hated Thomas something fierce. Couldn't blame him. She ended up giving him back to me a couple years after I got out. He passed away last year."

Her eyes fill with emotion. "I'm so sorry, Ridge."

"He was a good dog. Lived a good life too. I like to think he's up there with Harold now."

I feel the squeeze of my hand, but by the time I look down to confirm Camila's touch, she's already pulled away. The loss of her aches, and I curse myself for feeling like I deserve her comfort. I lost that right long ago.

We follow the path to another private trail with a wooden sign that reads Wake Up Time, and Camila throws me another curious glance. She's beginning to catch on, but she hasn't figured it out yet.

This cabin is a little bigger, with one master bedroom, an upstairs loft with room for two beds, and a wood-burning stove downstairs.

Not until we get to the next wooden sign, which reads Wildflowers, do the clues start to make sense. She stops as soon as she reads it and turns to me. The smile that seemed glued to her face for the first part of the tour starts to slip as emotion creeps in. "Are all your cabins named after Tom Petty songs or just the ones we've visited so far?"

I smile despite the feelings suddenly swirling in my chest. I can't tell what she's thinking, and I want to know. "It seemed appropriate."

When she frowns, dread sinks in my gut.

"How?" she asks softly, but her voice is as firm and fierce as ever. "How is any of this appropriate after all we've been through? You can't go around making girls fall in love with you, grinding their hearts into dust, then doing all of this. What is this, Ridge? Some sort of romantic gesture?"

I feel lost for words again. "No. I just—"

"You just what?" she demands.

"I wouldn't have done any of this without you."

Though I don't mean to sound so angry, I'm pissed off about what happened to us too. I may have been the one who ended things between us, but I wasn't the one who started the war. "You inspired me. It's as simple as that."

"It's not simple, and you know that."

"We have a complicated history, and you hate me, I know, but that doesn't change the imprint you left on me."

She crosses her arms and glares back at me. "But you ended it, Ridge. No matter your reasons, you were given a choice, and you didn't choose me. Take some responsibility."

"I have!" I yell. "What do you think I've been doing for the last ten damn years of my life? I've lived in my own personal hell, thanks to my decisions, but I never would have done any of it if I didn't think you were better off. Don't you see, Camila? Except for those few stolen moments I got to spend with you, my life was never mine. The only choices I was ever given end here. With me right here and you right there. There may not be a feud anymore with our fathers gone, but there's still a bridge, and it still divides us. If not for the hate that once existed, then for unforgivable hurt I caused you."

Her eyes are red and glassy as she backs away, shaking her head. "What am I supposed to do, Ridge, huh? I was so hurt for so long. One day, all that hurt hardened into this ball of anger that never stopped growing." Her chin quivers, and she drops her hands and balls them into fists. "I'm so mad at you, yet I want to forgive you, and I don't even know why."

My heart races. *Can she ever truly forgive me?* I've had so much doubt, even when she picked me up from that jail and rode me with so much aggression that I could feel it hovering around us like an invisible cloud. Back then, I couldn't have even attempted to ask for her forgiveness. I couldn't explain a damn thing. But things are different now. Patrick and Harold are dead, and the only war that exists is the one that rages on between two broken hearts.

"Have dinner with me."

My words shock me as much as they do her, and I can practically hear the breath expel from her parted lips.

"What?"

I step closer, committing to my words. "If you need to be mad at me, then be mad. But at least let me make you dinner."

Silence stretches between us, until she finally answers, "Okay."

CHAPTER 51

CAMILA

I strangle the steering wheel as I follow Ridge down the curvy gravel drive that leads to the main ranch house, my nerves firing off like fireworks the entire way. When I first saw him today, my heart did that fluttering thing. He was wearing a simple white T-shirt and jeans, but the way he filled them out, with his biceps stretching the fabric around his arms, and his jeans tight around his muscular ass, I'm surprised I was able to think clearly at all. Until I caught on to the significance of the fifteen different cabin names, I was doing pretty well. Now, I'm desperately trying to take control of my racing heart when his house comes into view. I feel like I've stepped back into my past.

When I showed up on his steps after hearing about Harold's death all those years ago, I was taken aback by the exterior changes to the home. The house was bigger and freshly painted, and even the roofing had changed from warped wood to metal. The crooked shutters had been removed and replaced with clean straight ones. The white window frames had changed to black. And grass surrounded the idyllic structure, as opposed to the dirt that was there before. I'd almost forgotten about the changes until now.

Ridge parks his truck and waits for me at the bottom of the porch steps, and as I move to join him, I'm keenly aware of how strange this all should feel. I was thirteen when I met Ridge, and I never once stepped foot inside his home. After so many years of hiding our friendship and more, a nugget of fear that we'll get caught is still in the back of my mind. But then I remind myself that we're both adults now. The feud is over. And this isn't a date. We're just two old friends who are trying to move forward.

When I approach, he reaches out, and I take his hand without even hesitating. *What is wrong with me? Why does it all come so easily to me when we are anything but?* Ridge has a habit of leaving me behind, and I have a habit of forgiving him without a second thought. I can't let my heart go back to that vulnerable place. Like I told Josie when I first arrived, I'll be cordial, but I'll never forget.

He pushes open the front door, releases my hand, and gestures for me to enter first. I step inside and am immediately blown away by what I see. From the shiplap walls to the natural wood flooring, to the beautiful open layout, I am filled with so many questions.

As a child, when I looked at the ranch house from the hilltop, I imagined Ridge's living conditions to be no better than wretched based on the outward appearance of the home. Seeing it up close is a whole other story.

"What is going on in that crazy head of yours?" He chuckles.

I let out an airy laugh, realizing I must look ridiculous, the way my eyes are wandering. "This is nothing like what I pictured you living in, Ridge." I struggle to find words that won't come out sounding offensive. "The way you used to talk about this place. The way you never wanted to be here." I shake my head, knowing my confusion is warranted, now that I remember those conversations.

Ridge smiles. "We have a lot of catching up to do, I see. Come. I'll pour you a drink."

He leads me down the hall and into the impressive kitchen. Everything is so clean and bright, from the white cabinets, to the stainless-steel appliances, and to the long pendant lights hanging over the long marble-top island. I'm in awe.

He pulls out a stool for me to sit at the island, and I accept with a smile. As he reaches into a cabinet, I suddenly feel my nerves take over again. I've never felt out of my element before, but I am aware of it now. So much has changed in the past ten years. Ridge has not only taken over Harold's farm but also started a new venture on his own. He's probably had a slew of girlfriends over the years. Maybe he's even fallen in love.

I stare at the bottle of red wine he's holding. "Um. Do you have anything stronger?"

He looks down at the bottle then nods before shoving it back into the cabinet. "Bourbon?"

"Perfect."

As soon as he slides my drink to me, I lift it to my lips and pour the smooth, fiery liquid down my throat. The burn is just what I need. That trail of fire leads straight to my chest, until a numbing effect takes hold.

He watches me over the rim of his glass as he takes a swig, then he leans onto the counter across from me, seemingly amused. "Better?"

Heat rises to my cheeks, and I'm not sure if I'm flushed from the bourbon or from his stare. "Getting there."

He smiles. "I have an idea." Ridge reaches into a cabinet below him and retrieves a basket. He points at the large window above the sink behind him, where a garden of fresh produce sits. "You choose the vegetables, and I'll make something with whatever you pick."

Narrowing my eyes, I bite down on my smile. "You can do that?"

Ridge shrugs. "Do it every night. I don't think too hard about it. I just grab what looks good and whip something up."

I take this as a challenge, and the gleam in his eyes shows he's not surprised. "Okay," I say cautiously. "Anything?"

"Anything."

With a quick hop off the stool, I take the basket from him, then I head out the kitchen door. It takes me a second to understand the layout of the garden. Herbs are in one plot of soil, fruits are in a second, and dark, leafy greens are in another. I walk by each plot, row by row, tempted to pluck everything I see. I manage to control myself and wind up with a basket of butternut squash, spinach, tomatoes, and a pomegranate.

"Okay," I say as I walk through the door to where Ridge is dicing garlic cloves. I come up beside him and place the basket on the counter. "Good luck."

He takes a good look at what I picked and smiles. "You went easy on me."

I shrug. "Whatever you come up with, I want it to be edible."

"Fair enough."

Taking a seat on the stool again, I raise my drink to my lips. "Okay, no more stalling. Tell me how I just walked into a farmhouse that belongs in a magazine."

He looks around then goes back to chopping the ingredients. "I think you had been away at college for three months when Harold asked me to come back to help him with the fall harvest. A lot changed after you left. Business picked up quite a bit, and I think it gave Harold a new lease on life. He gave up drinking and started spending all his off-hours doing projects around the house. And when winter came along, I started helping him. Over the years, we just kept at it. We added on to the house, updated the exterior, and totally remodeled every inch of the inside. You should have seen him, Camila. He was the happiest man."

I could sense the pride Ridge still feels for his father, and for that, I'm grateful they had all those years together. "I would have loved to see Harold like that."

Ridge nods. "He was a changed man. That's for sure."

A bitter thought warps our happy moment. "I guess you were his hero for putting an end to that rivalry. If business got better, and Harold didn't have all that nonsense hanging over his head, I can see why he would have been a changed man." *Even though you broke my heart.*

Ridge stops chopping and gazes back at me. He's always seen straight through me. I wouldn't be surprised if he could hear every thought swirling through my head too. "You said something to me five years ago that I couldn't answer then, but I can now. I know it's too late, and nothing I could ever say or do can fix anything, but there's no reason for me to keep this from you now."

I try to swallow past the lump in my throat then take another gulp of the amber fire that burns in my chest. When I set the drink down, my hand is shaking, but I nod to let him know it's okay to continue.

"You think I left you—left town—to end the rivalry between our fathers, and that's only partly true. Thomas Bradshaw came to me that morning. He knew about us and said your father knew about us too. He told me that if I didn't end things, your father would take everything from you. School tuition, the vineyard, your dreams. He forced me to make a choice—break your heart so you'd follow the path your father set for you or stay and let you forfeit everything. I couldn't let you do that."

It's like he's just dropped a bomb that I never had time to run from. The explosion blows through me and distorts everything I once believed. "And you didn't come to me about that?"

"I couldn't. If I had said anything to you, it would have just made things worse. I wasn't about to let you risk everything for me."

"Ridge, we could have talked. You and I had a plan. We could have stuck to it. I was going to go to college and come back after four years to take over the vineyard, then you and I were going to be together."

He clenches his jaw. "You think you would have come back in four years, and your father would magically be okay with us being together? No, Camila. I might have been in denial before everything blew up in our faces, but the reality of who we were and what we couldn't be was finally made clear. Being with me was only holding you back. And look, now you have everything you ever want-ed." He raises his glass. "Congratulations."

Anger burns in my chest. How dare he assume that his leaving could have done anything to benefit my life. He broke my heart. "Everything I've ever wanted? You're clueless, if that's what you think. Do you want to know the reality of what I came home to?" I hold up my pointer finger. "My parents fought constantly until they became as good as strangers." I hold up a second finger. "My papa died." I hold up a third finger. "The vineyard isn't even all mine." I hold up a fourth finger, but Ridge cuts me off.

"Wait. What? What do you mean, the vineyard isn't even all yours? That was the deal. You go to school, you get the vineyard, either by a transfer of ownership at the time of your choosing or by default after the death of your father. I read the terms, Camila."

My entire body shakes. "Right. I get whatever percentage of ownership my papa leaves me with. He left me with fifty percent. Guess who owns the other fifty percent now."

The fury that takes over Ridge's expression matches what I feel. "That bastard. He lied to us both and manipulated your father."

I nod. "Papa never said anything to me either. I'm still digging into everything, because it makes no sense. Even if Papa agreed to sell ownership, Thomas paid him millions over the last ten years. Millions that Papa turned around and invested in the vineyard."

"Millions? Where would Thomas get that kind of money?"

I shrug. "I'm trying to figure that out. I need to have majority ownership, Ridge. It's only a matter of time before Thomas tries to take the vineyard away from me completely. I don't know how he'll manage it, but I can feel the threat of it looming every single day. The Bradshaws have already moved into the guest villa."

Ridge's jaw tenses. "What?"

I scan his reaction carefully. "You really didn't know any of this? Raven never said anything to you?" I swallow. "I know you two are close."

His eyes lock on mine, and understanding registers on his face. "Whatever you're thinking, stop. Raven has been a friend to me, yes, but that's all."

Heat rushes to my cheeks as I shake my head. "It doesn't matter. You don't have to explain anything to me."

"What do you think we're doing here together, Camila? I'm explaining everything I couldn't before. I don't expect you to forgive me, but at least you have my full transparency now."

"Is that what you want? My forgiveness? I've been back in town for months, and you haven't even attempted to see me or talk to me."

"Because I don't deserve your forgiveness. I know what I did. I know what I lost. You were the only person in my entire life, other than my mother, who made me feel worthy of love, and I still broke your heart. But guess what? I broke my heart too. I can't take back what I did, and I won't fool myself into thinking I can."

I can feel my face crumble, and my heart is heavy with all the hurt I've been carrying around for too many years. "I hate when you do that. You make all these decisions without ever giving me a say. When are you going to start talking to me instead of trying to protect me? If I want to forgive you, then I will. If I want to stay mad at you, I'll do that too."

He slowly blows out a breath while assessing me. "Fair enough. As much as I'll always want to protect you, I know you're right."

A moment of calm silence passes between us. We've taken the first step toward each other since walking away all those years ago. It feels good.

"And for what it's worth," he says while holding my gaze, "I do want your forgiveness."

A slow smile lifts my cheeks. "Well, this is a start." I nod to the array of chopped vegetables in front of him. "You can continue earning it by making me dinner."

CHAPTER 52

RIDGE

Going by the guttural moan Camila expels, I think dinner is a hit. Her eyes are wide as she swallows her first bite of roasted squash, then she immediately stabs another and chews that one too. When she's finished, she sets down her fork and drops her jaw. "Ridge Cross, you can cook?"

I pick up a forkful of my own food and raise an eyebrow. "Apparently, I can cook very well."

She looks down at the colorful food spread out on her plate. "What do you call this?"

I shrug. "You picked the ingredients. You should name it."

She makes a face. "What? No. You added stuff."

"Not much. Only goat cheese, chopped walnuts, and a honey vinaigrette."

She points at me like I've just made her point. "See. Right there. Who makes honey vinaigrette from scratch? Who even thinks of that?" She shakes her head. "You do. That's who. You, with all these secret talents I'm just now learning." She purses her lips. "Okay. Let's call this meal You Wreck Me."

Laughter rolls through me at the Tom Petty song title. "Touché."

She smiles, pleased with herself, as she dives in for more food. Bob Seger's Greatest Hits spins on the vintage record player in the living room as we eat and drink our bourbon. We've eased away from serious conversation and moved on to lighter topics, like my plans for opening the resort and Camila's time in Italy. I love hearing about her adventures, and I only wish that her next one could be with me.

By the end of dinner, our plates are clear, her cheeks are flushed, and her eyes are wide and bright, just like when she would run through the cornfield. Camila's the beautiful and playful girl I started loving without even realizing when or how. She's the gorgeous woman who still holds my heart.

When "Old Time Rock & Roll" starts to play, a slow smile spreads across her face. She jumps up and walks around to my side of the table. "We can clean this later. Come with me." She holds out a hand.

Maybe it's the bourbon, or perhaps it's the drunk giggle that slips past Camila's lips, but I can almost pretend that nothing has changed between us as I wrap my hand around hers and let her yank me to my feet.

She tugs me into the living room and starts moving her body to the beat. Her arms swing above her head as she thrashes, and her hair whips around her shoulders as she twirls. No way will I move like that, but I'm enjoying the show. Every now and then, she grabs my hands and tries to get me to dance with her, and though I wish I

377

looked as good as she does doing it, I manage only a few shakes of my hips before the song transitions to a slow one.

The piano melody to "We've Got Tonight" is such a drastic change from the fast song before it, causing Camila to stop dancing completely. After a moment of awkwardness, she lets out an airy laugh and releases my hands. "Well, that's a mood buster. I'll change the song."

She starts to move past me toward the record player when something strong and instinctual—something that feels like fate—gives me a hard punch in the chest. I grab her hand and pull her back to me. Surprised, she stumbles a little, and her palms break her fall on my chest. When she recovers, she meets my gaze, and I don't try to interpret it. Instead, I move her arms around my neck, wrap mine around her waist, and start to move.

Her eyes narrow, but they have a glimmer in them. "Oh, so now you want to dance."

I cringe a little. "I don't think you can call this dancing. And to be fair, I don't think you can call what you were doing dancing either."

Not even her harsh glare can hide the amusement she finds at my joke. She purses her lips to hold back her laugh then swats at my chest before moving her hand back around my neck. "At least I was having fun."

"Oh, I was having fun watching you. Besides, you didn't seem to have a problem with my moves at prom."

Her cheeks redden, and when my gaze slips down to her neck, I find that part of her skin is changing color too. She's flushed all over, and I can't help but get excited that I'm doing that to her.

"Yeah, well, you also bribed me with a dozen pink

roses, a tent, and a pretty necklace, so we probably shouldn't compare experiences."

At the mention of her necklace, my gaze locks on her throat, even though I already know it isn't there. When she picked me up from the jail, she wasn't wearing it then either. The disappointment weighed heavily, and as much as I want to ask her where it is, I choose not to go there. I had no right to question it back then, and I still don't. "Just give me a few minutes, and I can rectify all that."

She smiles gently back at me, and the mood shifts from playful to serious. "You would, wouldn't you?"

My heart pounds so hard that I can feel it between my ears. I cup her neck while slowly moving a finger across her cheek, and I glance at her lips before locking on her eyes. "I would do anything for you, Camila. That hasn't changed, and it never will."

She blinks, as if she can't believe me. I drop my forehead to hers, and when her eyelids flutter closed as a shaky breath rushes past her lips, I know she feels the same.

"How does this feel so normal?" Her words are just a whisper. "I close my eyes, and it's like I'm right where I'm supposed to be." She shakes her head. "I don't understand."

"What's to understand? Our roots are deep, just like your vines, which adapt to every season. No matter the harsh weather, there's always new growth."

"Are you comparing our relationship to the life of a grape?"

The teasing in her voice makes me chuckle. "No. I'm comparing us to a whole damn vineyard. We're the root." I lean in, brush her lips with mine, and whisper, "You and me, Wild One."

A shiver racks her entire body, and I tighten my hold around her, as if it could help. The way she's engulfed in my arms brings me the most comfort I've felt in years. Camila's right. This feels so normal and natural, like we were always meant to fit.

I brush my lips against hers again, almost expecting her to pull away and tell me it's too soon or too late. Either one of those responses would be understandable. But when her fingernails dig into my back, I don't ignore the message. I mold my mouth to hers and kiss her hard.

Her firm lips respond to mine immediately, and she steals every bit of my air as she breathes me in. I explore the taste and feel of her like it's the very first time. In a way, that's exactly what this is. It's been ten years since our lips last touched, and though I've dreamed about it, nothing could have prepared me for the real feeling of our mouths moving as one, our breaths tangling with heat and desire, or our hands wandering as our mouths keep a slow and steady pace. The kiss is so consuming and powerful that I feel an awakening within me. And when she parts my mouth with hers and sweeps her tongue over mine, a growl rumbles through me.

I lift her by the backs of her thighs, and she eagerly wraps her legs around me then slips her fingers through my hair, gripping and tugging, and intensifying our lip-lock.

Years of pent-up feelings, secret fantasies, and unbridled desire sweep through me. Knowing what I lost and feeling the impossibility of never having it again has been worse than sitting in a jail cell for a year. That feeling of loss has turned me into a hungry, desperate man that only Camila has a chance of healing.

I walk the short distance to the couch and sit with her still wrapped around my waist. Her knees dig into the cushions on either side of me, and my hands begin to roam up her legs and under her dress, until I grip her ass with both hands.

Camila fits well over me, and I remember the feel of being inside her the last time we were together like this. Well, that time, she was in total control, and I was just along for the ride. And what a beautiful ride it was. But I want her beneath me this time. I want her so badly that I start to move her against me, pushing and pulling so that she grinds on my lap. Our mouths go slack the more we work ourselves into a frenzy.

I glide my hands up her arms and over her shoulders and find the thin straps of her dress to slip them down. Then I kiss her cheek, her ear, her neck, and her shoulder and stop at her chest, which heaves above the ribbed fabric of her dress. I slip a finger under the fabric and start to pull it back, but I pause to look up and ask for silent permission. Her heated stare is all the confirmation I need.

Looking down again, I pull the fabric down until it rests beneath her breasts. She's not wearing a bra, so her hard nipples are the first things I see. They're dark brown and firmly pointed back at me, and I don't waste a second. Leaning down, I swipe one with my tongue then close my mouth around it and suck. She gasps and squirms in response, only intensifying my hunger. My mouth is unrelenting as I palm one beautiful breast, then I transfer my mouth to the other.

"Ridge," she moans while trying to catch her breath. "Make love to me."

The final word is barely out of her mouth when I lift her from the couch, then I carry her down the hall to my bedroom, kissing her the whole way. She doesn't have to ask me twice. I've never wanted anything more in my entire life.

I breeze through the open double door that leads to my room without bothering to flip on the light then set her on her feet and yank her dress to the floor. With the faint light streaming into the room from the hallway, I can make out her strong, curvy lines, which appear soft in all the right places. She's naked, save for the scrap of black fabric of her panties. "You are insanely beautiful, Wild One." I gawk as desire tornadoes through me.

Her eyes flick over me before she takes a seat on the edge of the bed. "I want to see you too."

I lift my shirt over my head and unbutton my jeans to slide them down my legs, never once taking my eyes off Camila. Her eyes roam, and her mouth parts when her gaze locks on my erection fighting to come out of my briefs. Camila's seen me before and had me in her mouth. She's sucked my desire clean and swallowed me whole. Now, I'm going to return the favor.

As I lean down, her eyes go wide as she takes in my expression, and she inches backward on my bed. If I look anything like the beast of a man I feel like inside, then she has every right to be cautious. I kneel above her and grab her panties. With one yank, I rip them down her legs, then I toss them to the side before spreading her knees and getting a good look at her. She's so damn perfect, the way she opens up to me.

With a quick breath out, I lie on my stomach so that my ears are between her thighs and my mouth hovers over her pussy. I inhale her sweet scent like she's wine fresh out of the bottle. Then I slide my hands around her legs to grip her breasts and take my first long, slow lick.

She quivers, the skin over her abs tightening as I torture her with my tongue. I've barely even started, and she's already gripping my hair in a silent plea to release her. But I'm in no hurry, and I have too many years to make up for.

My tongue has a mind of its own as it plays with her clit in perfect time with the way her hips start to move against my face. I slip one of my hands from her breast to just above her slit while I place my other hand under her thigh. I work her skin toward my mouth while I deepen each swipe of my tongue, causing her to jerk hard from the pressure.

When I sense her climax building, I lock my lips around her clit and suck it into my mouth. She screams while she tugs at my hair, and I growl against her squirming body. I walk my fingers from her thigh to her opening, push them into her, and work them deeper and deeper until she moans her release and drips, wet and hot, around my fingers.

I breathe hard as I push myself back off the bed and onto my feet. My briefs are gone in less than a second, and I crawl back between her legs. I lean down and devour her mouth while fitting myself against her entrance. Her hands snake around to my ass as she lifts her hips, hinting for me to enter her. But I never forgot the way I pushed into her the last time and how greedy and aggressive I was with my first thrust.

My desperation to be inside her was almost as strong then as it is now. But this time, I have control, and I want to live in the moment as I feel her stretch around me. I want to hear each and every moan as it escapes those beautiful lips, and I want to reach deeper into her than I've ever reached before. I want to reach her heart and soul at the point of no return. This time, I want to stay there forever.

CHAPTER 53

CAMILA

I'm still coming down from my climax when Ridge starts to enter me. My breathing is erratic, my body feels limp and slightly out of sorts, my head is filled with white puffy clouds, and stars won't stop shooting behind my eyes. After the way he just consumed me, hot and vicious, like I'm his last meal, desire rages on in my core.

He's so thick as he moves into me, but my body adapts just like before, molding to him and engulfing him in a tight hug that ignites my center. He rocks inside of me, deepening his thrusts while kissing my mouth, my neck, and my breasts. Spreading my knees wider, I squeeze his ass and lift my hips to bring him closer and closer until his slow and steady thrusts hit the deepest part of me.

I move my hands to his face and bring his mouth to mine. But as soon as my lips touch his, I gasp at the first sign of another orgasm.

He quickens his pace, and I can feel his body tensing

too. Our eyes connect as he drives into me, and the wood headboard crashes into the wall as it moves. He doesn't let up until I scream his name and God knows what else as my orgasm blasts through me and carries me into a sweet, starry abyss.

I awake to the bright morning sun shining through the large bedroom window. Ridge's strong arms are wrapped around me beneath a white down comforter. I've never felt more relaxed in my life. A smile lifts my cheeks as I feel him stir behind me. He groans and pushes his naked body against me. His dick is already hardening between my ass cheeks as he grips my breasts.

"Good morning," I tease as his mouth begins to trail sweet kisses down my back.

"Yes, it is." His gravelly voice is thick with sleep as his words float down my back, causing me to giggle.

Suddenly he removes his mouth, and I'm hit with a breeze when he sweeps off the covers. Then he flips me over, crawls above me with a devilish grin, and pins my wrists to the mattress.

"I love your giggle." A smile slowly spreads on his face. He dips his head and kisses my neck, causing me to shiver. "I love this spot right here too." He moves down to my breasts and sucks each one into his mouth. "And these," he murmurs against my skin. Then he moves to my belly, sending my pulse soaring through my veins. "And this."

His hands are on my hips when he starts to move down my body again, but this time, he freezes. I lift my head, sensing something is wrong, and my heart immediately plunges into the pit of my stomach. His eyes are on my hip and the scar that will forever be a haunting reminder of that awful night that will never leave me. The hunter lives on in the darkest crevices of my mind, threatening to leap out when I least expect it. The scar is a trigger—whenever it aches, whenever I catch an accidental glimpse of it in the mirror, or whenever my fingers graze it as I'm dressing.

My throat clogs as I watch his face transition from curiosity, to confusion, then to realization as he starts to answer his own question. The scar isn't something a passerby would think was normal. It still tingles when fear spikes in my chest, and it makes me hesitate before putting on a bikini and saying, "To hell with it." It attracts stares and makes people wonder and turn away in disgust. Ridge won't do that, though. I wore a nude bandage at the dimly lit cabin five years ago when I undressed in front of him. He didn't even notice it then.

Suddenly, the light streaming in feels too bright. I reach for the sheet and pull it over my body, blocking my scar from Ridge's probing eyes. Even if he won't judge me for it, I'm aware of how grotesque the jagged and scarred tissue appears.

His gaze flashes to mine. "Where did you get that, Camila?"

Shying away from the conversation would be pointless. We've talked about that night only once, but it was five years ago, and he was too swept up in his own misery to ask any questions. He'd believed the lie that Harold told him. It had swept through the town in gossip channels until everyone knew, but they knew wrong.

"That night," I say quietly. "In the woods."

Ridge's eyebrows draw together. "Dave Lachey did that? Harold said you were fine. I didn't—" He looks lost and confused by the realization that Harold's version of what happened that night is grossly different from actual events.

A second later, I tell him everything I remember, from my search for the necklace to ending up back at the mine, where I spotted the hunter and his arrow aimed right for me. I recall each arrow that whipped by my head as I weaved through trees and brush until finally getting to the bridge.

"When I didn't see you there, I turned toward the cornfields, hoping you were on your way. And that's when he got me. It sliced open my side, then I tripped over a log and smashed my head on the ground. I don't know what happened after that. When I came to, Gus was with me, and Harold was standing over Dave's dead body with his shotgun."

I was shaking by the time I finished telling him my story.

Ridge had moved to lie beside me while I gave him the play-by-play, his expression only becoming more shocked and disgusted as my story went on. "But Harold said Dave was out hunting and mistook you for an animal."

I nod as the anger I've kept locked away for over a decade spreads through me again like wildfire. "Sounds about right. Everyone thought I was just confused. They thought I hit my head too hard and wasn't thinking straight and that Dave Lachey was nothing but a poacher, which he was. But he was also a psychopath who was trying to murder me."

"Why would he come after you like that? I don't understand."

I shrug. "I don't know. The weirdest part of it all was how he let me run right by him at first without trying to take a shot. It was like he wanted to chase me. Like he was in it for the hunt."

Ridge hugs me tight. "That's exactly how it sounds. Jason always said his brother was obsessive about hunting, but I got the impression he was a nice guy. I never asked too many questions. It didn't feel like my business at the time." His soft eyes rest on mine. "I'm sorry, Camila."

I don't know why I'm surprised that he believes me, but my throat thickens with emotion even more as I stare back into his eyes. "You're the first person who hasn't looked at me like I'm a crazy person."

"Why would you make it up? It's possible they dropped it since they couldn't prove what you were saying and he was already dead."

"That's exactly why the case was closed so abruptly, but it never sat right with me. Dave was a known poacher who took the hunt too far that night. Case closed. What if he *was* out to get me that night? What if I wasn't the only one he tried to hurt?"

Ridge shudders. "That's dark."

"Trust me. I've considered a lot of wild scenarios over the years. Maybe if they had just investigated my story a little, then I wouldn't be so obsessed with wanting to understand all the whys and hows. I don't know. But…"

Ridge pulls back slightly to look at me. "But what?"

I hesitate to tell him what I'm thinking. That night was so long ago, and despite what anyone believes happened, it's over. "I can't stop thinking about that mine."

He blows out a breath. "I told you not to go back to that mine alone. You promised me you wouldn't. It's creepy, and you know that area is dangerous."

"I was so upset about my necklace that I wasn't thinking. And you weren't answering your phone."

Guilt fills his expression. "I'll never forgive myself for not being there. At the time, I thought I was doing the right thing. I'm so sorry." He bows his head and touches his forehead to mine.

"Please stop blaming yourself for what happened to me. What Dave did was not your fault. But how did he enter that section of land? There aren't any roads at the edge of our property line in the woods, and beyond that, he'd have to travel over a massive mountain range to even get near an access road. So, how did he do it? No one even questioned it. And what if I wasn't the only one he hurt while hunting?"

"He couldn't have snuck into the woods through the vineyard roads?"

I shake my head. "No way. Not without security cameras picking something up."

Ridge shrugs. "Then I don't know, Camila. Dave was a sneaky bastard."

I search his eyes, hoping he doesn't think I'm totally crazy. "Do you think there could be an access road at the other end of the mine?"

He considers my words before he gives me a slow

nod. "That's very possible. But does it matter? Dave's dead. You can feel peace, knowing he can't hurt anyone ever again."

I shudder. "That's the thing. I don't feel peace. I don't feel closure. I'd thought seeing him dead that night was all I needed to put that terror behind me, but it's never left. I still feel like he's out there, spying on me, waiting in the weeds to take aim and shoot."

Ridge's face grows even sadder. "How can I help?"

"You already are," I whisper, blinking back tears. "Just by believing me. Just by listening." I don't want to keep rehashing that dark, lonely period of my life when he wasn't part of it. I just want to move forward with him now that there's nothing and no one in the world to try to stop us.

"I should go," I say softly. "Every second I'm not at that vineyard, Thomas Bradshaw is probably planning his next move to eject me from my livelihood."

Ridge hugs me tighter. "Don't go yet. I just got you back."

Smiling, I touch my nose to his. "You have me. Besides, I'm right next door if you need me." I wink and wiggle out from beneath him to search for my dress. It's still at the foot of the bed. I slip it on and glance at where Ridge is still lying, his eyes glued to me.

"I love you, Camila."

My heart squeezes. I missed those words so much and certainly did not expect to hear them today. Ridge and I had a great night, but we still need time to heal and figure out how to move forward together.

I walk toward him and sit at the edge of the bed as

he props himself up with his elbow, then I lean down and dust my lips across his. "I love you too."

His smile is the last thing I see before our lips meet in a slow kiss and he pulls me back into bed.

By the time I park in my driveway, it's nearly noon. I don't bother to change. Instead, I take a long walk around the vineyard, something I haven't done nearly as much as I thought I would do.

When I was a young girl and dreamed of my grown-up life running the land, the images that passed through my head were much like this one—slow Sundays filled with long walks, deep breaths, and big smiles. And the once-snow-covered aisles between the vines are filled with wildflowers that will be trampled by the time summer comes along.

I giggle at the hummingbird that zooms past my ear toward the feeder I set out last week, knowing that my soul needed this. With my mission to regain majority ownership, I started to lose sight of the reason I'd fallen in love with this place to begin with. This, right here, is it.

Tomorrow, the vineyard will be filled with activity. Now that the first buds have sprouted and foliation has begun, it's time for the growers to start the process of green pruning. They'll cut back the plant so that the molecules of the acids and sugars in the leaves and vines are concentrated on prime areas where the grape bunches will grow. Papa was so meticulous about it that I studied him like a hawk. The vintners in Napa where I last worked were impressed with my knowledge, and I always gave credit to the man who taught me everything I knew.

Thinking about my papa makes my heart heavy, but I can't be sad. I've grieved for him and celebrated his life, and now all I want more than anything is to honor his memory by continuing with the Bell Family Vineyard traditions he passed down to me.

When I unlock the casita and start my stride down the brightly lit hall to my office, I realize it's the first day in months that I didn't arrive before anyone else. Although the office is usually quiet on Sundays, it's always open. With winery sales coming in and employees from the field stopping by for paychecks and to talk, there's never a dull moment.

The door to my office is already open. I glare at it, annoyed at what feels like an intrusion into the only space I've been able to claim as mine. So far, Thomas hasn't fought me on that, but I can feel another war brewing as soon as I approach my desk and notice the items on it have shifted from their usual spots. In addition, a small unwrapped white jewelry box sits on my keyboard.

I pick it up, expecting to find a note underneath it or some indication of who it's from. When I see nothing, I open the delicate box and gasp. Emotion clogs my throat as I peer down at the handmade wire-wrapped arrowhead necklace. A silver plate with the words "Wild One," still etched into it. My hand automatically moves to that spot on my throat I always touch.

My heart beats fast as I search the space again for a clue as to who set the jewelry box here. *Who found it?*

Where *did they find it?* I shake as I notice again that items on my desk have shifted.

I'm meticulous about my work space. Before leaving to visit Ridge, I took the time to tidy up and place everything where I knew I could find them. But the computer monitor is angled in the wrong direction, a blue pen sits alone on my desk rather than in its normal place in the drawer, the notepad I keep next to the mouse pad has a tear, and the scent of cedar and musk lingers in the air. I wrinkle my nose at Thomas's signature cologne, then I charge back toward the hallway.

Thomas has an office two doors down the hall from mine. I normally avoid it at all costs, letting him come to me if we need to meet. But my patience is wearing thin. Now that he's invaded my space—not just in my home but in my office too—it's time we have a little chat.

Perhaps he's used to being all up in Papa's business, so I will give him the benefit of the doubt and assume he was at my desk for purely professional reasons. He'll learn soon enough that I work much differently from how Patrick Bell did. And if he's the one who found my necklace, then I have a lot of questions.

His door is shut, but light pours through the edges, so I knock. Classical music plays faintly on the other side, but I can't hear any other sounds. "Thomas, it's Camila. We need to talk." I knock again. Still nothing.

After a moment of internal debate, I turn the handle and push open the door to find the room completely empty. Irritation at his lack of care regarding the utility expenses gnaws at me. The least the jerk can do is power everything off before he leaves.

I stomp over to the ancient black stereo system and push the power button to cut the music then go to his desk and flip off his green lamp, a fan, and some electric serenity waterfall that surely serves a man like him absolutely no purpose.

I'm about to turn toward the door when the photos on the wall behind his desk catch my eye. Dread sinks low in my gut as a chill shoots up my spine. My heart races, and my palms start to sweat. I don't fully realize why I'm having such a physical reaction to what I'm seeing. All I know is I need to see more.

I flip back on the light and move around the desk to take a closer look. Dozens of photos with family, friends, and from his hunting days are arranged in a mosaic pattern on the wall. Papa has plenty of hunting photos just like these packed away in boxes at the main house. They've never bothered me before.

I find my papa in every photo possible, smiling at how happy he looks in each and every one. One photo in particular makes me think my mind is playing tricks on me. I shake my head and lean in to look again. My papa and Thomas are standing together with a man in the middle. But when the man in the middle's camo skull mask stares back at me, just like that day near the mine, my blood runs cold. The man who I now know as Dave Lachey is holding the same bow that he aimed at my head, and the same cold, dark eyes meet mine.

A shaky breath slips past my lips as I fall back and have to catch myself on Thomas's desk. My heart thunders, but I can't look away from the photo. Each passing second that I study the image makes the fear slithering through me intensify. Terrifying memories from that night flash through my mind until I reach the point that it all went dark.

When I force myself to look away, my gaze lands on a second photo of Thomas Bradshaw and a maskless Dave Lachey shaking hands and grinning while one of their recent kills lies between them at their feet. And I don't know what's more disturbing—seeing the man who hunted me displayed proudly on Thomas Bradshaw's wall, or the fact that they all—my papa included—used to be hunting buddies.

I'm so consumed with my thoughts that I don't hear the footsteps behind me until it's too late.

"What the hell are you doing in here?"

CHAPTER 54

CAMILA

With my hand flying over my heart, I gasp and flip around to face the deep voice. As soon as I see Trip in the doorway with a giant grin on his face, relief whooshes through me. Tears threaten to surface as my fear starts to slip away, and I realize just how shaken I still am because of that night.

"That's a first," he says with a chuckle before stepping forward. "We've known each other for twenty-eight years, and I have never seen you react like that." He scans my face. "You look completely spooked."

I shake my head, and his amusement eases my nerves a little. "I was just—" I look over my shoulder and gesture to the photos. "Just looking at old photos of my papa. I've been missing him, and Mama packed away a lot of his photos."

Trip adopts a sympathetic expression. "He was a good man with a strong work ethic. I really miss seeing him around here. He taught me so much."

I can't help but smile at his kind words. "I believe

that. You couldn't ask him a question without his turning it into an hour-long lesson."

Trip chuckles. "Sounds about right."

I frown, unable to stop thinking about the photos of his dad and mine hunting with the man who tried to kill me. "Trip, what do you know about Dave Lachey?"

Something flickers in his eyes before he frowns. "Outside of what I learned after what happened to you, not much. I'd heard his name before that. Everyone knew he was a poacher and a reckless one at that." He waves a hand over me. "Clearly, since he wound up hurting you that night." He tilts his head and narrows his eyes. "Why?"

I blow out a breath and shake my head. "Nothing. I just didn't realize he used to hunt with our dads." I assess his reaction as I speak, but Trip gives nothing more away than what he's already expressed. "Anyway, my curiosity was just getting the better of me again."

Trip smiles. "Careful there. This town doesn't need Camila Bell to go searching for trouble again. I think we're all still recovering."

I laugh. "I promise those days are behind me. You won't find me galivanting around the woods again."

An awkward silence follows as our broken friendship, which we've been masking, finally rises to the surface.

Trip kicks the floor before meeting my gaze again. "I know we haven't talked all that much since you've been home. And this shared ownership has been a big pill to swallow for everyone, but I really hope we can be friends again, Camila. It just feels wrong, walking around this place with this giant wall between us. That's not how I imagined all of this going down."

Trip is being completely genuine, but I also grapple with how he can be so naive. "What did you think, Trip?" I ask, genuinely wanting to know. "That I would be happy to share ownership of my family vineyard? That I would be fine seeing another family move into my home? I feel like I got the rug pulled from beneath my feet and I'm still trying to get back up."

He bows his head. "I'm sorry about all that. I really am. I never wanted you to feel that way. You were gone for a long time, and I don't know, things just kept changing. We all love this vineyard, but I see now why you could feel the way you do. No one even gave you a choice."

Just hearing him say the words makes me feel like I've won some small battle. I walk toward him and meet him at the halfway point in the room. "Yes, exactly. I was just an afterthought to everyone."

Trip shakes his head. "Trust me, Camila. You're nobody's afterthought. That's not it at all." He lets out a laugh, and his eyes softening. "You know our parents always talked about our future like we would end up together. I guess part of me believed that would be true too. In the back of my mind, I always pictured us running this place together one day."

My eyes widen slightly. "Really? We've never even dated. I mean, I know you asked me to prom, but—"

One side of his mouth curls up. "But you were already seeing someone else in secret."

My face heats. "Well, yeah, I suppose you were at a disadvantage there."

A dark cloud crosses his eyes before guilt takes over his expression. "Speaking of prom, I never did tell you how sorry I was about ratting you out the way I did. I don't know what came over me."

I purse my lips in amusement. "C'mon. You were always getting me into trouble. Like when you promised that you would be nice to Ridge if I stayed away from him, then you saw us get out of the gondola together. You totally told my papa, didn't you? That's why Harold started losing all his clients."

Trip cringes. "To be fair, my dad was the one I talked to about that. I never ratted you out to Patrick. Not ever. If Patrick knew anything, it was because my papa told him, not me."

"But my papa used to pay you to hang out with me."

"Yeah, to buy your lunches and to contribute toward gas since I was driving you girls all over town, but it wasn't like a job or anything. I liked hanging out with you, and I was happy to do it."

I made a face. "To think I've had it wrong all this time."

He chuckles. "Well, not all wrong. I was an asshole back then, but it was only because I liked you."

A laugh bursts from my throat. "You had a funny way of showing it most of the time."

"Maybe that was because I hated seeing how wide your eyes got for that farm boy." He rolls his eyes. "Between you and Raven, man, I had my hands full."

I tilt my head and purse my lips, trying hard to ignore the fact that he admitted to getting jealous of Ridge. "You still can't use his name, can you?"

Trip shrugs. "He'll always be Farm Boy to me. That's just the way it is." He nods at the photos above his dad's desk. "That all you came in here for?"

Discomfort snakes through me as I remember the reason I stepped foot in this office—because someone had been rummaging through mine. "Actually, I was looking for your dad. Someone left something in my office, and I think it was him. Do you know where he went?"

"He took off to meet some clients for lunch. That's where I'm headed too. Just swung by to grab some bottles to leave them with. Do you want to come?"

Trip seems genuine in his pursuit for us to coexist better than we have been. Surely by now, the tension between families has become obvious to our staff. Unfortunately, our problems are too complex for a friendly meal to fix. "I have a lot to take care of here, but thank you for the offer. I hope you two have a good lunch."

He hesitates, searching my eyes, like he has more to say but wants to assess me first. "Do you think you could ever be okay with us all working together like this? Maybe after some time?"

I take in a slow, deep breath and truly consider his words. It's already been months, and I'm more worked up now than ever. With a shake of my head, I give him an apologetic look. "Not with split ownership and not with your family living in my home. I'm sorry, Trip. It's truly nothing personal, but I will find a way to take back control. If you all want to stick around after that, the jobs are still yours."

Trip cringes. "Don't say it like that, Camila. Let me talk to my dad. Maybe he's willing to come to some sort of arrangement so you can hold majority share."

So much doubt clouds any sense of hope. "C'mon, Trip. He's not going to just hand back control after he worked so hard to get it. He doesn't strike me as the type."

"Just let me talk to him, okay?"

"Really? You would do that for me?"

He puts his hands on my shoulders and looks me straight in the eye. "I don't want you to be unhappy. There has to be a way for us all to work here without one person feeling like their livelihood is being threatened. This is your family home, and if I were you, I would feel the same. So I'll talk to him. I'll figure out where his mind is at and if I can sway him to give back a percent."

My heart races at the nugget of hope. "Okay." I nod emphatically. "Yes, of course. Thank you."

Trip takes a step back and smiles. "Just give me time with this. This isn't the type of negotiation I can have over one lunch, and we all need to try to get rid of this tension in the meantime. It could take weeks, but I'll wear him down."

Letting out a breath, I return his smile and walk him out, shutting off the light and closing the office door behind me. We say goodbye, and I stop by my office to lock up before heading to the main house. I'm too worked up to sit at my desk at the moment, so instead, I give in to my growling stomach and join Mama in the kitchen.

"Aww, is that for me?" I tease.

She's preparing a roast beef sandwich with her lips pursed and her eyes focused like she's in deep concentration. "No. You should be making *me* lunch." She nods to the ingredients still lying on the counter. "Make your own. If you can stay out all night, I'm sure you're quite capable." She winks, making me cringe.

Knowing Mama, I'm sure she's already figured out where I was last night, but I've already decided I'm going to keep my mouth shut. I have nothing to be afraid of anymore, but part of me wants to keep things just between Ridge and me for now while we're getting to know each other again. Maybe that's silly, considering we hated the secrecy back when we were first together, but it's been one day, and Ridge and I have a lot of time to make up for.

Smiling, I stand next to her and start to put together a sandwich. "Sometimes I really miss being young."

Her giggle is infectious. "Me, too, Camila. Me too."

We finish preparing our lunches and sit down at the round glass table in the dining nook. "Mama…"I need to figure out how to ease into this next, not-so-easy topic. "Do you remember that night?" I swallow. "After prom?"

She sets down her sandwich and closes her eyes, pulling in a deep breath. When she opens them again, I can see every thought in them, from her fear of hearing about what had happened to me, to her anger at my papa for letting his hatred for the Cross family result in my running straight into near-death, to the terror in her voice when she demanded for Gus to check the perimeter fence.

"Of course I remember," she snaps in a hushed voice. "How could I ever forget? It was the beginning and end of so many things. Must we talk about it?"

"Well, yes, because I just saw a photo of that psychopath, Dave Lachey, with Papa and Thomas." I shake my head. "I don't understand. Both of them acted like they didn't know who Dave was, just that they knew of him. Why would they lie?"

Mama's face contorts with confusion. "You saw photos? And you're sure it was Dave?"

"Thomas has a bunch of old hunting photos in his office, and Dave was in them. They were all younger then, but I'll never forget that face." I shudder.

She picks up her sandwich again, dismissing me with a shake of her head. "You said they're old, mija. Perhaps they didn't remember hunting with Dave. Their circle was very big back then."

Something about the way Mama has averted her eyes makes my stomach knot as my instincts kicked in. "But Dave was a known poacher, Mama. Why would Papa be hunting with him in the first place? Papa hated men like that."

She gives one of her heavy sighs that come out whenever she's frustrated. "Your papa didn't always hate poachers like that."

"What?" I ask with a laugh. "Of course he did. He told me all those stories about how poaching disturbs the natural order of things."

Mama studies me for a second then stands. "I suppose there's nothing to hide anymore, but I'm going to need wine for this. You?"

"Yes, please," I say, feeling anxious about whatever she's going to tell me. Revealing more secrecy and lies, only this time, they aren't mine.

She grabs a corked bottle of Bell Family Red and pours two glasses, then she sits again and turns her stool to face me. "Your papa was one of them, Camila. Before you were born, before I met your father, and before he acquired the vineyard from his parents, he was part of a group of hunters that poached for the sole purpose of making money to help them purchase land. I am not proud to say that there are plots of property now in your name that came from that money."

I don't know when my jaw dropped, but it's still hanging slack. "Are you sure? You're honestly telling me that Papa was a poacher? And so was Thomas?"

Mama nods before taking a gulp of wine. Her eyes close as she drinks, and when she pulls the glass away, she looks much more relaxed. "I didn't realize how good it would feel to tell someone that. Early on in our marriage, he kept things from me, the poaching being one of them."

"How did you find out?"

Mama smiles. "A friend. My only friend at the time, really. This was before I started volunteering at the country club. She was a sweet woman who worked at the Cross Ranch. We were secret friends, kind of like you and Ridge."

I laugh at the strange turn in the conversation. "Well, okay. So she knew about the men who were poaching?"

She nods, a dark look filling her expression. "The woman was very upset about it. Said she saw it for herself when she was taking a walk through the woods. Anyway, I confronted Patrick about what she'd told me, and he admitted it right there. That man looked as guilty as sin. I threatened to leave him if he didn't stop. And I'm the one who ordered for your papa to put up the fence around the perimeter to keep the wildlife out." She bows her head. "But that damn man cut it."

I shiver as I process everything. Men hunted on this land long before I was even born, and Dave Lachey was one of them.

"So, then papa stopped poaching. What about everyone else? With him fencing in the land, where did they go?" The questions wouldn't stop, but I tried to quiet them while I waited for her answers.

"I never asked, but I assumed they all stopped, since the land got taken away. Clearly, I was wrong. I fear poaching was an addiction for Dave more than it was about money." She furrows her brow and narrows her eyes at me. "What's going through that head of yours, Camila?"

I let out a sigh. "I wish I knew, but something doesn't feel right. The way no one tried to figure out why Dave came after me that night, the way they all acted like they didn't know him when apparently, they all spent quite a bit of time together, and how Thomas managed to take half of the vineyard away from our family the way he did. What's next? I need to get ahead of this, but I need to understand it all first."

"Oh, Camila," she says with a frown. "You're going to fight this battle until you're in the grave like your papa. He was always at war with someone because of this place. I wanted different for you. Honestly, you seemed so happy in Napa that part of me hoped you wouldn't come back."

"Mama!" I gasp.

She places her hands on my knees. "Look at how obsessed you are with this. You're going to make yourself sick, worrying about how to beat Thomas Bradshaw. Is it really worth it?"

I chew on my lip, thinking about the last ten years. "Yes. I don't care if I'm making myself sick or how obsessed I am with making things right." I shake my head. "I need to listen to my gut. Because something is very wrong in all of this. Papa loved this place too much to give it up so easily, no matter how close he was with the Bradshaws. Someone convinced him to sell. And I'm certain that same person encouraged him to turn around and put that money into the vineyard, leaving Papa with nothing. And before you tell me I'm reading into things, I'm telling you I'm close to something. I've pored over those documents. Nothing makes sense."

Mama swirls her wine, appearing stoic. "I'm not telling you you're wrong, Camila. I'm telling you that better men have tried to fight that man… and they lost *everything*."

I push off the stool, no longer hungry. "Well, then it's a good thing I'm not a man. I'm a woman. I won't let Thomas take any more than he already has. And I certainly won't let him keep what he's practically stolen beneath all of our noses."

With that, I take my wine from the counter, carry it all the way back to my office, and slam the door behind me.

CHAPTER 55

RIDGE

"Happy opening day," comes a chipper voice from outside of the main welcome cabin.

I look up from the computer, where I'm training a new hire. Camila stumbles in, holding a stack of boxes.

"Whoa!" I say with a laugh as I see them start to wobble. I jog around the counter and relieve the weight by pulling off each box and uncovering her smile, which does something to my insides.

Her cheeks are as dark pink as the sleeveless dress she's wearing when I lean in to give her a quick kiss to save Lucinda from too much PDA.

Camila has slept over every night. While we've made being together no secret, we avoid her villa, mostly because of the Bradshaws but her mama too. Neither of us wants any trouble, especially after everything we've already been through. We just want to enjoy this time together, and that's perfectly fine by me.

"What are you doing with all these packages?"

"They aren't packages, silly. I brought you wine. At least enough for the next couple weeks for welcome gifts for your guests. "

The boxes have the Bell Family Vineyard logo. "You didn't have to do that. I was going to purchase wine from you."

She waves a hand. "And let the Bradshaws get involved? Sales is their department, and I want to keep you all to myself, thank you very much. Besides, I figure you can point your guests in our direction if they like the wine."

There she is—my girl with nonstop ideas and energy. Thomas Bradshaw doesn't stand a chance against her. They've continued to work in a thick cloud of tension, while Trip says he's chipping away at the old man to try to get him to budge. I don't believe it for a second, seeing as Trip would do anything to get back into Camila's good graces. She hasn't said so, but I think she's doubtful, considering she's still digging around and reporting back to me.

"I'm going to put one in each of the cabins. Come with me? I'll show you what to do." Camila picks up one of the boxes. "Can you get away?" Her eyes dart to Lucinda then back at me with a mischievous grin. By now, I know exactly what that look means.

She's barely asked the question before I take the box from Camila and call over my shoulder, "Hey, Lucinda, why don't we break for lunch and meet back here at one?"

The older woman with bright-red hair and a beautiful smile lights up. "You got it, boss."

With the box under my arm, I tug on Camila's hand

and lead her into the woods, toward the first cabin I ever showed her. Shutting the door behind me, I look over my shoulder to see her already climbing onto the bed. "I thought we were dropping off wine."

She raises her eyebrows. "Then why are you shutting the door?"

I narrow my eyes playfully then pounce onto the bed, tackling her and planting a kiss. These last few weeks have shown me everything I've been missing without ever knowing it. Even during our separation, I've only wanted Camila, but I never truly knew what that meant until I got my second chance. I live for making her smile. Without the ranch, without the resort, or without anything at all, I would still be wrapped up in her and be perfectly fine for the rest of my life. I would be home.

Deepening the kiss, I try not to crush her while keeping her close. I can't stop kissing her when she makes those little moans when I slip my hand under her dress, when she spreads her knees just enough to fit me into that space meant only for me, and definitely when her hands start to roam beneath my shirt and she rakes her nails up my back.

"F-Fuck," I say, shivering.

An airy laugh escapes her. "I love when you cuss."

This makes me smile. "Why is that, dirty girl?"

She grins and moves her hips so that she glides across my erection. "Because I know you're only saying it because you've lost control. It's not every day that Ridge Cross loses control, and I happen to like that I can make him do that."

"Why are you talking about me like I'm in the other room?" I rock into her center, gasping at how good it feels even though I'm not inside her. "I'm definitely here."

She bites her lip. "I wish you were closer."

That's all she has to say before I strip off my clothes and push up her skirt. My patience is gone, and I flip her around, lift her hips, and pull her onto her knees. I hover near her entrance, running my finger along her slit and feeling her excitement. She's ready for me, but I'm not so sure I'm ready for her.

Her cheek is flat against the pillow as she looks back at me, waiting with those wide green eyes that captured and sentenced me to a lifetime of unexpected challenges. This is my payback.

I push two fingers into her, trying to hide my groan at the feel of her—soft, wet, and so fucking tight. She gasps as she pushes back against my hand, rocking into me like she could come at any moment.

"Holy shit. That feels so good."

I slip my fingers out and replace them with my erection, pushing in slowly, inch by inch, as I succumb to the bliss of the beautiful devil beneath me. She molds to me, reminding me that I've only been hers and she's only been mine, and I fill her so completely that there's nowhere left to go.

Her eyes are closed, her mouth is open, and I drive into her, rolling my hips as curse words pour from my mouth. She's right. With her, I can't help it. I lose all control. Her skin feels so soft beneath my digging fingers, and the apricot scent that rises from her skin puts me under the same spell it always does. I can't get enough of her, and it always yanks at my heart to say goodbye to her when we part.

I slam into her one last time before we both let go. She cries out and grips the comforter while I fill her with every last ounce of my release. Then I lie down beside her and pull her into my arms.

She rests her cheek on my chest, curls her leg around mine, and sighs. "I love how you give me what I need without asking questions."

"I'm sorry, would any other man deny you that? I highly doubt it."

She slaps my chest. "I don't just mean with sex. I mean emotionally. You could tell I needed you in the exact way you gave yourself to me, no questions asked."

My heart squeezes. "Okay, but... is it okay for me to ask what's wrong now?" I smile and weave her fingers through mine. "I knew something was wrong when you didn't try to roll me over and ride me."

"It was just a hard day. Thomas wants to have a meeting after lunch about adding an entire plot of vines, and I just don't want to deal with him. On top of that, I'm starting to get really frustrated that Trip hasn't come through for me yet. That can't be an easy conversation, and Thomas is more likely to tell his own son to fuck off than listen to any logic, but I haven't gotten any closer to finding a way out of this mess my papa got me into. Everything Thomas did, while it was definitely manipulative, was all on the up-and-up."

I squeeze her hand. "It's only been three weeks. Trip warned you it could take time, and it's not like the vineyard is going anywhere."

She groans. "I know, I know. Okay, I'll be patient."

I run a hand up and down her thigh. "Good, and

don't give up. Your gut is telling you something, and you should definitely listen."

I look at the spot on her throat where her necklace now hangs again. "No one's fessed up to giving that back to you, huh?"

Camila shakes her head, a dark look crossing her eyes. "No. I wish it didn't still bother me, but it does." She looks up at the ceiling for a few moments before sighing and sliding her body so that she's straddling me. "Now for the other reason I'm here," she says as she slowly drags her wet opening against my length.

My stomach muscles clench. "There's another reason?"

She nods, and her palms fall to my chest as she moves her hips against me, working me like a Slip 'N Slide between her lips. "I want you to take me on a date."

I chuckle, despite the fact that she's got me so hard that I can barely see straight. "We've gone on dates, Camila."

"Dinner, sure." She leans forward and brushes her lips against mine. "I want you to take me to the rodeo, and I don't mean right now." She grins. "Saturday night. You pick me up. You formally meet my mama. Then you take me to the rodeo, where the entire town will see us. You hold my hand. We'll eat deep-fried cookie dough, and I'll pretend to be frightened of the bulls so that I can snuggle up close to you." Her smile is infectious. "A date."

I cup Camila's cheek and press my lips to hers, then suck in a breath before releasing her. "Yes, Wild One. I'll take you on a date."

She kisses me back just as she reaches down to slide me into her, then she's off to the races. Camila is as wild in bed as she is in life, always an intoxicating mixture of reckless and uncontrolled as she tries to break free from whatever reins hold her back.

Well, she's free now. And it's like she's channeled all of that energy into making love, just like how we were always meant to be.

CHAPTER 56

CAMILA

When I leave Wild One Ranch, Ridge stops at the main cabin, where Lucinda is already inside, ready to go back to work. I smile and wave one last time at Ridge as I step into my Jeep, realizing for the millionth time how strange it is for me to be driving when there's a cutaway through the fields and over the bridge.

I haven't gone near those woods or that bridge since that awful night, and I don't plan to again, even if I do miss the hilltop. The hilltop was a place where I would dream of my future as vineyard owner. Now that I'm living that, my time is best served here, anyway.

Back at the villa, I walk straight into the casita, irritated again that I'm not the first one here. Three weeks have crawled by and still no word from Trip on the status of ownership, other than the random "I'm still working on him."

Not good enough! I want to scream, but at least Trip is trying. Meanwhile, I haven't let up on my hunt for information that may have fallen through the cracks. I'm convinced that evidence exists—something that proves Thomas Bradshaw forced Papa's hand to get him to sell.

I enter my office, and Thomas is waiting for me on the couch with a disapproving stare.

Speak of the devil.

"For someone who says they need this entire villa for themselves, you sure don't act like it. You're rarely here during your off-hours."

I laugh and toss my handbag onto the couch. "And it didn't occur to you that I stay away to avoid the thieves who are trying to run me off my land, my home, and my family business?"

"Oh, calm down, Ms. Bell. No one is trying to run you away. This is all yours *as much* as it is mine. I find that our disagreement comes primarily from you under-standing what shared ownership means."

"I understand just fine, but it doesn't mean that I agree with it." I take a few steps forward, refusing to sit down. "Please don't get me wrong. You've worked hard for this vineyard for many years, and you deserve your rightful spot. But what good does fifty-fifty ownership get us if we can't even agree on which varietals to use for our next vintage?"

He nods. "So then how do we settle this, Ms. Bell?"

"For starters, I want majority ownership of what should already be mine."

"And what stops you from running this place into the ground when you're the sole decision maker?"

"The same thing that stopped my papa from doing it. Love. Love for this vineyard and for the land it was built on. I won't let anything happen to it, which is why I think it's best that I take control back." I'm trying to be as civil as possible while letting Thomas know he's not going to push me around the way he did my papa.

"I'm not giving up a single percent of my rightful shares."

His tone is so smooth and airy that I can see how he became such a force in the business world. People listen to him. They're lulled by the hypnotic effects and believe everything he says, especially if they're the type who can be easily convinced.

"Thomas, it's the only way we can get out of this damn deadlock we always seem to find ourselves in."

He chuckles. "You could just as easily sell to me. Though considering you've been using your influence to convince my son that your way is the way it should be, you probably won't consider that option."

"*No,*" I snap. "I will *never* consider that option."

He shakes his head, frustration making its way to the surface. "Well, then maybe you should marry my son." His words roll off his tongue so easily, like he's planned this very encounter. "Your father and I always imagined for you two to end up together. The Bell-Bradshaw partnership was a dream of ours from the moment you were born. It's too bad that Cross boy got in the way, but you're all older now. You know what's good for you. Trip would make a fine partner, and you'd share ownership of the vineyard with him."

Rage blows threw me at the asinine suggestion. "You don't even like me. Why would you even encourage that notion?"

Amusement beams back at me. "I'd have more trust in you running the vineyard with my son than on your own, but I'd be much keener on you selling to me. I'll even let you keep this office."

I fume so hard that I can almost feel the steam blowing out of my ears.

Thomas leans forward. "When all is said and done, you have three choices, Ms. Bell. Sell to me, marry Trip, or fight me until one of us is dead."

"Marrying Trip isn't an option, considering I'm in love with Ridge."

Thomas's eyes go dark. "Ah, yes. An old love resurrected. I should have seen that coming. You could never stay away from that boy, could you? I figured it was only a matter of time until you started sneaking around with him again—now that your papa is *dead* and all."

The disdain in his voice grinds against my nerves. "You're impossible. I'm an adult now. I'll do as I please."

"Haven't you always, Ms. Bell?"

My eyelids narrow. "That's right. I have. So I don't need your comments on my personal business, dickhead. I can make decisions for myself just fine."

Thomas's laughter booms through the air. "You certainly have a strange recollection of your youth."

I've had enough. "This conversation isn't going anywhere. Get out. I have work to do, and I don't need you in here, distracting me with your empty taunts. And knock next time. If I'm not here, don't come in."

Thomas chuckles and stands to face me. "I think I'll stay and peruse these"—he tosses a pile of papers on the coffee table between us—"documents."

I look down at the financial papers I had left on my desk before leaving to visit Ridge at lunch. Though I don't normally leave my work station untidy, I was excited to deliver wine to Ridge for his opening day.

"May I ask what it is you're searching for, Ms. Bell? Maybe I can help."

"Again, that's none of your business."

His lips go flat as his eyes flash with anger. "That response reeks of evasiveness."

"Good."

A chill sweeps the air. "Let me get one thing straight, Ms. Bell. You don't want to fuck with me. I've been playing nice out of respect for your old man, but my rope is thinning. If it's not clear to you yet, then let me help. I make the decisions around here. It's why Bell Family Vineyard is what it is today."

My face twists with disgust, and a laugh tumbles from my mouth. "Who the hell do you think you are? I know you manipulated my papa. And I know it's only a matter of time before you try to manipulate me. So let me make this clear." I raise my eyebrows. "You're not going to win."

Thomas looks amused as he starts to walk toward the door. "We'll see about that."

Every word that comes out of his mouth triggers me. I suddenly feel desperate to call him out on all of his bullshit. It's like a tornado whips through me when my next words fly from my mouth. "I know you talked to Ridge after prom. I know what you told him to make him leave. I've figured out enough to realize that you wanted me gone, which is why you were always in my papa's ear about sending me away to college. All so that you could manipulate him into selling off his shares. So while my papa was investing in this business, you were creating more reasons for him to go broke while you sat back and purchased what he could no longer afford. It's the only reason he would ever have sold off what should have been mine. Papa would never have given up this vineyard in a million years, unless his legacy was at stake. I just don't know how you did it. What could you have possibly said to him to make him feel like there was no other way? And how the hell could you have afforded it all?"

Thomas gives a hearty laugh that shakes my core. "Oh, Camila. When are you going to open your eyes? You're not going to find your answers in those papers. What you will find are all the client signatures, all the long-term contracts, and all the guaranteed profit they could make by signing their contract agreements. None of that came for free. There's a price to pay for the type of assurance our clients need, and you, my dear, were a risk."

I scrunch my face, trying to make sense of what this monster is telling me. "So, you're saying they would only sign the contracts if my papa sold to you? That doesn't make any sense. I'm no more of a risk than you or Trip and Raven are."

Thomas shrugs. "But they knew me well. They invited me into their homes, and I got to know their families while they got to know mine. All they knew about you was that you were a hellion of a little girl."

I shake with rage. "You son of a bitch. You talked me down to your clients, and they all fell for your bullshit."

He chuckles. "Wasn't too hard, considering you were always getting yourself into trouble. Getting drunk at family events when you were just fifteen," he spits out.

"Running hikers over down the mountain when you went biking. Always traipsing off into those goddamn woods like you were invincible."

He opens the door. "Whatever you're looking for, sweetheart, you won't find it in those documents. You might as well give up now and consider your options."

I swallow, trying to maintain my cool while my insides roar with anger. "Sounds like we're at a stalemate."

Thomas's lips tip up in an evil smile. "Nah, I think I have another pawn to play." He winks. "See you tomorrow, Ms. Bell."

CHAPTER 57

RIDGE

On rodeo day, nervous doesn't even begin to describe how I'm feeling when I pull up Camila's driveway to her villa. The long, winding entrance is as magical as Camila once described, with its large arched gated entrance, a thick tree covering on either side, and a long paved road that eventually opens to an ornate fountain at the center of the circular drive.

Once parked, I blow out a quick breath and suck in a deeper one, trying to steady my racing heart. Not only will this be our first major public outing, but I'll be meeting her mama officially for the first time. While I've seen Camila's family in passing many times growing up, we've never spoken.

Reaching over the bench seat, I grab two brown-paper-wrapped sets of flowers, then I step out of my truck and head up the steps to reach her front door. To my surprise, her mama answers with a wide, beautiful smile. She's obviously where Camila gets her gorgeous looks and soul-deep spark in her eyes.

"Hello, Ridge. It's nice to see you again."

Even her tone sounds so much like Camila's that it's uncanny.

"Hello, ma'am," I say with a nod. "These are for you." I hand her the bundle of sunflowers, and her green eyes light up in surprise.

"Thank you so much. They're beautiful. And please call me Selena." She steps back, pushing open the door. "Come in. Camila should be down shortly."

The second I step into the villa, the stark contrast between her home and mine hits me hard. She grew up in a mansion, while I picked up Harold's empty beer bottles from all over the run-down farmhouse. I'm glad I didn't have the full picture of Camila's lifestyle when I was a teen, because I would never have had the courage to pursue her after seeing her in Ouray. My self-esteem back then was low enough without the intimidation that one look at this place brings.

But I'm older now, and I realize how deceiving looks can truly be. It's not about what you have. It's about what you do with what you have. As soon as the Bradshaws are out of Camila's way, she'll do amazing things and make her father proud. To her, the land is about more than money and power and making a name for the vineyard in the community. She wants to preserve nearly fifty years of wine production, using nature as her guide, and focus on organic growth, natural resources, and everything that Thomas Bradshaw forced Patrick Bell to do away with over the years to increase production at a rate the vineyard could barely keep up with. Camila knows the value of producing less to uphold the quality, and I believe she'll have everything she dreams of and soon.

Selena brings me into the kitchen and waves at a set of stools under the island. "Have a seat, and we can chat for a bit while we wait." She pulls out a vase from a cabinet and fills it with water before placing the sunflowers into it and setting it on the island with a smile. "Beautiful. Did you pick these from your farm?"

"I did. I'm expanding our sunflower plot and reducing our corn production. It's been a project we just started this past year."

Selena's eyes widen just as Camila's did when I explained the new plans for the farm.

"Oh, that's quite the change. Won't you miss out on business?"

I shrug. "Yes and no. Corn was never my favorite crop." I chuckle, thinking of Camila's nonstop comments about how much I hated the farm. "My plan is to create a place where the community can come and pick their desired flowers and produce. We'll have corn mazes, wildflowers, and sunflowers. And I'll rotate the corn with alfalfa seasonally. I'll keep the selection manageable while I spend most of my time at the vacation property."

Her smile is infectious, and my heart skips a beat at the thought of Camila's mama approving of anything I do.

"I love that idea, Ridge. And with your new ranch right there, your guests will love it."

"That's the idea. I'm building a small barn and a round riding pen right now. It will be great for kids, and I can offer trail rides for the older riders."

Selena's smile turns soft as she scrolls over my features, like she recognizes me from somewhere else. It's a silly thought. We've seen each other around town before, but it just feels like she knows me.

"You remind me of a friend I had once. She was beautiful and strong, and her dreams were as big and exciting as her beautiful brown eyes. They'd light up at the thought of all the good that could be done in this world, if people would only change their perspectives. If greed and wealth weren't solutions but the enemy instead."

Her words trigger something deep in my chest. My heart squeezes, and the familiarity in the message blasts through me. "That sounds a lot like something my mother used to say to me."

Camila appears by my side and slips her arm around my waist. I hadn't even heard her come in. I can't seem to take my eyes off Selena after what she just said.

"Wow, this feels intense," Camila says. "What did I just walk into?"

I wrap an arm around her shoulders. "Your mom was just telling me about an old friend of hers."

Camila perked up. "Are you telling him about your secret friend who used to work on the Cross Farm?"

Frowning, I look at Camila.

She seems startled. "What? I told you about her over dinner one night. She's the one who told Mama about the poachers."

I remember the conversation well, but I don't remember Camila mentioning that her mom had a secret friend. Turning back to Selena, I nod. "I'd like to hear more about your friend, if that's okay."

Selena smiles. "Of course. She was a brave one. That's for sure. Always on the lookout for new adventures. Like I already told Camila, we often met at the bridge and would chat for hours. She was a sweet, sweet soul, and her connection with nature was so strong." Selena laughs. "I could have sworn she could feel the rain coming before it arrived."

In my peripheral vision, Camila's head whips toward me, but my eyes stay on her mom. My heart thundering so loudly that it's drowning out all thoughts. "What did you say your friend's name was again?"

Selena gives me a knowing smile. "Molly. She never did give me her surname, but I do know she was pregnant with a little boy, whom she already loved very much. She was to name him Ridge, and I believe she did."

The backs of my eyes prick with unshed tears, and my throat closes up. Selena was friends with my mother before my mother moved us to the rez.

I was already nervous coming here, but now my emotions are overflowing. It's my first time meeting Camila's mom, and I'm on the verge of tears.

"Mama, you were friends with Ridge's mom? Why didn't you tell me?"

"It was for Ridge to hear first, mija. Part of me has always harbored guilt over the way your mother left. I've always felt to blame. Once I confronted Patrick about the poachers, all eyes were on me. My next meeting with Molly at the bridge was when everything went wrong. Thomas held a bow and arrow to her head and ordered her back to the Cross Farm. Next thing I knew, she was gone."

"But Papa said someone from the rez paid him a visit with a list of girls and boys that had gone missing from there," Camila says.

Selena nods. "Oh, they did. Right after they received a call from Thomas Bradshaw. Your papa felt like he was doing the right thing." Selena leans over the counter and wraps her hand around mine. "I'm so sorry, Ridge. For everything. And I'm sorry to you both. For not fighting harder for you two to keep the love you so clearly share."

I turn to Camila just as she's swiping away a tear, and I cup her face. "Don't cry, Wild One."

Her eyes meet mine, and no dam can stop the emotion being unleashed from the deepest parts of her. In the strangest way, it feels as if everything we've ever been through together is coming full circle, but I still have so many questions.

"It's not your fault, Selena." My voice is gravelly when I turn back to her. "Camila and I understand the sacrifices we make for family all too well. The things we do to protect each other, even though everyone still suffers. All we've wanted is an end to the war that ruined so many lives, and we have that now." I hug Camila from the side and kiss her cheek. "And we'll move forward together with a bridge that connects us instead of separates us."

Camila eyes are red and still filled with tears. I feel the first warm drop slide down my cheek.

"I love you," she mouths.

"I love you," I mouth back. Leaning my forehead against hers, I pull in a deep breath, then I let it out with my laugh. "Wow, and here I was, nervous your mom wouldn't like the sunflowers I brought her."

"You brought my mama flowers? You're the sweetest, Ridge Cross."

Selena and Camila laugh. "And he brought you flowers too. Look."

Camila smiles as I hand her the paper-wrapped bouquet of wildflowers. "Of course he did." Then she wipes her tear-stained cheeks and sniffles. "We really don't have to go to the rodeo after all that."

"Nonsense," Selena says. "Go and have fun. Please. I have a date with some girlfriends at the country club, anyway."

She shoos us to the door, where she gives Camila a big hug and a kiss on the cheek. Then she wraps her arms around me. Just from the hug, I can see where Camila gets her warm strength.

Selena pulls herself closer to my ear and whispers, "You should know that your mother loved your father very much. You were born from that love, and it shows." She pulls back, her eyes red and misty. "Okay, I'm done. Have fun tonight."

Camila pulls me out the door and looks up at me with a smile. "See? Nothing at all to be nervous about."

CHAPTER 58

CAMILA

A thick cloud of dust floats through the air as we round the corner of the bleachers to where Josie said to meet her. I search the crowd and spot my friend just as an announcer's voice booms through the speakers. He's commenting on the current barrel race, his excitement fueling the fan noise all around us. I'd almost forgotten the natural high I get from being at these events. The crowd gets so into it, and the bulls are all charged up, pounding their hooves in the dirt as they grunt, snort, and drive their horns angrily into their miniprisons.

I start to move forward again, then a bell dings loudly followed by a blare of a bullhorn, causing me to jump as my heart flies into my throat.

Ridge grabs my waist and leans down, laughing in my ear. "You weren't joking about getting scared of the bulls."

I smile. "It's so loud. I can't help it. C'mon." I lead him up the bleachers to where Josie and Abner are. Not until we reach their section of risers do I notice Raven and Trip sitting above them, both sets of icy-blue eyes glued to us.

Ridge must see them, too, because he takes hold of my hand and squeezes. He's trying to comfort me, but I can sense the looming awkwardness that we've managed to avoid until now. Rumors have been circulating about our relationship, but it's a much different thing to expose that relationship to the public eye.

"Geez, you'd think the Capulets and the Montagues were among us." Josie looks pointedly at the folks with their eyes trained on Ridge and me. Then she stands. "The star-crossed lovers are alive and well!" she booms, waving her hands at us.

Laughing, I tug her back down to her seat and cover her mouth to shut her up then release it. "How much wine have you had?"

Josie throws a look at her husband, who is now rolling his eyes in amusement. "Too much. Right, Abs?"

Abner nods emphatically. "I cut her off just before you got here."

"Aww, we missed all the fun."

Ridge leans in. "Is that my cue to go get you wine?"

I grin. "I would love you forever."

He narrows his eyes. "That's nonnegotiable."

When his expression slips into a smile, my insides start to melt. He leans in and kisses me and is in no rush to pull away. When he finally does, a buzz of electricity is still on my lips, and the heat of our first public display of affection rises to my cheeks.

"Be right back." He winks and heads back down the steps.

I watch him walk away, feeling the same flutters in my chest I felt back when I first met him. He's the epitome of man now, in his tight Wranglers that hug his muscular thighs, and his plaid shirt that does nothing for the erotic hunk of a man underneath it. It will be my pleasure to tear off each one of those buttons tonight as soon as I get him alone.

"So." Josie turns my attention back to her. "How was the visit with Mama Selena?"

A chill sweeps over me as I remember our conversation back at the house. Her explanation for why she didn't tell me was acceptable, but I wish I'd been prepared for the emotional afternoon. I can't remember ever seeing Ridge cry, and witnessing his tears just about broke me. At the same time, the conversation also felt like closure, in a sense, something Ridge may have needed without ever knowing it.

I fill Josie in, and her mouth hangs open, just like mine did when I heard the news.

"It's like you two are true fated mates, destined to be together no matter what."

I laugh at my dramatic friend, though I don't disagree.

Her eyes go wide. "I mean it, Camila. Your pull to him has always been so strong and intense. In the beginning, I didn't understand it, but then I saw you two together, and it was so obvious. And I'm not just talking about the fangirl vibes you were shooting off. I'm talking about Ridge too. I've never seen anything like it." She squeezes my hand, adopting a serious expression. "I'm glad it's working out this time. I'm not going to lie. I was a little scared to see something like this happen after last time."

My heart swells. "I know you were, but this time is different. No more feuding fathers, no more secrets, no more creepy mines…" The words are out before I can stop them when I remember how Josie gets about that night.

"Don't even bring that up. I could have lost you. For a long time, I thought I did."

I hug her arm. "But you didn't. I'm right here, happier than ever. I shouldn't have mentioned it."

She shudders. "Please don't mention it again."

We watch the end of the barrel racing events, then cattle roping begins, and I look toward the stairs to see if Ridge is heading back. He's been gone awhile, and I know he doesn't want to miss the bull riders coming out next.

When I still don't see him a minute later, I stand and yell over the crowd noise to Josie, "I'm going to find Ridge. Be right back."

I jog down the stairs and round the bleachers, then I spot him in the distance with his hands full of goodies. Laughing, I race toward him, accidentally bumping someone on the way. Popcorn flies everywhere.

"I'm so sorry!" I gasp, turning to find an older man looking around at the mess. "I'll buy you another one, sir. I didn't see you there."

The man looks up, and my heart jolts into my throat when I realize it's our family's old groundskeeper. "Gus. It's so good to see you." I throw my arms around my old friend, who doesn't seem to hug me back. Ignoring the strange vibes, I step back and smile. "I'm so sorry about your popcorn. I didn't even see you, but I'm happy to buy you another one."

When Gus is still looking at me as if I'm a strange person, I figure he doesn't remember me. "I'm sorry. You probably don't remember me." I laugh, feeling flustered. "I'm Camila Bell. You used to work at my vineyard." I search his eyes, waiting for a response, and I get one, but it's not the one I expect.

Gus glares at me as he chucks what remains of his popcorn into the trash. "I remember you all right. Wish I could forget, if I'm being honest."

His hostility is a shock until I remember that it's been over ten years since I've seen the man, and the last time I saw him was right before he got fired. Then I remember how angry Brody was toward me at High Pie when I first arrived back in Telluride. Guilt lashes at me.

"Gus, I'm so sorry about everything that happened back then. You should never have been fired because of that fence. You weren't the one who cut it. You weren't the one who shot at me that night."

His face twitches, like he wants to say something, and my heart beats fast. I'm probably reading into things because I want him to say more. I want him to tell me that he believes my story and that Dave knew exactly what—or who—he was hunting that night.

"You have nothing to be sorry for, Camila. You were just a young girl doing what young girls do. Me, on the other hand, I should have known better."

His sour expression irks me. The damaged fence that let the wildlife wander in wasn't the problem that night. "What do you mean, you 'should have known better'?"

His eyes dart around before he takes a step closer and

lowers his voice. "I should have told them all what I knew—the truth. I should have told them all that you weren't the crazy one." His expression softens from uneasy to apologetic. "I should have told them about that damn mine."

I blink, digesting his information at a rate much slower than I should be. "Wait. Told them what about the mine?"

Gus cringes. "Your papa wanted to know how Dave Lachey gained access to the land. Told me to check out the mine that night after everyone went home, and I did. That mine was our secret underground to access endless miles of hunting ground when no one was the wiser. When your pops demanded it be forbidden all those years ago, he ordered me to padlock that thing shut. I'm not so proud of my hunting days, and I thought it was all dead and laid to rest until that terrible night. No one was supposed to have access to that mine. But Dave was clearly still using it."

"Where does the mine go?"

Gus shakes his head. "You don't need to worry about that."

His omissions are so frustrating, but he's already told me more than anyone else ever has. Everything he's saying reopens the sealed box of memories that I've been trying to suffocate for years. "I don't understand why you're telling me all this now. Why didn't you say something then?"

"I was scared, Camila. I had a family who needed my protection. I took the threats given very seriously."

"Threats? What threats? From whom?"

"Threats to keep my mouth shut. But don't you

worry about who. That doesn't matter. After I got fired, I would have just looked like a disgruntled employee if I had fessed up." He waves a hand at me. "At least you were safe. Crazy Dave is dead, and to me, that was what mattered most."

I give Gus my best smile then hug him again, unable to help it. "I'm still thankful to you for taking care of me that night. You were always sweet to me, and I'll never forget your kindness. Your job is waiting, if you ever want to come back to the vineyard."

Gus bows his head. "I appreciate that, but I won't be stepping foot on that property again with Thomas Bradshaw still working there. I always hated that man." His eyes fall quickly to my neck then back up. "I'm happy to see your necklace was returned to you."

I touch the arrowhead, my eyes widening. "You knew I lost it?"

He nods while wearing a deep frown. "I found it that night near the entrance of the mine. When I remembered it, I had Brody give it to Raven." He takes a step back and waves. "I'm glad you're well, Camila. Tell your mama I said hi."

"I will."

Ridge finally gets to me as I watch Gus walk away, wishing he had stayed and that I knew all the questions to ask him right then and there, but I'm still processing everything.

He admitted to keeping the mine a secret. *But why? What would be the purpose of hiding the passageway Dave Lachey used to poach on our land?*

Ridge gives me a strange look. "You okay?"

Still stunned, I shake my head and force out a smile.

"Gus was the one who found my necklace." Then I lose some of my smile as I consider telling him more about our conversation. But I decide to let it go for now. Ridge and I are on a date. I'm not going to let more thoughts about that awful night take this night away from me too.

CHAPTER 59
RIDGE

C amila seems distracted for the rest of the rodeo. She's in her own head with her eyes glazed over while the crowd laughs and cheers for the rodeo clowns as they escape the bulls just in the nick of time. Even Josie throws me concerned glances when she notices how off Camila is acting. She is with us physically, but mentally, she's somewhere completely different.

At one point, I search the crowd for Gus, who I find sitting with his wife and two adult kids. Whatever he and Camila talked about earlier seemed pretty intense. While I'm dying to ask Camila what was said, now isn't the right time, with her peers surrounding us, and I can anticipate what she'll unleash.

As soon as we're back in the truck, I start the engine and turn to her. I've never seen Camila so consumed by her thoughts. Even when we sat up on the hillside for hours at a time, she always felt present in the moment with me.

"Okay," I start gently. "You're kind of freaking me out."

She turns to look at me, void of emotion, which only worries me more. "Huh?"

"Camila," I say, leaning in. "You've been on another planet ever since you talked to Gus. What happened?"

She shakes her head, looking almost pained. "Nothing happened. He just—said some stuff about that night. I guess I'm still trying to make sense of it."

Camila doesn't need to say anything more for my blood to start running hot through my veins. We don't talk about that night. I can sense that it still troubles her deeply, and I don't need any reminders of my guilt in what happened. If I hadn't left that night, she would never have been out in the woods alone.

After learning Camila's side of the story, I had to combat my rage at the thought of Dave Lachey coming after her. The sick fuck hunted her down like she was game. Her story still haunts me, especially since I wasn't even there.

"That's right. Gus was there that night." I knit my brow. "What did he have to say about it? Why would he even bring it up?"

"I brought it up," she says, surprising me. "I apologized for the way my papa treated him because of what happened to me. I wanted to tell Gus that I knew it wasn't his fault. I even offered him a job."

"That was nice of you."

She lets out a small laugh. "Yeah, well, he didn't want to take it. He said he won't step foot on that land again while Thomas is still working there. Can't blame him for that. He also told me he knew about the mine.

Papa told Gus to go there that night to see if that was how Dave accessed the property. Apparently, their whole hunting group used the mine to access thousands of acres of hunting land." Her eyes settle on me. "That was where Gus found my necklace."

"What?" My blood boils as I try to comprehend what she's telling me. "Where does the tunnel go?"

She takes in a slow breath and shrugs. "He wouldn't say, but they all lied that night. They all knew Crazy Dave and knew how he got onto the property. My guess is they were trying to protect each other and what they all took part in years ago."

"Shit, Camila. This is starting to sound even more fucked up than before."

"I know. I'm still trying to process everything, but now I can't get that damn mine out of my head. Like it contains the missing piece of a puzzle that's always felt unfinished."

"What are you saying?"

"I don't know. All I know is that when I was younger, I never feared a damn thing. Then that night happened. Now it's like I'm paralyzed with fear at any recollection of it. I haven't even tried to go back to the bridge or the hilltop." Sadness fills her expression. "I miss it, Ridge. I miss it all."

"We can go back to the hilltop together. We can go back to the bridge too. But it's natural for you to want to avoid those places. What happened that night is incomprehensible. You could have died."

She shudders. "I know. But every other time in my life when I've encountered something that should scare me, I face it head-on. Maybe I need to do the same thing with that mine. Maybe I need to go back."

"No!" I don't mean to sound so forceful or even tell Camila what to do. But the last thing she should do is go back to that place. I won't let her. "We'll go to the hilltop, and we'll go to the bridge, but we're staying away from that side of the mountain. There's no point in going back there, Camila. Don't even try to fight me on this."

She sits back against her seat with a huff while I drive us to my place. But even though I slammed the door on her suggestion, I know better than to think it will remain closed for long.

CHAPTER 60

CAMILA

My calves feel like lead as I try to push forward, and an arrow whizzes past my head. A sob bubbles up my throat as the weapon splinters in the tree directly in front of me. He's gaining on me, and I can't seem to get away from him, no matter how hard I try.

The bridge is up ahead, and I put all my focus on it. If I can reach it, it will all be over.

Whoosh.

Another arrow flies by me, followed by another menacing laugh.

The soil draws me down, sucking me in like quicksand and making it impossible to escape. Then I feel the hot graze of an arrow slicing at my waist. Mewling in pain, I fall hard to the ground. Dirt and grass cake my face, and I spit it away as I start to crawl.

Searing pain explodes through my arms and waist as blood pools beneath me. Heavy footsteps crunch closer and closer. When I realize I can't crawl any faster, I flip around to find myself staring back into dark, beady eyes. The man's face is cloaked by a skull *mask, and he lowers his weapon as he takes his final steps toward me.*

I'm completely paralyzed, and I cry out in frustration when my limbs refuse to work for me. Then he stands over me, feet planted on either side of my body, raises his bow, and cranks his arm back just enough to pin me to the ground with one easy shot.

A scream bursts from my throat, piercing my lungs, and only stops when my entire body pitches forward, making everything around me go dark.

The hunter is gone, but so is my sense of everything else— everything but one voice.

"Camila!" the frantic voice calls. "Camila, wake up. It's just a dream."

My heart crashes against my ribcage as I reach for my side, expecting to feel blood oozing from the tear in my skin. But there's no blood. The hunter is gone. And everything feels still.

"You're okay, Wild One. You're okay."

I gasp, recognizing Ridge's soothing voice, then cling to him like he's my last breath of air. Sobs rack my chest, and tears rush from my eyes. He holds me, skin to skin, but the tears don't stop. A decade's worth of pain and deep-rooted terror that I've stuffed down deep in my chest is seeping to the surface all at once.

He wipes my tears and kisses my cheeks, my hair, and my lips. Then he pushes me down onto the bed and hushes me with his soft, sweet, and loving words, which eventually bring me back to the here and now. I'm okay. I'm safe. Dave is dead, and I'm in Ridge's arms. I suck in a deep breath and let it out slowly. I can finally breathe.

The relief that rushes through me is almost as over-whelming as my dream was. I wrap my hand around the back of Ridge's neck and pull him down to kiss me. Our mouths crash together, and I run my hand down his perfectly lined muscles until I get to that deep *V* that points to his shaft. I take him in my grip and stroke him until he's as hard as a rock. He groans out his pleasure.

I don't know what has come over me, but I want him so desperately that my entire body aches for him. I need him, and I need him now. Quickly spreading my legs, I line him up at my entrance and let him take over. Inch by thick inch, he snakes into me, fulfilling me to the very end.

Our mouths never let up as our tongues lash against each other, and he drives into me over and over again. Our skin turns slick as he wraps his arms around me and pulls me onto his lap. With my feet pressed into the mattress on either side of him, I move over him, and he holds me close. I feel him deeper this way, like we're more connected, if that's even possible. He's sparking my core and creating the type of friction that drives me delirious with need.

I press one hand back on his muscular thigh while I reach my other around his neck and weave my fingers through his hair. Desire mounts as I quickly work my hips, hungry for the fire to burn its path through me and detonate at my center.

He leans in and latches onto my breast, his mouth greedy and unrelenting as his thick cock fuels my every movement. His passion, his love, and his desperation for me make me insane with each moment that passes. Those same things also give me the strength to trust in what I know I need to do next. As insistent as Ridge was that I don't go back to that mine, I know I don't have a choice.

So after we move closer to the edge and our cores ignite, exploding together in the most intense orgasm I've ever had, I let him hold me until his deep breathing tells me he's fallen asleep. Then I slip out of bed, throw on a pair of sweats, and sneak off toward the woods just as the sun begins to peek over the horizon.

CHAPTER 61

RIDGE

I awake to cold sheets beside me, and my heart instinctively jolts. I know Camila is gone before I can confirm it. Camila isn't the slip-out-of-bed type of woman. She has no problem with finding creative ways to wake me, no matter the time.

Camila is clearly still upset about her run-in with Gus. Her nightmare spoke volumes in that regard. I've never seen Camila so completely out of sorts. And while I didn't mind the sex that followed, it came from a place of coping. She would have done anything to get her mind off what troubled her, but I know better than to think a mind-blowing orgasm could eliminate that kind of deep pain.

I don't waste a second before my phone is in my hands. I call her and message her but get nothing but her voicemail with every attempt. If nothing is wrong, then she'll think I've become a stalker kind of boyfriend. *Let her.* Camila is hurting. She probably rushed off to find another kind of coping mechanism. *Work.* I swear the

445

woman would work twenty-four hours a day, if I didn't entice her with dinner and sex every night.

Seconds later, I'm dressed in just enough clothes to hop on the tractor. I pass the cornfields and move toward the woods, not stopping until I reach the end of my property line. After a quick jump off the tractor, I make my way across the bridge.

The strangeness of charging up the vineyard, as though my ancestors weren't banned from the property for over a century, doesn't faze me. Camila would probably love to see this too. My walking through rows of grapes is quite the role reversal to when Camila used to run through Harold's cornstalks.

I can't help but smile. Despite everything going on and all we've yet to overcome, Camila and I are finally free to live our lives together, and I never saw it as possible. I hoped, prayed, and dreamed, but our time always got cut short.

Once I get to the top of the vineyard, I ask one of the field workers where to go. He points me in the direction of a small building set off from the villa, and I thank him before taking off. The blue door to the casita is propped open, and wooden doors line the narrow hallway. Each office door has a name plaque, so it doesn't take long to find Camila's.

I knock and wait then realize she's not going to respond. A quick jiggle of her doorknob proves what I already know. It's locked.

"Camila isn't in yet. At least, I haven't seen her this morning."

I turn quickly to find Raven walking down the long hall. She stands in front of me, and something shifts in my chest at the sight of her—guilt for the way our friendship ended. Seeing her at the rodeo last night didn't help matters either. Camila and I haven't been flaunting our relationship, and Raven is one of those reasons why. No one needs to get hurt while we're enjoying our time together.

"Hey, Raven." I should say something to her about how sorry I am, but it's not at the top of my priority list right now. "Do you know where she could be?"

Raven looks around and seems to be thinking. "I don't know. She walks through the vineyard a lot to check on the workers. Some mornings, she meets with my dad. Usually, she's the first one here, though."

I try to decide where to look for her next.

"So, that's it, huh?" Raven asks, turning my attention back to her. "You and Camila are an official thing now?"

"You can say that, yeah." I think twice about continuing this conversation when all I want to do is find Camila. "I'm sorry, Raven. You and I were good friends, and I hate that it ended the way that it did."

She gives me a smile that tells me she doesn't believe me then shakes her head. "Yeah, me too. But to be honest, I saw it coming from a mile away. Even if you didn't. That's why I got so freaked out in the end. I realized that if anything more was going to happen between us, then it would have, and our window of opportunity felt like it was closing in on us. For what it's worth, I don't regret being your friend."

"You were good to me, Raven. I'll never forget that."

Her smile is kinder this time. "All right, then. Well, I hope you find Camila." She backs away and points at a door on her way past it. "That's my dad's office, if you want to check in there."

I start toward the office with a grateful smile. "Thank you."

The light to Thomas Bradshaw's door is on, and his door is propped open. I knock, accidentally pushing it forward and getting a good look inside. His office is empty, but I step inside anyway, my eyes catching on the hunting photos Camila mentioned.

Curiosity brings me forward to take a closer look, and after a quick search, I find the photo of Dave, Thomas, and Patrick, all dressed in gray camouflage. A chill sweeps over me when I look at another photo and see the skull mask. Camila described it so clearly that I'm surprised his image hasn't haunted my dreams too. She must have been terrified, running from that psycho in the woods.

I'm drawn to another photo, one that grips my chest and makes me take a step closer. I think I'm seeing double, and I shake my head and squint at the photo. In this picture is a man in a skull mask, and at first glance, I assume it's Dave Lachey. But then I look to the man's right to see Dave, who's wearing a smile and holding another skull mask.

"What the—?"

My gaze travels over the rest of the framed photos, but they're mostly of family or of Thomas with Patrick, working in the vineyard. My insides knot, and a nagging thought tells me that something is very wrong. Then my eyes lock on the corner of a photo that has slipped behind another. When I pull it up to take a better look at it, my heart stops.

The photo is of Dave Lachey holding up his kill in a clearing of red rock at the base of a mountain—a steel-gated tunnel, and a wooden-framed entrance with Cornett Creek Mine etched into it. Thomas has a photo of the mine. *Why?*

I start for the exit, panic quickly working through me, but again, my eyes catch on something *off*. A wooden wardrobe sits in the corner of the room, which would be completely normal, if it weren't for the sliver of gray camo poking out. I go to it and yank the doors open, and my stomach churns when I see a wall of weapons lining the back of the closet. Shotguns, rifles, and ammo take up the majority of the space, while hunting clothes take up the rest. None of what's inside the wardrobe is what sends me into complete panic-mode. But the empty hook of where another weapon should be twists the knots in my gut even tighter.

"Looking for something?"

I whip my head toward the accusing voice to find Trip's angry scowl. This isn't the time for one of our stare downs. Trip might be the only one who can help me at this point. "I'm looking for Camila."

Trip's eyebrows knit "And you're looking for her in my dad's office. In his hunting closet?"

I step forward, trying to stay calm even though desperation wants to take over. I slam the wardrobe doors closed and walk toward Trip. "No, the doors were open. I was just admiring his, um, collection." A quick change of subject is my only hope. "You haven't seen Camila, have you? She's not in her office, and she left kind of abruptly this morning."

"Haven't seen her." His eyes narrow. "What? You two have some sort of lovers' quarrel or something?"

Irritation chips away at my patience. "Look, I'm worried about her, okay? You and I don't have to get along for you to understand that. I need to find her. Raven mentioned that she and Thomas might be having a meeting." I wave my hands around the room. "Clearly, they're not here."

Trip's frown relaxes a little after he looks me over. "Nah, my dad's hunting in Ouray today. Won't be back until tonight."

Hunting. Ouray. "Hunting in July? What's he trying to catch? Coyotes? Squirrels? That seems a bit odd."

Trip shrugs. "Not when you own the land you're hunting on."

I squint, thoroughly confused. "You said he was in Ouray."

"That's right. He owns a plot of land out there. Goes hunting whenever he wants."

I'm sure he does. "What does he usually hunt with?" I point at the wardrobe. "I noticed there's a shotgun and a rifle in there."

Trip shifts. My questions are obviously making him nervous. "He's a bow hunter primarily. He likes the challenge. Says it helps him with his focus." He tilts his head. "I thought you were trying to find Camila."

"I am. I just got distracted, I guess." As I take a step toward the door, my heart thunders. Different pieces of the puzzle begin to click into place. I think I know where to find Camila.

CHAPTER 62

CAMILA

I reach the hilltop nearly an hour later. My trek was a slow one, as I fought off every thought that told me to turn around. Everything looks just as I left it. My favorite tree still stands tall and twisty, the large rock is still near the cliff at the edge of the hill, and the landing reveals a sparse covering of wildflowers.

My heart beats faster than it used to at the end of the uphill trek, and I blame that on the amount of time I've spent away. *How could I fear such a beautiful landmark from my past?* But the hilltop isn't the problem. I've feared the entire lineup of events that led me into the hunter's path. My natural instinct to stay away from the hilltop was a casualty in a long list of fears that I collected that night. But it's time I realize I don't have anything to fear anymore, since that madman is rotting six feet underground. I need to put my nightmares to rest once and for all, and as much anxiety as the mine has given me, I can't think of a better way than to face my fears head-on.

As I sit here, working up the nerve to make my way down the other side of the mountain, I can't help but feel a speck of guilt for leaving Ridge while he was asleep. He might worry, or he might assume I've gone to work. I could have left him a note, but telling him the truth wasn't an option, and I didn't want to lie.

Ridge doesn't understand what it's like for me to feel so trapped in my past that I can't escape it. My nightmares, like the one I had last night, were constant before I found Ridge again. He still has that magical ability to calm me, but after one trigger—one conversation with Gus last night—suddenly, everything rushed back, like I was walking through the woods all over again.

I can't live like this. I need to find a way past this other than through it. Going to the mine is the only way.

One thing became clear after my conversation with Gus then with Ridge—the events of that night don't haunt me as much as the questions that remain. Dave Lachey might be dead, but there's more to fear than I've ever allowed myself to admit. And it's time I fight for closure.

After a long, deep breath, I stand and start walking toward the mine. I try not to think about what awaits me at the bottom of the hill or what happened the last time I made this journey. Instead, I find comfort in knowing that I've been through the worst of it.

I use the bigger boulders as leverage to help me go down. The landscape has definitely shifted over the years. Not much, but it's enough to catch me off guard a few times. I slip on pebbles I don't expect to land on, and some of the rock I used to scale down before is missing completely.

When I make a leap onto the flatland at the bottom of the main hill to avoid a pile of bigger rocks, I cringe while in midair, anticipating the hard landing to come.

My feet hit the ground, and the impact shoots through my legs, but a second later, I'm able to stand and continue. The mine is just below the next drop. I can see it, and my heart starts to beat faster.

When I make the final jump off the roof of the mine to the landing in front of it, a flashback from that night lights up my thoughts. *How long did Dave stare at me through the tall grass before I saw him?*

What's even more chilling is that the mine itself looks exactly the same. It has the same steel bars and the same kind of padlock. The same ore-mining car is positioned on the rail tracks, and the dark tunnel seems to go on forever. The wooden frame still surrounds the entrance to the mine.

My spine tingles. The image from my past is still right here, still real, and just as terrifying as ever. My mission was to return to the mine and journey through it to see where it leads. Now that I'm here, I have so many other ideas that don't include traveling through the dark mine alone with nothing but the small flashlight I took from Ridge's utility cabinet.

I can turn around, go straight home, and forget this mine ever existed. Gus is right. It doesn't matter what I'll find on the other side of it anymore when the only threat that came from it is dead. Or I can call Ridge to tell him I'm here. Maybe then he'll meet me, and I won't have to go through the mine alone.

My options and what would happen if I tried them

cycle through my mind as I stare into the black hole of emptiness.

Just then, rustle of tall grass shakes me from my thoughts. I freeze, and my hair stands on end. Fear clutches every inch of me, and all I can think about is that feeling I got that day of someone watching me.

Spinning to face the tall grass, I expect to find those same dark eyes staring back at me from inside that terrifying skull mask. Meanwhile, I try to remind myself that there's nothing to be afraid of. The day is windy, and cloud cover is low. When another gust blows through the weeds, I allow the relief to consume me. My body shakes as all the emotion I've been hanging on to for so long tumbles through me in waves.

I came to this spot to deal with the constant reminder of what happened that awful night and to push past all irrational thoughts that continue to haunt me. What I need is for the surrounding woods I once loved to feel like home again.

Adrenaline suddenly charges through me, and I turn back to the mine, determination hitting me hard.

I grab a large rock, and with all my strength, I smash it down onto the padlock. A chunk of brass falls to the ground, and I rip the remaining piece from the door. I wrap my hand around one of the steel bars and yank it toward me before I can second-guess what I'm doing.

Carefully, I take my first step into the mine and walk around the ore car while placing my hand on the nearest wall.

Drip, drip, drip.

A puddle has formed from the water that glides down the pinkish rock. I would expect my fingers to come away with a gooey texture, but all I feel is wet rock. I dry my hands on my pants, then I spot something on the opposite wall.

With cautious steps, I walk around the ore car to get a better view and see a light switch there. I flip it up then gasp as the mine becomes illuminated in a yellow glow. A string of lights lines the top corners of each wall, reaching as far as I can see.

I start walking while blowing out another shaky breath. "Well, here goes nothing."

CHAPTER 63

THE HUNTER

Long brown hair, caramel skin, and wide green eyes stop the hunter in his tracks. He knew it was only a matter of time before the hunt continued. Camila could never stay away. Her curiosity was too strong. Of course she'd traveled back to the mine. With Dave Lachey gone, she had nothing left to fear. So she thought.

On that unfortunate night in the woods over ten years ago, during a chase gone all wrong, the hunter lost his focus, and Dave was the one who came out ahead. It looked like he was going to be the winner too. *Shoot to kill* was what they'd decided. They both chased her that night, and they were both so close. The hunter had broken the girl's skin enough to create a lasting wound, but Dave was the one who ran ahead and got in the way of Harold Cross's bullet.

The bastard had lain there dying while the hunter crept back into the woods, stripped off his hunting gear, and tossed his belongings into the ore car before getting the hell out of there. Gus, along with everyone else, thought it was just a hunting accident turned deadly. In a sense, they were right.

If it weren't for Dave's death, the hunter would still have his right-hand man in a territory they'd dominated together for the past twenty years. In an agreement they both shared, it was always Dave who took the fall if the authorities ever got involved. For that reason alone, his death was unfortunate. And it was all thanks to Camila.

The hunter slides the mask over his face then stalks through the tall grass toward where Camila has already entered the mine. Unlike last time, he carefully avoids the snap of a twig or the crunch of a branch that might give his presence away. His target will be more vulnerable, the deeper into the mine she goes, so he allows it.

Everything has to be perfect. More is at stake than last time. He has more to win if his aim finishes off the woman completely.

This time, the hunter is ready. He won't let the thrill of the chase distract him. This time, he won't miss.

CHAPTER 64

CAMILA

My heart pounds erratically with every step, and I try to take control of the sudden panic attack that floods my body. Looking back toward the entrance of the mine, I watch the rectangle of light get smaller until it disappears completely. If it weren't for the lights strung above me, I would be in complete darkness.

My breathing is shallow and slow as I focus on what I can see ahead. The tracks are bending slightly, and I have no concept of distance or time, but I think I've been walking for over ten minutes with no end in sight. My phone signal is completely shot in here, too, and I'm starting to consider turning back.

I've done stupid shit before, but this might just take the cake. Who knows how long I could be walking, though I keep reminding myself that if this really was a passageway for Dave, then it's a distance I can handle too. The mine itself is nothing to be afraid of. It's nothing but ore tracks, red dirt, a basin of water that flows like a river against one of the rock walls, a steel pipe that runs across the corner of the ceiling, and electric wires that are most likely what power the lights. The unknown is what fuels my anxiety.

Other than the drips of water echoing off the tunnel walls, all I can hear are the sounds of my breath, the crunching of rocks, and the buzz of overhead lights. I stop completely, shut my eyes, and pull in another deep breath to try to ease my nerves while filling myself with the courage to continue.

I'm still analyzing my next move when I hear footsteps approaching at a speed that makes my heart rate accelerate. Every ounce of progress I've made up until this point vanishes quickly, and my anxiety spikes once again.

I flip around, trying to make out something in the darkness to indicate that I'm just imagining the sound of heavy steps coming toward me. But I can't see a thing past the last bend in the tracks. I walk backward, away from the approaching steps, then a shadow reflects against the rock before the figure emerges in front of me.

He must be over a hundred feet away, but the moment I see the gray skull mask, the matching hunting clothes, and the bow in the man's grasp, a scream bursts from my throat.

Shock paralyzes me as the man quickens his steps then raises his bow and slips an arrow from the pack over his shoulder. He's my worst nightmare, no longer a taunting image from my past but very much in my present. And now that he's standing in front of me with that same deadly approach as before, I can't move a muscle.

"You won't escape me this time, bitch." The man's deep roar travels through the mine, blasting me with another dose of fear.

I need to turn around and run. But even if I start running now, I'll end up with an arrow through me. He's got a straight shot for God knows how long. I don't know where this mine tunnel goes.

"What do you want from me?"

He takes another step forward while his chuckle reverberates off the walls. "Nothing, Ms. Bell. I want nothing from you. And I'll kill you to get it."

Everything registers in that moment—his voice, the way he called me Ms. Bell, the photos in Thomas's office, and what Trip said to me about his father being the one to tattle on me.

"What the hell, Thomas?"

He reaches behind his head, rips off his mask, and tosses it to the mine floor. His salt-and-pepper hair is completely disheveled, and his dark eyes intensify as he regains his grip on the bow. "Surprise. Remember that final pawn I had left to play?" He flashes a grin. "This is it. Guess it's the right time to tell you that our business arrangement isn't working for me. I'm gonna have to let you go."

Terror races through me. I have no way out. Thomas's aim is steady on me, while I'm shaking from the inside out. "You don't have to do this. If you want the vineyard, it's yours," I lie.

Booming laughter echoes through the mine. "I'm afraid you're too late for that deal, Ms. Bell. Negotiations ended the second you stepped foot on my land."

Disgust tears through me. *"Your* land? We're on public land, Thomas. No one owns it."

Thomas's expression distorts into something menacing. "That's where you're wrong. This land has always been mine, and every time you stepped foot on it, you came that much closer to getting yourself killed. But I was good. I waited. I tried to give you the benefit of the doubt and hoped that you'd never want that vineyard, and if you did, I hoped you would share it with my son. When I realized that would never happen, after you came home looking like a whore the morning after prom, I knew I'd have to take measures into my own hands."

I shake my head as confusion snakes its ugly scales around me. My only chance at surviving this is to talk Thomas out of it, as impossible as that seems. "But Dave died that night, not you."

Thomas smiles. "Dave was obedient. Did whatever I asked without hesitation. We both hunted you that night. After old man Harold killed him and you left town, that left me only one other choice."

"Get my papa to sell you shares to the vineyard so I'd have nothing when I came home."

Thomas nods. "You're smart, Ms. Bell. I'll give you that. And perhaps you would have done a fine job with that vineyard, but now I guess we'll never know. You'll die today, and the vineyard will be mine tomorrow. And when my family and I stomp grapes at the next fall festival, we'll do it in the Bradshaw name."

I catch a glimpse of another shadow on the wall behind him just before Ridge emerges and scoops up a large rock. I gasp in surprise, causing Thomas to lower his weapon as confusion transforms his face. But it's too late.

Ridge already saw Thomas with the arrow aimed at me. He lifts the rock over his head. Just as Thomas turns to face Ridge completely, Ridge smashes the rock against Thomas's skull with enough force to cause a loud grunt to leave Thomas's body.

Thomas crashes to the ground, his eyes falling shut. Ridge doesn't waste a second before scooping up Thomas's bag of arrows and running toward me.

I'm so relieved to see him. I take off running toward him to meet him halfway and leap into his arms. He squeezes me, blows out a breath of relief into my hair, and curses. "Why would you come here on your own?"

My body shakes with panic that Thomas is still on the ground, less than one hundred feet away. Knowing Ridge took his arrows, my relief expels in doses of intense emotion. "You wouldn't have let me come, but I had to." I shake my head. "I can't explain what compelled me. I just knew I had to come and see what's on the other side of this mine." He might not understand the desperation I feel to finally uncover this last clue, but it's important to me, and maybe now he'll realize that nothing will stop me from getting the answers I seek, not even my own fear. "Is he dead?"

Ridge nods. "I hit him pretty hard. I think s—"

Before he's even finished answering, a groan sounds from where Thomas lays.

"Oh my God!" I cry.

Ridge grips my hand, and we take off in the opposite direction.

"Whatever happens, don't stop running," he says.

CHAPTER 65

CAMILA

Ridge is right on my tail as we haul ass through the mine. It feels like we've been running forever, and the end is nowhere in sight. The only comfort I have is that Ridge is with me.

With fear propelling me forward at a speed faster than I'd ever moved before, I try to imagine that I'm running through the cornfields like I used to. Back then, running felt effortless, like I could go forever. I do my best to channel that same energy now, all while trying to hold back gut-wrenching sobs.

"Thomas is trying to kill me," I say, gasping for breath. "He and Dave were both after me that night." I have so many more questions but no time to sort through them. Fear and anger continue to pump through me. I have no concept of distance or time or even whether Thomas is still behind us, only that it feels like a lifetime until I see another glimmer of light at the other end of the tunnel.

"There." The word comes out on an exhausted breath. "We're almost there."

"I see it. You're doing well, Camila. Keep going. Let's hope he's still out of it."

Using all the strength I can muster, I push forward and ignore the shooting pains spreading through my legs and lungs.

I crash against the gate just before Ridge runs up behind me. Another padlock has us locked in. A cry bursts from my throat. "We're trapped!"

He searches the space for something, and when he picks up a rock from the other side of the door, I turn to find nothing but the twisty tunnel of the mine behind us.

"Hurry," I whisper. Then I listen as hard as I can, trying to sort the dripping water from the sound of footsteps approaching.

"Got it," Ridge says, relief in his voice.

He pushes open the door. I look behind us again and scream when Thomas rounds a corner. He stops, his gaze falling on us. Blood runs down his head, coating his hair and dripping into his eyes as he stalks forward, a handgun dangling from his grip.

"Shit. Let's go, Camila."

Ridge tugs me, causing more adrenaline to burst through me. I turn and run with Ridge. At first, all I see is woodland around us.

"Look," Ridge says through heavy breaths. He points at something in the distance.

Hope fills my heart when I see a long dirt road. We turn toward it then follow its path while staying cloaked by thick tree trunks.

"Holy shit," Ridge says.

I look in the direction his eyes are pointed to find a small cabin with a truck parked in the driveway. "What?"

"I know that cabin."

Furrowing my brow, I ask, "You do? How?"

A gunshot rings through the air, and another burst of energy shoves me forward. I'm afraid my legs won't be able to hold out anymore. "Ridge, I need to rest."

"Just a little bit more. You can do it, Wild One. I know where we are."

Though I want to ask him how he knows where we are again, I push through the pain and follow him, but as soon as we reach a clearing with a mountain backdrop past a line of old wooden fencing that seems oddly familiar, my muscles give out, my feet drag, and I trip, sending me face-first to the ground.

Pain shoots up my arms.

Ridge bends down. "C'mon, Camila. You need to get up."

The fear in his voice makes me want to sob. I want to move, but I can't. He lifts me to my feet, wraps his arms tightly around mine, then picks me up and carries me as fast as his legs will allow. I'm just starting to make sense of our surroundings when I look over Ridge's shoulder and see Thomas dart around a tree and aim right at us.

"He's right behind you!"

My warning is too late. The shot rings through the air, and Ridge howls from pain. I don't know where he's been shot, but the damage is enough to toss us both to the ground. A loud growl comes from deep in the woods, then Thomas charges forward, running and pointing his gun at us.

"We're going to die," I say with a sob just as Ridge covers my body completely.

Ridge's eyes find mine, and pain shines through them. He's scared, too, but he doesn't say it. Instead, he presses his lips to mine, and our mouths shake as we kiss for what feels like the very last time. "I love you, Wild One."

Tears fill my eyes. "I love you, too, Ridge. Forever."

His face is the last thing I see before another gunshot rings through the air.

CHAPTER 66

CAMILA

The gunshot echoes at the same time as a loud howl. Next comes the sound of footsteps approaching. I can see nothing but Ridge, who's still cloaking me with his entire body. He's still breathing, even though his eyes are squeezed shut.

When the footsteps run past us and another gunshot sounds, Ridge opens his eyes to see what's going on.

"Ridge, talk to me."

He lets out a heavy breath, shock etched into his expression as he starts to peel himself off me. "It's okay. We're okay." He blinks and looks down at me. "We're going to be okay."

"You were shot." Panicked, I look him over, trying to find the wound.

He clutches his waist. "I'm fine. I think it just grazed me."

Relief tumbles through my body, but I still don't understand. Ridge helps me to a sitting position, and I look toward where I last saw Thomas standing. All I see are the bottom of his shoes, and just like that awful night over ten years ago, a man is standing over him with a gun.

My jaw drops. "Is that Jason?"

Ridge lets out an unbelieving laugh. "Yes, it is."

"Wait." I look around. I recognize the glamping tent against the old wooden ranch fence that faces Jason's livestock farm. "Are we—no." I shake my head. "We can't be in Camp Lachey. Ouray is nearly an hour from home."

Ridge looks thoroughly amused. "Apparently not through the mine tunnel. If you think about it, you just have to drive around the San Juan Mountains to get here. But these old gold and silver mines created passageways like this long ago."

"And the cabin? You said you recognized it."

"That's Dave's old cabin. And I'll give you one guess who owns it now."

"You think Thomas bought Dave's cabin?"

"That's my thought. Trip told me Thomas owns property here now."

"Trip told you? When?"

"I went looking for you at the vineyard, but you weren't there. So I went into Thomas's office because Raven said you might be in there and I saw the hunting photos. There was a photo of Dave and another man wearing the same mask, and I saw a photo of the mine. And then Trip walked in. He told me Thomas was hunting in Ouray, that he owned land here, and that he took his bow and arrow."

My eyes squeeze shut as I'm reminded of the conversation I had with Thomas in the mine. "I don't know how you knew where to find me, but I'm so glad you did. Thomas wanted me dead because of the vineyard."

Ridge shakes his head. "I can't explain it exactly. But after I saw the photo of the mine and I thought more about what you said last night, I just knew."

As much as I want to keep talking about this, I'm fully aware of the wounded man in the distance.

Ridge helps me to my feet, and we walk toward Jason who still has his gun aimed at an unmoving Thomas. I walk faster.

"Did you call the cops?" Ridge calls to Jason from behind me.

"Sure did," Jason says.

My heart crashes against my chest the nearer I get. "Please tell me he's dead."

Jason shakes his head. "He's still breathing. You two okay?"

I look back at Ridge, who's still clutching his side. "Yeah, we're okay. Thanks to you."

Jason glares down at Thomas. "Trust me. It was my pleasure."

All the anger, fear, and sadness I've felt over the years because of Thomas and that awful night come barreling out of me in uncontrollable rage. I kick Thomas's side so hard that he groans. Ridge puts his arms around me and tries to pull me back.

Thomas's eyes shoot open, and he glares up at me. With the blood pouring from his shoulder and leg, he's obviously already in pain.

"You missed again, you son of a bitch." My words drip like venom from my mouth.

He growls. "I should never have let you get by me

that night," he croaks out and coughs. "You'd be dead, and the vineyard would be mine. I gave you too many chances to live."

"If you wanted me dead, why wait? We've worked in the same building every single day for the past five months."

His lip curls up at the corner. "I'm a professional, Ms. Bell. Besides, it's harder to toss your bloody pieces to the coyotes that way. It was only a matter of time until we found ourselves together again in the woods. It felt just like old times, didn't it?"

"Yeah. You were a shit shooter then too."

Thomas loses his smile. "Yeah, well, you're still a whore."

All of the pieces quickly fall into place. I would never have taken Thomas as a man out for blood, but he's been the puppet master of everything, from having Trip spy on me when we were younger, to breaking up Ridge and me, to taking over half of the vineyard. He's an evil man, but it finally ends today.

"I wish my papa were here to see this. He trusted you, and you betrayed him in every way imaginable."

Thomas chuckles. "Your papa was a clueless fuck. He didn't know how to run a business."

Fury swirls through me. "It seems neither do you. I've been piecing together your business transactions, and the only thing that seems to be missing is the extra cashflow that magically made its way into your pockets. I think my attorney will have enough after today to turn you in to the authorities for poaching. We'll find your contacts, Thomas, and they'll give up your name. Then you'll lose everything."

His face turns beet red with anger. "You can't prove a thing."

"You've already underestimated me enough." I place my heel at his throat and push down. "Like right now. If you think that I won't kill you myself, you're wrong."

My body shakes as Ridge manages to pull me back. "You're done!" he yells down to Thomas. "If you don't die today, then you'll rot in prison for the rest of your sorry life."

Thomas chokes up another laugh. "That's fine. Half of the vineyard still belongs to me. I can easily turn that over to my kids. I've set them up to one day take over that property, and that's exactly what they'll do."

"Not when I prove that the way you purchased your half was through illegal means. All I have to do is speak to one of your clients and threaten them with turning them in, and it's all over for you. Then the vineyard will be mine again. Think about that while you're rotting in prison." I spit, aiming for his face, and internally applaud myself when it lands in one of his eyes.

"That vineyard is mine!" he roars.

"We can agree to disagree on that."

"Fuck you."

"No, thanks."

Ridge tightens his hold on me, telling me to calm down. Sirens begin wailing in the distance. Part of me hopes Jason takes a shot between Thomas Bradshaw's eyes, but I just might enjoy watching him rot behind bars more. Either way, the nightmare is finally over. Thomas Bradshaw can never hurt me, or anyone else, ever again.

CHAPTER 67

CAMILA

It's over.

I blink at my computer screen and reread the news report for the hundredth time since it came out that morning. An investigation started directly following Thomas Bradshaw's arrest two months ago, and the preliminary hearing came to a close yesterday. While he's being tried for willful destruction of big game —for poaching—it's the double-attempted murder sentence against me that will land him in jail for the rest of his life. According to my attorney, Thomas has all the odds stacked against him. He'll lose his shares to the vineyard, rot in a prison cell, and I'll happily wait for the final trial to see it all through.

A knock on my office door pulls me from my thoughts. I look up to find Trip standing there with a grief-stricken expression. I swallow, the former contempt I held for my old friend waning now that my head is clearer and I start to view the situation from his perspective. Or, at least I try to. No matter what Trip has done over the years to aggravate me and stoke the fires between his father and me, he had absolutely nothing to do with the crimes his father had committed. Trip and Raven are innocent in all of this, and I asked for them to come here today so that I could acknowledge that.

"Trip, hi." I push my seat back and stand before making my way toward him. We're a few feet away when I stop, hesitating to come any closer. We haven't talked in person since before Thomas came after me in the mine. I can't imagine what he must be going through. I glance behind him. "Is Raven with you?"

He shakes his head. "No, she-she couldn't make it." He opens and closes his mouth like he's struggling with the right words to say. "I'm sorry, Camila, this isn't easy."

"Do you want to have a seat?" I gesture to the couch which he looks at, then he shakes his head again.

"No, I just wanted to see you and tell you how sorry I am about everything." His jaw hardens and then he locks eyes on me. "I should have come sooner. Raven and I have been processing everything, and we're just so sorry. We had no idea that he…"

The crestfallen look on Trip's face breaks my heart. The evidence stacked against Thomas is too much for even his own children to disagree with. "Of course you didn't. I imagine your father got very good at keeping secrets over the years. It's not your fault."

He nods and a few beats pass between us before he lets out a sigh. "I just—I'm not really sure how to move on from this, Camila. The vineyard is all my sister and I know. But of course we'll resign. It's the right thing to do."

My throat squeezes and my eyes widen. "I would

hate for you two to resign. I mean, I understand if that's what you need to do, but the job is still yours if you want it."

Trip blinks out his surprise. "Really? It wouldn't be too hard working with us after—?"

I shake my head, letting him know there's no need to finish. "Gus already accepted my job offer to return as groundskeeper. Things won't be the same around here without you and Raven."

He shifts while he assesses me with his stare. "Do you mind if I take some time to talk to my sister? I feel like this is a decision Raven and I should make together."

"Of course. Take all the time you need."

I'm met with a small, thankful smile, and a hesitant embrace. "Thank you, Camila."

It's late afternoon when I see him out. I grab the duffel bag I packed this morning and lock the door behind me. While there are so many unsettled feelings still swimming through me, I feel a sense of a new beginning, too. Not only will the vineyard be completely under my ownership soon, but Ridge and I have plans to open access to the bridge between both properties. Our childhood dreams are coming true, and it all finally feels like a reality.

There's an unstoppable smile growing on my face as I walk between the vines down the slope that leads to the opening in the woods. I'm in no rush today. There's no one to hide from, no one lurking in the bushes. It's just me, closing up shop early so I can visit my man who's currently busy in the cornfields.

I opted out of putting together a fall festival this year, but that doesn't stop the harvest from taking place. The vineyard is full with locals who are hand picking grapes and adding them to the baskets that get picked up and taken to the presses. Bin after bin of redolent grapes are being coaxed into the early makings of wine at this very moment.

I know just where to find Ridge once I cross the bridge and enter the dry yellow field. While he spends the majority of his time at Wild One Ranch, he's on a tractor today. He prefers to be the one out there on the first day of the harvests to open up the field in Harold's honor.

I dash between a row of stalks and run between them until I hear the roar of machinery near me. Pushing my way through tall leaves, I find myself in a newly mowed clearing where Ridge is currently riding his tractor.

I drop my bag at my feet. With a wave of my arms, I catch his attention.

He shuts off the large tractor and stands up with a frown etched into handsome face. "Are you crazy? I could have run you over! Will you ever learn?"

I burst into a grin even bigger than the smile already on my face, and take off toward him. He laughs when I jump onto his tractor, throw my arms around his neck, and kiss the anger right off his mouth.

He pulls away from me with narrowed eyelids and an amused expression. "What's gotten into you, Wild One?"

"Nothing. I just wanted to see you and I couldn't wait until tonight. Can you take a break?"

He chuckles. "For you? I think I can manage that. Want me to drive us back to the house?"

"Actually, I have a better idea." After hopping off the tractor, I walk toward where I dropped my duffel bag and open it. I pull out a wool blanket and spread it out before plopping down and reaching back into the bag for more surprises. There's nothing but corn stalks on three sides of us and Ridge's tractor blocking us from the opening he'd just mowed. There's something so romantic about being surrounded by the field that first brought us together.

"What's the occasion?" Ridge asks while sitting and accepting a wine glass and letting me fill it for him.

"It's the first day of our harvest. I figured since we weren't having a big festival, you and I could celebrate together."

We clink glasses and he pulls his drink to his quirked lips. "That's awfully sweet of you."

I bat my lashes. "I might have had some less-than-sweet ideas after cornering you in the field."

He gasps, feigning shock. "You don't say. I'd love to hear what you had in mind."

Giggling, I set my glass down in the field debris and pluck something else out of my bag. By the bend of his brows, I can see his curiosity written all over his face. I hold up the bunch of red grapes and move to straddle him, then I dangle the fruit between us with a teasing smile. "Usually, there's a grape stomp at the festival."

"And you want to stomp those in my cornfield?"

Laughing again, I shake my head. "Not exactly." I lift the cluster so it's dangling right above his mouth. "Take one."

His teeth move around a grape and then he tears it off the stem with a quick move of his head. Moving closer to him, I bite down on the exposed end of the fruit and crush it between us. "Oops," I say.

He glares back at me as juice spills down our mouths and over our clothes. I lick across his lips before placing another grape between his teeth and doing it all over again. Before I can crush the next one between us, Ridge is tossing it aside and taking my mouth with his. Our kiss is wet and sticky, but I don't care. He still makes my knees weak and my stomach flip, like he's the one in control now.

I miss him the second he starts to pull back from the kiss, but I'm intrigued when he places his glass of wine to my lips.

"Drink."

I do as he says, loving his hooded gaze while he grows firm beneath me. I barely sip the wine before he pulls the glass away and continues to pour the dark liquid down my chin. "Oops."

Wine drips down my neck and between my breasts, then his tongue is lapping up the liquid in one clean stroke. When he reaches my breasts, he stays there. My game just turned into his, and I'm not complaining.

He pushes down the fabric of my dress and stretches my straps as he exposes the pink lace of my bra. Without bothering to remove the garment, his mouth closes around my nipple sending a ripple of shivers straight through me. His tongue feathers me as he shifts me against his lap with his other hand.

I'm warm all over and I'm already so wet. I can feel my sopping panties as I rub against his hard cock. The friction makes me dizzy. Just the thought of taking him inside me causes my belly to flip in anticipation.

I throw my head back as he teases my breasts—one and then the other—before a moan slips past my throat.

He growls in response and makes quick work of my dress straps, pulling them down along with the rest of my dress until it's bunched around my waist. My bra snaps open behind me as he frees me for his greedy mouth. Teeth wrap my nipple next, sending a shock wave to every nerve ending. He isn't biting down on me, but the threat of him doing so is electrifying and so stimulating.

The ache between my thighs becomes unbearable. He knows it, too. I shiver again in his hold, and the corners of his mouth turn up while it's still wrapped around my nipple.

"Ridge," I beg, and I don't have to say anything more.

He places me on my back and moves down my body, leaving my bunched up dress around my waist as he spreads me. He pushes away the fabric of my panties and leans down until his hot mouth is hovering over me. His licks that follow are gentle and slow as he laps me from my back to my front. I squirm, forcing him to hold me in place as he eats me just the way I love.

Finally, his mouth moves back to my clit and his tongue flicks over me without mercy. He's growling into me like a starved man, and sucking me hard like he's desperate for more. He's unrelenting, torturing me with all the pleasure he knows I need before letting me give him anything in return.

This is us. Like everything else, sex isn't an act, it's a journey. We aren't afraid to take the uncharted path. We aren't afraid to take the long road. In fact, we revel in it.

I moan when two thick fingers push inside me as his tongue continues to whip my clit. I'm so close to an orgasm when I slide my hands through his long disheveled hair and hold him down between my thighs. But Ridge apparently has other plans. He rips his finger and mouth away simultaneously and crawls up my body, taking my mouth with his.

"I want you on my tractor." He's breathless with his request.

I look over his shoulder at the large red machine with a single seat that rests close to the giant steering wheel. "Is that possible?"

He grins. "We'll make it possible."

He helps me to stand and kisses me while he slips off my remaining articles of clothing, and I help him undress, too. Then we're climbing onto his tractor and he's pushing his seat back as far as it will go before he guides me over his engorged cock.

His thickness is never something I'll get used to, I've already figured that out. And when I sink down around him this time, I'm just as shocked by the sensation of him as I was that very first time. He spreads me wide and enters me, sinking so deeply I can barely breathe once I'm completely seated. And then I'm moving, with my hands pressing down on his shoulders and his rough hands gripping my ass. He moves me at a steady pace, building my orgasm slowly before I warn him of my pending release. Our eyes burn into each other's, his gorgeous chocolate ones into my green ones, and he's right there with me.

"I love you, Wild One," he says against my bruised lips.

I quicken my pace and kiss him right back. "I love you so much, Ridge." I breathe out, my energy nearly gone as I give him the last of me, riding him as the sun dips beneath the horizon.

It's total darkness, save for the bright beams of the tractor lights into the cornfield, as I bring us both to climax. As our release shakes through us and our moans dissolve past each other's lips, our bodies start to weaken. There's something about today, this moment, that feels momentous. We've been through so much to get here, and it's finally our time. This is our beginning to a full and meaningful life together. We've surpassed our greatest odds and become stronger for it. And it's all thanks to a bridge between us ... a bridge that now connects us in all the ways we've always dreamed.

EPILOGUE

EPILOGUE

M y Wild One is back in every sense of the word. Whatever Thomas and Dave stripped from her that night over a decade ago is completely dead and buried. She's currently running through the cornfield, with her hair tossing in the wind and her cheeks pointed at the sun, as her feet carry her toward our hillside. She has everything to smile about and nothing to fear, and so do I.

Thomas went to prison and was sentenced to life behind bars, but that life ran short after Camila worked with her attorney to prove what she'd suspected and worse. Thomas Bradshaw was not only a poacher but also the leader of a poaching ring gone awry.

Over the years, the original poaching ring had disbanded, leaving Dave and Thomas as the last remaining members before Thomas began to recruit new ones. Some of them used Dave's property to access the mine, giving them thousands of acres to hunt.

Once all evidence was presented and Thomas Bradshaw was forced to forfeit all shares to the vineyard, he completely lost it. He stole a prison guard's gun and killed himself, leaving his two kids nothing.

Camila, being the beautiful human she is, offered Trip and Raven an opportunity to keep their jobs. In the end, they both remained, since the vineyard is all they've ever known.

With Thomas removed, they had their challenges in the beginning, but it was all worth it. Together, they spent the past year building a new business model, one that saw less value in quantity and more value in quality, which Camila oversaw with grace and a determination to carry out her family's legacy.

Today, I follow Camila to the top of the hillside, but this time, we sit at the edge of the peak that overlooks our neighboring properties. We've opened public access to the property via the bridge. I take her hand in mine and smile as her eyes mist with tears at the sight below our dangling feet.

"We did it," she says as emotion spills out of her, which seems to be happening a lot lately.

I wrap an arm around her shoulders and press my lips to her cheek. "We did it. Just like you said we would."

"Look at how happy everyone is," she gushes as we watch families stroll through the vineyard and little kids chase each other through the cornfield mazes I set up for the fall festival. This year, we decided the fall festival would be one giant party, celebrating the Cross Farm, Wild One Ranch, and Bell Family Vineyard. Guests pack both properties, and the real festivities haven't even started yet.

"I just had to see it from up here." She looks back at me with a bright smile. "We changed the future, just like we said we would."

"To be fair," I say with a smile of my own, "I think that was all you. I'm just along for the ride."

She chuckles and shakes her head. "You're so modest."

"I'm not being modest. You're the one with all the ideas."

"Maybe." She tilts her head, giving me that adoring look that makes my heart skip beats. "But you're my hero, Ridge Cross. You save my life every single day just by existing. None of this could have happened without you. We did this together."

I lean in and kiss her, loving the way she melts to me like it's the very first time when we sat on that mountain in Ouray. "Okay, you win."

She grins against my lips. "Don't I always?"

I nod and push her back into the wildflowers. "Yes, Wild One. Always."

By the time we get back to the festival, it's time for the grape stomping to begin. Familiar faces crowd the barrel as an announcer invites Camila onto the stage, where she slips off her shoes and steps into the large round bin. She laughs as she picks up the fabric of her white dress and waits for the music to begin.

We've talked about this day over the past year, since last year's festival was canceled. Camila was nervous to even hold another event now that her papa isn't there to step into the grapes. But her mama is there, right by her side.

I laugh as they dance, their dresses getting more stained by the second as they slip and fall together. When the song is over, Camila's mom looks over at me and winks, telling me it's my cue. I smile and hop onto the platform before stripping off my shoes and jumping into the grapes to join Camila.

We dance and laugh, then I pick Camila up and spin her while placing a kiss on her mouth for everyone to cheer for. And at the precise moment that Camila turns back toward the crowd and away from me, I kneel and slip a velvet box out of my pocket.

A hush falls over the crowd as the music stops, and Camila looks around, thinking something must have gone wrong. When she finally turns around and looks down at me, her eyes turn misty as her hands fly to her mouth. "Oh my god."

I can't stop smiling. "Camila Bell, Wild One, what do you say we officially end this feud once and for all? Marry me. Be mine forever."

More tears spring to her eyes, and she nods. Her words come out strained at first. "I've been yours since the moment I laid eyes on you, Ridge Cross. I'm yours forever. Always." She laughs. "Yes, of course I'll marry you."

I open the box and have to choke back my own tears when she realizes it's the ring her father gave her mother when he proposed. Selena wanted Camila to have it, and after I asked her for her blessing, she was all too eager to hand it over.

Camila's hand shakes as I slip the ring onto her

finger, then I stand and take her into my arms while the crowd around us explodes with cheers and congratulations. The music starts again, and we finish our dance with Camila's arms glued around my neck.

"I have news for you too," she says against my ear.

I laugh, thinking nothing could top my proposal. "What is it?"

She giggles and whispers, "I'm pregnant."

Surprise! Read the Bonus Epilogue
www.smarturl.it/abbu_bonus

If you loved *A Bridge Between Us* then you will love *Waterfall Effect*, a small mountain town romantic suspense.

CONNECT WITH K.K.

I hope you enjoyed *A Bridge Between Us*! If you would like to drop a few words in a review on Amazon, Goodreads, and/or BookBub, I would be forever grateful.

You can also connect with me on social media and sign up for my mail list. Be sure to never miss a new release, event, or sale!

Subscribe for Updates: smarturl.it/KK_MailList
Instagram: www.Instagram.com/KKAllen_Author
Facebook: www.Facebook.com/AuthorKKAllen
Goodreads: ww.goodreads.com/KKAllen
BookBub: www.bookbub.com/profile/k-k-allen

BECOME A FOREVER
facebook.com/groups/foreveryoungwithkk

Enjoy special sneak peeks, participate in exclusive giveaways, enter to win ARCs, and chat it up with K.K. and special guests ;)

ACKNOWLEDGMENTS

I'm sitting here staring at a notepad filled with people who supported me throughout my writing *A Bridge Between Us*, and I'm overwhelmed with gratitude. My tribe is strong and growing, you guys. It's an incredible feeling. As always, I could not have done this without them.

I want to start at the very beginning of when this idea came to light. It was just a spark of an idea, fueled by a location, and burst to life with every bit of research I dove into—some of which was used in this story, some of which was not. Like all my books, *A Bridge Between Us* started as something completely different—a love story born on farmland, yes, but with every bit of information I learned about Telluride and the surrounding areas, the rich history, the beauty found in every single season, it's safe to say this story grew into so much more than I ever could have dreamed up on my own.

With all that being said, I want to first thank you, T.R., for letting me talk your ear off at the very beginning stages of this novel. You provided invaluable reference material and ideas to help me keep the authenticity I aimed for.

To my son, Jagger, for accompanying me on an unforgettable research trip in Colorado—from the small campsite in Ridgway where we made our basecamp at a glamping site, to our day of hiking and swimming in the hot springs of Ouray, to taking an adventurous drive through the San Juan Mountains to reach Sutcliffe Vineyards, and then finally getting to spend a day riding gondolas and eating at High Pie Pizza in the town of Telluride. I could not have written this book without you, babe!

Speaking of our trip to Colorado, I want to thank the wonderful Basecamp 550 owners, Sam and Heather. I was completely out of my element and you two made me feel right at home. Thank you! I also want to thank John and Chloe and all the lovely people at Sutcliffe Vineyards for the tasting and tour. John, you are an extraordinary talent. I'll be the first to read your book as soon as you're ready to hit publish.

Sammie and Cyndi, as always, you two came through for me in a way that I could never ask of anyone else. I can't count the number of times you read this story and provided your honest, no bullshit, feedback. Thank you for all the ass slaps it took to get us here.

Patricia and Brenna, you two stepped in earlier than normal, and wow, thank you so much for the incredible notes, the encouraging feedback, and putting in all the time that you two did. I am forever grateful.

Kimberly and Emily, I adore you two so much. Thank you for stepping up to be first-time beta readers for me! Having your farmland experience and your amazing eyes on the second draft of this story was something that was desperately needed. I hope I did you proud.

A major holler to Sarah Plocher and Karina Giblin for your last-minute eyes on my baby. I appreciate you both so much.

A special thank you to all my Native American sensitivity readers, two of whom are tribe members who have requested to remain anonymous, along with Patricia, who not only lives in Colorado, but has experience growing up near a Native American reservation in northern New Mexico, and Kimberly who has experience working with a Native American tribe. Thank you all for everything.

One of the most difficult tasks in publishing is coming up with the perfect cover. I struggled with the direction to go in for this story, but like a boss, Najla from Najla Qamber Designs was right there to hold my hand. I'm so impressed with the attention to detail, not only with the design, but throughout the process of designing. Thank you to you and your team, Najla.

Thank you to Regina Wamba who just so happened to have the perfect photos to bring Camila and Ridge to life. The combined effort of photography and design created perfection.

To Lynn and Susie at Red Adept Editing, thank you isn't even enough. Lynn, your understanding and willingness to work with my timelines is such a blessing. I am so appreciative. To Susie, for your badass editing skills, it truly felt like we were the dream team. You are incredible.

Thanks to you, Lindsey, for your positivity and daily reminders, and everything you do for me. I love you to the moon and back.

To Renee, for all your incredible support and friendship. It means the world to me, an I just love you so much.

To my boo, Harloe, my writing buddy, and my dear friend. I love you so much. Thank you for always being there for me.

To Shain and Maria who lifted me at a time I desperately needed it. Thank you two babes so much.

I need to thank Sarah at Social Butterfly for being so wonderful to work with. This year has been crazy, but your constant positive energy is the best ever. You're amazing.

To my street teams, Angsters and Booksters. I love that you guys ask me for more to share when I'm always trying not to bother you. LOL. You're such a social media force, and I'm so blessed to have you all cheerleading me on.

A huge thank you to all the bloggers who supported this novel in any way. I don't know how you all keep up with so many releases and promotions going on, so thank you so much for being there for me. I will forever be grateful.

To all my readers, I know you have a million choices when it comes with what to read. Thank you for choosing *A Bridge Between Us*. I truly hope you enjoyed this journey, and I hope to see you again.

Much Love XO,
K.K. Allen

NOVELS BY K.K. ALLEN

British Bachelor

A steamy enemies-to-friends-to-lovers romantic comedy.

Coming January 24th!

Up in the Treehouse

Haunted by the past, Chloe and Gavin are forced to come to terms with all that has transpired to find the peace they deserve. Except they can't seem to get near each other without combatting an intense emotional connection that brings them right back to where it all started . . . their childhood treehouse.

Under the Bleachers

Fun and flirty Monica Stevens lives for food, fashion, and boys ... in that order. The last thing she wants to take seriously is dating. When a night of flirty banter with Seattle's hottest NFL quarterback turns passionate, her care-free life could be at risk.

Through the Lens

When Maggie moves to Seattle for a fresh start, she's presented with an unavoidable obstacle—namely, the cocky chef with a talent for photography and getting under her skin. Can they learn to get along for the sake of the ones they love?

Waterfall Effect

Lost in the shadows of a tragedy that stripped Aurora of

everything she once loved, she's back in the small town of Balsam Grove, ready to face all she's kept locked away for seven years. Or so she thinks.

Center of Gravity (Gravity, #1)

She was athleticism and grace, precision and passion, and she had a stage presence he couldn't tear my eyes from. He wanted her...on his team, in his bed. There was only one problem... He couldn't have both.

Falling From Gravity (Gravity, #1.5)

If I hadn't considered Amelia dangerous before, I certainly did now. She wasn't anything like I had expected. Even after all these years—of living so close to her, of listening to her giggle with my sister in the bedroom next to mine—I hadn't given much thought to my sister's best friend.

Defying Gravity (Gravity, #2)

The ball is her Amelia's court, but Tobias isn't below stealing-- her power, her resolve, her heart... When he wants a second chance to reignite our connection, the answer is simple. They can't. Not unless they defy the rules their dreams were built on and risk everything.

The Trouble With Gravity (Gravity #3)

When Sebastian makes Kai an offer she can't afford to refuse, she learns signing on will mean facing the tragedy she's worked so hard to shut out. He says she can trust him to keep her safe, but is her heart safe too?

Dangerous Hearts (A Stolen Melody, #1)

Lyric Cassidy knows a thing or two about bad boy rock stars

with raspy vocals. In fact, her heart was just played by one. So when she takes an assignment as road manager for the world famous rock star, Wolf, she's prepared to take him on, full suit of heart-armor intact.

Destined Hearts (A Stolen Melody, #2)

But with stolen dreams, betrayals, and terrifying threats--no one's heart is safe. Not even the ones that may be destined to be together.

ABOUT THE AUTHOR

K.K. Allen is a *USA Today* bestselling and award-winning author who writes heartfelt and inspirational contemporary romance stories. K.K. is a native Hawaiian who graduated from the University of Washington with an Interdisciplinary Arts and Sciences degree and currently resides in central Florida with her ridiculously handsome little dude who owns her heart.

K.K.'s publishing journey began in June 2014 with a young adult contemporary fantasy trilogy. In 2016, she published her first contemporary romance, *Up in the Tree- house*, which went on to win the Romantic Times 2016 Reviewers' Choice Award for Best New Adult Book of the Year.

With K.K.'s love for inspirational and coming of age stories involving heartfelt narratives and honest emotions, you can be assured to always be surprised by what K.K. releases next.

www.KKAllen.com

WORKS CITED

Editors, Charles River. *The History and Culture of the Utes: Native American Tribes.* Createspace, 2005.

Decker, Peter R., *"The Utes Must Go!": American Expansion and the Removal of a People.* Fulcrum Publishing, 2004

Jones, Sondra G. *Being and Becoming Ute: The Story of an American Indian People.* The University of Utah Press, 2019.

Dalton, Susan. *Telluride: A Silver Past, A Golden Future.* Strasboourg Cedex, France, Editions du Signe, 2017.

Elliott, Stephen. "Righting Old Wrongs." Telluride News, February, 18, 2015. Updated May 27, 2015, https://www.telluridenews.com/the_watch/article_392b1422-04b6-11e5-b099-0b464c6e2d6e.html.

The West: A Film by Stephen Ives and Presented by Ken Burns. PBS, 1996.